CW00859518

Return of the Maca

Return of the Maca

Chronicles of the Maca IV

Mari Collier

Published 2015 by Creativia
Book design by Creativia (www.creativia.org)
Cover art by http://www.thecovercollection.com/
http://www.maricollier.com/

To the Reader: The lilting speech of the Thalians is not Scottish. Their words are similar, but do not necessarily mean the same thing. They use the letter T before words like is, was, would, were, etc. so that the sound is tis, twas, twould, twere. You is pronounced "ye," and your as "yere." All of these sounds are alien to our ears. Their speech is used once in a short section. To avoid confusion, I have kept the accents to a minimum and included a Glossary.

Contents

Chapter 1

The Kenning Woman Speaks

The Ab woman, Di, stood between the merchant stalls located close to the waterfront's walkways and piers in the city of Bretta. Her massive fists were clenched and her eyes a vacant stare. The wind tore at her long, thick, chestnut-brown hair. Her short, brown kirtle flapped against the muscled thighs. Her body quivered while her mouth drew in and blew out air in short, quick gasps. At first some in the crowd had jostled against her, but others backed away, unsure of what held that magnificent Thalian body enthralled. Soon members of the Sisterhood in their black warrior uniforms, Abs in their brown garments, the Tris of Betron in their light green summer outfits, and Krepyons (derogatorily called Kreppies) in their green uniforms gathered around her. A sturdy man child of about five held onto her left leg and looked upward. He was shaking her leg to draw her attention, but nothing could break her concentration. Finally she turned to the crowd, her eyes cleared, and she pointed to the people directly in front of her.

"Thalians, Abs, Tris, people of the Houses, and Krepyons listen to me. I am the Kenning Woman, and I have a message." Her voice was as strong as her body, and it rolled over the crowd.

"Llewellyn, Maca of Don, will return. With him comes his laddie, the blind-eyed Laird of Don. Together they will restore Don and their House will be alive with new people. The false prophet will be destroyed. Beauty, Counselor of the Realm, will be forced to honor her debt to him."

Her voice rose as she pointed a finger at one from each group standing before her. "The Tris will supplant the Abs, and the Sisterhood is doomed."

"Ye Krepyons will rue the day ye stripped Thalia of her wealth for ye will be crushed like the chalk from the cliffs of your planet. The Justines will rule no more, and LouElla will be avenged!"

She stooped, picked up the wee laddie and strode through the hissing Abs, the growling Kreppies, and the smiling Tris, her long legs eating away at the tarmac. A desire to hide and sleep overrode any desire to explain away her outburst. What madness had possessed her? There was no Kenning Woman for the broken land of Thalia; none for almost eighty years. She was Di, the magnificent Ab, once the Handmaiden to Martin. Now she had damned Martin as the False Prophet and there would be retribution from that bitter, aging man. She hugged Wee Da closer.

"Ye must go to the Laird of Don when he comes," she whispered to him. "He will be your fither and your protector."

Di knew she must find Is. He would guard them while she slept. She unlimbered her legs and began to run. She disappeared from view among the broken storefronts of what once was the proud city of Bretta on the continent of Betron.

She found Is in the old inner district as he returned from a day of scrounging. He was dirty, unkempt, but unbowed. Since Martin had decreed he was not acceptable to the other Abs until he proved he would do the menial tasks of Abs during the work season, he was denied the rations and the safety of Martin's House of Abs. The House of Ishner still managed to get supply packets through to him and his condemned younger sister, but he had given the last packet to his renamed sister, Il, who was allowed to remain with Martin. The Handmaiden claimed she would protect Il, but Is wondered if that were possible. At least his sister had a place to sleep, but she was having difficulty adjusting to the life of an Ab, the loss of her name, and the security of the House of Ishner.

His bag was slung over his shoulder and he was congratulating himself on his take when Di ran up to him.

"We must hide. I spoke the vision." Her light brown eyes were wide with distress.

Is gaped at her. "Ye did nay." Horror was in his voice.

"Aye, and I named Martin as the False Prophet. Take my Wee Da and hide him."

Wee Da, however, had a firm grasp around his mother's neck, and she could not remove him. Is shook his head.

"Nay, we'll go to this new place I've found. Quickly." He turned and sped up the broken street with Di loping behind.

They were in a part of Bretta once lined with small craft shops and Tri housing overhead. Before the Justines had enforced their rule with Krepyon guards, Tris and members of Thalia's Houses would fly in on their flivs, the four-seat vehicles of Thalia, and park at the padports for a fee on a celebration day or to shop. The rounded buildings of concrete and Ayranian alloys were deserted; the padports vacant. The remaining Tris had left this area for the waterfront where food was distributed. In the back of one building, Is had found a door that opened. For over one hundred years the owners never returned to lock it, nor was it likely that they would return now. The three disappeared within and Is blocked the doorway with a carved statue of a wild elbenor raised on hindquarters showing fangs below the snarling lips.

"Come, we'll go upstairs. The furnishings are quite good. Ye can rest there and Wee Da can play. I'll prepare the meal."

Di bounded up the steps. "Will they nay see the light up here?"

"I've blocked off the windows, and I've been outside at night to verify that nay light escapes. We are safe as long as Martin's minions nay ken where I rest."

Di spied the long couch and then the hall leading to the still furnished sleeping areas.

"Dear Gar, a real bed. Is, tis perfect." She swept into one sleeping room and set Da on the bed, pulled off her brown, ankle boots, and collapsed.

"I must rest. Wee Da, be good for Is." She closed her eyes.

Is set his bag down and looked at the child. Wee Da regarded him with a smile and started to run. Is shrugged and ran after him. He did nay mind watching the wee one, although he kenned it was Troyner's get. At present Troyner, Maca of Troy, stood in the docket before the Council of the Realm. Is doubted if Troyner could fend off the Sisterhood much longer. They would bar Troyner from House and make him Ab. Damn the Sisterhood and their strict obedience to the rule of the Justines and the Kreppies. Only once had a Justine died on Thalia since the war ended and that had been in Ayran, deep in the mines, a dangerous place in the best of times.

Di woke with shadow light enfolding her and Wee Da patting her cheek and saying, "Mither, tis sus."

She sat up and her vision of the bulky Maca of Don and his handsome, hard-faced laddie with the strange grey, blind eyes faded. She hugged Wee Da and sniffed. The smell of food and the burning of oil came from the front area. She pulled on her boots, swung Da onto her hip, and walked out into the front.

Is had devised some sort of lamp from a slender-necked ceramic vase by filling it with oil and inserting a wick twisted from an old mat. A golden flame from the wick wedged into the vase stood above the neck. The improvised light cast a glow over the table. At least there was bread and a spread for it made from onions and some sort of shriveled red vegetable or fruit.

Is smiled at her. "I sorrow that there tis nay milk for Da, but I had nay anticipated guests."

"Tis all right, Is, he still drinks from me. Tis there a working lav here or must I go outside?"

"Tis best to go outside. I'll help with the door and the guarding."

As they went down the stairs, he asked, "Did ye sleep well?"

"Aye, but I dreamt the vision. It will return. The Sisterhood will come for me." She turned to him.

"If they take me, ye must see that Da gets to the Laird of Don when he arrives. The Sisterhood canna hurt Da then."

"Ye worry too much. They will ignore ye."

"Nay, they are already angered. Twice I have almost been House, and the Sisters have noticed. Ayranians hate me for luring their Maca into my arms. They believe I coaxed her into a life as an Ab as the Handmaiden to Martin. The Sisterhood found out I was safe with Troyner of Troy. They mean to control his House and see him reduced to Ab or dead. My time with Rocella of Rurhran does nay count for Rocella would nay defy her Maca."

"The Sisterhood goes after any Maca that tis male. It has nay to do with ye." Is held the door for her and they went outside. Di handed Da to Is before scooting around the corner of another building.

Chapter 2

A Reprieve

Is' assurances about the Sisterhood proved correct. They scorned the Kenning Woman's words from a vision. What the Counselor of the Realm found annoying was the green clad Kreppie screeching at her about the Maca of Don returning prophesy given in a public place. Beauty wore her official Counselor of the Realm white uniform and listened patiently. The Kreppie's greenish cheek scales were almost jiggling by the time he screamed at her, "You will arrest that woman and send her to Ayran!"

"We will nay give credence to her words." Beauty sat straight in her rounded chair, glaring down at the official. "If we send her to Ayran, Jolene will smack her bottom, put her to bed, and shower her with gifts from House. That tis nay punishment."

"You forget. This Ab is responsible for the Maca of Ayran defecting to the Abs and to Martin."

"I have nay forgotten. Ye and the Justines approved it as fulfilling the old prophesy that Ayran would become Abs. As for the former Maca, she was always whining about the old religion. Di did nay persuade her. All Di wished was to become House and she thought Jaylene would grant it for the love of her body." Beauty practically spat words at him.

"The Ab must be made an example of for others to see." The Krepyon put his hands on the desk and leaned towards her.

"I demand to see the Guardian of the Realm."

"My mither, the Guardian, grows eld and she tis resting right now. She will awaken within the hour." Beauty smiled at him. "I will, of course, discuss this with the Great Betta and will defer to her wisdom."

The Krepyon, appointed envoy and administrator of Thalia, glared at her. He knew full well that Beauty ran the day-to-day functions of Thalia. Beauty, he thought with abhorrence, was a complete misnomer. The woman stood at least six-foot four and was muscled from head to toe, plus she possessed but two skimpy mammary glands. Thalians had a strange concept of beauty, He shuddered. His policy would be carried out.

"That woman must be silenced!"

"I agree with ye, Coordinator Balen. She must be silenced, but not by making a spectacle of her. If she does nay spout those words again, they will be forgotten and go nay further than Betron." *The woman will die*, she thought. The words about her long-ago betrayal must nay be repeated.

"Do you believe that?" Coordinator Balen pounded at the desk. "The Abs will sign for work duty by the end of this cycle. They'll carry it to every continent on Thalia. She must be confined."

Beauty sank against the back of the chair and smiled. "Coordinator Balen, I promise if she speaks again, she will be silenced, but nay by condemnation. There are other ways." She leaned forward.

"Consider how ridiculous her words are. It has been over one hundred and twenty years since they left. The Maca of Don is dead."

"We have no proof of that. The Justines do not believe that one of their own has been lost out there. When Ricca returns, he will tell us how he disposed of Llewellyn."

Beauty looked at him. *Stupid Kreppies. Always they credited the Justines with Gar like powers.* She made her voice all innocence.

"We believe they've disappeared into space. Even if they return and the Maca tis with them, he canna have a laddie. He tis a mutant and there tis nay seed, or so the Justine teachings go."

Balen's face whitened with horror. "You doubt the Justines? I'll report you."

"I? I doubt the teachings of the Justines? Ye must be mad. I used Justine teachings to remind ye of the foolishness of her words."

"The Tris and Abs of Thalia give too much credence to the words of the Kenning Woman."

Beauty straightened, her hands grasping the chair's arms, her eyes becoming brown agate, her voice rising in protest.

"There tis nay Kenning Woman! She tis a fraud."

They were reduced to glaring at each other when Betta entered the room. Her white hair glistened, and the white, full length over-gown hid her aging body from view.

"Ye both are nay thinking." She looked at the two. "I had the troller on so I have heard your words. Beauty tis correct. If the woman holds her tongue, all will be forgotten. If she speaks again, we will deal with her and she will die, but nay as a condemned in Ayran. There are other ways." She went to the other side of the desk and sat.

"Now, tis there anything else?"

Balen looked dubious. "Won't a death of such a young, healthy Ab be suspicious?"

Betta gazed at him complacently. "The old prophesy from the last Kenning Woman said, 'the new Kenning Woman would stumble.' She will stumble." Betta smiled at them both.

Chapter 3

The Stumble

Is returned the next afternoon when he finished trading some of yesterday's scavenged finds. His bag was partially filled with food. He was confident they would survive until Signing Day. His Guardian should send another packet then. He had sent an urgent plea for two packets and hoped that Ishmalisa would heed him. It was fortunate that the seasons were warming, and he no longer risked freezing outside. He knew he was strong enough to work, but how he longed for his fishing vessel.

Wee Da met him at the top of the stairs with a bellow and ran straight at him intent on continuing the wrestling match of the morning. Is swung him upward and grinned at Di.

"Does he nay tire?"

Di smiled and stopped her pacing. "Of course, he does nay. What did ye find out?" She needed air. She wanted exercise. Confinement was more wearying than work or working out.

"They are nay looking for ye. I was correct. They dinna care what ye said as long as ye nay say it again."

"How can ye be sure?"

"One of the Sisterhood's low ranking patrollers was kind enough to pull me aside and suggest that ye nay drink so heavily of the brew that loosens your head and your tongue. They nay wish to hear such words from ye again."

Di heaved a sigh. "I dinna wish to speak such words, but when the vision comes it tis hard to ignore." She made a slight face and shrugged her shoulders.

"Signing time tis soon. I'll choose Ayran. Nay there care what I say, and till then, we will enjoy our time together." A smile lifted her cheeks.

The days grew warmer, and the Houses began to assemble in Betron for the monthly meeting of the Council, and the day when Abs signed up for any agricultural or menial work offered by each House. The discussion of wages wagged every tongue. To show their good will, the Houses sent extra provisions for Martin to distribute. Ishmalisa had sent the extra packets, and Is felt his strength returning. He and Di strolled among the booths decorated with each House's colors and looked at the posted work. Abs refused all schooling, but so many of the Tris had voluntarily joined the Abs to procure food that someone was always available to read when the crowd gathered around each screen displaying the work list. The former Tris and life-long Abs pretended to ignore those condemned to servitude from the Houses, but found it difficult not to give way or bow.

The Abs ignored Is as he was too apt to incur Martin's wrath; a situation that could dramatically decrease their food allotments. Di pushed the people away from the posted work assignments and smiled at him.

"Read aloud, Is, so that all may hear."

As she turned, she saw the breadth of Llewellyn, Maca of Don, and his face was stern. Behind him stood his laddie, the blind-eyed one, his grey eyes like slate glaring at a hostile world, and in his hands was a Justine sprayer. She saw Llewellyn point at her and heard him roar, "Speak."

Unable to disobey, she turned to the crowd and raised her arms. "People of Thalia listen to me. I am the Kenning Woman appointed by Gar. Llewellyn, Maca of Don, is returning with his blind-eyed laddie to free Thalia and complete the revenge of LouElla." Her arms dropped down and she swayed back and forth not hearing the gasps and the laughter rippling through the crowd. There had been no prolonged vision, but the words had flown from her mouth.

Is scooped up Wee Da and put his free arm around Di, pulling her back, away from the crowd, guiding her toward the back streets. It was time to hide again. Their progress was interrupted by the Lad of Don, his dark, blue hat sat jauntily on his head hiding the graying hair, and he smelled of the brew he had been drinking. He stood well over six feet, had the straight even features of Don, and he still possessed the body of a Thalian warrior. His withered right arm was held against his side, but he raised his left hand to halt them.

"If ye run in the streets with your wee one and your companion, they will find ye."

Is trusted this man of Don, one of the last of the surviving warriors from the Justine War. As the last of the House of Don, Lamar should have been Guardian of Don. His laddie or lassie would have become the next Maca, but the Justines had taken his seed when they withered his arm. Now he passed his time talking with old friends or drinking the Rurhran brew offerings from the Houses. Is had not spoken with him since being condemned to the life of an Ab.

"Lamar, can ye think of where we should go? There will be Army and Betron Enforcers looking to drag her before the Council."

"Ye should nay go back where ye were lodged." He used his left arm to point over towards the unused streets. "They ken where ye were hid. I heard that from my Counselor.

"Ye," and he pointed at Is, "should take the wee laddie to the Handmaiden. She will care for him, and then ye may stay at the Ab compound or wander the streets. If they ask about this one, ye can truthfully say she ran off.

"And ye," he turned and smiled at Di, "will come with me. We will saunter back towards the port and find a friend of mine."

"Nay!" Di snapped at him, her brown eyes determined.

"I am still a bit of a strategist." Lamar favored them with a smile and ran his left hand down his chest. "They will nay look for ye so close to the official gathering."

"Mayhap he tis right, Di. If the Sisterhood kens where we lodge, there tis nay safety there. They will nay look for ye in House."

"Aye," Lamar broke in. "They will think ye are cowering like a Kreppie in some back alley." He smiled inwardly with satisfaction as Di snapped her head up, kissed Da, and handed him to Is.

"How long am I to hide?"

"Nay, long. My friend will arrange a way to transport ye elsewhere and get the message back to the Handmaiden for your wee one."

Di took a deep breath. "Let's go."

Lamar used his left hand to grasp her arm and they walked back towards the port, Di walking nearest the buildings.

Di was as tall as Lamar and they matched each other's step as they made their way to what was left of the shops in Bretta. Lamar propelled her into a brew hall reserved for House members and their highest ranking retainers. The few patrons gave a guarded look and ignored them, although later the gossip would spread that Lamar was bedding outside of his marriage vows for they had seen him guide an Ab woman into the hallway towards the lift.

Inside the lift Di closed her eyes and expelled a huge gust of air. She had not dared to breathe while walking across the floor with so many eyes flicking toward her and then snapping back to their companions as though she did not exist. In truth, House members never really looked at Abs anyway. The thought stirred something in her being. Why was this prominent House member helping her? Was it because she had predicted that Don would be restored and he was grateful? The door slid open for them.

"The lift tis safer than the stairs. We are going to the second room to your right." Lamar leaned his head in that direction as they stepped from the lift. "Hurry now."

Di matched his steps, but once again her mind nagged at her. How did he so conveniently have this room waiting? Had there truly been time enough? The door opened at his touch and he stepped in, nodding his head in approval.

"Aye, Rollie was right. This tis a good place. The windows are lightly tinted. Ye can see the street below, but others canna see ye. I suggest ye nay look too oft or someone might catch your shadow and realize ye are hiding here."

Di stepped into the room. "Do ye mean Rollie, Counselor of Rurhran?"

Lamar looked at her. "Who else would I mean? I shall be back in less than an hour with the arrangements."

He smiled at her and ran his left hand up over the muscles on her arm. "Ye have a magnificent warrior's body." He bowed his head and stepped outside and turned as he put his palm on the keypad. His eyes softened as he looked at her. "Tis almost a pity." And the door slid shut.

Di looked around the room. She realized this was a trap, and she needed a way out. The furniture was soft and round, ready to accommodate those who wished to relax or engage in a bedding away from prying eyes. She pushed some of the heavy, ornate golden chairs against the door. Rurhran's color was gold; at least Lamar had not lied about that, but why, why? Did Lamar nay wish Don to be restored? She finally settled on the round solid, molded table as the only weapon available.

She turned the table over and leaned all her weight down on the leg: it held, the rim of the table coming up from the floor. She had less than an hour. How long would it take to break the window reinforced with protective metals from Ayran? Di lifted the table and aimed one of the legs directly at the center of the window, then rammed it into the metal infused glass. Nothing. Again and again she rammed the leg against the window, sweat started to gather in beads on her forehead and body, and time lost its meaning. Suddenly there was a crinkling noise, overridden by a burning smell. She whirled to face the door and realized the Sisters must have been given permission to up the charge in their stunners, or else it was Kreppies that were after her. Fear put strength into the next ramming and the window started to crack into fine glazed pieces.

Blue flame licked at the side of the table and she flung the table back towards them. Di jumped up and through the window, using her left shoulder to break through the last of the glass. Too late she remembered she was on the second floor and there was nay time to tuck and roll to correct her landing.

Chapter 4

The Handmaiden

Is held the squirming Da and started towards the Ab compound, his thoughts bitter at the turn of events. He had walked less than a mile when he met the Handmaiden hurrying towards the backstreets and hailed her.

The Handmaiden turned her dumpy figure, fully encased in a brown robe, and let out a gasp at the sight of them.

"Did they get her already?"

"Nay." He stepped closer to her so his words would nay carry. "She has gone with Lamar, Lad of Don, to another place. I am to give Da to ye." Is tried to hand Da to her, but she refused to take him.

"Where did they go?"

"I dinna. Lamar said that a friend was waiting and that betwixt them they would send her elsewhere."

"Folly!" came out of the Handmaiden's heavy face. She was barely one hundred years of age, but she resembled the Ayran Abs rather than the Ayran Warriors with her dumpy body and face set with small black eyes. Her thin black hair was covered by a brown scarf. "Which way did they go?"

"Towards the port. Lamar was certain they would nay look for her there."

The Handmaiden lifted her long robe in both hands and ran towards the port. Is shrugged and followed as Da bellowed in his ear, "I want Mither."

They were almost to the main section where the rounded shops were two or three stories high when they heard the breaking glass. Is stopped to look up and his heart hammered in his chest. Di hurdled out of the second floor of the building in front of them and dropped to the cement, landing on her left side. A wild keening noise erupted from the Handmaiden's throat and she rushed to the fallen woman. Two of the Sisterhood looked down from the broken window and then disappeared.

Is hurried to where the Handmaiden stood disrobing herself.

"Help me move her onto this," she hissed at him. Then clad in her thong and strap and still keening, she knelt beside Di.

"Ye have killed my beloved! Ye are wicked, wicked! Oh, my magnificent Di, my love," and her wails grew louder. A crowd of Abs and Tris began to encircle them, hoping to catch more of the drama. Di's left arm was bloody and immobile. Blood was coming from her left side, her left leg horribly bent, and blood flowed from her nose and mouth.

The Handmaiden looked up at him. "Quickly, I must wrap her. The world should nay see her like this." There was desperation in her voice, and Is knelt, not sure what the Handmaiden was planning.

He stood Da beside them and asked. "Won't we hurt her more?"

"Ye canna hurt the dead, and even had she lived, there tis nay medical for Abs." The Handmaiden glared at him and put her hands under Di's shoulders. Is put his hands under her hips, feeling the familiar rounding wrenched at his stomach and he closed his eyes.

"Lift," commanded the Handmaiden.

Together they moved Di's body onto her robe, and the Handmaiden used her belt to tie the gown around the inert body. Is wanted to believe he'd heard a moan when they moved her, but he could nay see if her eyes were closed or open.

The Handmaiden bent lower and ran her hand over both eyes. "There, I have closed her lids," she announced to the world as two of the black clad Sisters burst through, moving the crowd back.

The sight of the Handmaiden stopped them, and they glanced at the predominantly Ab crowd. They kenned that any move against the Handmaiden would ensure a riot.

"All we need to do is make sure she does nay speak again," said the one with the rank of Sargent.

The Handmaiden looked up at them. "I have already closed her eyes, and the blood has stopped flowing."

Is looked down at Di. How had the Handmaiden worked that miracle? He listened to her words.

"Since she tis Ab, she tis my responsibility. This Ab," and she waved her hand at Is, "will help me move her to the compound. The burning will be in the morn. Please, request that the Byre Berm be open. Ye may bring word to Martin this eve about the time of the burning tomorrow."

She turned back to Is. "Put the laddie on your shoulders, and we will carry her home."

Is picked up the wailing child and whispered to him, and then set him on his shoulders. Wee Da continued to cry, but hung on to his hair. Is nodded at the Hand Maiden, and together they lifted Di and began the long walk to the Ab compound. Inside he was shaking. It would not have surprised him if the Sisters had arrested him and sent him to the mines of Ayran. In his mind, he blessed the Handmaiden for his salvation from that indignity.

The sun still beat its rays against the world when they staggered in, their burden sagging badly. The few Abs that were there stared at them and then broke into fierce whispers.

"She's dead."

"The Kenning Woman has been punished."

"Gar took her."

"Nay, it was the Sisterhood."

"The Sisterhood hated her."

The Handmaiden led the way through the chattering Abs to the Healing Quarter, and one of the male Abs pulled open the door for them, stood back respectfully, and closed the door after they entered the hall.

"We'll take her to the back room. There tis already one dead woman there." She stalked through the first room with its crude stools and tables and brushed aside the curtain. They laid Di on one of the tables that lined the room, and Is removed Da from his shoulders, his chest heaving from the walk. The Hand-maiden's dumpy figure belied her strength as she was breathing normally.

In the middle of the room was another table already occupied by an older, dead Ab woman. She was skinny, wrinkled, and her open mouth gave the observer a view of missing and broken teeth while her unclosed eyes looked up at the dingy ceiling.

"Help me move this table over to the middle of the room," commanded the Handmaiden. Both of them ignored the squalls from Da. Once the table was beside the other one, the Handmaiden picked up Da and whispered to him.

"Your mither can nay hear ye. Ye must remember how much she loved ye. Now kiss her one last time."

She held Da down to Di's face, and he tried pulling her hair to wake her while screaming, "Mither."

The Handmaiden pulled him away and gave him back to Is. "Take him to my laddie, and tell Pi to put Da with Ka. They are close enough to the same age and may console each other. Then have Pi bring me another robe. I'll nay be able to wear that one again." She motioned to the table where Di lay wrapped in her gown.

Is nodded and was about to leave when the curtain was swept open by Martin's staff of authority, and the brown-robed Martin entered the room. His grey hair was mostly gone, but what was left fell in wispy lengths to his shoulders. He cultivated a beard, but his attempt was thwarted by the nature of Thalians. The beard, like his hair, was sparse and grey. It fell in strands from his cheeks and chin giving him a grimed, striped appearance.

The Handmaiden pointed at the opening. "Ye may nay enter here. I have work to do and am nay clothed."

"The Sisterhood wishes assurance that the false Kenning Woman has died ere they deliver tomorrow's food allotment. I must verify this."

"Ye just did. Use your nose as tis the stink of death that dwells here. Ye may tell them their treachery has killed the magnificent Di. Now go away as tending the dead tis my province." Tears were rolling down both sides of her face, but her voice did not waver.

Martin twitched his long beak of a nose, glanced at the table and saw no movement. He noted the yellow pallor of the face that comes from losing too much blood and saw the pooled, thick blood and the death stains spread on the robe. He shrugged, nodded at her, and walked out.

The Handmaiden's shoulders slumped, but she had two more orders for Is. "Once ye have given Da to Pi, ye are to find Ki. She tis supposed to be here helping with her mither or her brither. Ye must also find the Ab sea captain, Bi, who sails from Don this eve. Ke's casket goes with his sailing, and I must have her ready. They will nay need Di's body until tomorrow. Bi was here, but has probably gone with Ki to some swill room. Now go."

She turned away from him and picked up a bucket of water and some strips of cloth. The bucket she placed on the floor next to one of the tables and the cloths on the table. She then began to clean the dead.

Is held the crying Da and stepped out of that dimly lit room; relief then sorrow swept over his face. The eating hour was approaching and more Abs were in the compound, but they had lost interest now that death was accomplished. He carried Da through the empty rooms to where the younger laddies had their sleeping quarters, and found the thirteen-year-old Pi holding ten-year old Ka in his arms. Pi was fairly tall for someone of Ayran descent. His upper was body slender, but he had the wide hips and heavy thighs of Ayran. Is handed Da to him.

"Ye are to put him with Ka so that they may console each other over the loss of their mithers. Once ye have them calmed down, ye are to take your mither a clean robe as she has nay on but her strap and thong."

Sadness shadowed Pi's dark eyes as he reached for the wailing Da and put him next to Ka. Ka was red-eyed, but had stopped crying some time ago. He put his arms around Da, and they clung to each other. After a few minutes, Pi decided it was safe to leave and entered the small, neat room he shared with his mother. He took the spare robe from the hook and hurried to the Healing Quarters. Since Abs were never given medical treatment, Pi thought of it as the Death Quarter. He took a deep breath and entered.

"Make sure that curtain tis locked in place."

His mother's voice brooked no questions, and he used the tags at the bottom and top to keep it from blowing or being pulled aside. He turned to greet his mother and saw the position of the box for Ke and the tears streaking down his mother's face. His eyes widened and his mouth opened in a big O.

Chapter 5

The Justine Refuge

The Captain of Flight looked at those seated around the command center. His Director of Flight was to his right, her mouth in a straight line, and her muscles rigid. His Second in Command was to his left. The rest of the command staff was his Second's various blood kin into the third generation. All but one were descendants of the Captain's own dear Earth counselor, Anna. They numbered nine; six men and three women. Red O'Neal was seated at his Director's right. Red twas related to his Second in Command through their biological Justine fither. O'Neal's title was Captain, although he had requested Commodore, a notion rejected by the others.

"It tis decided then, when we make contact we twill take out any space craft at the Justine Refuge."

"I'd rather be able to utilize any space craft that is at the Justine Refuge." O'Neal wanted another vessel and conquest was one way of securing it.

"Nay!" Both the Captain of Flight and the Director spoke at once.

The Second in Command interrupted. "Be patient, Red, y'all will get your own ship for trading. It's not worth the risk. Why bring it up? We need to take them out at the first strike. Then and only then will they be willing to listen to a bunch of mutants demanding a new treaty in the galaxy." A faint scar pulled the right side of his mouth higher as he gave a quick smile. "Papa and Grandmère are correct."

"I do have one suggestion." The only completely grey-haired member spoke out. "You three," she pointed to the three at the command console, "are better at maneuvering and firing than the rest of us. I believe until we make contact that one, or all three of you, should bed down in here. If we are surprised or need to attack, we can wake you instantly."

"Agreed." The Director of Flight stood. "We twill bring in the bedding now."

* * *

Lamar, his counselor Beatrice, Lass of Betron, and Tamar, laddie of Betron, the sixteen-year-old they were raising, were seated at one of the gold and cream booths in the Justine Refuge lounge. Like Lamar, Beatrice's hair had grayed. They had been sent here to give Rennie, Lady of Rurhran, and her counselor, Rhodan, laddie of Rurhran a long needed break from their stint as envoys to the Justine League. This provided the Justines the opportunity to have Lamar where they could observe him while their one remaining *Golden One* had scheduled maintenance in its bio level.

While the Brendons performed the needed agricultural tasks, a Krepyon craft patrolled the surrounding space. Both Krepyons and Brendons where overseen by a Justine.

No meetings were scheduled, but the Justines required all Thalians and Brendons to be present and visible during the daylight hours. Tamar had appeared for the midday meal. He was allowed to study with the one Justine youth and sessions were over for the day. Like his appointed Guardians, he was clad in the Thalian skin-fitting, dark blue of the House of Don. His dark brown hair was cut short. His eyes were the lighter brown of Troy. His mither, Belinda, Lass of Betron, Counselor of Army, had decided she did nay wish to raise any child; particularly a male child since she had wed Beauty.

The Thalians had greeted each other warmly by hugging, laying their head on the shoulders, and making a tsk sound in the ear. So far, the Justines had not forbidden the ritual, but the Kreppies would frown.

An excited Krepyon voice came over the com. "We have made contact with Ricca's *Golden One*. It is not known at this time if Toma is aboard. We will…"

An explosion in the background was heard and the com went silent.

The Justines, Krepyons, Brendons, and Thalians gathered for the meal sat in stunned silence. What had happened? The Thalians held hands, worry briefly appearing on their faces, then hidden. Llewellyn, their Maca of Don, had been with Ricca. Had he been marooned or would he be returning?

Three Kreppies followed the one Justine up into the control tower.

"He tis trying to contact the *Golden One*," Lamar whispered. "If that twas an attack, they had best man their remaining *Golden One* or any attacker will destroy us."

Beatrice nodded and she gripped his right thigh rather than his useless hand. The Kreppies would kill them if they suspected them of being in league with an unknown assailant.

The Justines' practice of permitting the Kreppies to patrol while the crew of the *Golden One* rested was a dangerous tactic in Lamar's mind. To him, all Kreppies were treacherous.

A *Golden One* appeared on the scan screen. It was high in the northern sky above the Justine created biosphere, and the com returned to life.

"If your *Golden One* shows any signs of lifting, we'll blast it into dust. We are here to discuss a treaty, but will not tolerate an attack." It was a male baritone voice with an unknown accent. The words were in the Thalian language.

"We need to know who you are and why you attacked our ally." The Justine's voice filled the spaces.

"Go to hell." The voice was flat. "Do you wish to talk or not?"

Lamar and Beatrice noticed other Justines flying to their grounded spaceship. The Justines in the lounge area had already left. A bolt of golden light hit the space near the *Golden One*. The ensuing explosion flipped one of the Justine's four-seater Scouts and dust and rock debris flew into the artificial sunlight. Kreppies were running to assist the Justines and then stopped. What if they fired again?

"We need to speak with Ricca or Toma."

Another voice came through the com. "Tis tired I am of this dilly-dallying. Ye had yere chance. Do ye sit at a treaty session with us or nay? If nay, yere Refuge tis nay more."

The voice of Bolly, the Justine in the tower, responded. "Your words are Thalian. Who are you?"

"I am Llewellyn, Maca of Don."

A ripple of murmurs swept through the scale-faced Kreppies. The Thalians fought to keep joy from their faces.

"Llewellyn, do you realize we have your elder Lamar and his counselor Beatrice here? They will die if you do not surrender immediately."

There was a longer pause than normal transmission time.

"They are Thalians and my heart twill break, but if ye dinna negotiate with us, ye are nay more."

"Before we answer you, tell us where Toma and Ricca are."

"Toma tis aboard. He twas most helpful on the journey. Ricca twas a fool and tried to impose his will on the beings of the planet where Toma was trapped. The beings there killed him. Beat him to death with clubs. They are fierce opponents."

The Justine paused before speaking.

"May we see Toma at the controls?"

There was another silence.

"The consensus tis that ye may see Toma, but he tis nay at the controls. Nay may ye speak with him till we have landed."

The scan came alive with a Justine facing a screen in a *Golden One*'s crew quarters. He inclined his head and the scan went blank.

"We need a moment to confer. Will you grant that?"

"Aye, that we twill give."

Grim faced Kreppie guards appeared at the table occupied by the Thalians. Their long stunners were laid across their left arms.

Finally, Bolly spoke again. "What kind of treaty are you requesting?"

Llewellyn's broad face appeared on the screen. "We wish a new treaty for all in this galaxy; including the Brendons. I assume they have an envoy at your Refuge." His pronunciation implied refuge was a dirty word.

Kreppies and Justines could be heard taking a deep breath.

"If ye dinna agree to a treaty, this place, yere *Golden One*, all twill be blasted away. We then continue to the Kreppie's planet and destroy most of what tis there. Thalia twill be free."

The Justines conferred with mindspeak before Bolly spoke.

"You are a Thalian Maca. Will you agree to a challenge to fight one of us? The winner will then dictate the terms."

"It twould give me great pleasure. We twill use a Krepyon ship to land. The *Golden One* remains aloft. If the person manning the controls sees or hears any betrayal of yere words, this place and the Kreppie planet twill be gone."

"Toma would not betray us like this. What have you done to him?"

"Toma twill accompany us when we land. He has agreed to immediately leave the field. We have done nay to him.

"Are we cleared for passage through the biosphere?"

"Where did you acquire the Krepyon craft?"

"Ye equivocate. Do we land or nay?" The voice had grown stern.

"Very well, you are permitted to land."

Kalen, eldest of the Justines, approached the Thalian and Brendon tables.

"All of you are to march behind us. The Krepyons will be your guard. You should be there when Llewellyn loses. No talking."

The Kreppies motioned with their stunners, and all rose to begin their walk. The Brendons' faces were worried. They marched behind the heavier, taller Thalians. Their green hair had begun to turn to the red of old age. They would soon return to their families to be properly buried in the earth to replenish it. Would they not be allowed to complete their final life task?

Lamar noticed the Justine remaining in the tower. Did he plan to fire at the *Golden One* from the tower controls? How could his younger fight a Justine? Llewellyn was a mutant. A mutant twould nay be able to stop the mind control of a Justine.

The Kreppie craft left the *Golden One* and a pulse of energy came from the tower. An answering golden bolt from the *Golden One* met the pulse in the air. The blast rocked the ground and Justines, the two Brendon envoys, the Thalians, and the Krepyons fell. Dust rose and filtered downward in the golden light. A second, slender bolt demolished the upper portion of the tower, leaving a jagged line of concrete, silicon, titanium ribs, and insulating electronic slurry creeping down the outer golden walls. The fallen beings looked around and rose as the Krepyon craft wobbled to a landing.

'They have killed Bolly. Who can be at the controls if Ricca or Toma are not there?' A group mindspeak by the Justines tried to make sense of what they had just witnessed.

The Krepyons were scrambling to retrieve their weapons as the Thalians were on their feet and towered over the Krepyons. Beatrice was positioned on Lamar's right side, Tamar on Lamar's left.

"They've killed a Justine." Lamar muttered to Beatrice. "Be ready to die." His voice faded away as the Krepyon craft's opening panel slid upward to half-position and the landing platform edged out.

"Something tis wrong with that craft." Beatrice tried to keep her voice low.

"No talking," commanded the Krepyon behind Beatrice as he nudged her back with his stunner.

Three people appeared on the ramp. The man in the middle was Toma, red hair, copper eyes with golden bands around the pupil and extremely slender: a typical, tall Justine in appearance. It was the other two that made the watching group look in amazement.

The man and woman were the same height: six feet. Both had red hair and were heavier than the Justine, but they matched steps with Toma as they walked down the ramp. It was the woman who caused mouths to drop. Her mammary glands were large by any known planetary standard; yet her body was slender, the green clothes clinging to her, and her mid-calf shoes had high heels. They were carrying what looked like Krepyon stunners. It wasn't until they were closer that the watchers realized the two had Justine eyes.

The next four caused Beatrice to take a huge, gasping breath and tears began flowing down Lamar's face. Tamar looked in wonderment. To his teenage eyes, two were Thalians; huge, muscled bodies and dark, straight hair. The male had to be Llewellyn, Maca of Don, but who was the older woman dressed in black?

On Llewellyn's left side walked a slender (to the Thalians' eyes), wide shouldered man wearing a kineman's hat like they wore on the continents of Don and Rurhran. His trousers were a heavy material in blue, the shirt Thalian blue, and strange boots were on his feet. His gait was slightly rolling, but nay a Thalian's. The other man looked Justine: tall, extremely slender, but his red hair was thinning. Behind them came a motley group of twenty beings, mostly men but some women, dressed in a wide variety of clothes, hats or hair bands, and boots. All of them carried weapons that resembled long, primitive forms of stunners.

As the group approached, Toma gave a curt nod to his parents and used mindspeak.

'My parents, you are thanked for greeting me, but I must go to the Reflection Room. I have been too long among these primitive beings.'

Kalen and Malen exchanged glances and the group tried to speak to Toma, but his mind interrupted their mindspeak.

'You must forgive me, but three of these creatures are from my spermatozoa. One is their descendent; the others are adventurers from their planet. These beings will take what they want. All of them are capable of violence and you will be unable to enter any of their minds.' He walked away.

"Who tis my opponent?" Llewellyn's voice rumbled out over the assembled beings.

The Justines shifted their gaze. As one, they raised their index finger and pointed at the Thalian woman. A sudden orange burst sprayed the ground in front of the Justines and they stared at the man wearing the kineman's hat.

"Stay out of her mind. She's the only one that cannot protect herself." It was the strangely accented voice heard on the com.

Stunned silence settled over the group. How could any of these beings defy a Justine? An indignant Krepyon standing guard on the left end of the Justine group raised his stunner and died from the man's stunner's orange beam hitting and dissolving him.

As a group, the Justines turned their mind on the man beside Llewellyn, but Kalen fell, writhing in agony.

"Stop, Lorenz, he tis yere biological elder fither."

Thank Gar, thought Lamar. Llewellyn had finally issued an order and then he, like everyone else, realized that man must be one of the three that Toma had sired. All looked at him, but none could detect red hair, and the eyes, the eyes were blind and yet he saw. Was there an implant? Surely, that being could nay have downed a Justine with his mind, and how did Llewellyn ken? A kernel of disquiet grew in Lamar's gut.

Malen used mindspeak with the stranger. 'How can you deny your natural parentage?'

The man responded aloud. "My natural father is a vicious killer. He tried to murder us all. He succeeded in killing a six-month-old baby. This man, Llewellyn, rescued my mother and then me from the hell we'd been thrown into. He is my father and he has my allegiance."

The grey eyes were slate. "You all have tried your tricks. Now which one takes up the challenge or do we end this now?"

A smile flitted across Llewellyn's face. "Tis his way, but he tis correct. Does one of ye fight or do we win by default?"

"I am Adrian and I have the task."

Both men shed their upper garments. Llewellyn was in superb condition. Muscles ran from his neck to his ankles. The Justine was whip-hard, but easily weighed one hundred pounds less; however, the beings inhabiting the Justine Refuge expected him to win. No Thalian could fend off mind control.

The man beside Llewellyn spoke again.

"Remember, this is a physical fight. Both of you can use a mind block, but neither is permitted to enter the other's mind. If any Justine watching tries to interfere, Red, (he waved a hand at the first male to appear) will order his troopers to attack."

Llewellyn went into a half crouch and the two began circling each other looking for an opening. The Justine shook his head, annoyed. He could not penetrate Llewellyn's mind block. Then a stab of pain hit him and he heard the words in his mind.

'I warned y'all. Don't try it again.'

And Llewellyn was at the Justine swinging his powerful fists, landing blows.

Adrian brought his mind into focus to control his muscles and nerves. His mind began to work in perfect unison with his body, sending blows and kicks at Llewellyn. The Justine meld of mind and body meant their physiques possessed strength far beyond their appearance, and their movements were rapid. Adrian's fists and kicks began to land, but Llewellyn continued connecting with his blows.

For ten minutes they fought, sometimes blocking, sometimes bringing blood. Both were bleeding from facial cuts. Adrian danced away, swung back in and landed a blow at the side of Llewellyn's head and tried to execute the same maneuver.

Llewellyn watched him move away and dove for his midsection. His weight brought Adrian to the ground. Llewellyn grasped Adrian's arm and leg and rose, swinging the man in an arc before tossing him to the ground.

Adrian's momentum made him do a slight spin on the tarmac, and then Llewellyn dropped his knees and weight onto the man's chest. Bones could be heard cracking. Llewellyn began to raise the man again for another toss.

"Enough. You may have your treaty. Let us heal our injured."

Kalen spoke through whitened lips. "We will withdraw and you may assemble in the lounge. We'll speak over the com."

"Ye will nay withdraw." It was the Thalian woman with the group. "All of ye twill face us and ye twill hear our words and our terms.

"Captain O'Neal's troopers will disarm and guard the Kreppies." She spat the words out. "The Brendons twill be seated with us. I am sure they have concerns for their planet that we dinna ken."

Chapter 6

The Maca of Don

Llewellyn piloted the Kreppie ship towards the Maca of Don Compound in the city of Donnick. He ordered Jeremiah "Red" O'Neal commanding the *Golden One* to destroy the Kreppie ship rising from Thalia's surface and then three Thalian fighters trying to intercept him. His mission was to access the Maca's Tower and regain control of Don.

This was a confiscated Kreppie ship they had found in the underground research center and manufacturing plant of the Krepyons. They had destroyed everything but one of the two freight ships the Justines had granted the Kreppies. They had modified the seating arrangements ere they left, but it remained a tight fit for his six foot nine frame and corresponding bulk. His dark eyes were on the panel coordinates and he aimed for the padport within the walled compound. The crew behind him consisted of his mither, his laddie Lorenz, his elder Lamar (mither's brither), Beatrice, Margareatha (the lassie of his own, deceased counselor Anna), and four of the adventurers from Earth. They had gone over and over this plan from the time they left the Justine Refuge.

Beatrice had assured them his mither's prints had nay been erased from the security system. The Sisterhood wiped out her ability to change data when they were appointed to the Justine Refuge as envoys.

The landing was perfect and they deployed as practiced; Llewellyn leading the way and the others behind him. At the back double doors, he stepped aside, and his mither came forward, her eyes on the elaborately carved middle door section that hid the screen and placed her hand and fingertips in the panel to the right. In less than a second (to Llewellyn it seemed equal to the one hundred and forty years spent in exile) the doors swung open.

They ignored the lifts to the right and ran down the short hall into the main foyer, Llewellyn leading the way, his mither, his laddie, and Margareatha behind him.

Named Margareatha at birth and Rita by usage, she was part Justine and none here could stop her. As they ran into the foyer, she pointed her finger at the woman sitting at the reception area and commanded, "Lock the doors."

Benna obeyed by clicking in the commands and then fell to the marble floor, moaning and holding her head. To Lettuce, the youngest Don Enforcer, the strange, heavy-topped frontal shaped being was a Justine gone mad. Lettuce had turned from the upper viewing screen and ran to the top of the stairs going down to the foyer. She snapped her weapon into position when a blow from the back sent her sprawling and the weapon dropped to the floor.

The Justine swept her cowl back and seated herself at the front desk. "Can anyone see in?" Her cold, copper eyes with the gold-circled pupils bored into Lettuce who was looking downward and then up towards the figure behind her.

Lettuce heard her Director, Leta, answering.

"Nay, nay can see," quickly to avoid Benna's fate.

Lettuce tried to figure out why Leta had struck her when she saw Lamar standing in front of the hall from the walled courtyard. Then realization registered. It was nay Lamar. This man was younger and possessed a normal right arm. She groped for her weapon.

This time Leta tromped on her hand. "Ye fool, tis our Maca,"

Leta's foot went out and kicked the offending stunner down the stairs. Then she addressed the huge form below. "My Maca, I welcome ye back. How may I help ye?"

Llewellyn, clad in the dark blue of Don, slowed in midstride. "Do I ken ye?"

"Aye, Maca, I am Leta, and I would lay my head on your shoulders."

A wide smile lit the man's face and he shouted, "That must wait, my sweet one. Tis the Ops Room door open?"

"Aye, and I will show the person at the console how to keep it so; if a Justine is to be trusted, that tis."

"Trust her, and confine that one if she tries to stop us." He pointed at Lettuce and whirled to run down the hall. The other beings behind him followed just as rapidly. Lettuce had little time to ken who they were other then Lamar and Beatrice. Two strange beings entered from the hall and carried weapons at chest level. They took up a stance at the entrance as guards.

Lettuce slowly pushed herself up to a sitting position while Leta put the wires around Benna's wrists and ankles. The Justine woman was flicking her eyes between the console screen and them. Lettuce was shocked to see the Justine wore vivid red lip coloring on her full curving lips. Why would a Justine follow primitive ways? The thought was frightening. So were the two strange clad beings of different skin coloring standing guard. Screams came from the Ops Room and Lettuce closed her eyes.

Llewellyn burst into the Ops Room and leaped over the first seated woman to take down three Sisters standing at the screen watching the wrecks and the people congregating around the front of the Maca's Headquarters. The rest of the group entered single file. One black gowned figure smashed into the woman at the main panel, her fists rising and falling, then whirling to meet the next one.

Lamar and Beatrice worked as a team, she standing on his right side to prevent anyone reaching his bad arm.

The strangely garbed grey-eyed man ran at the other Sister at the main panel. Another Sister tried to stop him by leaping in front of him. As she landed, a blow from the man struck her forehead. It was followed immediately by another to the chin. She fell backward against the chair as the man sought to protect Llewellyn and the other figure at the panel. He slammed into one Sister who had managed to grab the attacking woman's left arm and they went down in a tangle. He rolled away and shot upward swinging his fists and connected with another Sister's chest; his second blow landed on her temple. He whirled to meet the next one coming towards them and realized this one would not be so easy. She was taller, heavier, and looked to be a guard, not a technician. He began to bob and weave, trying to give those at the main console time.

"I am Llewellyn, Maca of Don and I issue my call to any that are Don!" The voice boomed out in the small room.

The Sister in front of the strange blind-eyed one stopped. Her fist ready to strike and he saw the look of puzzlement wash over her face. He held up his hands and nodded in the Maca's direction. Confused, she turned and looked.

Llewellyn smiled and opened his arms. "Are ye Don?"

The Sister nodded and took a hesitant step forward, then two, then three, and walked stiffly into his embrace. As tall as she stood, she had to stretch to lay her head on both shoulders.

Her face was dazed as he released her. "My Maca, the Sisterhood will destroy ye, and my family." The last words were bitter.

A soft smile played with the straight features of the Maca. "Nay, we will persevere. Why would your family suffer?"

"I joined the Sisterhood so they would have food. We are from the Third Sector of Don, the poorest in Donnick. They have nay else but my wages."

"Then how would ye like to be part of the Don Enforcers. Leta will arrange it. What tis your name?"

"I am called Lena. Mayhap the Enforcers will be like the Army."

"Good, and mayhap, when the treaty tis read, the Army will have a place for ye again."

Lena shrugged.

Llewellyn looked at the Sisters beginning to stir and then at the console. Beatrice anticipated him and pushed a circle on the raised panel. He nodded to her and bent.

"Leta, we need to confine these people. Will ye direct things? If I remember, the cells are below. Tis that correct?"

"Aye, Maca, I'm on my way, but the Sisters can open all locks from their headquarters. I'll bring wires."

Llewellyn turned to the one working on the console. "How goes it, Mither? Have ye blocked them?"

The woman smiled with satisfaction. "Aye, they are blocked. Now I need to enter your eyes and palm print for transferring the command to ye. Then it will be Lorenz's turn. Thank Gar, they had nay changed the technology in all the time I have been gone."

"How could we? The Justines closed the schools, and nay new systems were allowed." Beatrice's face was grim.

Chapter 7

The Blind-Eyed One

Da, Ka, Pi, and Ur were examining the booths set up in Donnick, capital and port city of Don, this year's location for the Ab Signing Day and Council of the Realm meeting. The Thalian Guardians rotated their Council of the Realm meetings and the Compound of the Abs from continent to continent after every work season for each House to enjoy the economic benefits of members of the House visiting their continent and sharing in the responsibility of caring for the Abs. It was a rotation that had existed from the time Thalia had first united and elected a Council of the Realm.

Da, at age twelve, was large and muscular. Ka at seventeen was still the skinny, dark-reddish brown-headed land Ab from Don. Pi was the tallest, but now his right arm was bent from the injuries in the mines of Ayran. Ur had joined the group two years ago when the Tri family he lived with kicked him out, claiming he was an Ayranian Ab born to their lassie and they could nay longer afford to feed him. There was wonderment on all sides as to why a Tri family would have kept the broad, ugly Ur for as many years as they had. His dark hair was straight and coarse. His teeth gleamed white, but the large teeth were separated by spaces. His one redeeming physical feature was his magnificent, muscular structure. At the age of sixteen, still more than fifteen years away from full maturity, he looked brutal.

Signing Day for the work at the different Houses was in three days, but the weather was not as balmy as a normal spring for the air had a chill to it. Most Abs wore a jacket or extra shirt to keep away the cold; all except Pi and Ur. Pi and Ur had both roused the ire of the Handmaiden and Martin by refusing to accept their assigned roles. Pi had been in training as the new Martin, but

Martin and the Handmaiden had decreed, "Ur tis the chosen by Gar. He will be the new Martin."

Ur laughed and spent his days hiding from them. "What folly," he complained. "All ken that I am a Warrior. Someday I will make the Flight Lists." He remained vague on when there would be any possibility of the Flight Lists being reopened.

Pi had defiantly gathered a group of Abs and spoken to them about their duty to Gar and his own duty to speak the few known word remnants from the pages of the Book Thalia once possessed before the Justines destroyed all copies as barbaric myths and folktales. As punishment, he had been banished from the Ab Compound and then to Ayran on a sham charge of stealing. Since his return, he was allowed on the Ab perimeter and would be permitted to try to sign with one of the Houses. He kenned his chances were ill. He was but twenty and considered young for prolonged physical work, his arm hampered his strength, and starvation was a reality in the coming months. Ur drifted in and out of Martin's control. It depended on how hungry he was and how successful he had been finding clients with money to pay him to procure young girls or boys. He didn't care if the buyers were Tri, Sisterhood, House, or Kreppies, nor did he care if the procured were Abs or Tris. Ur never mentioned his sideline to the others, and, so far, nay had found him out.

Da and Ur looked at the last two wrinkled pina pods they had snitched from the vender's stall and handed them to Pi.

"At the next stall Da and I should wrestle like we are in the Arena," suggested Ur.

"Nay," said Pi, "there would be all sorts of objections. Ye are far too big for Da."

"I can whip him and I'll be on the Flight Lists." Wee Da favored them all with a smile.

"Bah," shouted Ur and went into the stance of a fighter flexing his biceps and raising his arms. "Try me."

Pi sighed and shoved the pods into the pockets of his ragged trousers. "This tis nay the place to raise a crowd." His logic prevailed, and Ur dropped his arms.

"Aye, there tis nay to filch here."

They started back toward the row of stalls and had just turned the corner onto the broad thoroughfare that once thronged with members of House and Tris ready to spend their credits at the shops and eateries. Now only members of the Sisterhood, the alien Kreppie guards, or Abs had any funds. Signing Day had nay brought in any early arrivals from the Houses, and even when they came, they would nay bother with such ill goods except the pina pods from Troy. A Kreppie vessel rose rapidly and silently from the Army Administration quarter and began streaking to the west when a golden beam shot from above and scored a direct hit.

They watched open mouthed, necks craned upward to keep the vessel in sight as smoke poured out of the top and it spiraled downward. As one, the crowd started towards the craft, then the people hesitated, caution overriding curiosity. Only the Justines possessed the golden beams. Had war been declared again? Where would they hide? Nothing could stop the Justines if Thalia and all on it were to be demolished.

Three smaller, black Thalian fighters rose and just as rapidly three golden beams felled them. As the fighters crashed, the crowd stopped moving to watch the smoke billowing upward. "Do ye think we should move away from here?" asked Ka.

"I dinna," whispered Pi. "They have nay fired at the buildings, but they may."

An uneasy quiet crept over the crowd. Black suited Sisters burst out of the Kreppie compound armed with their hand stunners. Three Kreppies armed with their longer, killing weapons ran with them. They seemed to be heading towards the destroyed fighters and the Kreppie vessel. The boys looked at each other and decided to follow.

"Where are the medical?" asked Da.

"They would have to fly here from their own quarter. I dinna think they'll try that right now." Pi's voice was awed.

Ur kept searching the sky. Any attack meant there should be other crafts, he knew it. He was the Warrior. He found what he was looking for and pointed. "See, there."

A green Kreppie craft broke free from the clouds, and to the amazement of the onlookers landed at the back of the Don Compound on the western rim of the bay. The crowd surged westerly. There had been little to amuse them in the past months and they assumed the Kreppies were bent on destroying the last of Don. If they were fortunate, there would be something of value left in the rubble that they could claim.

There was no rubble. The Don banner floated above the door and the rounded blue dome glistened in the sun. The narrow windows of all three levels cast their blue tint around the area. The Kreppie vessel was hidden by the wall.

A contingent of armed Sisters milled around the front, speaking into the back of their hands. They tried waving the crowd back, but by now curious Abs, Tris, and members of House were jostling each other for position to see what would happen.

A unit of Kreppies marched through the milling ranks of the black clad Sisters, wheeling smartly at the front to face the bulk of the crowd. Some in the crowd found it hard to contain their smirks as the Kreppies were nay taller than Da. Balen stepped forward and placed his hands on his hips. The Thalians glared at the self-important pose, but waited, unable to initiate an attack. The Kreppies smirked back. They had weapons, and reprisals from the Justines would be swift if Thalians did not obey their jurisdiction.

Balen, in a loud voice announced, "I am here by the command of the Golden Ones. Everyone is to leave this area. My men will be stationed here to prevent any mischief. All your questions will be answered tonight at the Guardian's Council of the Realm. The Justines will reveal their purpose. Two minutes after I leave, my men will start to clear the area." He marched off surrounded by five of the armed Kreppies. The other Kreppies remained on the steps casually pointing their weapons at the crowd. Everyone realized they had important business elsewhere that needed immediate attention.

The blue, opaque glass doors set between two columns prevented any viewing as to what the Enforcers of Don were doing. The limestone columns and rounded mass of the building reflected blue and white; a cold, impersonal monument to the once proud House of Don, and no one appeared to explain.

"Where do we go now?" asked Ka as they walked away.

"To the Guardian Complex." Da was shocked at such ignorance.

Pi nodded his head, but Ka was puzzled. "Why? Tis but a little after the midday. Nay will be there now."

"But there will be cleaning for hire, and nay else will want to do Don's section." Da was impatient with the rest.

Ur felt they should try for a different section and objected. "Don nay sets out the required food or clothes. The Guardian of Don and her Counselor arrive as the session begins and leave as it ends. I prefer Rurhran. They put out a feast and give out the required clothing."

"And the work goes to Martin's minions." Pi's voice broke in derisively. "We are but laddies. Don tis all they will allot us, if that. If we get it, at least we can shower while we clean."

"Tis something the rest of us will appreciate." Ur grinned at him and threw a fist at the good shoulder. The rest whooped with laughter as they ran for the Guardian Complex.

They were lucky. As the first to arrive, they were allowed to be among those that bid for the cleaning. When the other Abs willing to work for food and clothes declined Don's section, the Keeper of the Complex pointed at them. "Tis yours and the cleaning must be accomplished by seven when the doors are open and all arrive."

Ur took one look at the years of untended dirt and grime in Don's section and shook his head. "This tis folly. Ye are welcome to the rewards, whatever they may be." He bounded over the low wall in front of the seats without a backward glance and headed out the door. The other three looked at each other. Finally Pi spoke.

"Why tis this so important to ye, Da?"

Da looked at his friends. "I ken that something truly important has happened today. Tis like Mither tis whispering, 'Go to Don.'" His lower lip protruded and his soft, child's face hardened.

Pi smiled at him and touched him on the shoulder. "I will help ye then."

Ka shrugged his shoulders. His elder was in Don and she would make certain that he received his allotment of food. Da never worried about food for the Handmaiden always had a roll or sweet for him, but he worried about Pi. So far, betwixt the three of them, they had kept Pi supplied with enough to survive. Since Pi felt this was important to Da, then he too would stay and help for he did nay believe Da would stick with the chore of cleaning.

Hours later, all three romped in the huge shower built for two adult Thalians, perhaps with dalliance on their mind. They whooped as the cold, then warm stinging needles of soapy water ran full force on their bodies. They had finished pulling on their clothes when two of the Keepers of Don entered carrying platters of food. The boys almost laughed at the relief on their faces when they saw the cleaned rooms, but wisely swallowed it down. There was food for the House of Don and the requisite two Ab loaves made of coarse grain. They set the covered platters on the heavy table and handed the loaves to Pi.

"Ye are allowed the clothing ration, but I canna promise the compartment will open, or if your size will be there," said one. She was dressed in the medium blue of a Don retainer and the dark blue belt denoted her rank as Keeper. Her dark hair was cut blunt on top and shaved down the sides and from the crown to the nape in the manner of the Sisterhood. She spun on her heel and led the way towards the back. In the hallway, she pressed a symbol on the panel.

One wooden wall slid into another and revealed empty shelves from floor to ceiling. The dust of over a hundred years floated out and coated the floor. The woman shrugged and anger laced at her words as she glanced at the empty shelves.

"Ye are out of luck. Nay has been restocked. They that claim to rule Don are negligent." She touched the symbol and the wall slid shut. She stalked out, the younger women following her.

They looked at each other in silence and ran back into the main room, all three heading to the table. They stopped, grinned at each other, lifted the heavy, silver domes, and gazed in wonder at the array of food. Pi felt his stomach contract and his knees turn wobbly as the smell of meat and peppers fought with the cloying sweetness of sugar from the yeasty rolls and daintily wrapped special candies. Da's hands shot out and he began stuffing the candies into his pockets. Pi and Ka started on the meat pies. Da grinned at them and reached for the small, silver rearing elbenor statue guarding the candies when a cold voice snapped them to attention.

"What the hell do you all think you all are doing?"

The language was similar. There was no misunderstanding the words and the authority in the voice. Da hurriedly stuffed the elbenor in his pocket while turning. They found themselves looking at a handsome, male being with wide shoulders, slim hips and flanks, a black kineman's hat set on his head, and clothed in the dark, blue hue of Don. More amazing, the eyes were grey, flat, and hard, but this being, despite the blind eyes, could see, and he was looking straight at them.

The candies in Da's left hand fell to the floor and he stammered, "My, Laird, I sorrow." And the rest of the words he meant to say would nay come as he gazed at the man his mither had died for. How could he go to this man who saw him as a thief?

All three clasped their hands behind their backs and bowed. Pi could think of nothing to say, and the food weighed heavy in his gut. Any Ab caught stealing was sent to the mines in Ayran and he was certain he would die there this time.

The man moved from the door and walked with long strides toward them, his shoulders swinging, his rolling walk of a man long in the saddle imitated that of a Thalian, and yet to their eyes his body was too straight, the gait wrong. In the doorway loomed another man. This one was taller, heavier, his bodysuit of navy blue material accentuating every muscle that rippled and rolled down from his neck, through his shoulders, arms, torso, thighs, and legs. He walked with the normal, rolling, rocking gait of a Thalian, but it did little to assure them. Behind the strange Thalian, Lamar, and his Counselor, Beatrice, appeared.

The blind-eyed one's hand was on Da's shoulder and another hand gripped him under his chin and lifted it up. "Y'all were stealing."

"Tis ye, Lorenz, ye, nay you all." The huge man stood beside them, glanced down and said, "They are the Abs hired for the cleaning."

"Y'all don't call this clean."

"Considering the condition over the last few years, aye, it has been cleaned." Beatrice was as uninterested in Abs as Lamar, but she felt the truth was necessary.

The man's face remained hard as he looked down at Da. "Y'all want to hand me that…" He saw the blank look in Da's eyes and switched his wording. "Show me what ye put in your pocket, or do I turn ye upside down and shake it out?" His voice was mild, but there was no mistaking his intent.

For a moment Da hesitated, his face reddened, and then anger burst through. "Tis your fault. Ye dinna come! They killed her!"

"Whoa, back up. Killed who?"

"Mither. She said ye'd come. Ye and him." Da pointed at the Maca, who was eating a meat pie and watching with narrowed eyes. "Ye are to restore Don and I would be in House and a Warrior."

"Why would anyone kill your mother-mither-over what she said to ye?" Lorenz was puzzled. The kid was truly angry and blamed him.

"She was the Kenning Woman and she proclaimed it to all. That tis why they killed her!"

"There tis nay Kenning Woman." Lamar muttered.

"And when was this all supposed to have happened?" Lorenz continued his questioning.

"Seven years ago. And she was the Kenning Woman. All listened to her."

"Boy, (Lorenz switched to Thalian again) laddie, seven years ago we were loading the ship to start here. How could she know, ken, that?"

Wee Da looked at him in amazement. He was spent inside. All he wanted to do was crawl away and hide, and still the man held him firm in his grasp, looking at him with those strange, grey eyes that should nay see, but did.

Lorenz started to say more, but time shifted and he wasn't looking at a boy's face. It was a muscular woman with long, dark brown, wavy hair and light brown eyes, holding out her right hand to him, a pleading look on her face and in her eyes. For some reason her left side was obscured as though floating in fog. He blinked his eyes and he was staring down at the kid. Kenning he understood. Often his father had called Mama a Kenning Woman and said that he had some of her abilities.

"Who killed her?"

"I nay ken. Most say the Sisterhood, but others say it was House too."

"Why do ye call him Laird?" The huge Thalian asked.

"The Kenning Woman said that you, the Maca of Don, would return with your blind-eyed laddie and restore Thalia." Pi was trying to find words to save them all.

The Maca gave a tight smile.

"Who can verify, hell, tell me what ye are saying tis the truth about your mother, mither."

Pi cleared his throat. "She told her vision on the waterfront of Betron. There were many there for the Council and for the Ab signing."

"All Abs lie." Lamar admonished. "Ye must hear it from House or a House Tri."

Pi straightened, his face red. "I would be House if Mither had stayed in Ayran. He tells the truth. The Sisters came to the Ab quarters to make sure she was dead."

"Did y'all see or hear them." Lorenz ignored Lamar's snort.

"Well, nay. They sent in Martin to verify her death."

"Uh huh, and I suppose he's somebody important too." Lorenz inclined his head towards Ka.

"Nay, Laird, I am but an Ab and I will leave now." Ka started edging toward the door.

"Stay right where y'all are."

They could hear the bustle of a crowd outside and Llewellyn wiped his hands. "Tis time we made our appearance."

"You all stay here until I get back to sort this out. Eat all the food you all want." The hands released Da. "After y'all take out what's in your pocket and put it on the table." The last words snapped out.

Wee Da swallowed and drug up the silver figure. "I sorrow, Laird. I will nay touch it again." He tried to make his face pathetic and then bowed.

37

"Abs canna remain in here during a meeting of the Council." Lamar was outraged.

Lorenz turned on Lamar, his face a cold mask when Llewellyn stopped him. "Why tis this important to ye, Lorenz?"

"It's hunch. I'm going with my gut."

Llewellyn smiled. "Aye, in that case, they stay." He saw the disappointment on all three faces. "Mayhap ye should turn on the viewers and eat all ye wish," He turned and walked for the door.

"Llewellyn, ye have forgotten the ways of House. Ye canna do this."

Llewellyn stopped for a moment, his voice hard. "Ye forget, my Elder. I am Maca." He strode out of the room.

Chapter 8

The Treaty

Attendance at a Council of the Realm meeting by the Tris and those of lesser standing in the Houses was but a fraction of bygone days. What few Tris of Don and other Houses were in the audience were in the middle sections on either side of the reserved boxes. Once Abs were excluded but now their brown garments filled the side rows from top to bottom. They were a bitter reminder to the Houses as to who really ruled Thalia.

As the members of the House of Don emerged, the crowd became silent. Beatrice and the blind-eyed one stayed in the open Don seating area while the Maca and Lamar moved to join the procession ready to take the Guardian and Counselor chairs. The Council of the Realm would nay be dull this evening.

Ilman from Ishner, appointed Counselor of Don, wedded to the appointed Guardian of Don, rushed at Llewellyn, her palms extended to push him out of the line. "Ye are nay fit to sit." she was reduced to screaming when Llewellyn's hands came out and encircled hers. Agony etched her face as he tightened his grip and she went to her knees before being lifted and thrown towards Ishner's place in line. She landed with a thump on her backside. The people in the stands gasped, then laugher rippled in small waves.

"There tis your trouble maker, Ishmalisa of Ishner. Do with her as ye please. She tis barred from Don." His roar filled the auditorium. Llewellyn turned to the appointed Guardian, Lavina, and his words rumbled out.

"I am Maca, and to ye I issue my call. Ye may take your seat in Don's seating, or ye may leave. If ye leave, ye will be banned from Don."

Lavina lifted her arms for the Maca to pick her up so she could lay her head on his shoulders, confused as to how she should react until she felt the burning, nerve tingling command of the Maca's hands. She first laid her head on the right shoulder and then the left, but instead of the clucking sound of greeting, she was whispering, "Maca, they have my laddie," in the right ear, "and my beloved," in his left ear.

Llewellyn responded in like manner laying his head on one shoulder and then the next as he whispered, "Tell the man standing outside the door that Mac says ye may leave by fliv." He then set her down and gave a quick smile.

"Since ye have acknowledged me, ye may stay or leave, with my blessing." He moved to stand beside Lamar as the trumpet sounded to signal the Guardians to convene.

Beauty held up her hand to stay the line and started towards Llewellyn. "Ye are an interloper here. Nay male may sit as Guardian." Her voice rang out.

Llewellyn placed both hands on his hips and a wicked grin lashed across his broad face. "Beauty," he greeted her, "I remind ye, I am Maca of Don. Ye still owe me bedding for the time I beat ye in the Arena. Do ye intend to honor your word now in front of all?"

Beauty stopped as laughter ran through the crowd again, and Betta put a restraining hand on her wrist.

"Nay now." Betta's voice was sharper than normal.

Beauty swung to face her mother. "Mither, we canna allow this breach." She ground the words out.

"He tis Maca," came the complacent words of her mother. "Come, ere the Kreppies complain we delay the Golden One and make us small in the eyes of Thalia." She turned and started up the middle staircase that ran inside the round stone column holding the Guardian's rostrum. Two lines of Guardians and Counselors started up the left and right staircases that led to their seats. Beauty quickly caught up with Betta, her face flushed and her fists clenched as tightly as her teeth.

Betta seated herself and watched the others emerge from the stairs and take their seats. To her right and left the seats curved around her and Beauty. Army, Betron, Ishner, Medical, and Rurhran were on her right. Ayran, Don, the empty chairs of Flight, Manufacture and Trade, and then the appointed Guardian and Counselor of Troy were on the left. All of the seats for Guardian and Counselor, except Ishner, Rurhran, and Don, were occupied by women. Ishmalisa was allowed her mate to be her Counselor since he always deferred to her. The Counselor of Rurhran never contradicted his Guardian and was the last of the male Warriors that fought the Justines. The last male warrior, if one did nay acknowledge Lamar. It was painful to look at Lamar and see what he had sacrificed for Thalia. His existence shamed them all for their adherence to the rule of the Justines and the Sisterhood. Now there was another treaty. How many new humiliations would be demanded from Thalia? Llewellyn was the focal point. Why had the Justines permitted him to live and to return? Her forefinger touched the audio circle and her words came out strong and clear.

"Welcome Thalians and honored guests." In her mind she saw all the Kreppies crumpled on the floor with broken necks and backs. "We are here to approve the new treaty from the Justine League."

The Kreppies were seated below and directly across from the Guardian and Counselor of the Realm in the House section. Balen touched the amplifier button on his chest and stood. "Prepare to welcome the Golden One. Honor him."

The double doors opened and the Justine appeared. His copper hued hair was mid-length and bare of covering. His copper eyes with the golden circle around the pupils were fixed on his reserved seat. His golden robe barely covered the shimmering bluish white gown that swept to the floor. The robe swung easily as the man moved with measured steps across the arena, his longish face in complete repose. Balen and the rest of the Kreppies dropped to their knees and lowered their heads. A murmur rose and flew through the spectators as another figure appeared. This one was not as tall as the Justine, only about three inches over six feet, and was covered by a long, black Thalian warrior's cloak. The cowl was pulled forward and effectively hid the features, but all could see this one moved with the rolling gait of a Thalian.

"Who?"

"Who?" The word buzzed through the crowd.

Their attention was diverted as more beings entered and the crowd gaped in wonder. The first was a tallish woman with exquisite even features, high cheek bones, and full red lips. Her curly hair was as red as an angry sunset. The thick mane of curls spilled down past her shoulders and the sides were pulled up and tied back with a shiny green ribbon. Her cape of green was thrown back revealing a dull green, tight fitting garment that showed every curve and line. Her boots had slender, spiky heels that would nay permit running. Never had any of the spectators seen a female with such heavy mammary glands, not sensibly flattened, but pushed up and outward by her clothing, unless she was due to birth, but that did nay seem probable since the woman was slender from the glands down. They gasped as they saw her Justine copper, golden pupil circled eyes look at them and at the Guardians as she moved a few feet to the left of the door.

The next being was a male dressed in clothes of mottled browns, tans, and greens. His hair under a kineman's hat was the red of a young Justine. His eyes were Justine, but his build was wide in the shoulders, more muscular down the middle, and slim hipped. In his arms, he cradled a weapon. More beings followed. Their clothes were mottled like the first man, but most were hatless, and two of them had bands tied around their heads. In their arms were the disallowed weapons, but it was their appearance that struck the crowd. These were no known beings. One was but medium height, his skin coloring like a Thalian's and his eyes were blue. A woman with fewer curls and sensible warrior shoes was dark haired with brown eyes and could have passed for a smaller Thalian. One man was the color of the darkest brew from Rurhran and his black hair looked permanently crimped. Two other men were medium in height, with bronzed skin like land Abs, but their hair and eyes were dark. The last man was so blond he could be a Slavey's slave if there were any Slaveys left in the galaxy.

The Guardians were as astounded as the crowd, but Betta managed to keep her face neutral as she tried to calculate how many new planets and cultures these beings represented. Betta surmised that there might be three, possibly four, and Llewellyn had contacts with them. The figure beside the Justine was the puzzle. Nay Thalians had been permitted to leave other than the appointed envoy to the Justine League. Lamar and Beatrice had returned with Llewellyn and the robed figure was nay the daughter of Rurhran, nay her counselor as they were here, not yet scheduled to leave for duty. It was time to speak and she addressed her remarks to the Justine.

"We request that ye advise your people that weapons are nay allowed in the Guardians Council."

The Justine looked up at her. "Guardian, I have no control over those beings. Our minds cannot penetrate theirs." Silence filled the hall and Betta considered. Were they superior beings? She looked down at them and spoke to the strange woman. "Will ye have them disarm?"

The woman lifted her head. "No, not at this time." Her face showed no emotion, nor was there any in her rich contralto.

Betta started to object, but the Justine began speaking.

"Guardians and Counselors of the Realm, the Justines have agreed to deliver this new treaty that has been imposed upon us. This treaty affects the Justine Refuge, Thalia, Krepyon, and Brendon. The harsh terms we extracted from Thalia and Brendon are rescinded.

"The treaty itemizes the freedoms you are given back and the restraints and obligations of the Justines and Krepyons. It includes the name of the Thalian that sent us word of your attack, the money we have paid her and your Sisterhood over the last one hundred and sixty-three years as you implemented our policies and removed the dissidents from the Houses. At this time, the Thalian responsible for the new treaty will read it to you."

At his words that told of a betrayer in their midst, Betta reached out and clasped Beauty's hand, and brought Magda of Medicine to her feet, her wrinkled face contorted in anger. The hands of the Guardians and Counselors of Ishner and Rurhran were tightly clasped. Betta glanced at her miniature screen. Jolene of Ayran, her face tightened, had a thin smile of satisfaction. Brenda, Maca of Betron, was scowling, and Betta kenned that Brenda was thinking of her laddie, Laird of Betron, recently condemned. Bobinet, Guardian of Army, was looking wildly at everyone, and Betta's heart sank.

The Thalian beside the Justine reached up, undid the cape and cowl, swept the garment back and off, lifted her head, and with arms and fists pumping upward, screamed, "Thalia, I have returned." Her grey hair was a short bob and the black warrior's suit accentuated every muscle. Although she neared the declining age, absence from Thalia had nay diminished that magnificent body.

For a moment there was silence, and then the people rose and screamed as one, "LouElla, LouElla!"

Betta was on her feet with the rest, ignoring Beauty who remained seated. It was LouElla, the finest Warrior Thalia ever birthed. LouElla who while exiled had stolen the Golden One and used it as a huge weapon to crash into the Justine planet in revenge for all of Thalia's dead. Thalia mourned at her passing and appointed LouElla as honorary Guardian of Flight. The remaining Justines had permitted it as all of Thalia's space transports were destroyed, the factories deactivated, and the schools closed.

LouElla lowered her arms and held forth the thin sheets of metal with inscribed words. "Valun of Justine has given ye the gist of this treaty, but tis nay I that am responsible. It tis my Maca, my laddie, Llewellyn!" The pride in her voice blasted to shreds the very basis of the Sisterhood's oldest tenet that LouElla had decreed there be nay male Macas. "His laddie, Lorenz, my younger," the pride still in her tone as she looked at the blind-eyed one in the Don section before continuing, "their kin and hired retainers." She swept her hand, indicating the group at the door. "They are responsible."

"Llewellyn, tis ye who should read this treaty as ye are the one who won the challenge."

Betta stood. "LouElla, beloved, we welcome ye back into our hearts, but what challenge?"

"When we surprised the Justine League and demanded a new treaty, they scoffed at us and challenged my laddie as befits the ways of a Thalian. They could nay defeat him by mind and nay by bodily combat. The Justines were so confident they offered that winner take all. They signed our treaty as promised, and they divulged their secrets. Now hear our rights. Then I shall finish what I started and challenge the one who betrayed my beloved Jason, our Mithers, Fithers, our youngers and elders, and destroyed Thalia."

Betta sat, her eyes fixed on LouElla. Dear Gar, the woman meant to destroy all the governmental changes the Sisterhood had won.

Llewellyn's deep voice rolled over them. "We, the Justines, relinquish all right to govern Thalia, Brendon, and Krepyon. Each shall have the right to govern their own worlds as they had before we destroyed their capabilities with the help of Thalia's, Bobinet of Betron. For her information of the date of your combined attacks, we paid her the sum of ten million Justine credits.

"During the occupation, we also paid the Sisterhood the sum of five hundred thousand credits for the dismantling of the cattle and sheep herds of Don, the mammals called kine and bucht in Thalia. For each dangerous Thalian male or female removed from Houses and made Ab, we paid the Sisterhood twenty-five thousand credits and deposited all amounts for them to use in trade with the other planets. At present this account totals five million, five hundred thousand credits. Don has been awarded the five hundred thousand credits to compensate them for the temporary loss of their cattle and sheep. We deliberately depleted the Houses of Thalia so they would never become a viable armed force again. A list of those charged is provided. We admit that none of those from the Houses charged as our enemies ever tried to fight us. The only Thalian to fight us after the first treaty was Lamar of Don and we eliminated his ability to reproduce."

Lamar sat straighter at Llewellyn's words. Magda of Medicine tightened her grip on the symbolic spear. Brenda of Betron had her arms crossed over her chest and was glaring at Betta. Tears rolled down the cheeks of Ishmalisa of Ishner as she thought of her dead parents, her siblings, and her Counselor's two youngers condemned as Abs. Rurhran had nay lost their members to condemnation, but the Guardian and her Counselor remained with their hands clasped, and no one could read the heavy face of Jolene of Ayran.

"The Krepyon ships in our possession have been given to Llewellyn, Maca of Don. The Krepyon ships on Thalia and Brendon will be given as compensation to the respective worlds. The Krepyons on these worlds and our renovated asteroid will be transported back to Krepyon by one of the *Golden Ones* in the possession of the Maca of Don, and under the control of an Earth being by the name of Jeremiah O'Neal." Betta drug in a huge gasp of air as Llewellyn read these words. Control of the ships was disaster for the Sisterhood. She forced her mind back to the reading.

"While at the planet Krepyon, Llewellyn and LouElla with the assistance of their crew were to dissemble and destroy all but one of the remaining Krepyon crafts capable of interplanetary travel as well as their manufacturing plants. This will place all known beings on the same technological level."

Balen had jumped to his feet dragging at his holstered weapon when the woman at the door stepped forward and pointed her right index finger at him. Balen dropped to his knees and crawled to her whimpering for forgiveness. None of the other Kreppies moved. Wherever the origins of the red-headed woman, the spectators grasped the fact that she was Justine, and she could inflict pain with her mind. She held up her hand and the crawling Balen stopped when he approached her feet.

"We the Justines will no longer interfere with the governments of the other planets. We are offering our services as teachers and mediators and our living space as somewhere others may come to learn and discuss their differences or to rest from their journeys. The knowledge we have acquired over the millenniums will be available to all. One of the Earth descendants of our own Toma will run the education unit. We will continue to pay a fair price for the imported food for our needs. There will also be a unit devoted to relaxation for travelers. This unit will be commanded by the Earth female issue of Toma. All rights of trade will be returned to the respective planets, and they are free to trade with all others."

Betta could imagine the great joy this would bring to Brendon with its lush fields and greenhouses, and she ground her teeth knowing that she would lose the support of agricultural Rurhran if the Sisterhood no longer controlled the sale of grains, fruits, and meats going to the Justines and the Krepyons. The Guardian of Rurhran was squeezing the hand of her Counselor wondering how she could keep the kine and sheep herds away from Don and not lose the profitable export of meat, grains, fruits, and clothing. At least the Justines had allotted Rurhran a portion of the trade. Would the Kreppies buy from Rurhran if they could buy food elsewhere? They watched Llewellyn retrieve the crystal from his unit and nod at his mither.

LouElla smiled up at him. "Thank ye, Llewellyn."

She moved down from the platform, raised her face toward Bobinet, Guardian of Army, and roared.

"Bobinet, ye traitor of Thalia, ye are challenged to the death for the Thalian deaths ye caused."

Chapter 9

Restoration Delayed

Bobinet stared straight ahead and touched her audio. "LouElla, my beloved, think what ye do."

"Ye are nay and were nay ever my beloved!"

"LouElla, all ken that we spent those last three nights together ere the attack on the Justines."

LouElla whirled and looked up at Jolene. "Tell the truth, Jolene, I charge ye. Tell them who I was with and where."

Jolene of Ayran's face was triumphant and her brown eyes gleamed. "LouElla was with my brither, Jason, at Don's Laird's and Lady's Station. I did nay speak previously or the House of Ayran would have suffered the depredations of the Sisterhood."

Betta noted her choice of words.

The crowd was silent, watching the woman in the middle of the Arena.

LouElla looked to Jolene's right. "Llewellyn, will ye attend?"

"Aye, Mither." He stood and moved towards the stairs.

LouElla looked back at Bobinet. "Will ye answer the challenge or be ranked as a coward and condemned to the mines of Ayran for your betrayal?"

Still Bobinet did not move, but Magda, Guardian of Medicine, her gray hair slicked back, was on her feet. "She fights or I will impale her now!"

Her right hand held the spear aimed at Bobinet. "My fither, my mither, my whole House died in that battle, and now my eldest lassie has been sacrificed to the Sisterhood's greed."

Stone-faced, Bobinet tried one more time. "LouElla, consider, ye are about to destroy the Sisterhood ye created."

"Ye lie," LouElla shouted. "There were so few Thalian men left that my words were for the small fighting force that remained on Thalia because of youth or pregnancy, and so I addressed ye as sisters. Look at ye now. Where are your wee ones?"

Her question stung deep. Birthing had been curtailed or aborted. Who wished to raise a wee one to be sentenced as an Ab to the mines or the fields?

Bobinet rose. She had nay fear of LouElla, and she nodded at her lassie, the Counselor of Army.

"Will ye attend?"

Belinda was white faced under her dark, straight hair, and her lips were drained of color. "Mither, I canna."

"Ye must." Bobinet reached down and pulled her up. "Come." As they descended the stairs, she kept up a line of chatter to reassure her lassie.

"'Tis true, LouElla was once stronger, but I am faster. LouElla has been gone these many years, and has missed honing her skills in the Arena or Flight Lab with nay way to test her moves and keep her fighting skills sharp. I shall be merciful and tell her that a bedding tis preferable to her death." Bobinet smiled with satisfaction as they walked out below and she began stripping out of her black, Army uniform.

LouElla pulled open her suit and used Llewellyn's arm to steady herself as she stripped off her suede boots. These had been cobbled to be as close as possible to Thalian footwear. Then she shed the body clinging clothing to stand before the crowd in her strap and thong. Bobinet handed the rest of her clothes to Belinda and looked at her opponent.

Both women were over three hundred years of age, but LouElla was taller by two inches and she had never let her body sag. She plotted for years to take her final revenge. Her body was as hard as it had been when she was younger and the crowd roared her name as she bent the bar. Bobinet no longer deluded herself as to muscle mass, but still believed her moves would be swifter and surer as they moved toward each other.

Bobinet feigned to one side and swung her left fist at LouElla's nose and missed. LouElla had squatted and lunged forward, faster than Bobinet imagined possible. When had LouElla quit meeting every opponent head on? The crowd roared again as LouElla stood, Bobinet's legs were locked in her arms and she went into a spin, tossing Bobinet into the middle of the Arena.

Bobinet ignored the superfluous skin burns and jumped up to face LouElla who was bounding forward, fists swinging. They stood toe to toe, landing blows to head and body. Bobinet managed to step back, whirl, and aim a kick at LouElla's hip. Once again LouElla moved faster than Bobinet anticipated. The kick hit further back on the buttocks than planned, and LouElla remained on her feet to close in, landing her massive fists against Bobinet's flesh.

The greater muscular strength of LouElla took its toll, and Bobinet faltered as a fist cracked into her head. She dropped her arms for a moment and felt herself lifted into the air again. This time LouElla dropped her flat onto the floor of the Arena and then landed with her knees in the middle of her back. Bobinet's lungs collapsed as her ribs cracked, and she tried to put her arms under her body to push upward.

LouElla grabbed Bobinet underneath the chin and with her other hand, the hair on the top of her head. Then LouElla twisted the chin to the side and upward. The crowd had grown silent and the crack of breaking neck bones could be heard by everyone. Belinda screamed for Medicine as she rushed forward and knelt at her mother's side.

Babara, Director of Army, touched her audio circle and hissed an order.

"Attack." Then she rushed from the Army viewing box, tearing her tunic up over her head and flinging it wide, revealing the flat, altered chest of the newest Sisterhood fashion as she rushed to take LouElla down. Llewellyn dropped LouElla's clothing and stepped in front of LouElla, his fist coming up and connecting on Babara's chin. She dropped as though dead.

The door at the far side of the Guardian's Hall opened and a squad of Army troopers manned by members of the Sisterhood ran in. The alien being with grey eyes tossed aside his hat, vaulted over the low wall, and grabbed the bending bar stuck into the rack. He held it midlevel and ran forward to meet the black clothed warrior women pouring in from the back door.

Betta was on her feet, trying to be heard over the tumult. "Order! Order! LouElla has won the Challenge!"

Llewellyn scooped up the prone Babara and flung her at the advancing troopers. Three of the front women went down at the impact and those directly behind fell over them. The being with the bar stepped aside as two came at him, whirled and swung the bar behind their knees, dumping them on the floor. He whirled again, and continued swinging the bar, catching the legs of three more attackers. Those running behind the front lines on his side fell and started to rise, when the loud report of weapons echoed in the round Hall. The silence was complete.

The female army of Thalia looked at the door where the strange beings stood with weapons pointed at them and a red-headed Justine in strange clothes spoke in a calm, steady baritone.

"That was strictly a warning. The next volley kills. LouElla, darling, if y'all would be so kind as to get those two fools out of there, we can avoid hitting them when we fire. The rest of you be assured; we will kill if you attack again."

The crowd, the Houses, and the Warriors all understood the words that were so familiar, yet pronounced so differently. Betta was still standing, and she looked down at O'Neal.

"Would ye allow our Medical to verify whether Bobinet still lives?"

The man looked up and a smile curved his mouth. "Of course, Guardian of the Realm, our purpose here is to keep order and corral the Krepyons for their ride home. We don't want to interfere with your traditions."

Betta looked at Magda and her Counselor. Magda gave an abrupt nod and Melanie rose and descended the stairs. All waited in silence.

The young man with the rod and Llewellyn had slowly walked backward until they were beside LouElla. Betta had noticed his grey eyes sweeping the crowd, the room, every corner during the seating and the reading. She had wondered how such a skinny bodied one or the other strange beings would react when faced with fighting Thalians. The outcome was nay what she expected. Nay had run or cowered. True, two were Justines and the others had weapons, but none had shown any fright.

Melanie gently moved Belinda out of the way and knelt. She held the scanner over Bobinet, shrugged, then stood, closed her fist, and laid the closed fist on her heart to signal one and all that Bobinet was dead. Belinda's sobbing became screams and she rocked back and forth on her heels.

Beauty rose and ran to her counselor. Betta spoke to the crowd, "In view of the death of our Sister, I believe we must stop all proceedings until after a proper grieving time."

Magda rose. "That Sister," her voice registered somewhere between a hysterical screech and a sneer, "was a traitor. We vote on the treaty now, and then we bring our loved ones back to House."

Betta tried reason. "Magda, we are all upset over the news and events of today. That tis why I suggested waiting rather than vote now. I hate to be the one reminding ye, but your lassie disobeyed the rules of the Arena, nay Sisterhood. She could nay be one whose removal was paid for or instigated by the Justines.

Magda shook her spear in the air. "It was the Sisterhood under the guidance of the Justines and Kreppies who changed the punishment from banishment in the Arena to being declared an Ab. All those punished and condemned as Abs must be returned now. My lassie returns to House!"

Betta could not offend Magda for her support of the Sisterhood was vital. She wished Beauty would leave that twit she had wedded and return, but Beauty was carrying the sobbing Belinda off to the Army's section. "Council of the Guardians, do ye believe we should vote or wait?"

"We vote." The roar came from all but the appointed Troy Guardian and Counselor.

Betta took a deep breath. Her allies were the two appointed to Troy; nay else. The only way to stave off complete debacle was to allow the vote and let them reclaim the members of their House. She had tried to warn Beauty and Bobinet.

"Ye canna take the lads and lassies away from their Houses," but they would nay listen.

She watched with misgiving as Llewellyn escorted LouElla to her seat as Guardian of Flight, but she smiled at LouElla and said, "Since the others are in such a rush, ye may wish to appoint your Counselor later."

LouElla turned. "I appoint Llewellyn, my Maca and my laddie, as my Counselor of Flight. He has flown the Golden One and the Kreppie vessels." She gathered her cape around her and both sat in the chairs of Flight.

"As Maca of Don, I, Llewellyn, appoint my elder Lamar as Guardian and his counselor, Beatrice, as Counselor of Don. They have served Don well in my absence."

Betta clenched her jaws and forced a smile for the crowd. Silence reigned while Beatrice made her way to Don's Counselor Chair. Then she began the roll call by calling on Ayran. As she expected, all the Guardians and their Counselors approved the treaty. Even the two from Troy knew better than to protest and voted, "Aye."

"The treaty tis approved. Do ye now wish to consider the matter of those condemned to be Abs?"

The question was answered in the affirmative.

"Very well, this tis a major change which requires a discussion before we vote. Do we rescind the sentence of Ab for all condemned since the end of the war or merely those on the Justine list?" Betta paused. She was trying to contact Beauty, but their private link remained silent. She noted that the one LouElla called 'her younger' had returned to the Don section and was searching everywhere with those strange grey eyes.

"Army tis absent. Guardian of Ayran, do ye have any thoughts on which condemned Abs to consider or should it be all?"

"When ye say 'all,' do ye mean those condemned for thievery? Releasing them would be a mistake. Why loose such on Thalia again? I think we should limit the release to those who were House."

The Tris in the audience began booing and yelling, "Nay!"

Betta pounded her fist for order when the voice of Beatrice, her sister, began speaking against the Sisterhood.

"Jolene errs. Too many stole for food, or became Abs so the food allotment for the remaining Tris would be larger. All of Thalia needs to start over after years of repression. The thieves will steal again and Ayran will still have cheap labor." The Tri spectators cheered their approval. The Abs remained silent.

Betta spoke again. "Betron, how do ye speak?"

"There tis nay need to discuss this," said Brenda, Maca of Betron, Betta's own first birthed. "I vote now. Free all House and Tris who became Abs. My laddie returns to House this evening." She glared at Betta.

Betta smiled at her daughter and wondered how Brenda had kenned to be here. She had refused to attend since Benji had been condemned. Betta suspected the House of Don somehow had sent her word of the new treaty.

"Don, what say ye?"

Lamar swelled with importance. "My beloved Counselor and I are one. Two votes from Don that all return now."

"Flight, how do ye say?"

"Two ayes for release," LouElla shouted.

"Ishner?"

"Ishner grants two votes to release all now. My youngers are to return to House." Ishmalisa's clear voice rang out.

"Medicine, state your vote."

Magda rose. "Two votes for release now. Why did ye call for a vote on this? If ye think ye can order the Sisterhood to stop us, I will issue a Maca's Call for my House to oppose them."

Betta realized her control had evaporated. "Magda, I am but following the rules of order. We have been given back much this evening, and I want nay further stain on the Guardian Council of the Realm."

Her voice was firm and she continued. "Rurhran, how do ye speak?"

The Guardian and her Counselor were still holding hands, and Ravin spoke, her voice full of joy. "LouElla, we thank Gar that ye live. Whilst Rurhran has lost nay to the condemnations, we both heartily support the release of all." She wanted this over. There would be no discussion of kine or sheep transfer tonight. It was a bargaining tool. The rest were fools. She and Rollie had sensed the grey-eyed one was a true kineman. She had nay doubt that the Maca of Don would try for a Claiming Ritual to name him Laird of Don.

"Guardian and Counselor of Troy, how do ye vote?"

The two women looked at each other, and the appointed Guardian raised her chin. "We vote nay."

Betta considered. "My Counselor has absented herself, and I apologize; however, as Guardian of the Realm, I cast my vote for release, and declare the measure passed. All other matters will be considered after the burial. We meet again after the three day mourning period and the Signing of the Abs." Before Betta could close the audio, Magda was on her feet again screaming at her.

"My lassie tis here. She returns to House now!"

"My youngers are here also." Ishmalisha's, voice was gentler, but firm.

Martin stepped forward, motioning for two of the larger Abs to attend. "We give up nay of ours!" He pounded his walking staff to emphasize his point.

The red-haired, strangely dressed Justine, spoke, his voice carrying over the crowd. "Guardian of the Realm, my apologies, but until we have gathered all of the Krepyons, no one is permitted to leave this Hall or fly without registering through me. There is no limit on how many are in your vehicle, but any unauthorized flight will be shot down. Since many of you may wish to return to your own residence this evening, you can reach me by using the Justine frequency."

Martin glared at the man. "Ye canna stop me. I am Martin."

Red barely glanced at the man. "I don't care if you're the Pope. God didn't appoint you over me. Go sit down and take those two apes with you."

Shock ran across Martin's face as his eyes opened wider. The Justines had nay interfered with him or his Abs. Gasps went up from the crowd. No one, not even House spoke to Martin in that manner. Did these people have nay respect for the representative of Gar? It mattered little that few but Abs had such respect. What mattered was that Martin represented an earlier time when there was order and Thalians retained their beliefs. Who cared what Martin proclaimed as long as he directed the Abs and kept order?

Betta watched with distaste as the Houses of Medicine and Ishner clambered down the stairs to stand in front of the crowd.

The one called Jeremiah O'Neal bowed to the two Guardians. Magda and Ishmalisa took this as their due, not realizing the bow was for their sex.

"Which of those people belong to you ladies?"

Another slight intake of breath went through the crowd. To call someone from House lady implied an expected favor from their House. Few would be so bold as to do it in public.

Magda was the first to recover. She had been puzzled, then realized the man's outlandish words were but part of his speech. She inclined her head towards him and turned to the Abs. "Marta, Lady of Medicine, come to House with your laddie. Ye are both welcomed in my heart."

A plump woman with dark, flowing hair in the back stood. She held a dark-haired boy child on her left hip. "I dinna if they will let me pass."

"They will or they will have a severe headache."

All heads turned to the red-haired woman at the door. Margareatha remembered her own separation from her family and glared up at the group surrounding the woman. At first they showed no signs of moving. Suddenly a man standing in front of the woman collapsed. The others quickly made a path for the woman and child.

As Red turned to Ishmalisa, two slender Thalians in the Ab crowd rose and made their way down the tiers. Lorenz noted that these two, like Ishmalisa were slender, both looked to be about the same height as Margareatha and O'Neal. They would be unrecognizable as aliens on Earth. The man and woman made straight for Ishmalisa, both throwing their arms around her at once. The other called Marta was introducing her laddie to his grandmother.

"Anyone else up there from House?" Red was impatient to take his captives out before a general riot erupted. He didn't believe mowing people down with bullets was a way to foster trading negotiations.

People in the middle section rose and a white thatched man spoke, hope in his eyes. "I was Director of Carving for Don. My laddie and I went voluntarily to increase food for my Counselor and youngers."

"Welcome back," boomed Llewellyn.

"They have nay kine," muttered Rollie to Ravin.

The Guardian of Rurhran kicked her Counselor on the ankle.

Another of the Abs stood. "I am Ma, once Laten, laddie of Magus, Keeper of Agriculture for Don. I was training for a Keeper position at the Laird's and Lady's Station of Don when declared dangerous."

Lorenz straightened and looked at the man. He was tall and blocky, well-muscled, and self-assured.

Ma continued to speak. "I canna return without my Ab counselor, Do, but I am willing to sign as an Ab early. My counselor has worked kine and zarks and will sign early."

"Hired," shouted Lorenz.

Llewellyn grinned. "Ye are Laten and House. Your counselor may sign early. Her name tis Dolo, and ye will both work with my laddie, Lorenz."

Lamar frowned. What was wrong with Llewellyn bestowing workers to that alien?

The brown clad Abs returning to their Houses were few. Many had died off in the ensuing years, others were unsure of the food situation, while others were quite to content to remain with their Ab families.

No one but the Counselor of Ayran noticed Jolene anxiously searching the crowd of Abs for a familiar face, and she assumed her Guardian was looking for Janet, the previous Counselor responsible for the death of a Justine. *It was pitiful.* She carefully framed the words in her mind to use when relating tonight's events to other members of Ayran. *Ye could see how deeply she grieved at nay finding her.*

Betta remained deadpan as the members of House and their Tris went to their boxes.

Red turned and bowed to the crowd and then to her. He signaled his group to march out the Justine and the Krepyons. What type of beings were these that could defy the Justine mind? She kenned that Don had the answers, but Don would nay speak. The crowd cheered as they left.

Betta watched with a satisfied smile. It was pure pleasure to see the Kreppies under guard. She touched the audio. "Our Council tis officially closed for this eve."

"It tis nay!" Llewellyn was speaking. "Ye will note that Troyner of Troy was nay there. He tis locked away on Troy as tis Benji, Laird of Betron. Ye will also note that both are on the Justine list."

"And the Sisterhood guards them for the Justines." Scorn rang in Brenda's voice. "They must be guarded else the Tris of Troy would free them."

"They will be freed when we have time to contact our Sisters." Betta kept her voice steady.

"Nay!" Brenda was on her feet. "How can ye do this, Mither? Ye imperil the life of your own younger!"

"Brenda tis correct." The Maca of Don remained seated, his face and eyes hard. "They were condemned by the Justines, and Council has just ruled them released. Ye will contact your minions now and alert them that the Maca of Betron will arrive for her laddie, and the Maca of Don for his friend Troyner, Maca of Troy. If they offer resistance they are defying the Council of the Realm and those that live will be Abs."

Betta went white. "Are ye now the Guardian of the Realm that ye give such orders?"

"I am but reminding ye of the laws of Thalia before the Justines took over and the Sisters obeyed their will."

Betta glared at him, knowing that the Council meeting was being aired to all the House members and Tris at home or in a brew hall. How she wished the screens had remained blank but the Justine envoy had ordered them opened. She glanced at the rest of the Council. Already Magda was tight-lipped, Jolene too bright eyed, and Ishmalisa's mouth was pulled tight. Only Ravin seemed to send a message of sympathy with her eyes, but remained silent.

Betta looked at the crowd. They seemed to be waiting for her command and she knew the wrong one would throw Thalia into a war for power.

"Babara, the Director of Army, tis nay present. I shall issue the order myself once the Council tis adjourned." The lie flowed more freely than she thought possible. "If there tis nay else, the Council of the Realm tis over till we meet again."

Betta sighed inwardly when the Guardians of Ayran and Rurhran rose and started toward their quarters. Betta almost reached for the button that would send the audio from below to her ears, but she refrained. There were too many and the sound would be garbled. Llewellyn might have taken precautions. Llewellyn was connected to the aliens and they had mentioned trade. Such talks would need to go through her office. She did nay want them going through Llewellyn. She rose to follow the remaining Council members down to the lower level wishing she could hear what Magda was saying to her lassies or Brenda to Llewellyn. She kenned Brenda would nay uphold the Sisterhood.

Brenda had pushed her way through the crowd to stand beside Llewellyn as he came down the stairs. "Ye promised to rescue my laddie this eve if things did nay go well." Her voice was almost an accusation as though Llewellyn had changed his mind.

She stood two inches over six feet and was almost as heavily muscled as her younger sister. Beauty. Her dark hair was longer and not shaven in the manner of a Sister.

"Aye, we leave at once. I dinna trust the Sisters anymore than ye."

He turned to Lorenz who was talking with Ishmael, the returnee to Ishner. "Are ye ready to leave, Lorenz?"

"No, I need to question those boys."

"Take them with us. Ye can sort out the other later."

"What about the members of House y'all have collected?"

"They go with us."

Chapter 10

Rescue

Lorenz sat in the third row of the cairt, a transport for ten people. The Director of Carving, his son, and three other Tris still had relatives in Donnick willing to take them in. Lorenz's face was taunt and his grey eyes glittering. He resented Lamar's objections to Abs sitting with House. To not have taken them would have been a betrayal. It was difficult for him to accept that Lamar was his great-uncle when comparing Lamar with the men he had called uncle in his youth.

Lamar sat stiffly beside Beatrice in the front row of seats during the journey. His younger, his Maca, had ignored his vigorous objections to Abs in the cairt. Llewellyn's brown eyes had reflected puzzlement.

"Laten tis of our House, and we canna leave the lassie or the laddies."

The rule of the Sisterhood had been brutal to Thalia and most Thalians, but Lamar, insulated by his status as a Warrior against the Justines and counselor to Beatrice, had led a comfortable life discussing affairs with his friend, Rollie. That Rurhran controlled the livestock from Don was of no consequence to Lamar. He detested animals as nay fit for a Warrior's consideration. He had love, companionship, food, and brew. His one regret was losing Llewellyn to the Justines, but even that had worked out well. He was baffled by Llewellyn rejecting his counsel and agreeing with that grey-eyed, arrogant being called Lorenz. Lamar assumed the Thalians stationed at Troy would obey the dictates of the Council. Troyner, Maca of Troy, and Benji, Laird of Betron, would be released upon hearing of the Council's reversal of the condemned. It was nay necessary for the members of Don to accompany Brenda and her fighters.

Llewellyn, who was piloting the craft southward, could feel the dislike generated by Lamar and Lorenz. He chose to ignore the tension as he knew Lamar would fight with Beatrice as a Warrior when the time came. As for leaving the renamed lassie, Dolo, Llewellyn had lived too long on Earth to be swayed by the caste customs of House. If Lorenz felt the laddies could provide information, then he would back him.

He was piloting according to Brenda's coordinates. When over the Troy headquarters, he swung the craft down for a smooth landing. He could sense the coming battle. His eyes brightened as the musk smell of a fighting Thalian swelled from his body and he gave his brief order.

"All but the laddies may join the festivities." He left the craft's light aimed at the low building with the barred windows, jumped the few inches to the ground, and ran towards the building, Lamar and Beatrice following on his heels.

Brenda, Maca of Betron, had landed closer to the door of the building and was running towards it screaming, "Benji, ye will be free!"

Lorenz dropped to the ground and stood looking towards the one-story buildings off to their left. A door burst open and several black clad women came running towards them. They were unarmed and a quick smile went across his face as he heard Laten and Dolo behind him. He bent down and picked up a rock, hefted it for a moment in his hand, and threw it at the lead runner's fore-head. The heavily built woman sank to her knees with the others piling over her. He put his hands on his hips, a wide smile on his face as he watched his father's group roll over them when a second contingent rounded the corner at rapid march.

Ah shit ran through Lorenz's mind as he realized this group of five was moving in a tight formation straight at him.

"Spread out don't let them bowl us over," Lorenz shouted over the noise of yells from the other group.

Just as the Sisters neared them Lorenz stopped, braced his feet, waited for one second, dropped into a quick squat and rose straight up his right fist preceding him in a straight upward thrust. It met the jaw of the oncoming woman and rocked her. He twisted and slammed his elbow into the side of her head. She started to slump and he grabbed her left shoulder with both hands and pushed her into the two on her right side. He could hear the blows Laten and Dolo were landing on the two to his right. One of the Sisters avoided the woman he pushed and swung, striking a blow to his shoulder. He backed away and brought his right fist across his body towards her face; a blow she blocked. She threw her left at him, and he was able to block it with his right and send his left fist into her middle. She whirled away as the other two started coming at him. He jumped to the side as one rushed in, but the other took him down, grabbing at his hair and neck. He punched his left index finger and middle finger straight into her eyes. She lost her grip and he rolled away as a kick from one of the others caught him on the hip. His hand closed over a fist-sized rock and he came up on his knees and flung it into the face of the heavier woman hurtling through the air to land on him. Momentum slammed her body on top of his and he rolled into the feet of the other Sisters slowly retreating from the first fight. For a few minutes it was a confusion of falling bodies, elbows, legs, fists flailing, and a mass of churning bodies, blows and grunts.

The members of Betron's House surrounded them and began restoring order. The Sisters were herded to the side of the building. One Sister stepped forward and addressed Brenda. "Maca, ye must send those mutants and the Abs to Ayran. The Abs fought against the Sisterhood and that alien has blinded our sister. We need Medical."

"Ye ken that we have the blessings of Council to be here or ye would nay have named them mutants." Brenda was almost spitting at the woman.

Beatrice was stroking Lamar's arm. Touching his face and he in turn had his arm around his counselor as he surveyed the group in front.

Llewellyn, like the rest had suffered minor damage to his face, a bruise was growing on the left cheek. He surveyed the group long enough to say, "Watch them for now. I must attend to Troyner's release." He and Brenda hurried to the door of the stone building.

"Benji, stand away from the door. Tis locked. I must burn it."

Llewellyn shoved her hand weapon upward. "They may nay be able to back far enough away. This tis a small building. Mayhap the key tis in the Admin."

"I will have my laddie ere they send others against us." Brenda was glaring at him.

"Here comes someone else, Papa." Lorenz winced from speaking and licked blood from the corner of his mouth. A tall, muscular woman clad in umber tights was approaching. Her hands were in the air in the acknowledgement of surrender.

"I am Triva, Director of Labor for Troy. I warned them that ye were following orders from the Council of the Realm. My hand will open the door."

She bowed when she was three feet from them. The broad planes of her face were composed into straight, determined lines.

Brenda stood aside for her. Triva held one hand against a block. Soundlessly the door slid open, revealing a dark interior and she stepped back.

"Benji," Brenda's voice wailed out.

A slender young man appeared in the murkiness supporting the body of a taller, emaciated man. "My fither tis in dire need of assistance, Mither."

Llewellyn sprang forward and embraced Troyner. "Ye are going to House with us."

Brenda pulled her son close to her and embraced him, both laying their heads on each other's shoulders and stroking the arms and body of the other.

Triva took a step forward. "Take me with ye, Maca of Don. The Sisters will have their revenge."

The Sister that had demanded Medical began yelling. "We need Medical, and ye canna take that one. She tis the one that kens the raising of the pina pods. Thalia will be in turmoil without pods."

"Thalia tis already in turmoil," snapped Llewellyn.

"Lamar, call Medical for that one," he jerked his head at the wounded Sister, "and to attend Troyner when we return to Donnick."

"Lorenz, request a transport from O'Neal for the rest of these Sisters. Beatrice, ye contact Ayran and tell Jolene to expect seventeen new Abs. They had the audacity to fight two Macas without one of them issuing a Challenge."

A shocked silence fell on the muttering group. Beatrice cleared her throat and began to explain the situation. "We dinna ken if Jolene will take the Sisters as Abs. She has nay revealed her position, and she may turn them loose."

"The law protects us. Ye canna turn the Sisters into Abs. Tis our law." This time the Sister doubled her fists as she spoke. "Ye are the ones who will be Abs."

"Then we'll lock them up with the rest in the cells at Don."

Lamar stepped forward. "My Maca, heed our counsel. Ye had the right to lock up those who were on Don and opposed ye. These, however," and he swept his hand in the direction of the Sisters standing against the building, "are here at the direction of the current Maca of Troy."

"Who tis a fraud." Llewellyn gritted out.

Beatrice nodded, "Aye, but I fear that Troyner will nay get his rights back till the Counsel of the Realm restores them, and that would be at the next meeting, if then. All depends upon the votes ye can gather from the other Houses."

"Papa, it'll take Red about fifteen minutes to gather his crew and get here."

"Lamar, when will Medicine arrive?"

"Ah, I was listening to ye." He hastily called the House of Medicine.

Lorenz went over to Laten and Dolo. He noticed Laten had his arm around her and she was nestled into his chest. "Are you two all right?"

Dolo raised her head and turned. She was sporting a nasty blackened and closed eye, plus a split lip.

"Looks like y'all could use a doctor, uh, medical too."

"Laird, Dolo tis still Ab. They will nay treat her."

Lorenz started to swear and changed his mind. "Follow me. We brought our possible bag along." He led the two puzzled people into the craft, pulled out a black, leather bag by the handle from the overhead compartment, and set it on the front seat before opening it.

"Like the Boy Scouts, we're always prepared." He grinned at them and dug into the bag to locate a tin.

He held it up and removed the lid. "This salve works wonders. It can even take away proud flesh." The stunned looks on their faces almost stopped him. "Hell, this scar was four times as large and purple when Papa and Mama started using it on me." He pointed to the scar running from the temple, down his cheek, and under the collar of his shirt. "It's nothing that will hurt y'all." To demonstrate, he rubbed some on the split at the corner of his mouth.

"Laird, she tis Ab. They are forbidden Medical."

"The hell! That's one custom that ends in Don. Now hold still." He liberally applied the salve to Dolo's face. "Y'all might as well make her comfortable. I'll go help guard those out there. It looks like Brenda wants to take her group home."

He looked back at the boys who were watching with wide, disbelieving eyes. "Men, you all sit tight. We still need to talk." He stepped back out into the night.

Llewellyn approached guiding Troyner to the craft. "We need to help him inside." Fury made his face red and his lips tight. "It seems Medical still considers him Ab since he canna be Maca till Council rules. He needs water, sustenance, and rest. He goes with us."

Llewellyn settled Troyner into the seat behind the pilot and reached up and brought down a water blad. "Here, my friend, drink." Then he brought down the traveler's wafers used as quick sustenance on flights. "These will have to do till we have ye to House."

He eased the man back and turned to Lorenz. "We need to help the others till O'Neal arrives. We'll lock those Sisters in Don's cells. They are a bargaining tool."

Llewellyn's eyes widened when he saw Dolo's bruised face. Dolo made a rapid bow and Laten spoke. "The Laird put on the medication. He would nay listen that she tis an Ab."

"Good. Ye fought well, lassie." He turned and followed Lorenz outside.

A slow smile spread across Laten's face. "The Maca has returned. Dolo, we have our chance."

Troyner slumped in the seat, too weary to raise his head until Lorenz returned.

"The prisoners will lift off shortly," Lorenz announced. Troyner reached out and grasped his wrist as he walked towards the back.

"I dinna why the Ab laddies are back there, but Martin will use Da to destroy the Houses."

Lorenz looked at the man, an emaciated skeleton of someone whose frame said Troyner once might have rivaled Llewellyn in size. The eyes were hollow sockets and the bleached lashes framed light brown eyes in a taunt, drawn skin.

"Tis already whispered that Wee Da tis Maca of the Abs," Dolo added.

Laten snorted. "The Abs have nay Maca."

"Ye ken that the land Abs do," Dolo retorted, her bronze skin flushing to a deeper color.

"Aye, one to each group; nay one over all."

"But Wee Da tis from House." Dolo refused to back down.

Lorenz was puzzled. "Why didn't the House just keep him?"

Laten inclined his head towards the recumbent Troyner. "The Ab born remain with their mither. House canna claim him without the mither's permission, and Troyner was condemned right after the Kenning Woman died. Once he tis House again, he will have the right to claim him."

Lorenz shook his head and moved to the seats where the boys sat. "All right, Da's mother is dead. Are both your mothers gone too?"

Pi rose and bowed. "Ka's mither died the same day as the Kenning Woman, and my mither follows Martin's authority. I am being punished and excluded from the Abs till Martin decrees otherwise."

Lorenz's eyebrows went up. "And just what did y'all do?"

"I refused to let Ur take my place as the next Martin in training."

Lorenz fought down the urge to ask who Ur was. "Who is going to raise a rumpus when you all aren't there?"

His response was three puzzled looks.

"Who will try to find ye?"

Ka swallowed. "My elder Ki will look for me on Signing Day."

Pi threw a hasty look at Da who was looking at the Laird. "My mither, the Handmaiden, will have all Abs looking for Wee Da. Nay will care about me."

Lorenz looked at the well-muscled Da and decided the wee must be for his size; a fact that raised another question. "Just how old..." again blankness descended over their faces, "eld are ye."

Pi bowed again. "I am twenty-five, Laird." He would do anything to stay and work for this man. If lying about his age would allow this, lie he would.

Ka looked rapidly at Pi and then Wee Da. They had already decided that Ka would say he was eighteen to sign on as a working Ab and he stood and bowed before replying. "I am eighteen."

Da realized the Laird was not disputing them, but had no chance to tell his lie.

"Laird, they all lie," Laten interrupted.. "Pi tis but twenty, Ka tis seventeen, and Wee Da tis twelve."

Pi closed his eyes waiting for the blow or the bellow that would throw them out, leaving them stranded on Troy.

No blow came; nor did a bellow hit his ears. He opened his eyes to see the man shaking his head and grey eyes staring at him, measuring him.

"Y'all have a reason for lying?"

"Aye, Laird, if we are too young, we canna sign for the work season. Tis our only chance."

Lorenz looked at Laten who nodded his head in agreement.

Llewellyn appeared at the doorway.

"Any messages for O'Neal?"

"Yeah, tell him to have coffee ready when we get there in the morning."

Lorenz looked back at the doleful faces of three boys and added. "You all just sit down and stay quiet until we reach home. We'll arrange somewhere for you all to sleep."

Chapter 11

The Sisterhood Regroups

Gloom presided in the Army Section of the Don Guardian Complex among those gathered to console Belinda after the Burning ceremony. Missing were Medicine, Rurhran, Ayran, Betron, Don, and Flight. Betta looked at Beauty stoking a sobbing Belinda. How could she bring Beauty back to reality?

Magda solved the problem by entering with her Director, Millay. Their purple robes added to the somber background of black Army attire. Magda carried her ceremonial spear with the carvings of centuries ago: healing herbs entwined around the staff. Betta doubted that she really kept it sharp enough to impale anyone.

"Why are ye gathered here to mourn? Ye have lost the goodwill of all Thalians. Ye compound your errors by mourning for a traitor." Magda leaned on her spear and glared at them.

Babara stood, her fists clenching and unclenching. "How dare ye speak of our beloved as a traitor? She gave her life for our Sisterhood."

Magda turned her back, the response of House to a mere Tri, and spoke to Betta. "Because my eldest was torn from me in the time of her greatest need for support, she has joined Troyner with their laddie. She fears to dwell in my House. If ye wish to restore the Sisterhood, ye must immediately change our rules to include those who prefer males as their counselors, and announce this new order at the next Guardian's meeting. Do ye so intend?"

Betta's shoulders slumped. "We have nay discussed such a change."

Beauty stood. "The Sisterhood still reigns. Last night was but a temporary setback. Males are needed only for their seed and that can be replicated.

Llewellyn canna possibly restore Don. Rurhran and Ayran are with us, and we control the Army."

Magda looked at the small group. "If they are with ye, where are they? Shall I tell ye? Rurhran tis meeting with the Maca and Guardian of Don to discuss a Walk the Circle agreement for one of Rurhran's available lassies. This will forestall turning over the kine or the sheep. As for Ayran, Jolene kenned the lie that Bobinet had spread of LouElla's last days here. She waited all these years to speak and when she did it was against us. Jolene has returned to Ayran and tis plotting her own plots. She will bide her time till the next Guardians Council meeting. Gar kens what she tis plotting, but I tell ye now, she did nay speak of LouElla's and Jason's bedding till it would nay endanger her. She has nay made an enemy with her knowledge, but she has made friends and will use any quarreling to her advantage."

Betta closed her eyes. She was too old for this dissention. She opened them to see Beauty pacing and then patting the hiccupping Belinda on the back while refuting Magda's statements.

"Rurhran would nay wed Rocella to the Maca. She tis a hundred years younger."

Magda looked at her with scorn. "Ye are correct. The negotiations are for the blind-eyed Laird."

"He canna be Laird. The Council has nay accepted him." Beauty was raging. "Both are mutants and nay Thalians."

Magda grasped her spear with both hands and leaned forward. "I'll grant that the one dubbed the Laird tis nay Thalian, but after last evening's performance, Llewellyn has shown he tis an archetypical Thalian male. He dumped her," one hand loosened from the spear long enough for a thumb to jerk in Babara's direction, "with one blow. When they landed at Troy's Ag Station, Llewellyn directed the fight, and according to the accounts of the onlookers, he fought them three at a time. Who will challenge him? Beauty lost to him when they fought in the Arena that one time and he will nay doubt challenge her again for his bedding that she welshed on fulfilling."

She turned her dark eyes on Beauty. "I dinna believe ye wish to fight him. He will win."

Beauty flushed. "He has nay workers, nay the animals to feed any retinue he gathers, and nay the credits to rebuild Don. Tis a destroyed continent."

"True on the animals," conceded Magda. "The Justine League, however, has granted Don a portion of Thalia's credits. There tis the possibility that he will wed. Nay all of the Tris of Don are gone, nay are they all idlers. There are Tris ready to work."

Magda turned back to Betta. "I have almost lost one lassie to your concept of Thalia. She will let me visit them, but she will nay risk their laddie in my House." Magda's voice was filled with bitterness. She kenned that upon her passing into the Darkness, Lady Marta, her eldest daughter, would birth the next Medicine Maca. The risks were great. Medicine was populated by some of the most fanatical of the Sisterhood.

"My youngest lassie helped them leave. I have nay guarantee Melanie will remain. Do ye intend to change the rules?"

"Nay change!" Beauty's voice lashed out. "The Army tis ours and we will use it when the accursed *Golden One* returns to their planet. Those beings will go back to the places where they are from and we will overrun Don. We are the Sisterhood." Beauty intoned the last sentence and the others took up the chant.

"So be it." Magda shrugged and turned to leave. Her passage through the door was halted as Ravin and Rocella of Rurhran entered. They were clad in elaborate metallic worked golden tights, black mourning sashes, and covered by heavy, brocaded golden capes. Their wide brimmed golden hats sat jauntily on their dark hair.

Ravin stepped forward and removed her hat. "It seems ye need a bit of counseling, and then mayhap we can bargain."

Betta rose. "We welcome your wise words, Guardian of Rurhran. Both ye and your Lass of Rurhran have too long been absent from our gatherings." She and the two women formally greeted each other.

"We were told ye were negotiating with Don for a marriage." Betta began.

"The so-called Laird tis an arrogant male, nay capable of kenning our ways. He refused to attend." Rocella stepped forward and removed her hat. "He claims that he does nay "love" me or ken me, and Walking the Circle for political reasons tis nay civilized. It was a wasted morn."

Betta nodded and thought *Don had rejected their suit. Good.*

Ravin glanced at them and advanced to Belinda. "We sorrow with ye at the loss of your Mither." She embraced Belinda and laid her head on each shoulder of the sobbing woman. "Ye must, however, learn that crying nay brings her back, but revenge tis at hand." Her speech raised eyebrows, and all waited for her to continue.

"Don canna prosper if we, the Sisterhood, isolate them. They have nay kine to fill the meat demand and nay the people to carve, process, and deliver it. Without the sheep, they have nay wool for a non-existent clothing industry. If ye back the House of Rurhran in retaining the kine and the sheep, Don will sink into abject poverty as the rest of our Houses thrive."

Betta's eyes lit up. "Magnificent! That will keep Jolene from interfering and civil war from erupting. Do ye have else to say?"

"Aye, we and all Thalia need the assurance that laddies remain with their Houses."

"Agreed. Beauty, how say ye?"

Beauty sat down beside Belinda and looked at Betta. "Mither, do ye truly agree with that policy?"

"Aye, ye need to permit them to keep their laddies, and their lassies that prefer laddies."

Beauty's shoulders straightened. "I dinna agree with either assumption. We will have the next Council meeting in two days. The Houses will see the importance of the labor when nay Ab signs with Don. Martin will arrange it. He has cause to hate Don."

Betta sighed. Don had Tris, reclaimed some made Abs, and would reclaim more. To what end she could nay discern as Don had nay kine to carve, nay agriculture but small gardens, and thousands of Tris were available for work that did nay exist. She did nay believe the Tris would work long for just food and promises. Don would capitulate if they could unite the other Houses against them.

"Beauty, listen to my counsel. The Sisterhood will rule if we can isolate Don. To do that, we must prove a mutant canna be trusted in Thalia. Ye must accept the fact that laddies are part of the Houses and they are needed; even loved and protected. Jolene will vote with us if Medicine's and Rurhran's acceptance of males is adopted.

"Look at what has happened. Our wee ones are few. We have become like the Justines. We will lose Rurhran, Betron, Medicine, Ishner, and Ayran if ye dinna compromise. LouElla and Llewellyn canna rule Thalia without them. Thalia would be torn apart. This time there will be no Justines to stop the Kreppies."

Beauty's face became as stone. "Tis a bitter thing, Mither, but I will concede. Make the ruling the first thing to be considered at Council. Llewellyn will think he has won."

"Good. Now ye must excuse me as I have arranged a meeting with Jeremiah O'Neal, the Captain of the *Golden One*. We will be discussing trade."

Ravin stepped forward. "After the vote on laddies, Don will wish the beasties. Ye must have the votes to stop them."

Betta looked at her. "Then I suggest ye start talking to the Guardians now." She softened her voice. "Who kens, perhaps these other beings will trade with us. Mayhap their world needs agricultural products."

Chapter 12

House of Don

Lorenz woke as the twin moons were swinging low to meet the graying of dawn. It was the morning after rescuing Troyner and for a moment the huge, round bed confused him. Nothing on Earth that he'd ever slept on matched this in size, and years of enduring the narrow confines of a spaceship bed left him unprepared for Thalian comfort. He was in Don's Guardian's House. Yesterday's events filtered through his mind and scattered the confusion. Cattle; they were out there waiting to be found. The boys could wait until later. He rose in one smooth motion, grabbed his clothes, and started to dress. Then he remembered the Thalians had a penchant for bathing and anyone that didn't would be shunned. He headed for the shower. Within fifteen minutes he was downstairs and banging at the door of Laten's and Dolo's bedroom.

"Rise and shine. We've work to do. Meet me in the kitchen."

Dolo looked at the grey outside the window and groaned. "When did House rise so early?"

Laten rolled out of bed and aimed a slap at her backside. "I'm House. Remember? Only the Abs nay worry about morn's light. Tis shower time."

She made a face and aimed a playful kick back before rising. "He tis worse than a Slavey."

After a shower, they pulled on their clothes and walked down a hall. "Do ye ken where a kitchen tis?"

"Aye, Dolo, I was here often as a laddie. We take a right turn and pass a couple doors, turn right, pass through the Keepers section and we are there."

They found Lorenz balefully eyeing the contents of a built-in cold cabinet. "Where the hell is something to grab for eating around here, and what do y'all have to drink that's hot and quick?"

Laten shook his head. "Laird, I have nay been here for years. Tis possible the corner cabinet will be stocked with some quickbars for sustenance, and there should be some pina tea."

"Get them. We're wasting daylight."

While Latin located the items and handed them to Dolo, Lorenz poked at the circles on the communication screen set in the wall over a small desk.

"Red, are y'all up?"

A blurry eyed O'Neal appeared on screen. "Hell, no. It's not daylight yet."

"I'm going on a scouting expedition in ten to fifteen minutes. It'll be from the position we gave y'all for landing last night. Alert Melissa that I'm in the air. Papa and I will be flying to the Maca's Tower by eight. He's sent messages to the Directors of the Centers to meet him there. That means three small flyers will be going there. When I return, y'all better have a pot of coffee going or I'm going to be in a foul mood. There's nothing like it here." He broke the connection and looked at Laten.

"How long does it take to fix that tea?"

"A couple of minutes after I locate the cups."

"We'll get some when we're back. Did y'all find those bars? What's in them?" Lorenz was thinking of Earth's nineteen-forty's candy bars.

Laten shrugged. "Different grain proteins, pina nuts, and a sweetener. It works as a snack. We should leave a note for the Keeper that we have taken some of their stock."

"Let's go. I'll tell them when we get back."

He led the way towards the outside while pulling on his jacket. He stopped at the door and looked at them. "Hell, you all need some coats." He pulled open a door. "Papa said extras were kept here."

"Laird, those are for House and Tris. Dolo is still Ab till she fulfills the work season." Laten was convinced the man needed a Keeper.

"The hell! Papa took y'all back into House last night."

"Me, yes, but Dolo must complete the time. She tis Ab." Laten's voice was patient.

Lorenz looked at him puzzled. "Look, we're wasting time. I don't care what she wears and there's no one else here. Now put on these damn coats. We have work to do."

Laten's face softened. He had lost his prejudice against Abs long ago and this man really didn't care whether one was House, Tri, or Ab. Laten wonder what was driving this being from another world. Both of them put on the dark blue jackets and followed Lorenz to the padport.

Laten found the answer to what was driving the man when they flew over the plains of Don. Lorenz swept the craft low over the meadows, small stands of oaks and dwarf pines, draws, gullies, rivers, and creeks. Excitement was building in all of them as they watched the loose kine feeding.

"There they are! Look down there. There must be at least fifty in that bunch." Lorenz jabbed a finger at the coordinates every time they spotted a herd. Most were still on the ground, their legs folded under them as they chewed on their cud. Lorenz estimated the number of each herd before transmitting all the information to the Maca's headquarters.

Dolo was puzzled. "I thought Rurhran had taken all on this side of the mountains."

"Papa told me that kine had ranged over most of Don and weren't penned until fattened for processing. Unless they rode out here and checked every draw and shady spot, they were bound to miss a few, and kine will do the same here as they do in Texas: propagate." Lorenz turned to her.

"What do y'all mean on this side of the mountains?"

"The Justines left some herds for the land Abs. It would have been cruel to leave them without work or food."

"How many kine were left?"

"I dinna. Whenever we stayed there over the winter months, meat was plentiful. Laten will agree."

A huge smile lit Lorenz's face and the grey eyes gleamed with joy. "And how many land Abs are there? What kind of a society do they have?"

Dolo shook her head in puzzlement.

Laten answered for her. "There tis nay way to count the land Abs as they come and go with the seasons. There are some fishing clans that settled along the coast. I have heard of groups of Abs and some Tris that have built homes with logs and are surrounded by high walls to fend off the raiding Abs, but I have nay seen such places. Then there are the Abs that move from place to place."

"A fly over will answer the question, but right now we need a place where the kine can be slaughtered and butchered. What about where Lavina lives. Would it have such a place? And where is she located? Y'all would probably like to see your brother again too, right?"

Laten smiled. The man was a bundle of energy. Thalia hadn't seen the like for years. "Aye, Laird, I would like to see Luman again. Ye need to swing two degrees to the south and head to the southwest coast, but the Laird's and Lady's Station of Don has pens and slaughtering facilities. They have nay been used since the time of the occupation."

Lorenz nodded and continued to fly low over the plains. He took a quick swing by the foothills before turning west when something caught both his and Laten's attention. He slid the cairt nearer the grove of trees that blanketed the land turning into hills.

"There tis a fliv down there under the trees, Laird."

"Aye, we'll check it out." As he lifted over the trees, the scanner showed a land combo (LC) rolling towards the fliv. Five black clad Sisters were in the vehicle. The scanner picked up three people hunkered down behind the trees and shrubs.

"Laird, that tis my brither and family."

"How'd they get there in a fliv without being shot down?"

"If Lavina skimmed the ground, she would nay have been detected, but here she would need to go higher."

As the LC came to a halt a man emerged from behind a shrub, his hands clenched into fists and a woman joined him. The Sisters were out of the LC, hand stunners aimed at the group.

"Damn! Laten, can y'all fly this thing?"

"Aye, Laird, but tis been twenty odd years. I'm apt to be a bit rough."

"Take it and fly over the Sisters heads and then between them and the people down there. How high will the energy level of those stunners be?"

"The Kreppies disabled most of their stunners to stun. Those canna kill a being." Laten moved into the seat as Lorenz vacated it.

Lorenz moved back one row and reached overhead. He brought down his canvas bag and pulled out his Winchester and shells. He inserted the shells and asked, "Where's the gadget to open these windows?"

Dolo was staring at him and Laten gave a brief look. A 30/30 might not look like their energy weapons, but the shape was similar. "That tis but one weapon against their five, however, we've given them pause as two are looking up. Where do ye wish to land?"

"I want the damn window open."

Laten pushed at one of the circles on his left, and the window on Lorenz's side slid down into the wall.

"Swing along side of them so that they are directly in front of my sights."

Laten almost protested, then did as directed. The sound of the rifle surprised them both. Dolo bolted upright, thumped her head as the cairt turned, and went to her knees, her hands clapped over her ears.

Lorenz fired again.

"Now land right beside them. There's two of them down, and you all stay behind me."

Dolo later swore the man's eyes were ice. When she glanced out the window, she realized that primitive weapons could kill. Two Sisters were down on the ground, and red was spurting from one Sister's leg. The other Sisters were scrambling to get into the LC when the Laird shouted, "Stop right there. The next one to move takes the next bullet."

The whole thing became surreal to Dolo as the morning breeze blew Lavina's hair across her face and two birds flew over the newly leafed out trees. One Sister sat up moaning as blood spewing from the other Sister began splattering across her face and upper torso.

Lorenz stayed at the window. "Everyone toss their weapons, now!"

The black stunners landed on the ground. "Lavina, y'all and your man use a tree limb and get those stunners back out of the way. Don't walk in front of them or my rifle. Once that's done I can tend to those two before they bleed to death."

His words goaded the two at the trees into action. Lavina and Luman found the needed branches and swept the stunners within their grasp. They turned the stunners on their attackers, but held their fire.

Lorenz strode up to them and motioned at the Sisters to move back away from the LC. "Keep those things trained on them." He stripped off his shirt and used a knife stowed in his boot sheath to cut off one of his sleeves. Then he knelt beside the Sister whose leg spurted life's blood, wrapped, and tied the sleeve. He pressed down with his hand and looked up.

"Somebody get me a sturdy, small stick."

Leman, Lavina's laddie bent and found what the Laird wanted and brought it over.

"Walk behind me." Lorenz's voice was quick. He took the stick and used it as a brace while he finished tying off the sleeve.

He looked at Lavina and Luman. "Are there any suggestions as to what to do with those three?" He nodded at the Sisters still standing as he moved toward the one holding her shoulder, the blood from her wound seeping downward to mingle with that spewed from the badly injured woman.

When no answer came, he continued. "Watch them while I contact Red and the doctors." Lorenz stood up and looked at five baffled faces. "O'Neal and Medicine," he said as an explanation and strode to the cairt.

He was back within minutes. Laten and Luman were standing next to each other, Laten had his arm around his brother.

"We'll take these two with us. If it's not safe to return to the Zark Station with these people running around, you all can ride with us. It might be best as that arm of yours looks like it might need a doctor."

"Nay, Laird tis stiff, but I can move it, and I dinna trust Medicine. I am male," he added by way of explanation.

Laten removed his arm and turned. "Laird, if ye would permit, Dolo and I will go with them. We can take the LC and Lavina and Luman the fliv. We'll leave the Sisters out here to find their way back. The zarks at their station need tending."

"Tis nay a solution," shouted one of the Sisters. She moved a step closer and stopped as the stunners were trained on her. "I challenge ye now, ye so-called, Laird."

Lorenz looked at her. "Another time, ma'am, I have to be back at the Maca's side within the hour." He turned back to Laten.

"I'm going to need you and Dolo later tonight. Don't get too exhausted in your reunion."

"Laird, my counselor, my laddie, and I would lay our heads on your shoulders." Lavina bowed as she intoned the words.

"As long as someone keeps them covered." Lorenz could think of no way to refuse that would not have offended them. He heard the Sisters gasp as the still Ab clothed Laten took the stunner from Luman. Lorenz realized that this society was far more stratified than what his father had told him.

After the greetings, they tied the wounded Sisters to the seats and Lorenz headed for Donnick and the House of Medicine. He was on their padport in eight minutes.

They were waiting for him and rushed forward. Melanie entered the cabin, set down her scanner and the stretcher, reached back and pulled up an eight-year-old Timor. Marta, eldest daughter of Magda, followed Timor.

Lorenz wondered why the boy, but said nothing as Timor sat quietly out of the way. Melanie knelt to examine the two. "Med now," she muttered at seeing the woman with the tourniquet around the leg. The two sisters sliced the ropes and hefted the Sister onto the stretcher and carried her to the door. Willing hands grabbed the stretcher and placed it on a hover carrier and rushed towards the doors.

Lorenz untied the other woman as Melanie and Marta returned. The Sister was white-faced, but stood unsteadily. They supported her to the door and helped her onto the stretcher placed on another hover carrier. She too was whisked away.

"What did ye use to cause such wounds? I must ken for treatment." Melanie's distressed face showed disbelief. A stunner set to stun would knock an opponent down. Set to kill, the stunner did, but no one arrived at medical with loss of blood and so much damaged tissue from being stunned.

Lorenz held up the rifle. "I used this, a rather primitive weapon by your standards. It shoots lead bullets."

"Dear Gar, I must attend." Melanie turned to Marta. "Are ye sure ye wish to do this?"

"Aye, Melanie." Marta walked closer to Lorenz. "Laird, we have heard that Troyner tis at Don. This tis our laddie, Timor." She smiled at the solemn, brown-eyed boy.

"Tis nay safe here for him. My mither's Directors, Keepers, and Tri workers of House hate him. They hate me for bearing and keeping him. Please, take me to Troyner. I beg ye for the friendship your fither and Troyner had as youths."

Lorenz realized the pleading in the brown eyes was real. He didn't need to dip into a mind to see that.

"Tis true, Laird," Melanie spoke. "Two of the Medical were completely hysterical at the thought of a laddie in our home. More were spiteful in their sayings. If Mither had not intervened, they might have refused him food. As tis, I worry that they may poison him."

Shock went across Lorenz's face. Someone harming a child went against everything Papa had told him of Thalia. Could one hundred and twenty some years make such a difference? He doubted it.

"Of course, it will be my pleasure."

Melanie threw her arms around him and laid her head first on one shoulder and then the next as her tongue made the tsk sound in each ear. Like the others from the House of Medicine, Melanie was shorter than most Thalians, just six feet in height; and she was but eighty-five years of age. Her body was feminine, not hard and muscular like his grandmother or the rest of Don's House. Even the slender Dolo was hard and muscular. He hugged her back with pleasure.

"Go," muttered Marta. "The others are coming this way. We must leave."

Melanie extracted herself and jumped from the cairt to hurry towards the coming Medical women. Lorenz closed the door, went into a climb, and then leveled off.

"I will lay my head on your shoulders, Laird, as soon as we land." Marta had seated herself and taken Timor onto her lap.

The House of Medical was located but a mile or two from the Guardian's home and they were there in seconds. Lorenz opened the doors and used the communicator to inform Red he was back and the coffee had better be ready.

As they stepped onto the tarmac, Marta bowed formally and went through the ritual. The years as an Ab had not made Marta slender. She is the second Thalian woman to feel like a woman, thought Lorenz as he hugged her in return. Marta lifted Timor and he shyly did a childish imitation of his mother's hug, his eyes remaining wide and solemn.

"Where tis Troyner?" Marta asked the attendant who stood at the door.

"He tis in one of the upper rooms, Lady of Medicine. They have taken breakfast to him."

"I remember the way." Marta turned to Lorenz. "My thanks again, Laird of Don."

Lorenz headed for the room where he'd left the boys. They were sitting on the floor with sad faces and stood and bowed as he entered.

"Have you all eaten?"

Pi was their spokesperson. "Nay, Laird, we canna enter the kitchen and the keepers will nay serve us."

Da decided the Laird's face became an interesting shade of red.

Lorenz sucked in air to keep from swearing. Da, he decided was looking too intently at him.

"Follow me," he commanded as he stripped off his shirt and grabbed another out of the closet. He whirled out of the room heading for the kitchen. At least eggs and fat meat had the same smell whether on Earth or Thalia, he thought.

"Who the hell didn't follow my orders to feed these kids?"

The various cooks and helpers (mostly short haired women) stared at him. His abrupt entry into their domain had nay precedent.

"They are Abs," was the disdainful answer.

"Either they are fed now or by God, I'll throw everyone out of this room."

Mouths dropped.

A well-muscled woman in a dark blue uniform rose from the table and announced. "Ye are outnumbered."

"Right, but it just takes the word of the Maca to empty this place. Want to test it?"

Lorenz noticed two of them shifting back and forth on their feet.

"Dish up three plates." He turned his back on the group and looked at the boys. "There's a small table over in that alcove, or would you all rather eat in the room?"

Pi was stunned and his stomach growled at the smell of food. "I think mayhap the room would be better, Laird."

"All right. Bring the dishes back here when you all are finished and then wait at the padport for me. It'll be awhile before I'm back."

Lorenz looked at the man who was slowly filling the plates. "Someone get a pitcher of milk or juice to send with these three." With that he turned and made his way to what he considered the dinning room as he had seen a huge table there last evening.

Llewellyn, Lamar, Beatrice, and Tamar were seated at a massive round table. His father was in the middle of one side. Lorenz noted an empty place next to his father's right, slid into the chair, and smiled at them.

"Good morning, you all." He turned to his father.

"Papa, I was right. The cattle are there, pockets of them. We logged over a thousand head and didn't have time for a full sweep. There's probably even more on the other side of the mountains."

"Ye have been a busy man." Amusement glittered in Llewellyn's brown eyes.

Lamar cleared his throat. "Ye left out the part about leaving three Thalians to die in the wild, almost killing two more Thalians, the stealing of Lady of Medicine, and asking your fither's kitchen workers to feed Abs."

Lorenz lifted his head, the slight scar on the left side of his face became redder and his eyes hardened.

"Marta and her sister, Melanie, asked me to bring her and Timor here. The two of them went upstairs to Troyner, and anytime somebody works for me or I'm protecting them, they eat where and when I say. As for those three out on the prairie, I suggest y'all send somebody after them and throw them in the pokey or turn them into Abs. They were after our own House."

Llewellyn held up his hand. "Lorenz, first tell me about the kine ye saw this morn, then where the Sisters came from."

"Papa, all we need to do is round up the kine and drive them in to where y'all have the butchers and processing plants ready. That's meat we can sell now if Rurhran is less than ready to hand over our beeves.

"As for the Sisters, we were going towards the Zark Station when we saw Sisters in a LC bearing down on Lavina and her family. The Sisters wouldn't back off when we flew lower, and they had stunners trained on the three. I used my rifle and shot two of them."

Lorenz dished out his eggs. "Then I left Laten and Dolo with Lavina and Luman. They took the LC as we figured Don would send someone to arrest the Sisters. I took the wounded two into Medicine where Marta and Timor came aboard and requested a ride here."

Llewellyn set back. Beatrice and Lamar were too dumbfounded to speak.

A low, rumbling laughter emerged from Llewellyn's full throat. "Ye've managed to throw all of Thalia into a tizzy in a few short hours. I kenned ye'd be good for Thalia. Eat up, laddie. We have a meeting with the Centers' Directors and Keepers in twenty minutes."

He turned to Beatrice and Lamar. "Do we have enough enforcers to pick up those three?"

Not knowing the answer, Lamar shook his head.

Beatrice answered for him. "Mayhap, Leta will ken who to call in. I dinna think we can use the Army, nay should we use your troops from another world."

"Aye, see to it." Llewellyn returned to eating.

Lamar stood. "I have a meeting with Ravin and Rollie regarding the negotiations for the return of our kine."

"What negotiations? Those kine belong to Don. Why not just ask when they are going to deliver them, and if they won't set a date, demand it." Lorenz couldn't comprehend the man who in this world was his great-uncle. Lamar risked his life raising Papa, but he sounded like the cattle should stay where they were and Don should accept that.

"Tis a bit more delicate than that. Tis that nay right, Llewellyn."

"Mayhap, but I too wish to ken when the kine and sheep will be delivered."

Lamar straightened. "The negotiations involve Lorenz and Rocella Walking the Circle before delivery."

Llewellyn's eyes widened.

Lorenz hurriedly swallowed his food before speaking, "Hell, no. I don't know the woman and I certainly can't be in love a stranger."

Lamar ignored him and smiled at Llewellyn. "Ye can see the wisdom of this. Rocella will provide the political alliance we need with Thalia's most powerful House."

"And I sure as hell don't marry anyone for political reasons. It's not civilized." Lorenz stood.

"Papa, explain things to the man. I'm going to see about those kids and get my coffee before I tear somebody's head off." Lorenz stalked out.

Llewellyn looked at his elder. "Lamar, ye dared raising me and giving me a safe haven, and for that ye have my love and my thanks. But my laddie will Walk the Circle when he tis ready. Arranged marriages are considered a primitive practice in his land." He set his mug down.

"Remember, when ye meet with Rurhran, the kine and sheep are Don's. Ye are to arrange a time for their arrival, nay else."

Lamar voiced his irritation. "Ye have forgotten the ways of House. We dinna quarrel. Nay do I consider livestock worthy of our Warrior status."

"Lamar, what else will enable Don to provide employment and education for our Tri's? We need to rebuild our facilities for spaceships, clothing, and leather products. Don tis in sad repair and needs to be rebuilt. I dinna blame ye or Beatrice. The Justines and the Sisters created these deplorable conditions."

"LouElla tis Director of Flight and ye are Counselor. That will be enough for our needs." Lamar remained unconvinced.

"It will nay be enough. Don will be a prosperous land again. A date for their delivery must be set."

Chapter 13

Directors Meeting

Lorenz was carrying his coffee mug as he and his father met at the back entrance to the Maca's domed Headquarters.

"Has the coffee put ye in a better mood?"

"Yes, it has, but importing coffee from Earth will be an expensive proposition. Would coffee flourish on one of the continents here?"

"Mayhap on Troy. Part of it has a high, humid climate where they grow a different variety of Pina pods. Can ye nay develop a taste for the tea?"

"It tastes too much like fake hot chocolate." Lorenz made a grimace. "Y'all got your list?" They had gone over and over the plans to revitalize Don on their journey. The Centers were the key. They functioned as food distribution stations, the social hub of each sector, and where the few items of clothing or other available goods were sold. Future retail shops would be located in the area of the Centers.

"Aye, the list of projects has been entered into the records, and I will have it on screen."

"Wait a minute before we go in, Papa." Lorenz stopped and lit a cigarette. Llewellyn raised his eyebrows.

Lorenz smiled at him after blowing out the smoke. "Yeah, I know. Importing cigarettes would be even more expensive than coffee. Right now, I don't want anyone to overhear us. Something's been nagging at me, but first I need to know how many people y'all have left in Don."

"According to the rations dispersed, there are about ten thousand in the First Sector, seven thousand in the Second, and five thousand in the Third Sector of Donnick. Nay ken how many live out their lives without the rations. Medicine, which has their House and facilities here, has five thousand drawing rations. There are five thousand one hundred and seventy-eight Abs drawing rations in Don with two hundred more sentenced to Ayran, and the Army has two hundred Sisters here for keeping order during the Guardians of the Realm Council. They will leave once the Abs depart."

"Is that all the people there are? Is the rest of Thalia so sparsely populated?"

"Rurhran has the most people with some fifty thousand. Betron has about thirty thousand, Troy has at least twenty-five thousand, and Ayran lists twenty thousand, but nay ken how many there are on Ayran. Some of the Tris on all planets trade with the land and fishing Abs and both go back and forth for a living. The Justines did as almost as much damage here as Mither did when she blew their planet apart."

Lorenz let out a stream of smoke, shook his head, and changed the subject. "Did y'all know the Kenning Woman had more of a following than Lamar insinuated? It seems the Tris listened to her also. Da is her laddie, and according to the one called Ka, some of the land Abs already consider Da their Maca."

"Why? Such beliefs nay make sense. The Abs rejected the Houses when they revolted against technology." Doubt was in Llewellyn's voice.

"Call it part of my kenning abilities from Mama; plus last night, Troyner said that Martin was going to use Da as Maca of the Abs to destroy the Houses."

"Bah! Martin tis but repeating the old legend that the House of Abania will once again rule all of Thalia."

"When did they?"

"Over three thousand years ago when technology developed to the point that Thalia could have been destroyed, but we had nay yet journeyed to the stars. After a few centuries of Abanian rule, several Houses revolted. We had another world war like your land tis trying to prevent. The continent Abania was partially destroyed. Later, when the other Houses prevailed, the Abanians eschewed technology and refused a new Maca for the people. Abanians that wished to remain part of the Houses elected to follow the man who was dubbed the Maca of Ayran for the renamed Abanian continent and isles surrounding it. Ye will notice that Jolene's complexion has a deeper rose tinge and her hair tis a dark brown, nay black. Martin tis but stirring up trouble and will nay succeed. Tis this the reason ye are keeping all three laddies?"

"That and I've a hunch we'll be getting all sorts of flak over this once Martin figures out where they are."

Llewellyn thought for a moment and then shook his head. "We've enough problems to solve without worrying about future revolts."

"The one called Ishmael thought it was important enough that he needs to talk to me about Da. That should be House enough even for Lamar. I need to talk with Ishmael before I send the boys back." *If I do*, he thought and snubbed out the cigarette before they entered the door into the hallway.

As they entered the round lobby, Llewellyn greeted Leta who was manning the console. "Good morning, Leta. Did ye find any Tris for Don's Enforcer Service?"

"Good morning, Maca. I have two coming in this morn." She saw the Maca's eyebrows rise and added. "Five more from the outer sectors will arrive as rapidly as they can. Our biggest problem tis transport and that will continue after the other beings take the Kreppies out of here."

Llewellyn nodded. "When Mrs. Andresen arrives, she'll take over your post. She will coordinate the flivs when O'Neal permits the other crafts to fly. I need ye in the Ops Room to eliminate prints and irises. Have the Directors and Keepers arrived?"

Leta made a face. "All but the Director from the First Centor as she tis attending the Burning and Mourning for Bobinet."

"Her name, prints, and irises are to be erased now!" Llewellyn swung on his heel and headed for the elevator. Lorenz tipped his hat at Leta and followed him.

Llewellyn's face remained smooth, but his lips were drawn into a tight line. Lorenz watched the door to the lift close and asked, "How many others in Don are going to snub y'all?"

"Everyone that has been appointed by the Sisterhood, and that may mean the rest of the Directors will look for a chance to leave."

They wasted no more words on the ride to the third floor and walked briskly into the room. There were four people seated at the round conference table. The Maca's chair by the inlaid table console was wide and covered in dark blue leather as were the Guardian's and Counselor's chair set on either side of the Maca's. The windows reflected the light from the sun and cast a faint bluish light into the room lit by lowes. "Lowe comes from our eld word for flame," Llewellyn had explained to Lorenz on his first visit to the *Golden One* once hidden in the earth of Texas.

The bluish white light did little to lighten the sallow skin of an elderly man seated on the right side in the Head Keeper's chair. His thin, grey hair barely covered his skull, and the wrinkled face and hands conveyed a sense of extreme tiredness. Lorenz realized with a shock that this was the first really old person he had seen on Thalia. The man was dressed in the light blue of Don's Tris trimmed with a sash of darker blue. A woman clad in the darker blue of House and a man dressed as the older one sat on the left. Their clothes were tight fitting as were all outfits Lorenz had seen. The other man seated on the right was clothed as the other men. For some reason, his clothes did not fit as well, nor did his hair look as neatly trimmed. The three appeared to be in their mid-thirties, but then to Lorenz, most of the populace of Thalia appeared to be about thirty to forty when they were between the ages of thirty and three hundred. All of the people at the table rose, put their hands behind their backs, and bowed as they entered.

Llewellyn put his hands on his hips and returned the bow. Then he looked at all of them. "Since ye have attended, I shall take it ye have answered the Maca's Call. The older man fidgeted, and while the one in the middle looked a little uncomfortable, they bowed again.

"Please be seated. We have much to discuss."

Llewellyn turned to the older man. "Ye are Minn from Medicine. The records say that Minnay, your lassie, was appointed Director of Don's First Center. She tis nay longer my Director."

The older man bowed his head.

"I have decided to replace ye also. However, since ye answered my call, ye will receive half pay as your pension. The ability of either of ye to open or close the First Center tis removed. If ye need assistance to leave, it will be provided."

The man's head snapped up and defiance showed briefly in his eyes. Then he rose and bowed formally.

"Thank ye, I need nay assistance; nay do I think Don will have long to pay my pension."

He left the room as Llewellyn entered the information and hit the transmit command. The others at the table sat straighter.

Llewellyn smiled at them and looked at the woman. "Ye are Levin, Director of the Second and Third Center."

The woman's angular face softened as she nodded.

"And ye are Linan, her counselor and Keeper at the Second Center."

Like the woman, the man nodded. He was softer looking until one noticed his large hands. His dark hair was cropped short.

Llewellyn gave a brief nod and looked at the last man. "Ye are Lecco, Keeper of the Third Center. The Second Center tis open five days and the Third but one-half day during food distribution. Tis all this true?"

"Aye." The Director's voice was a soft soprano which did not match her harsh facial angles.

"Tell me, how did two males acquire such a high post in Don?"

"Our fithers served on Lamar's warcraft during the Justine War." Linan's voice was a pleasant bass. "While she was Guardian of Don, Beatrice was able to secure us both a position. There was no opposition to my counselor becoming Director."

"I've noticed the First Center's retail, gym, and pool are opened much longer, yet the Second Center has a higher percentage of profitability. How have ye achieved this?"

Levin and Linan exchanged quick glances and Linan cleared his throat. "I'm at fault. Rather than have the stands with uh, less authorized merchandise set up outside, I've allowed them inside. People can then see the authorized goods and oft times make a purchase of them also. The Director of the First Center will nay allow any but authorized goods inside as the others pay nay to the Sisterhood, or Don."

Llewellyn smiled. "Where do they acquire the credits to produce the nay authorized merchandise, and how do the people acquire the credits to purchase them and the authorized goods?"

The man and woman were now holding hands, but Linan's voice remained steady. "There are still technicians to run and maintain the energy panels and the transports Don tis allowed. Most of them live in the Second Sector as the first tis reserved for House and for their Directors and Keepers."

"Who was responsible for allowing the stands inside?"

"I allowed it," Levin answered as she shifted her body slightly as to shield Linan.

Amusement lit the Maca's eyes. "Tis nay what your counselor just said. Tis he better at selling products and arranging the Center than ye?"

Levin nodded her head yes and worry creased her forehead.

"In that case, I appoint Linan as Director of the First and Second Centers. Ye will be Keeper of both the First and Second Center. If ye find that ye need another employee to stock shelves, keep an eye on the customers, or for any other reason, ye will contact me or my named intermediate for assistance. As for the nay authorized merchandize inside, once they interfere with selling authorized goods, they may band together and request a building of their own next to ye, or close by. There will be a slight charge, but they will earn enough for profit."

Llewellyn ignored the startled looks on their faces and swung his gaze to Lecco. "If I appoint ye as Director of the Third Center, can ye remain open for at least half days all week? Could ye find someone, I dinna care whether male or female, to work as Keeper for the time ye are open?"

Lecco dumbly nodded, then realized he was suppose to say something. "Thank ye, Maca. Uh, what do I offer to pay the man?"

"Man?" Llewellyn's eyes lit up. "Ye have someone in mind?"

Lecco glanced at the far wall, squared his shoulders, and firmed his lips. "Aye, as this man helps me when necessary. I admit that I allowed him and his family the use of the pool on the rare days I was allowed to fill it and used part of my pay when nay else covered his hours."

"Ye Gods, are all the pools dry?"

"All but the First Center, Maca, and that tis open but twice a week." Linan's voice was crisp. "We have nay swim guards, nay teachers, and nay allotted water. We have nay gym equipment either."

They watched Llewellyn's hands clench. "What happened to the equipment?"

"The Sisters took most of it and the rest tis locked away and we have…"

Llewellyn stood. "Tis it locked away on the premises?"

"Aye." The three answered in unison.

"Then those doors will be opened. All of ye are to proceed to the Ops Room below and the information entered. As for payment, I have reserve amount of credits from the Justine's profits off of Thalia. Ye two will receive the Director and Keeper salary for the First Sector's Center. When profits rise, ye retain your wages and hire another Keeper. If ye earn enough, ye both will have a Director's salary. Ye, Lecco, will have one-half the Director's salary for the Third Center and it will be open five half days. If ye make a profit, ye will need to stay open all day during the week and your salary will be a full Director's pay. The man ye hire will receive one-half of a Keeper's salary. His pay will increase when your pay increases."

"I've sent a list of needed workers to your Centers. They are to be posted in a prominent place. Do ye ken?"

He watched them nod and continued. "Schools are to be reopened. I need a Director of Education for Don, but he seems to have disappeared. Tis he still alive?"

Levin looked at Linan, and then answered softly. "His laddie tis counselor to the Keeper of the Laird's Home in Donnick. They are there every day as her mither tis the Director of the Home, but too far into her decline to do anything. Her counselor attends her."

Lorenz was amused. He was accustomed to his father calling a house an abode or home. House stood for the ruling families, but he had to ask. "Why is there a Laird's home, if there wasn't a Laird of Don? And who's paying them to be there?"

"The Lady's and Laird's Homes have always been here, but the Justines and the Sisters made sure that every penny was drained for their favorites." Linan's voice registered his disgust.

Llewellyn grimaced and said, "Contact any known technicians, manufacturers, and the Director of Education. Tell them they are to report to me tomorrow. I also need men and women now for transporting goods from the Golden One to your Centers this afternoon.

"Now there is someone ye need to meet."

His index finger touched a small rectangle. The door behind them opened, and a slender, tall, white haired man entered the room. The three Thalians stared at him. His clothing was outlandish and there was a wide knotted ribbon at his throat tucked inside a vest. The shoes looked awkward and heavy; nay supple, and they contained lacing. His light blue eyes were almost as distracting as the Laird's grey eyes.

"This tis Andrew J. MacDonald, one of my youngest from the planet where I resided."

Andrew inclined his head and studied them. The Thalians were impressed. To them, the length of a name bestowed status, the white hair meant he was destined to be an administrator, and his eyes were cold and intelligent as he met their gaze.

"Andrew will be in charge of starting the different manufacturing units we need and will confer with all of ye about the Centers, their profits, their needs, accounting methods, and staffing. He will ensure all are run as businesses should be run. He reports directly to me and will occupy an office on this floor. Are there any questions?"

Linan, Levin, and Lecco swallowed and shook their heads no.

"I need to meet with each Center Director to set up the accounting procedures. I'll be at the First tomorrow, the Second the next day, and the Third the following day. I also recommend you make Levin the Director of the Second and hire a Keeper to work between each. By all of us coordinating our efforts the Centers should begin to show a profit within six months. All have been poorly run and audited, although it's not their fault." Andrew inclined his head at the assembled Thalians.

"Thank ye, Andrew. Ye've wasted nay time. Your recommendations are noted."

Andrew nodded at all and withdrew as Llewellyn looked at the rest and continued.

"If Andrew has the same recommendations after meeting with ye, I will implement them. All view screens in individual homes will be activated within the hour. My laddie and I will send out a message to all of Don, and we will keep sending it at intervals."

"Y'all didn't mention we need butchers—meat cutters for beeves, kine now. Just the one isn't sufficient." Like his father, Lorenz stood.

"Ye have the kine back from Rurhan without the carvers?" asked Levin.

"Don has kine without the ones held by Rurhan. There are more than enough on the southern prairies to feed Don. We also need people to clean out the facilities, and to make sure they are in working condition."

That tis Ab work and Signing Day is two days away." Linan looked concerned.

"What's wrong with Tri's? It seems to me anyone who wants extra rations or credits would be willing to work."

"Aye, if nay wish to work when ye offer a job to them, reduce their rations. Transportation or a fliv must be offered along with the opportunity to learn to pilot fliv. Does anyone have any questions?" Llewellyn looked at the three.

Linan smiled as he rose. "I'm sure there will be requests for transportation and learning to pilot the flivs. I and my counselor would like to lay our heads on your shoulders and be welcomed into House."

Lecco stood, his pasty face almost glowing. "Aye, we must lay our heads on your shoulders, Maca of Don."

Chapter 14

Restoration Begins

Lewellyn and Lorenz rode down the lifts and walked into a madhouse.

"Ye will be silent!" Leta was shouting from the hallway, her stunner in her hand, but not really pointed at anyone.

Margareatha was surrounded by Tris of all ages from all Sectors of Donnick begging for an audience with the Maca, for food, and for jobs. Silence descended when they noticed the Maca and surged towards him.

He stepped forward, raised his arms, palms out, and spread his feet. "People of Donnick, I am Maca!" His voice thundered in the room.

"Who dares to challenge me?"

Quiet settled over the room and Llewellyn smiled. "In that case, your Maca welcomes ye. Here are the new Directors of the Centers. Linan directs the First and Second, Levin the Keeper for Linan, and Lecco tis Director of the Third. They have lists of people needed for the work of rebuilding Don. They will take your applications now."

Lorenz lounged back against the wall, a small smile on his lips as he watched his father control these people. Here the man might not dwarf everyone as he had on Earth, but his size meant he could be a dangerous Thalian.

One wide faced man with spaces between his teeth and dark hair (to Lorenz it looked like an old-fashioned bowl cut) pushed forward. His light-blue Don Tri clothing was clean, but showed the signs of wear. The man was clenching and unclenching his fists.

"Lists do us nay. Truly, we are desperate and soon what jobs there are go to the Abs."

Mummers of agreement came from the people behind him, and they started forward again.

"Lelan, the Maca has already told me to hire ye as the Keeper at the Center. Tis for half days until business improves." Lecco's face betrayed his uneasiness, but once again the crowd stopped.

Lelan looked at the Maca in disbelief, but Llewellyn was speaking again.

"Leta, would ye show everyone to a spare room with tables and screens. Let them ken where the facilities are. This may take time. Lecco, tis up to ye whether this man tis hired or nay."

Lorenz stepped forward. "Is anyone here a butcher?"

"That tis carver, Lorenz."

"All right, if anyone is a carver by trade, or knows, kens anything about carving up kine, we need them now."

All looked at Lorenz as though he were deranged. "There are nay kine in Don," several muttered.

"There will be by tomorrow." He turned to Llewellyn, gave a quick smile, and stepped back.

"The positions for cleaning the facilities are on the lists." Llewellyn nodded to Leta and stepped out of the way.

Chapter 15

Trade and Other Issues

Betta kenned she looked magnificent with her white hair swept upward and back. She was dressed in the flowing, white robes of the Guardian of the Realm. She remained seated at her desk when the Keeper announced, "Captain O'Neal to see ye."

O'Neal entered, removed his kineman's hat, and bowed. He was still dressed in his mottled colored clothing, but at least he had removed the weapons.

"It was good of you to meet with me on such short notice. There are three topics of trade we need to go over as we will leave as soon as the Guardians guarantee there are no more Krepyons on their continents. The Krepyons should have all the personal articles we are allowing them to take by tomorrow afternoon."

Betta raised her eyebrows, but made no comment other than to indicate the chair on the other side of the desk.

O'Neal sat down and extracted a small case from inside his shirt pocket, and placed the crystal in front of her. "You'll find the items listed that we've brought to Donnick and the credits subtracted from Thalia's account. We're ready to unload the merchandise. Mac assures me that he has the laborers. You'll find that everything is properly sealed if you wish to examine them."

"Did Beatrice give ye the right to bring this information to me or did LouElla?"

O'Neal's eyes lit with amusement, but his face remained bland. "We took delivery at the Justine Refuge as we would not allow the Krepyons to deliver the freight. Since I'm going to be responsible for any trading or hauling with the *Golden One*, we thought it expedient that I handle this with the other matters."

Betta fought the impulse to ask "We?" Instead she gave a slight smile and asked, "How is that expedient, and who tis Mac?"

O'Neal seemed to relax and leaned back into the rounded chair. "Mac is Llewellyn, Maca of Don, and I'm the one designated by our corporation to recoup our expenses and then develop a profit. I'm sure you can understand the benefits of one person being in charge, and I still need to know if you want the merchandise."

Betta was bewildered. Whoever heard of a trader being in charge unless said trader was Guardian of House and responsible to the Guardian Council? What, she wondered, was a corporation? Information, she desperately needed information. Finesse was needed for she did not intend for Don to benefit from any trade.

"The House of Medicine will take delivery and store the material. The Guardian of Medicine will supply the laborers and transport."

O'Neal's face remained bland as he made a bridge with his finger tips. "You forget, Guardian, we landed in Donnick. Under your own laws, the Maca of Don has the right to say where any trade goods are delivered within Don and who moves it."

Betta quickly clenched and unclenched her jaw. No, this Justine was not in her mind. LouElla must have instructed him.

"I dinna believe the Maca told ye true. Donnick's Centers are nay prepared."

A smile appeared on O'Neal's face. "He's already met with the Directors and Keepers of Donnick's three Centers. The Directors will have transport available and be allowed to fly.

"I'm surprised you haven't been apprised of the results," he continued smoothly. "There will be an announcement via Don's transmissions to the inhabitants of Don within the next fifteen to thirty minutes."

Betta tasted bile in her mouth. The session with Magda and Ravin had been worth the time, but it prevented close contact with her Director of Affairs and Beauty was useless until pried away from Belinda.

"Ye mentioned ye had three matters of trade," she said too swiftly.

"Yes, the Krepyons have developed a strong affection for the brew of Rurhran and wish to purchase a substantial amount to take with them. They wish to take the brew back to Krepyon for resale." He held up his hand as Betta started to protest.

"Remember, according to the treaty, the party in charge of the *Golden One* has destroyed any ability the Krepyons had to make wars or travel between the stars except for one freighter. It could be a year or more before they arrive. You'll both be depending on me to transfer any trade goods until then, if I have time or if it's profitable."

Betta mentally chopped the arrogant male into pieces and nodded. Thalia would nay have been able to destroy the Kreppies. Why should it matter to this being? Who was the power or planet that controlled him? She forced a smile.

"If I refuse to arrange the brew shipment, ye would go directly to Rurhran to arrange a purchase, tis that true?"

O'Neal's smile became affable. "Yes, Guardian, I would; however, I prefer to work through the proper government channels when possible."

"Does it matter who tis in control?"

O'Neal's smile became raffish. "As long as said government permits me to conduct my business, I see no reason to interfere." His face became serious.

"Are you interested in selling the brew to Krepyons, or shall I leave?"

Betta was convinced the man must be House. He did nay speak like a Tri; nay a Justine for that matter. "Aye, we will sell to the Kreppies at double the price that we have charged."

"They won't accept that. They'll buy from Brendon when we stop there. The same will go for their agricultural products. If you change your mind, you may contact me through Llewellyn before ten o'clock this evening. The next issue is the trade between the three planets of the Justine League and my home world. If you've read the codicil to the treaty, the MacDonald Corporation is the only party allowed to go there or do any trading. Since, returning there won't be immediate, that issue may wait." He stood, gave a mock bow, and headed for the door.

Betta took a deep breath. "How much did the Kreppies offer for the brew?"

O'Neal turned to face her. "One half of what they had been paying."

Betta rose, her face a mask to hide the anger. "They will pay what the Justines have said was fair."

"My thoughts exactly. Since I normally divide the charge on freight between both parties, I'll gladly sign a receipt when I accept the shipment and charge the Krepyons the full freighting costs. Their offer is an insult.

"Leave the details to me, Guardian. The credits will be applied to Thalia's account at the Justine Refuge."

"In the future such trade requests are to go to our Trade Director or the Thalian Envoys at the Justine Refuge. Any trade betwixt other planets would be discussed with them."

"Of course, as you wish, Guardian, but at present there are no Thalian Envoys at the Justine Refuge. Would you be willing to pay the cost of transport for one or two?"

Betta's mouth tightened. This had nay gone the way she planned. The man had told her little and the cost was rising.

"What are ye charging for the transport?"

"A mere five hundred credits for one, double for two. They would need to be ready when I return from my journey to Brendon and Krepyon. May I remind you that if they do not travel with me, any order or communication will wait until my return. In the future, the cost of passengers may double."

"When I return, all merchandise will be delivered here at Donnick and the Maca of Don will take his cut."

Betta nodded and then her brain started to work again. "Would ye object if I arrange delivery elsewhere?"

"Mac would need to agree."

"Why nay take control now and then ye would have the credits?"

Red stared at her. "Madam," he said using his own terminology, "Mac is quite capable of pounding me to a pulp."

"Ye are Justine."

"Part Justine and so is he."

Betta sat back in her chair and stared at her visitor. "But the Justines said he could nay mindspeak."

"They also said I could not exist, nor Llewellyn. There's also a matter of his descendents, Lorenz and his descendents, and Margaretha and her children. You may wish to review their other premises and see what else they have wrong."

Betta took a deep breath. "Are ye saying ye canna win in any type of fight with Llewellyn?"

Red grinned. "No, Guardian, I'm not saying that, but even if I somehow beat Mac, then I'd have to fight Lorenz. He wouldn't rest until I was dead." Red did not add, "And my sister is not here to stop him."

"Lorenz tis his laddie?"

"Aye, while Mac isn't the biological father, Lorenz's loyalty to Mac is beyond comprehension."

Betta was about to say he tis nay Justine, but realized she might be wrong. She had a myriad of reasons to stop Llewellyn and his so called blind-eyed Laird. O'Neal's trip would take several months. By then control of Thalia should be settled and they would have two from Rurhran's House ready to return to the Justin Refuge as envoys.

"There is one more trade item, Guardian. The Krepyons we already have confined in the brig revealed that they had been negotiating with the Justines for more Thalian timber. Are you interested?"

"Perhaps, but I will need to speak with the Maca of Betron. I will have an answer when ye return."

"I'm sure we'll both find it profitable." This time the bow was smoothly done and he contained a satisfied smile as he left the room.

O'Neal held his pace to a saunter as he walked through the building. Once outside, he went directly to the Scout and headed to LouElla's residence. She greeted him heartily as a proper Thalian, added a hug, and began stroking his back and buttocks. He returned all courtesies.

"Come, come, ye must see how my home tis returning to normal."

"Of course, but can we talk privately here?"

"As privately as anywhere in Thalia. Why?"

"I don't feel comfortable going to Brendon without you. We may have missed something when we destroyed the Krepyons' capabilities. I'd rather have someone with me that has fought more than once in space. From what I've read, the Krepyons reproduce at a rapid rate, and their population exceeds that of any other known planet. They may have other facilities we missed. They're a clever people and they've had years of practice avoiding mind contact with a Justine. I want someone like you with me when we take all those Krepyons back. Frankly, I need you. Everyone has already surmised we've been bedding. Let them think that's the reason you're going."

"Ye think of everything, don't ye?"

Red smiled at her. "You'd relish destroying the rest of the Krepyons' abilities, whatever they are."

"My Maca and Thalia need me now."

"And what good will you do them if the Krepyons destroy our ship?"

"Ye have the *Golden One* and ye have Melissa."

"Who is as good at killing as her father, but she has but one experience using the *Golden One* as a fighter and neither Rita nor Melissa pilot as I as I do."

He pulled her against him and buried his face in her neck. "You know you'd relish demolishing the Krepyons."

LouElla stiffened while she considered. Putting an end to all Kreppie abilities would be sweet; almost as sweet as a bedding, and this man was a knowledgeable lover. Gar kenned he had enough experience. She snuggled against him.

"We'll discuss this after the bedding."

But LouElla had already decided. Llewellyn and Thalia needed her here.

Chapter 16

Missed Opportunities

"Rise and shine, gentlemen, the sun's lighting the world and breakfast is almost ready. I'm expected in Donnick, and you all have work assignments." Lorenz's voice boomed over the com into the boy's room.

Pi nearly tripped as he flung himself out of bed in his anxiety to please the Laird by his speed in being present for a new day. Ka sat up confused by the soft comfort of the bed they'd slept in. His elder must realize he was missing from the Ab camp, and Ka wasn't sure how to explain to anyone that he had no business here. Wee Da, however, blinked his eyes, frowned, rolled over, and pulled the pillow over his head. Nay had he worked so hard cleaning one room. Could the Laird nay see that he, the Kenning Woman's laddie, was a Warrior and should be honing his muscles and movements? Besides he was to be the Laird's laddie. Mither had said so.

Pi and Ka pulled Da out of bed. Da bellowed his protests at the rude awakening. None of them were clothed and between them Da was pulled into the shower. Ka closed the door while Pi turned on the water. Who cared that work awaited them when they had spent the night sleeping like House and had eaten food fit for House? Ur had made a bad choice when he sought a better opportunity.

* * *

Ur had not slept on his usual pallet at the Ab Compound and had missed the Ab breakfast: fat meat or porridge, bread, milk, and some sort of fruit from the orchards of Rurhran. At least, he reflected sourly, the pallet would have been warm and the breakfast filling. He watched glumly as the sun rose. He had tried to find Pi in the usual hiding places, but they were empty. For some reason he had not seen any of the three since the Maca of Don arrived. Had Wee Da found refuge with the man the Abs whispered was the blind-eyed Laird the Kenning Woman had predicted? He shivered against the cold and looked over the crumpled fence wall of what had once been a prosperous Tri home. Since all he heard was silence, he urinated against the stone fence and trotted down the street. Yesterday had started out much more promising.

He paced the streets to see if there was something to steal or to sell. By midmorning, it seemed Donnick was coming to life. Vendors were being allowed to set up their stands, and more people than usual seemed to be heading for the First Sector's Center. He watched the two Kreppie vessels lift upward, and like everyone he cheered at the departing Kreppies. Even the black suited Sisters waved and cheered. He watched until the crafts disappeared into the *Golden One*. With that came the realization that he had missed an opportunity to snatch pina pods or one of last season's brools. Ur imagined his teeth sinking into the later: crisp with sweet juice under its red skin.

He set off to find another opportunity when one of the Kreppie crafts returned, landing within the Don Compound. For some reason, the Maca seemed intent on arousing the wrath of the Sisters. They would nay take lightly the thought that a male controlled such a huge vessel. That they possessed nay skills in navigation would nay matter. It was wrong for a male to yield such power. A member of the squad could be seen running for the Guardians' Compound.

Ur shrugged. He needed to find a customer and made his way towards the brew halls that lined part of the waterfront. They were convenient for those coming by sea; whether House or Ab. The brew halls were also close to the padports for incoming flivs and cairts from other Houses. Tomorrow they would all be here for Signing Day. Surely some were early and would need a companion. He needed a place that served those with credits, but were too crude for House. He would need to deal with one of the Sisters for the Tris of Don had few credits. He strolled towards the water, hoping one of the food vendors would set up by a brew hall. Mayhap the Sisters would close it down as a joke and distribute the food for free. They had a rare sense of humor.

He stuck his head into one doorway to check out the crowd and saw the Keeper frown and start towards him. He backed out. Had he angered the woman in some way, or was it the fact he was male? The day was warming rapidly and Ur flexed his muscles, feeling the warmth. Noises were coming from one establishment. That meant someone was celebrating or spending freely. He smiled to himself and walked behind the building to see if people were using the back entrance, but the alleyway was deserted. It would be a good place to return later when those inside had drank their fill and were looking for something new. He really wished all or one of the three friends were here. It was easier to grab something when they were there to distract the vendor. He sauntered back up the street.

Ur returned as the temperature began to decline and the sun began to move leisurely westward. It would be cool this evening and he needed credits or it would be another night of listening to Martin instructing him in the ways of Gar. He leaned against the wall and crossed his arms over his chest. From here he could watch the people entering or leaving and make his offer. He preferred more darkness, but the coolness said he would need refuge tonight, and there was barely time to accomplish a bargain and a snatch. His eyes studied anyone that came near. Some seemed to admire his frame, but he wanted nay of that. Far better to force someone else to play the pretty, and he cursed all the times he'd missed filching something today. For some reason the vendors were standing straighter while bargaining with the few people who had something of worth for their merchandise. It was as though they were watching for him. He was almost ready to leave when he saw a Sister being pushed out of the door.

"Your insults are nay wanted here, Mafy. This tis a brew hall, nay a home for pretties."

The Sister snarled something at the Keeper vanishing into the interior, straightened her cap, and glanced towards the waterfront. She then shrugged, turned, and watched Ur swagger toward her.

Ur bowed. "Good evening to ye, Sister. Mayhap I can supply something the hall lacked." He could smell the brew coming off her and noticed the uniform stained on the upper sections. Someone must have thrown a brew with great effect.

Mafy's hatchet face grew intent as she studied him. "I prefer lassies, young lassies, nay laddies." She reached out a hand and stroked his arm, feeling the massive muscle. "If ye cut off that below, ye would be acceptable."

Ur's stomach contracted, but his smile remained. "Sister, I did nay mean my-self. Mayhap I could bring ye someone to please ye; someone young and soft since that tis your preference."

Mafy stepped closer, practically rubbing against him, keeping the stroking motion going, moving it over his back and buttocks. "Ye are young also. Mayhap ye would join us."

Ur's smile was set, his eyes hard. "First I must have a place to bring ye what ye wish. The House of Army would nay admit us." Now he could feel her thin, hard muscles against his body and she put her mouth to his ear.

"Can ye remember the fifth building past the sunset side of the Army Compound? Knock three times. Nay will bother us."

"Aye, Sister, and the price will be five credits in coins for two of us." He felt her hand starting to investigate certain places and felt his nerves beginning to respond, the male musk rising from his body.

Her teeth found his ear and nipped. "That tis to remember me. Five it will be." Her hand clamped on his male part and she started to squeeze. "And that tis a warning as to what will happen if ye cross the Sisterhood."

She released him and strode down the street to disappear around the corner leading towards the Army Compound. Ur took great gulps of air. Somehow he would have to get the credits without entering her lair. First he must find a suitable offering, one that would make her pay on arrival and keep her occupied while he ran. Ur turned back to the vendors' area, running swiftly. The light was perfect as it was enough for him to see, yet almost dark enough to cloak his true age.

Running increased his awareness and he began to look everywhere for a lassie less than twelve. Mayhap the vendor with the carved wooden figures was still there. He had seen such a lassie nay more than ten years with swinging black hair, the plump white cheeks of Don, and her girlish figure nay yet ready to muscle. Ur began edging closer to the buildings, slowing his pace. He did nay wish to draw attention to himself as he neared the vendors. Most of the Tri vendors had left; the few remaining were packing away their merchandise for the evening, hurrying to avoid the dark to be safely at home, and their goods locked away.

Ur was relieved to see that the girl was not at the stand. Good, mayhap she was down at the waterfront watching the clumsy wood Ab boats bobbing among the few sleek House vessels built by Ishner. He picked up his stride to check the piers and found nothing but Abs leaving or returning to their sea crafts. Mayhap she was looking at the goods offered at the few remaining stalls.

Nightfall began its creep downward and he hurried, but once again he saw nothing, nor did he see anyone that looked like a replacement. There was one last place to check. He'd seen her once at the little pool and fountain behind the First Center. He trotted towards the Center and ran to the back of the building.

There she was! She sat cross legged, stirring the water with a stick, her black hair hanging down over her shoulders. She did nay see or hear him move behind her. He reached down, his left arm going around her chest and underneath her arms, his right hand clamping over her mouth. He hefted her off the ground and began running back towards the street when a lad of about her age appeared and started to yell.

"The Snatcher has Lida! Help!"

Ur almost stopped, his eyes seeking an escape route. Caught. Trapped. He dropped the girl and ran towards the street, not stopping for the lad in his way. The boy fell to the side, but his legs went out and Ur tripped. He fell, his face toward the cement, but he was able to block his fall with his hands. His knees felt the skidding impact and began to burn. He jumped up, ignoring the pain in his hands and knees. He charged out into the street and started to turn towards the Ab Compound. The girl's fither and other vendors were running towards him, staves and tubing in their hands. He whirled and ran towards the north, pushing for speed, knowing he had to find a side street and a hiding place soon.

The chasers were older; their legs longer. As he dashed into the street leading back through the homes someone threw a club at him and it struck his ear, threatening his balance. He stuck out his hand and pushed against the wall to regain his traction and ran harder. Dark was cloaking everything, and he prayed he would nay trip. The men behind him did nay ken this area as well as he.

His heart was pounding when he turned into the street where homes were filled with broken doorways and windows. He dove through a window of a home with a sealed front door. He rolled on the floor, hoisted himself up in the darkened room, and walked towards where the backdoor would be with arms outstretched. Now was no time to hurry. Steady, steady, his outstretched hands felt the opening and he headed for the back, following the night air blowing towards him. His hand felt a counter and he kept his steady pace. He could hear men yelling outside.

"I dinna see him."

"He's in one of the homes. Search them."

The siren, a shrill warning of the coming curfew, sounded to remind the inhabitants to be home within the next half hour. Twice more it would sound and any found outside were subject to detention.

Ur hoped the vendors lived far enough away to give up their pursuit. Instead, he heard banging on the walls and the sound of someone landing on their feet inside. As quietly as possible, he squeezed through the backdoor and stepped outside, his lungs pulling in the fresh, spring night air. He ran for more than a block and then headed towards the hills on the West side of Donnick; an area devoid of population where dark would thicken into blackness. Too late now to return to the Ab Compound for Martin would lock the doors when the next siren sounded. He'd have to find a hole or cellar to spend the night. He gnashed his teeth in frustration. Mafy would be looking for him tomorrow and so would the vendors. Ur doubted they were able to see his face, but they would remember his muscular body. If they complained to Martin about an Ab being the Snatcher, he would be in more trouble.

He was trotting now; more to keep warm than to evade the ones chasing him. If he swung back to the town area too soon, he would be discovered; too late and his night would be cold and miserable. He cursed at those who had thwarted his plans for credits to provide a warm meal and a rented bed. Tomorrow he would need to find a place to hide from all. How he wished he had asked Pi where he was sleeping. At least another body helped to keep one warm. All he could do now was hope Pi was as miserable as he.

Chapter 17

Signing Day

The morning sun rose above the pink and peach streaks lacing through the clouds to wash the streets of Donnick with light. The streets in the deserted sections were still littered with debris, but those from the waterfront to the First Center had been picked clean by Tris. Lorenz had been right. Employment had been so meager for the Tris many of them were ready to work anywhere at anything for a chance to earn food or credits.

The spring air slowly warmed the earth and the sun sent blue sparkles bouncing off the blue micaceous glass of the Maca's rounded compound. Tents dyed in the color of each House lined the area between the beach padports and the green area around the First Center. The smell of delicacies wafted from the tents overpowering the smell of the ocean. Tables set in front of the tents were draped in matching House colors. Flivs and cairts in the House colors rested on the padports signifying that all the Houses attended. Rurhran made certain their golden table was as far from Don's dark blue as possible.

Laten, dressed in House blue, set up the table and recorder outside of Don's tent. He brought out two blue chairs and smiled at a frowning Tri blue clad Dolo as she returned.

"Did ye nay find Ki?"

"Aye, I found her, but Martin has warned the Abs that to sign with Don means nay food when the work tis over."

"Did ye tell Ki the terms at the Laird's Station and she could have Ka there as her helper?"

"Aye, but she says she needs to dwell on it." Dolo looked at the Abs starting to line up at the tent of Rurhran as she slid into the other chair. "I did buy her another brew ere I left," she added. "At least she accepted that."

A squad of Sisters marched down the thoroughfare towards their area, wheeled as they came abreast and lined up on the edge of the green facing them. If Martin's orders failed to keep the Abs away, the Sisters intended to ensure that Don would have no workers.

Laten grew somber as he watched the Abs line up in front of Rurhran's, Troy's, Ishner's, and Betron's tables. Ayran lacked any volunteers, but there was sure to be a fight before the afternoon wore away, and Ayran would have extra workers from the condemned.

They watched the Laird approach the Guardian of Ayran and bow. For some reason neither laid their head on each other's shoulder. They were too far away to hear what the Laird was saying, but they could see the Guardian of Ayran's face darken. She put her arms akimbo and snapped something back. The Laird grasped the brim of his hat, tipped it to her, and stalked back to Don's tent, his face set and hard.

Dolo looked at Laten. "What was that about?"

"I dinna, but the Laird tis nay happy."

The Tri's of Don were gathered behind the Sisters, watching the Signing process. Some were hoping the Houses would distribute the uneaten food and some were there to watch any unforeseen show. Street vendors were openly working the crowd. From somewhere, people must have scraped up spare credits or found goods to trade. Their Maca was at Betron's tent visiting. The other Guardians and Macas were also visiting each other and sampling the provisions and brew.

"Mayhap I should get us a brew." Laten suggested as he watched the crowds grow around Rurhran.

"Nay now." Dolo was watching the broad shoulders of Ur making his way towards their table. His face looked wary and he was making short dashes between the assembled crowds. He sauntered around the last of the Sisters and headed straight for Don's table.

One of the Sisters sprang after him. "Stop ye abominable Ab! Ye are wanted."

Ur didn't bother to look behind as he increased his speed. He had spent the night hidden in the lower region of a deserted building. He'd foregone breakfast on the theory that someone would be looking for him at the Ab Compound.

His vantage point this morning had been behind the serpentine wall of the First Center. Abs were around all the Houses' tables but Don's. He'd seen the strange Laird stalk away from Ayran. So far only one or two extremely well-built Abs had approached Ayran's table, and when the Maca of Rurhan approached Jolene, Guardian of Ayran, both she and her Counselor left the table to confer with Ravin. It was his opportunity to disappear into Don as a signed Ab. Whether he would actually go or not hadn't entered his mind. He could remain hidden in the tent and there would be food.

Ur stopped in front of Laten and Dolo, and wet his lips before he trusted himself to speak. He was banking on the fact that his hard, sculpted body meant people thought he was older. Since he was nay born in the Ab compound, none were sure of his age.

"I wish to sign with Don as a general helper."

"Ye canna sign him," screeched Mafy. "I want that miserable Ab condemned."

"What offense has he committed?"

Laten halfway turned in his seat and then straightened. He should have kenned the Laird would see and intervene. He saw that Lorenz had beaten Lamar out of the tent, the Guardian of Don red-faced at being last.

Ur stood as straight and tall as he could, hoping his stomach would not growl from hunger and fear.

"He did nay fulfill his obligation." Mafy had her hand on her stunner.

"What obligation was that?"

"One that ye should ken well, mutant." Mafy's face contorted into hatred.

"Sign him, Laten."

Laten shrugged at the Laird's command and entered symbols on the screen and handed the stylist to Ur.

"Abs canna enter data! He tis a miserable thief." Mafy was shouting.

"What did he steal?" asked Lorenz.

"A good time and ye should be grateful I left his man appendage. Stand back."

Ur stood straighter and the Laird looked at him. Hard those grey eyes were, hard like the grey slate of Ayran.

"Woman in my land, no decent man hits a woman, but if y'all don't back down, y'all aren't leaving me any choice. Sign that list, laddie."

Ur bent and wrote his name and handed the stylist back to Laten. Then he put his hands behind his back and bowed. When he straightened, he saw the slight smile on Lorenz's face.

Lorenz looked at Mafy. "Get out of here. No one is backing your play."

Mafy looked around. Most of the Sisters didn't like her and she didn't have the authority to order them. She stalked off vowing to stun the mutant alien at the first opportunity.

Lorenz turned to Ur. "I believe at this point, y'all have the right to partake of the food inside the tent. Is that correct?"

"Aye, Laird." It was difficult to keep his voice from cracking. He decided it was the shock of seeing someone with grey eyes that saw. Ur walked around the table and towards the tent seeking safety from the outraged family of the lassie he had tried to snatch. Once inside he inhaled the long missed smell of meat and breads spread out among the sauces, plates, and utensils. One table was loaded with sweets and kegs of brew waiting to be tapped. Ur grabbed a plate and began piling it full after stuffing a slice of fatty kine into his mouth.

"Careful, laddie, eat too much rich food on an empty stomach and it will protest."

Ur whirled to see the Laird with a bemused look in the strange grey eyes studying him.

Balancing his half-filled plate, Ur gave a quick bow. "All Abs wait for this day to indulge, Laird."

"I am not Laird according to Thalian law. My name's Lorenz MacDonald. Y'all may call me Mr. MacDonald after the way of my people."

Ur ducked his head, looked up and grinned. "Aye, Laird."

The man was half-laughing at him, but the eyes were still hard as though seeing right through him.

"Eat away. Anyone with guts enough to defy the Sisters and Martin in one day is welcomed here."

Lamar appeared at the tent opening.

"I am going to find Beatrice. Ishmael tis here to see ye." His voice sounded angry to Ur.

Lorenz nodded at him and went towards the tent opening. Once outside he was caught in a bear hug by a young man his height and weighing approximately the same. He felt the head on his right shoulder and then on his left.

"I did nay properly thank ye the other night." Ishmael was beaming at him. "How do ye greet in your land?"

Lorenz put out his right hand and after a moment Ishmael grasped it and they shook. Lorenz noted that Ishmael wore a skin tight shimmering aqua suit with a V neck slashing to the beltline. His hair was neatly trimmed in the short fashion of Thalians.

"Y'all look much better than the last time we met. Come in, have a brew."

Ur was at his elbow handing them two filled mugs. He bowed and vanished.

Lorenz's eyes were wide with surprise. "What the?"

Ishmael laughed. "Ur tis being useful. He must be in trouble with Martin again." He took a sip of the brew. "Tis nay as I expected, but what body! Which House brewed this?"

"Nay House, but one of the foreign companies from my planet. Papa, the Maca, said that Thalians would appreciate this one. The English call it stout."

Ishmael shook his head at the strangeness of the words and drank again. "When I am able to sell my loads, I will buy some of this if ye intend to market it." He smiled at Lorenz. "Today I need to fulfill a promise. Can we talk inside?"

They drifted into the tent, and Ishmael continued. "I made a promise to the Kenning Woman while she lived that I would try to get her laddie to ye. Since my fish were dumped, I've spare time on my hands before sailing again."

"Why did the Kenning Woman want her son, laddie, to be with me?"

"She kenned she was in danger and that Martin planned to use Wee Da as the Maca of the Abs to rule Thalia. She could nay protect him from Martin. Since ye are to restore Don and Thalia, she felt he would be safe with ye. She hoped ye would allow him to become House. She did nay care whether it was Don, Army, or Flight. Di felt that being a House Warrior would be his best protection."

"I was told the Abs had no Maca."

"They dinna, at least the Abs that follow the work seasons. The land Abs are different. Each small group has a Maca. Tis laughable. They are deposed by a challenger regularly."

"According to Latin, Don has most of the land Abs."

"They are on the emptied lands of all of the Houses except Rurhran. Ayran may have a goodly populace, nay ken. There are fewer on Ishner and Betron, but they exist."

"How did they get there? I was told the Justines and Kreppies moved all of the people from the interior to the coastal cities."

"They cared nay where the Abs went afterward. Some Tris eluded them and they became land Abs."

"Do they live off the land or buy supplies?"

Ishmael shrugged. "They exist by hunting, fishing, and growing a few crops. If times are bad, they come to the mainland and join the Abs here and work for a season or two. Most of the land Abs move their camps in the spring and fall. A few have permanent homes. As far as I ken, the land Abs eschew all learning and technology even more than the Abs with Martin.

"If ye cross Don's mountains," Ishmael pointed to the northeast, "there are small fishing villages on the coast. Tis said that escaped Tris have put up a settlement inland rather than bow to the Kreppies."

"And they were left alone?"

Ishmael's face was bitter as he answered. "Aye, nay had to feed them. Other than living in one place, they are little different from the Abs. Ye are nay drinking your brew."

Lorenz looked down and gave a self-conscious grin. "I'm not fond of brew even though my mother, mither, made it."

"What do ye drink?"

"Whiskey, brandy, and sometimes wine with a meal. If y'all don't mind, I'm going to change the subject as I've much to learn about Thalia and Papa's been as busy as I."

Lorenz looked at Ur. "Why don't we go outside and y'all can tell me about the fish? Are y'all ready for another brew?"

Ishmael grinned. "One more, Lorenz, and then I must rejoin Ishner's tent. Ishner hires few Abs. We take enough to help with the cleaning of the catch and packing when the season tis in full swing. What tis it ye wish to ask about the fish?" He accepted the fresh mug Lorenz handed him.

"It sounded like y'all had caught a load of fish and just dumped it. Why?"

"Ishner tis overrun with Sisters. My elder does nay wish to offend them. If they revolt, or one challenges her lassie for the title of Maca, Ishmalisa would have to fight her. Ishmalisa tis nay the most magnificently built Thalian. The Sisters would nay let her counselor, Illnor fight. Tis their Sisterhood laws." His voice grew harsher as the explanation went on.

"The Sisters dinna like the fact that Ishmalisa has given me back my ship. They judged my catch as nay worthy and refuse to transfer it to the packers, or to the meal processing plant."

"That's wasteful. What would your Guardian say if y'all were to come up with credits for your catch?"

"How do I do that if I canna send them to market?"

"Y'all sell them to Don for meat or meat credits."

Ishmael took a long drink. "Ye could nay process them, or if ye did, nay sell them elsewhere."

"Agreed, at least selling them. I need to talk with Papa, Fither, and see what solution he proposes."

"Don has nay meat to sell." Ishmael hated pointing out the obvious.

"That's what the rest of Thalia thinks, and we'll let them continue to think."

"Continue?"

Lorenz's smile transformed his face. "Aye, we are already supplying all of Donnick with the beeves, kine, I've rounded up. There are kine on this side of those mountains and more where land Abs dwell."

Ishmael's eyes lit up. "Di was right. Don will be restored." He looked at the man in front of him. In truth, Lorenz could pass for a Thalian; except for the grey eyes that were nay blind. Perhaps they had more in common.

"I hope ye dinna mind my asking, but how close are ye to the wedding age? I canna judge by looking at ye."

"I've been married—wedded as y'all call it. My beautiful Antoinette died after sixty-five years of marriage. That was about forty years ago and I still miss her at times."

"Lorenz, I—I offer my sorrow. One should nay die so young."

Lorenz shook his head. "Ishmael, my world is completely different. Antoinette died of old age. I should be dead too, but I'm part Justine, and I do not die at the end of a normal Earth lifespan."

For a moment the bitterness flowed in his speech and Ishmael searched for a way to change the conversation.

Lorenz looked up and saw a well dressed Ab woman approaching the table. Her face was ruddy, her dark brown, braided hair swung over one shoulder, and her kirtle was new and clean. The brown blouse appeared satiny, and around her neck hung a carved bone necklace. She wore a rust colored vest and matching colored boots. Lorenz noticed that Dolo's shoulders stiffened. He walked forward and the woman looked across Laten and Dolo to study him as intently as he had studied her.

"I've come to see what tis still available." Ki spoke to Laten, ignoring Dolo.

"As ye ken, all but one of the listed positions remains open," Laten answered.

"Tis there one that offers a home with a garden if there are two?"

"Aye, if ye are planning on bringing the laddie. Won't Martin take it out on him next year?"

Her full lips pulled back in a grimace. "May Martin go to the Dark. I have more questions."

She looked directly at Lorenz as though to challenge him as she asked, "'Tis it true that ye have my younger, Ka?"

"There is a youngster, laddie, at the Laird's Station named Ka. He seemed to come with the Kenning Woman's laddie and the other one."

Ki's face softened. "Does Don intend to give rights to the Abs that sign?"

"Aye, that we do." Amusement flickered in Lorenz's eyes. "Y'all will have the right to a name, to learn, to keep the home, and mayhap work out a deal to remain on the same land for a per cent of what y'all grow."

For a moment the dark eyes flared, then she considered. "What tis a per cent?"

"Don would only tax, take a small part of what y'all produce. It would be your job to sell what y'all produce to the vendors or markets in town. If y'all don't wish to peddle your produce to individuals, Don would buy it, but at a lower price then y'all might get on the open market."

"There tis nay market and few vendor stalls."

"There will be more."

"Are ye saying, Laird, that the land I work will be mine?"

"I'm saying that the home and land will be leased to y'all for a set number of years if y'all sign. Ye could earn a lot more than Ab credits if y'all are as good as your clothes say y'all are."

"And tis there brew for the signing?"

"Aye, it is inside."

"And tis brew part of the weekly credits."

"Y'all will have to buy your brew out of the credits. It'll be served with the communal meals, if and when y'all eat with the others."

"Tis this how they do things in your land, Laird?"

Lorenz smiled. The woman had a mind. "Not quite. When my land had few people, the government, what ye call the Council of the Realm, gave land away free or sold it for a small fee to all who would work it."

Everyone was staring at him.

"The Houses gave away their land?" Ishmael could nay believe what he heard.

"There are no Houses in my land. Houses are what we call individual homes."

Ishmael looked at him in disbelief. The Justine did nay have Houses, but the Kreppies and Brendons did. "Who rules the land then?"

"It depends on the country. In mine, we elect, cast votes for those we want." Lorenz smiled at Ki.

"Well are y'all going to sign?"

"Ka will be with me and join me in the work. His food will be on top of my wages. I am worth it." Her head and shoulders were straight and the gaze straightforward as though none could dispute it.

"Sign away. The food and brew are in the tent."

Lorenz looked down at the list on the screen and frowned.

"How goes the signing?" It was Llewellyn returning with Brenda.

"Not good, Papa. I say open the jobs to anyone who wants them, and that means Tris."

"Maca, Laird, Tris will nay take an Abs job." Laten protested.

"The announcement was in the Maca's message I sent to all the homes. Tis been repeated every four hours. Mayhap that tis why so many are here."

They watched Llewellyn walk through the Sisters and up to where the Tris waited. Their mutterings had been growing louder.

"Laird, we should follow. There may be trouble." Laten stood.

They were in time to hear his words.

"I heard grumbling. What tis the problem?"

A man stepped forward, his chin out. "Ye offer jobs to Abs and nay to us."

"Ye are wrong, If ye want jobs, they are yours. If ye are nay sure what tis available, we'll be happy to tell ye. There are even more jobs than what tis on the Ab list. If someone is an excellent gardener or machinist, tell us. We'll place ye. I need men and women like every one of ye!

"This tis Laten, Director of the Laird's Station, Llewellyn continued. "He will sign up those that wish to work there. Those that prefer town living need to see the Director of each Sector's Center." With that he turned and walked back to the table.

He smiled at Dolo. "Are they following?"

"Aye, Maca, they are."

Laten resumed his seat beside her and she whispered, "I must tell Ki that we are filling the jobs with Tris and will leave soon. Else she will drain the brew and leave. If she leaves she will find a companion and start to drink elsewhere and nay return."

Chapter 18

Council of the Realm

Betta and Beauty watched as the Guardians and Counselors took their places.
For once the lower tiers were filled with Tris. Where did they come from?

Betta was puzzled. The light blue clad Tris outnumbered the brown clad Abs.
Was Llewellyn planning more trouble? She already had an accounting of the
charges Rurhan planned to bring and the list of grievances from the Sisterhood.
She turned on the audio and spoke.

"People of Thalia, much has happened these last few days and there tis much
to cover this eve. We realize that many are anxious to return to House after the
signing. We shall try to be as brief as possible.

"The Sisterhood has declared their laws against the males of Thalia nay valid.
We apologize to all we have hurt. This means all males may take their place in
society as Thalian laws have always dictated."

Cheers greeted her words.

Betta continued. "The Council realizes it will take time to implement. Before
we proceed, there is another matter that concerns us all.

"Llewellyn, ye who call yourself Maca of Don, are but part Thalian. I must
ask ye. Can ye enter another's mind?"

"Aye, I can do that, but ye have my word as a Maca and a Thalian that I will
nay enter any Thalian's mind."

Betta's face was stern as she spoke. "Ye say that, but how do we prevent it
from happening if ye appear in the arena?"

"Guardians of the Realm, ye will need to judge that if it ever occurs."

"Ken this, Llewellyn, ye will nay be Maca if ye do. Thalia has had enough
of Justine rule."

"Guardian of the Realm, I suggest ye are raising hypothetical situations when ye wish to avoid voting to restore Troyner to his rightful position and returning the kine and sheep to Don."

"Tis my kenning that Rurhran tis negotiating that situation."

"Rurhran tis refusing to return them. I have instructed my Guardian to request a vote"

LouElla leaned forward to speak. How dare they attack her laddie? "Before the Guardian of Don makes that request, I ask ye to restore Troyner to his rightful position. The Justines had him on the list of those deliberately removed. The treaty specified that Thalia return to the rules of Thalia ere their arrival."

"Troyner was nay even born then." Betta wished to return to the subject of Don.

Brenda, Maca of Betron, interceded. "What the Director of Flight has requested tis reasonable. There should be a vote."

"There will be nay else considered while we debate the validity of Llewellyn holding the title of Maca."

Betta noted that Llewellyn was clenching and opening his hands. Let him, she thought, we're ready for him.

She made sure her next words were measured with just the right spacing for emphases. "Council of the Realm, we now request your remarks before our vote on the validity of Llewellyn as Maca of Don.

"Jolene, what do ye say?"

Jolene's face remained bland, but her full lips curled. "I think ye have been very busy and have lined up Rurhran on your side. Ye canna dispose Llewellyn by decree. He has every right to be Maca and ye have nay right to do so when imposters are ruling Troy."

Beauty interrupted. "Guardian of the Realm, Llewellyn must be escorted out."

Llewellyn's roar interrupted her. "I am Maca! Let any who denies me or wants to be Maca challenge me now."

Silence prevailed.

"I thought nay." Llewellyn swung his eyes back to Betta. "On the contrary, Guardian of the Realm, tis the Council that must leave if ye pursue your stated intent. This farce of a meeting tis nay amusing. If ye reject me, Don will charge a fee for any meeting held here. As long as ye leave the Abs in my care their supplies will be delivered to the Director of the First Center and we will determine their distribution."

At this Martin stood to add his protests, but the stentorian voice of Llewellyn overrode his un-amplified voice.

"Be aware that as Chairman of the Board and President of the MacDonald Corporation, the ships I brought with me stay with Don."

Betta blanched. How could she stop this tirade?

Llewellyn's voice rumbled on. "The Golden One that left with the Justine and the Kreppies will be returning. When they do, the profits from that trip belong to the MacDonald Corporation and the goods will be stored on Don and Thalia charged for the storage. It will be the people of Don who have the jobs of storing and transporting the merchandise to the other Houses, if they have the credits to buy them. The Sisters also need to ken that Flight remains in Don. Tis here that the ships remain and new ones built. Any that pilot them must seek permission from the Director of Flight or the Maca of Don. Your threats are hollow. Ye can, of course, return to the true problems of Thalia."

"Llewellyn, by your words ye condemn yourself. Arrest him." The guards below loosened their metal bars at Beauty's command and started towards the stairs when another voice yelled.

"People of Don: To the Maca!" Lorenz was yelling as he, Laten, Luman, and Dolo strode towards the guards and the Tris of Don streamed from the stands. Lecco and Linan were in the foreground, their metal bars already swinging, the prospect of revenge against the Sisterhood sweet in their mouths.

The floor became a mass of whirling light blue and black. The outnumbered Sisters sank under the weight of the Don fighters. From the floor a woman screamed.

"My ear! Medicine!"

Llewellyn's bellowed out his command. "Attend, people of Don."

They stopped at his words. What had he bribed them with Betta wondered. She had heard rumors of extra meat being delivered, but how had Llewellyn procured it?

"Llewellyn, don't be a fool. Ye will isolate Don. From where would ye get your meat, flour, and grains if nay from Rurhran?"

"Great," and somehow the Great became a sneer, "Betta, mayhap ye will pay Don in grains and flour. I have found the people of Don are very resourceful."

"Llewellyn, ye have but Tris. Ye had best leave as ye will nay be allowed to vote."

"Betta, if ye were younger, I would challenge ye." LouElla stood.

Brenda was on her feet. "This tis a travesty. The Counselor of the Realm acted without a vote. Ye are trying to start a war with the House of Don. What tis wrong with ye?"

Jolene remained seated. "She tis right, Guardian of the Realm. Ye are acting like the Sisterhood controls every voice on the Council. They do nay. Ye have nay right to arrest Llewellyn for an offense that has nay occurred. I have nay heard of a Justine headache afflicting anyone, however, I do have questions for Llewellyn. If the Council of the Realm ignores all the false charges, do ye promise nay to use your Justine mind?"

"Both my laddie and I will swear to that."

Jolene swallowed. "I had nay realized he was capable." She switched the subject.

"Do ye intend to follow through with your threats or do ye intend to work within the Council."

"Guardian of Ayran, I have always meant to work within the Council of the Realm, but on the matter of Don's beasties, Rurhran tis leaving us little choice. I dinna ken why the Guardian of the Realm wishes to destroy Don. Mayhap she wishes revenge for Bobinet."

Betta was hiding her face in her hands.

Beauty swung to face him. "Ye mentioned a Corporation and gaining credits for it. Tis that the government from your land of refuge and ye intend to give them Thalia's credits? It sounds like ye wish to bleed us as dry as the Justines or Kreppies.

Llewellyn smiled at her. "A corporation tis a business founded under the laws of the country where the necessary legal papers are filed. It has nay to do with governing people. If this Council throws me out, I will remain Maca of Don."

"Ye are a mutant!" Beauty yelled.

"Guardian of the Realm," she continued in a normal voice, "I request that we consider him excluded and vote on a new Guardian for Don. I suggest someone from Medicine."

Shouts of Nay erupted from the Don's Tris.

Betta looked up. "Llewellyn, will ye step down for peace in Thalia?"

"I will nay. I am Maca!"

Jolene's face remained bland as she spoke. "Guardian, I suggest ye give up this idea of appointing someone else as Maca or Guardian of Don. If ye persist in this, I will leave with Don."

Brenda leaned forward. "I remind ye, Guardian of the Realm, that I am Maca of Betron. Betron owes a great debt to Llewellyn. He and his House rescued my laddie, Benji, Laird of Betron. If ye recall, Benji tis your younger. I insist ye stop this farce."

Ravin stood. "I thought ye meant it when ye said the males would be welcomed in the Houses and Council. For the first time, my Counselor and I let our younger attend this meeting. Now I regret that we were so foolish. If he tis nay safe, we will leave."

Beauty saw her mother's face sag as Betta sank back into her chair.

"My fellow Guardians, I did what I thought best for Thalia. Mayhap we should close our meeting until after the Feast of Beltayne."

"I suggest we vote on whether Thalia operates under our laws ere the Justines changed them. If we are nay clear, the Guardian of the Realm would have extraordinary powers to send the Army after anyone." Jolene smiled at Betta. "That tis the vote ye delayed at the last meeting."

Betta swallowed. "Very well, that will be our business this evening. The other matters such as Troy and livestock can wait until after Beltayne. The Arena banquet will be this eve. I regret to say Belinda is still in mourning for her mither. Out of consideration for her Counselor, Beauty will nay attend. The bouts will be short." She dared nay say, "I grow weary and the eve too long." They would accuse her of entering her decline and elect Ravin as Guardian of the Realm.

"There will now be a discussion about our laws. Ayran, ye may start." She kenned Llewellyn would win and remain Maca.

None saw the grey eyes of the new Laird grow hard and he motioned to Laten and Dolo to follow him.

Chapter 19

The Naming

"There are over one thousand kine missing from the Northeast pastures, Mither." Rocella announced as she entered the room where her parents were breakfasting. "Your plans to isolate and starve Don are nay maturing in the direction ye envisioned. They have nay begged for mercy."

Raven was startled. "Were the Keepers nay alert? Where were our scanners aimed?"

"If ye recall, ye said they would try for the fatted kine or for the processed meat."

"One thousand head will nay feed Don for long. How do they plan to supply the grains and produce?" Rollie was perplexed. Why had Lamar nay alerted him of any impending raid?

"It seems Martin 'stored' a goodly portion of the foods allotted the Abs over the years. Llewellyn has ordered all Abs transported as he will nay accept charges for their food or clothing. Martin, like a fool," Rocella's voice rose in anger, "tried to ship the stored food with them. Llewellyn confiscated every ounce of it and confined Martin to quarters until the last Ab tis shipped out, which will be soon. In the meantime, our efficient systems have continued to deliver the food allotment to Martin for all of the Abs. Don tis retaining the foods since the Council tis charging Don instead of paying Don to feed and quarter the Abs that remain. Folly!"

* * *

Lorenz looked up from his breakfast as the console sitting on the counter came alive and Llewellyn's voice filled the room.

"Are ye ready for visitors?"

"Aye, Papa, I'll meet y'all and Lamar outside." He stood and looked at Pi and Da.

"I promised them a tour of the barns and processing plant. Pi, bring brews for the Maca and his Guardian, and then do a physical inventory of all the Ab clothes in the warehouse. We'll dispose of any that are rotted and then decide what to do with the rest.

"Wee Da, y'all take care of the dishes and make the beds. Then start cleaning the great room." He swallowed the last of his coffee and headed out the door.

Llewellyn and Lamar were at the padport waiting for him. He walked over and formally greeted them. The ritual was as expected as shaking hands on Earth.

"Pi's bringing two brews if you all care to wait."

"Aye, laddie, a brew would be tasty."

The three men turned as they heard a shout from behind the wall. Lorenz saw Wee Da dash out the front carrying a tray with two mugs of brew. Pi emerged from behind the wall, mouth open and his eyes focused on Da.

Da looked up at Lorenz and bellowed, "I'm coming, Laird."

Lorenz yelled, "Slow down and look where y'all are going."

Da ran to the padport pathway and his foot stumbled on the rocks outlining the walk. Wee Da, tray, and mugs went airborne before he skidded over the gravel filling the path.

Pi started towards Da who was pushing himself up and looking at the spilled contents of the tray with crestfallen face and wide eyes.

All Da could think was *I've failed my Laird.*

Lorenz reached Da before Pi and lifted him up by grasping him under the arms.

"Fool kid, what did y'all think y'all were doing running with two full mugs of beer?"

"He needs a burning," came Lamar's voice.

Wee Da was staring at Lorenz with remorseful brown eyes, his mouth open but no sound emerging. Lorenz looked down and saw the ripped trousers and blood seeping through. He released Da and turned up Da's hands to show the embedded gravel.

"It looks more like he needs some medical attention."

"He tis Ab."

Lorenz ignored Lamar. "Papa, why don't y'all and Lamar take a look at our set up? Laten can show you all around until I get there. Pi can bring the brews." His accent was thicker than usual.

Llewellyn gave a brief smile. "Aye, Lorenz, Lamar and I will make a quick survey. I need to return and check with Andrew and Linan if they can use the spare Ab clothing and furnishings ye found. We still need to survey factories and I have yet to set up the tower's defenses." They walked off and Lorenz could hear Lamar protesting.

Lorenz looked down at Da. "Can y'all walk or do y'all need to be carried?"

For a moment Da's face softened like a boy's and then it hardened. "I can walk. Tis the place for the burning at the dispensary like all the other Houses?" He started to limp towards the warehouse.

"I meant to the home. My possible bag's in the pantry. I mean to clean that gravel out of your hands and knees and put some salve on them. Y'all are headed the wrong way.

"Pi, pick up the tray and mugs and then get the Maca and his uncle, ah, Guardian another brew."

He turned and Wee Da was running towards him, his arms outstretched. Within a foot of Lorenz, Wee Da leaped and landed on Lorenz with a thud, then laid his head on one shoulder, and then the next, sobbing. "I sorrow, Laird, I sorrow."

The sorrow washed over Lorenz like a grey shroud, a sensation he had not experienced since Papa and Grandmère had let the sorrow of their isolation on Earth pour into him so many years ago. It tore at his soul then and it tore at it now. Why did this boy grieve so? He could feel Da trembling, and he hugged him closer and whispered, "Ssh, ssh, tis all right, laddie, ye are safe." He walked towards the house carrying the boy.

Pi ran past them with the empty tray and mugs and palmed the door to open it for them. Lorenz nodded at him.

"Pi, get the black bag out of the pantry and set it in the kitchen. Then take the replacement brews out to Papa and his uncle. After that start on the surplus Ab clothes."

Pi deciphered his words and hurried inside to comply before carrying the brews to the Maca and his elder.

Instead of the kitchen, Lorenz walked directly into the backyard to the river's edge and set Da down on the sandy beach.

"Hold still." Lorenz pulled the trousers down and off. "This may hurt."

He proceeded to wash out the gravel from knee and hands. Wee Da did not make a sound.

"Now we'll get that salve. Y'all okay?"

"I can walk." Wee Da set off at a steady pace, his shoulders rigid. He was certain there would be a burning for the spilling of the brew and the ripping of the pants. He would nay act like a child. Yet the Laird had held him close and taken his sorrow. The man did nay make sense to Da's young mind.

In the kitchen Lorenz sat Da on the counter, opened his bag, and smeared on the salve.

"Now, y'all get another pair of britches and do the chores I outlined earlier. I've got to catch up with Papa." He smiled at Da and turned to go. At the door he paused.

"Why are y'all sitting there? There's work to do."

Stunned Wee Da jumped down and headed for the bedrooms. What manner of man was this? Mayhap Pi could tell him. It looked like another busy day for the Laird had decreed learning should be done after the evening meal.

* * *

To fill the long evening hours, Lorenz had set up impromptu classes for Pi, Ur, Ka, and Da. They had been studying for two hours when he decided to call a halt.

"Time for bed, boys." Lorenz changed the viewer. It was surprising how much Pi and Ur knew for two who weren't supposed to have access to any schooling. Ka and Da at least knew their alphabet and the number system for math.

"Mither taught us some, and some of the Tris were instructors before being Abs." Pi had explained their abilities. "Ur learned from the instructors in his sector."

"They had nay else to do." Ur yawned as he spoke. He used yawns to hide any expression. He had to get out of here before the Laird asked more questions. The man kept looking at him and when he did those grey eyes narrowed as though he kenned every secret hidden in his mind and heart.

"Same time tomorrow, lads. If something comes up I'll let you all know."

Ka stood and bowed. "Thank ye, Laird. Ki insists we rise early."

The rest bowed to him and left, Ur beating everyone out the door for the nearly barren Ab barracks. Da, as usual seemed to dawdle, but Pi grabbed his left arm and almost pulled him from the room. Pi was certain that there was never a man as kind as the Laird. This was a safe haven. The work of cleaning the processing plant had been hard, but nay like Ayran. The Laird even permitted him and Wee Da to sleep here in the main home. He would nay let Da spoil it.

Lorenz went to the built-in cabinets and slid the door open. He took out the whiskey and poured a drink. Danger he did not sense this evening, but he knew it would come. Rurhan would not take losing one thousand head easily. He wasn't sure when he would see his remaining Earth family again and he was thankful for the presence of the boys. On his ranch there had always been some visiting friends or neighbors. Relatives arrived for long visits. There were the workers, their families, and the people in Schmidt's Corner. Here he knew no one but his father, Grandmère, and Andrew. He was beginning to understand the loneliness his father experienced on an alien planet; both his father and biological father.

He had tried to bring some of his world's music, but there had been so little time to put everything together. Somewhere on the *Golden One* Melissa had the crystal with the inscribed music. When they returned, he'd have the technicians here replicate it. Until then he was left with the choice of singing the ballads and hymns he knew or attempt to hear them in his head. Reading what the Justines had left of the history of this world would be a better choice. He returned to the viewer and searched for any entry on the geography, climate, and various trades. He must have sat there for an hour when he felt or heard movement behind him. He picked up the empty glass and turned slowly as though going for a refill.

Da was leaning against the doorway, his arms clasped over his chest, and clad only in his thong. He was staring at him with sad, sad eyes. He looks, thought Lorenz, like a lost puppy dog.

"Aren't y'all suppose to be in bed, fella?" And he saw a look of disappointment and hurt fleet through the boy's eyes.

"Okay, Wee Da, what is on your mind?" He sat the glass back on the desk.

Da took a deep breath and stood straighter. "Mither said." He waited expectantly.

"Said what?"

"That I should go to ye."

"Aren't y'all here?"

"Well, aye, but ye have nay named me, nay taken me into House. Sometimes ye call me by names that nay make sense."

Lorenz coughed to keep from laughing. "Da, I'm not House."

"But ye are!" Da protested. "Ye are Laird! Mither said!"

"Wee Da, did your mother, mither, tell y'all this before she died?"

"Well, nay, but tis like she comes to me when I'm sleeping."

"Y'all mean a dream?"

"Nay, I would sleep and she'd be there, then gone. Mayhap I ken too."

"How old were y'all?"

Da shrugged. "I dinna, mayhap six or seven, the first time, but I have seen her many times."

Lorenz studied him for a moment. Children, he knew, could garble things. His own had been masters of garbling. Could Da really remember his mother and her instructions or had he dreamt it and then continued to have the same dream?

Da gave him one last resentful look and turned to go.

"Wait a minute, Da." Lorenz considered. He knew what it was like to have one's mother torn away when too young to understand. The beatings and no food were nothing compared to the empty gut feeling of too little affection.

"I thought that kind of naming came after the work season, but if I'm wrong, my apologies to y'all and Pi. I cannot be House until the Council of the Realm approves my father's request."

Da turned and held out his arms to Lorenz.

Lorenz lifted the boy and Da performed the Thalian ritual, but instead of letting loose he clung to Lorenz, his body shaking. There were no sobs, but he could hear Da sniffing. Stunned, Lorenz stood there and felt the loneliness sweep from Da's being into his. He knew this ability of Thalians from the first time his father had bent and pulled him close for no reason other than Earth had no Thalians.

"Shush, laddie, shush, tis all right." He used the Thalian speech to comfort Da.

Finally Da raised his head and looked at him, the boy's eyes still pleading, but lips were trying to smile. "See, ye are my fither just as mither said ye would be."

"Dear God, when did she tell y'all that?"

Da's lips became a straight line as though daring him to dispute it. "Dinna ye shake the first time your fither held ye?"

"True, but I thought he was going to beat the crap out of me."

Da stared at him in disbelief.

"He didn't, but I deserved it." Lorenz remembered the night he pointed a rifle at Llewellyn's gut and barely had sense enough not to pull the trigger. A few minutes later he was beating on the boards of the wagon and Papa was holding him close to stem the violence.

He set Da down. "Y'all are getting heavy, lug."

"Tis that my name?" Da felt a keen disappointment as it was nay a long name as befitted the Laird's laddie.

"No," Lorenz put his hands on Da's shoulders. "Your name tis Daniel. It was my brother's name and he was a very brave man; a warrior by Thalia's standards.

Da protested. "But tis nay a Don name."

"It's a name from my family. If ye are my laddie, ye must have one of my names."

And then he remembered the other ritual that both Papa and Grandmère performed. He took his right index finger and traced Da's eyebrows, ran the finger down the nose and across the lips while intoning, "Ye are in my House and in my heart forever." Daniel stared transfixed and then did the same.

"Now it's time for bed and don't ye dare wake Pi. I'll name him in the morning." He took Daniel's hand and walked him to the boys' bedroom.

Chapter 20

The Sea Ab

Bi docked his boat at the Ab quay and looked around, his dark eyes scanning the empty streets. Where were the Abs that usually greeted him? In some ways it was best that none were here, but there should be someone, anyone, vying to find out what goods he carried this time. And where in the Darkness was Ki? She was to meet him instead of signing this year. Was she trying to make him admit he depended on her for more than a bedding?

Irritation showed on his face as he went ashore and headed for the Ab Quarters. Where had the Abs gone? Bi was certain that Martin would oversee the last of the food ere departing to whatever House the Council had directed they be sent until the winter return of the working Abs, and wherever Martin lodged there would be the Handmaiden.

The walk to the Ab Quarter caused even more concern. There were several Tris at their fishing boats emptying their catch. It seemed to Bi that they had caught far more than what would feed their families. Had Ishner quit supplying Don? Was Don so broke it could nay pay Ishner?

As Bi fretted over the strangeness of Tris supplying Don's fish, he found the rest of the walk vastly more puzzling. Normally the Ab brew halls would be filled with Abs. One hall remained opened and there seemed to be but one or two Abs in there. The rest of the halls were shuttered as though all Abs had departed. This was too early. The ones who signed would be gone, but the dalliers, Martin's guard, the wee ones, the ones not chosen at the signing, where were they? He found himself nearly running the last seg to the Ab Quarter.

No one blocked his entry and he walked towards the room he knew was assigned to the Handmaiden. The curtain was secured. He removed his sailor's hat before speaking.

"Handmaiden, tis Bi. I have some wooden toys that ye may wish to purchase for the wee ones left in your care. Do I have permission to enter?" It was not entirely a lie. He did have some jointed, wooden toys that she might select, but the words were also a code.

"Enter, ye are welcomed here."

Her voice, thought Bi, was weary as he waited for her to loosen the tags. Once the curtain was released, he stepped inside. The Handmaiden's greeting was brief and then she walked back to the table. Bi noticed that boxes lined the walls, but the cot was still in place.

"Handmaiden, did all the Abs sign? There are few to be seen, and I canna find Ki."

"That slut has gone with the blind-eyed Laird." Her voice was vicious. She seated herself across from him and looked up.

The implication did not register and Bi tried again with lowered voice. "If I canna find her, mayhap ye can tell me where to find Da."

The Handmaiden stared at him and slowly closed her eyes. Then she used both hands to cover her face. Bi stared helplessly. Was Da dead? He was afraid to ask when finally the Handmaiden lowered her hands and spoke in an even tone.

"Da has gone to the one his mither bid him to find when she died."

"The blind-eyed Laird?" Bi whispered the words. "But he was to come with the Maca and Don would be restored. Tis a dead waterfront out there."

"Aye, but the Kreppies and Justines are gone from Thalia." Her voice was bitter. "The Sisters would love to emasculate the Maca of Don, but he will nay bow to them. Instead they tried to isolate him. He has ordered all Abs and Sisters out of Donnick, and the Council of the Realm tis shaken. Medicine canna operate unless Don collects its fee and allows the transports to land. Medicine has nay enough credits to move their facilities. Don tis off bounds to any that the Maca refuses. Rurhran has refused to deliver our food as Don will nay permit them to deliver to us. It must come through his House. If we dinna work, there tis nay food. We are to go to Ishner as assigned else we will be dumped with the land Abs of Don and starve."

Bi lowered himself into the other chair at the table. "Will I be detained for sailing into port?"

"I dinna." She gave a brief smile. "Ye'll have to ask the Maca. Now go away. I have work to do. We leave this afternoon."

Both stood and Bi tried again to elicit information. "I have trade goods. Tis Linan still Keeper of the Second Center? He tis a fair man and kens when there tis a possibility of a sale."

"Nay, Levin now runs the Second Center with a different Keeper."

Bi swallowed. "Did the Sisters dispose Linan?"

For a moment the Handmaiden appeared baffled by the question and then gave a bitter laugh. "I'm sure they wish they would have. Nay, the Maca has made Linan Director of the First Center. Ye will find him there."

"Ye have nay for me ere I leave?"

"Why? Wee Da tis with the Laird. Now go."

Bi nodded and left. The Handmaiden had dismissed him and he saw nay reason to cause a disturbance over Ab material and another crystal for another toy when he returned. He still had to find a way to talk with Ki and Da, but how? Where was this blind-eyed Laird? His seaman's legs gained balance as he walked to the First Center.

The First Center was one of Don's maintained, larger buildings with places for retail, an inside and outside pool, an exercise room provided with all types of weights, and often a trainer for movements, strength, and strategies. There was an electronics area for people to practice at the learned arts, but under the Sisters it had been little used. Tris were forbidden to enter and the Sisters usually stayed away from Don. Bi noted the street that ran from the Maca's Tower to the First Center had been cleaned. There were other buildings around the Center that were in the process of being cleaned. The main educational building set on the same campus had Tris going in and out carrying buckets and brushes. Puzzling, thought Bi. Nay Tri child was to be tutored, yet the Tris were acting as if the school would open. Mayhap Linan would be more forthcoming. Bi touched the opening panel for the double glass doors and entered after they slid open.

The merchandise was spread thinly on the counters, and Bi could see there were stalls inside fitted out for dispensing brew or pina tea. Linan was behind one of the displays talking into a screen. He looked up as Bi entered and waved him over.

"Ye have been long absent."

Bi was startled to see Linan wearing the blue of House, but at least Linan still talked with him, nay at him. The desire for Ki and information gave him courage. "Nay but a season, Director. Tis a bit changed here. Most of the Abs are gone and I have goods to trade; both toys and food stuffs. Would ye be interested?"

Linan pursed his lips. "I doubt if the toys would sell. What are they?"

"Cleverly jointed wooden toys of animals and beings. Some are clothed in Ab clothes and some of the animals are dyed or have the fur of the beasties on them."

"I'd have to see a sample. Right now there tis nay much demand for toys as the wee ones are few. The Maca may be interested in the food. What have ye on your ship?"

"Nay much," Bi admitted. "There tis some kernel meal that the Abs like for their special breads. I also have some dried fish from the shores and rivers of Betron." He pulled out a small sample enclosed in a leather pouch.

"Tis favored by the House of Betron if they can find the time to fish or purchase from their land Abs."

"Tis good, but a bit strong smelling. How long does it last?"

"Six months, but if ye use the cooling machines tis longer." Bi smiled. "Do ye have Ab cloth to exchange for it?"

"Nay, I have but Don credits, and a box of Ab clothing that needs sorted. Things have changed. Mayhap, I'll have brown cloth again if one of the House members disposes of their holdings."

"What would I do with credits? I canna swap them with land Abs. Tis the cloth the lassies are wanting for new clothes come Beltayne."

"Beltayne is but three weeks away. They would need to sew rapidly." Linan eyed the man.

"Why the meal? That tis nay anything that I have seen. Tis the meal a flour or a thickening agent of some kind?"

"Tis like a grainy flour."

"Ye'd best negotiate with the Maca."

Bi turned red. "A Maca does nay speak with Abs."

"This one will." Linan noted the stubborn jaw and the man's disbelief. "However, if ye rather, the Laird tis serving as a Director and offers the Maca counsel. Ye'll find him at the Laird's and Lady's Station."

Bi's face cleared. That could be his reason for approaching the Laird. Now if he could locate Ki. "Do ye ken an Ab lass named Ki?"

Linan nodded. "She tis the Ab that usually has credits enough to buy the Ab cloth or clothes when available. Both she and her younger are working at the Laird's Station."

"I will see if the Laird will trade. If there are Abs there, mayhap they will wish the meal or the toys."

Bi doffed his sailor's hat and hurried back to his ship. This was nay turning out as he had planned. He found his two crewmen in the Ab brew hall nearest the pier busily downing brews. He cuffed both of them on the back and ordered them to the ship. They took one look and decided not to refuse. They had already heard about the sorry aspects of an Ab finding a decent meal in Don without hard labor.

Bi ignored the soft spring air, the small birds chirping from their nests and let his foul mood continue. He bellowed for full sails as soon as he swung over the ship's rail. At least the wind held steady. He guided the two mast vessel between the smaller fishing boats until they were out of the harbor.

"Take over," he commanded one of the crew and went below for a brew.

Chapter 21

The Toy

Bi pulled into the small cove at the Laird and Lady's Station of Don and tied off at the pier. It was late afternoon of the next day. They'd been delayed by a squall, and his mood was still black. He wanted Ki and he was sure the Laird was bedding her. He started over the side when he saw a slender, wide shoulder man step out of the shade of the boathouse, a weapon causally held in one hand; at least Bi assumed it was a weapon though it bore little resemblance to the sleek ones of the Kreppies. This man wore Don's blue, a kineman's hat, and hard looking boots.

Bi decided to wait before disembarking. "Hallo the shore. Am I bid welcome or refused port?"

"Now that depends on your intentions."

The voice was a high baritone, mild, but the body looked ready to go into action if it were necessary.

"I was sent here by Linan. I have some flour that the Abs consider vital for Beltayne celebrating, also, some dried fish, and cleverly crafted wooden toys."

Lorenz narrowed his eyes. "Let's see the flour. Y'all are welcome to step off the boat, but I'd rather your crew stay put."

Bi nodded. "Bide a moment, I'll bring ye a sample." He hurriedly opened one of the barrels on deck and scooped a handful into his hat, and stepped onto the dock. It took him a moment to adjust to land and his Thalian roll in walking increased. He planted both feet and held out the cap to the man.

The man jabbed in a finger and brought up a taste to his mouth. "Hell, it's cornmeal. Man, y'all are a life saver. Do y'all have whole grain corn? If so, how many bushels?"

The man's enthusiasm was almost as disconcerting as the fact that Bi found himself looking into a pair of grey eyes that saw. How could House be excited over Ab food?

"Nay ken bushels, Laird, but there are ten barrels of ground if ye have the Abs that wish them."

The man grinned, revealing even white teeth. "The Abs won't get full credits until the end of the season, but I want the meal if it isn't wormy. Then I want to know where in Thalia this grows. I'm sure we can work out some sort of deal on credits."

"I dinna deal with credits. Tis trade goods or nay."

"And what would y'all consider trade goods?"

"The brown Ab cloth that Linan claims there tis nay."

Lorenz considered. "What would y'all say to the Ab cloth already made into Ab clothing?"

"If I may see them first, Laird, and then nay matter how I decide there tis an Ab lassie here I wish to visit, with your permission."

Lorenz was amused. The man was a full-blown trader one moment and the next servile. He nodded. "The Ab clothes are this way. They've been stored for years. Once we're back in full operation, we won't need much in the way of Ab labor."

Lorenz turned and yelled at a figure peeking out from behind the portage building. "Daniel, go find Pillar and tell him to meet us at the warevault."

"Aye, Fither, but may I bid Bi welcome first?"

Bi fought to keep his mouth closed as the one he kenned as Wee Da came running up, gave him a hug, and was about to run off when the grey-eyed one grabbed his arm.

"Y'all know—ken this man?"

"Aye, Fither, tis Bi. He always brings me a special toy. Of course, I am too big for wee toys now."

"Mayhap ye would like a small cart," Bi suggested, and he pulled out a wooden cart with tongue, wheels, and banded with colored glass. "The Handmaiden has traded for this," he assured the Laird.

The Laird was now studying him. "And do y'all always bring special ones for my son?"

Bi didn't ken son, but he kenned the suspicion. "Tis nay special, other than the Handmaiden sent it."

Lorenz put out his hand and took the toy, turning it over and running his index finger over the surface. He carefully eyed every portion of it.

"By the way, who is the 'lassie' y'all are looking for?"

Bi swallowed. "Tis the one called Ki. She may have her younger with her."

Lorenz looked at him. "And what is her connection to your toys?"

"There tis nay." Bi was honestly confused, and the Laird must have sensed it.

"Daniel, go get Pillar. Bi, the warevault is this way."

Lorenz didn't relinquish the toy, but tucked it in his waist pack. He led the way towards the main house with Bi walking awkwardly behind him. By the time they reached the warevault Bi's legs were once again operating on land and the one he knew as Pi drove up in a lander with Da as a passenger.

Seeing Pi clothed in Tri colors left Bi speechless. Dear Gar, what was the Laird doing? Turning every young Ab into House or Tri for beddings? Without a word he followed Lorenz and Pillar through the double door into the interior.

Chapter 22

Frustration

By the time Bi reached the dwelling of Ki, his legs ached and sweat was pouring through every outlet in his body. After he had selected the Ab clothes he would take in trade for the meal, Pillar had driven him back to his sailing craft where the restored Laten and Dolo greeted him. He erred in jesting about her new name and acquired Tri clothes.

When the ground meal had been placed on the pier, Laten had merely pointed at a house in the distant field and said, "Ye'll find Ki there near the time of sundown."

Bi flopped down at the door after pounding on it. He patted the leather bag at his side filled with six containers of Ki's favorite brew and a new bracelet before he closed his eyes.

He woke to Ki shaking him and laughing, "Bi, tis glad I am to see ye."

Bi looked up into her face reddened by Don's sun and wind and found her magnificent.

"Darling lassie, tis grand ye are. Give me a hug." With that he pulled her down onto his lap and proceeded to investigate her with his tongue and his hands.

Laughter brimmed in her throat as she responded. Suddenly everything changed. Ki rolled away and stood, her breath coming in and out in rapid sequence.

"Nay, I canna. Ka tis putting away the crawler and I must prepare the evening meal. Ye are welcome if ye have brought the brew. The Laird tis a bit stingy on that point."

Bi stood and hid his annoyance. "Aye, I've brought the brew, plus some mealie. Why prepare the meal now? Ye just came in from the fields?"

"Ka tis due at the Laird's for his schooling."

"Schooling?" Bi followed Ki inside. At least she was still wearing Ab clothes and her dark brownish hair swung in a long braid, nay cut in the House style that Tri's imitated. "Abs dinna have schooling and why are ye both driving mechanicals? Tis a Tri thing."

Ki snorted. "Bah, ye ken full well Abs working at Rurhran use the mechanicals. They dinna pay well if ye refuse. As for Ka, the Laird calls him Kahli and says he tis a natural artist with an excellent mind. Why object to Ka learning? Ye read and write quite well when it suits ye."

Bi swallowed. She kenned him too well. Besides if Ka went to the Laird's home, mayhap Ki would drive him to the boat. Right now he wanted Ki and then food, but realized he would have them in reverse order.

He watched with real disappointment when Ka drove off on the crawler. He hoped the laddie was back in time for Ki to drive him. Bi finished his brew and stood. His voice was husky.

"Ki, I have missed ye."

Something in his voice must have amused Ki for she smiled and opened her arms.

* * *

Lorenz had no welcoming arms from his feminine visitor that night. He waited until dark and took the wooden toy out of his pocket. He set it on the molded ledge by the bed. Nothing happened. Did it take time? He stared at the darkened shape. What was different? Then he realized he hadn't played with it like a child. On an impulse he pulled it back and forth a few times. He then turned off the lume and stretched out, but his eyes remained wide open.

First there was a light haze to the side of him. Gradually, a form began to take shape. It was someone covered with a shawl with the face barely showing. There was no movement until the figure leaned forward to show brown, wavy hair framing a weary face. "Ye must go to the Laird of Don, my wee one. He will be your fither." The image faded.

Lorenz's face was grim. The Abs had more technology than people knew or someone from one of the Houses was responsible. He'd have to see if the toy would project the apparition again.

Chapter 23

Fither and Son

Working from dawn until midnight became common for Llewellyn, Andrew, and Lorenz. The Maca was trying to find the educators to teach the young and not so young, overseeing the schools' repairs, locating equipment, lining up directors and keepers for the manufacturing to be, screaming for people, and railing at Lamar for not producing the kine or recruiting members of House to come forward. Every night he went over defenses with Leta, urging her to hire more people and appoint a Training Keeper. Andrew oversaw the Centers with an occasional input from Llewellyn and Lorenz.

Lorenz was in charge of the kine, the zarks, the dairy, the butchering, and the deliveries. Lorenz assured Llewellyn the kine would last, but Rurhran remained edgy, waiting for another raid. Let them wait, he thought. They'll believe their kine are protected. He continued the schooling for the younger ones at his ranch. All the ranch data was entered into Don's info banks once the boys had retired. The nights would be quiet and he could think and sometimes look at the sky, seeing stars and moons in the wrong place.

Daniel spent his time trying to drive Lorenz to distraction. He would be set to pulling weeds and Lorenz would find him examining bugs or swimming.

"Tis warm." His face was sad as he looked upward at Lorenz. "And there tis nay to talk with."

Lorenz figured he meant no one his own age and would send him to clean one of the ranch rooms or prepare lunch. Instead, he would find Daniel lifting weights.

"I need to learn how to be a Warrior." Daniel's voice was earnest, his shoulders and head held high.

When Lorenz found him digging a hole deep in the earth for a bunker instead of turning the compost for the back garden, he turned him over his knee and yelled, "Get back to work or y'all aren't eating tonight."

One night a week the two refugees from Earth would dine together; grandfather and grandson. Andrew was truly grateful as most Thalians viewed him with awe, certain that he was a leader in his land with his white hair. His blue eyes were another distraction.

Llewellyn had joined them this evening as he and Lamar had had words over Rurhran not returning the kine and the people from House continuing to shun actual work. Tamar had made a quick exit from the room as the words flew between the Maca and Guardian.

"Ye would think the instructors and administrators for the schools would step forward. They should be planning their lessons for fall. If Lamar can find instructors for Flight, ye'd think the ones for the rest of Don would appear.

"It was almost like he kenned why the kine are withheld and why my House tis shirking their duties."

"Maybe he does, Papa. What does Lamar say?"

"He claims Rurhran fears for their workers and the House members are worried the Sisterhood will return in force.

"Why not call a meeting, Grandfather Mac, and require their attendance and cooperation if they are to expect a normal food allotment?"

"I canna let my House starve, Andrew."

"I didn't say starve them. A reduction in food might make them more amenable."

"They would think the Sisters correct and that we were running low on sustenance. They might even consider deserting."

"So make the Tris House."

"That tis tempting, Lorenz, but there are too many connections with the other Houses." Llewellyn grimaced and changed the subject.

"Ye two have seen little of Thalia. How would ye like to attend the celebration of Beltayne at Betron? Their cured sausages, hams, the smoked fish from Ishner or Betron's lakes are superb."

"Why go to Betron? We could celebrate here."

"Betron tis where Beltayne started and tis the House of the Guardian of the Realm. All of Thalia will celebrate there and their booths and vendors will make an appearance."

"Does that mean we can take the best venders we have? Have y'all tasted or seen what they manage to produce?"

"Aye, we can. Andrew can alert the Center Directors and we'll coordinate taking them."

"Papa, there's no way we can transport all of Don."

"True, but those that have been working have their own flivs and have learned to use them.

"I also have a request for ye, Lorenz. Ye need to call me Fither in such a crowd."

"Why? Y'all never called me son."

"Just what do ye think I meant by calling ye my laddie all these years?"

"And just what do you think I meant when calling you Papa all these years?"

Llewellyn's face reddened and the sides of his cheeks puffed out.

Lorenz looked relaxed, staring upward, flat eyed and smooth faced. "Before y'all get too upset, Papa, it was the proudest day of my life when the judge said, 'Henceforth you are Lorenz Adolph MacDonald.'"

"Ye are enough to drive a man mad, son." The words almost gritted out.

Lorenz smiled and his face and eyes lit up. It was the smile that Llewellyn called Anna's smile and the anger left his face.

Lorenz stood, "Well, then, Fither, in that case I can probably throw in a ye or two instead of y'all."

Llewellyn was shaking his head. "All these years, ye could have asked or said."

"Why? I was a MacDonald and ye were Papa. It meant the same to me, and now I suppose the next thing y'all are going to tell me is that I have a laddie with the same semantic problem."

"Does he ken the context of 'son'?"

Lorenz lost his smile. "No, he doesn't. I'll take care of it. Maybe he will quit acting like a ten-year-old."

Llewellyn stared at his son. "Laddie, he tis the same as a ten-year-old Earth child. He tis bigger, aye, but nay in his maturity or attention span."

"What the hell do I do with a ten-year-old? Antoinette took care of them at that age."

"Father told me that you taught him to ride when he was only four."

"Andrew, most of the time I was gone on cattle drives or out on the range. The kids were schooled by a governess and then a teacher from St. Louis. If

I was home, I'd see them, but most of the time I was out on the range. From mid-May to August I was gone on a drive."

He looked at Llewellyn. "After Beltayne I'll find those teachers."

Chapter 24

Beltayne

Betron's buildings and windows were tinted green. To Lorenz it looked like moss had overgrown the round structures and would eventually bring them down. The Tris of Betron wore light green. House members wore a darker green. Those with status had a dark green sash around the waist or a sewn sash running up over the shoulder.

"Fither, it makes them look like they have liver problems."

"Ye Gods, ye call me Fither when ye insult Betron?"

"Maybe I said it because something's wrong. I can feel it, smell it. There are too many damn Sisters strutting around. We need to stick close." His jaw was tight and his words low.

They were standing in front of the stalls set up by the House Tris. Grease was running down Daniel's chin as he sampled a sausage and a cup of pina tea sweetened with brool juice. Pillar was breathing deep of the wooded, humid air and trying to decide which sausage he would try. Andrew was watching everyone with a bemused look. Kahli was devouring a wrapped sandwich of ham and bacon.

"I am expected at the Maca's Tower. Then Brenda and I will attend the booths and greet everyone."

"I should be with ye, at least keep your back in sight."

"When I am with Brenda, the guards will be close enough. Ye think that I am in danger?"

"I don't know." Lorenz shrugged. "The feeling is too vague. Something is being planned. I wish I had left the boys at home. At least Ur had sense enough not to come. What are we supposed to do? Aren't there any horse races?"

Llewellyn smiled. "Nay zark races, but there are contests for all ages; contests that test your strength and your skills. Thalians often wager on those the same as ye would races. Why nay take the laddies and stroll around. I will return in two hours. Ye'll find the different events in the tents. Don has some entrants in the wrestling and weight lifting."

"I don't like it." Lorenz's voice had dropped to gravely growl. "Where do we meet up?"

Llewellyn's white teeth flashed. "We'll meet here where the best of the sausages are. Brenda and I will be hungry by then."

Llewellyn left them sampling food and exhibits. Within minutes he entered the Maca's Tower where Brenda was waiting for him in her alcove off her office. She had shed her official Beltyane suit and turned as he entered.

"Llewellyn, ye are welcome."

He smiled and crossed the room, pulling her close to him. Her muscular legs came up and closed around his hips as he walked her to the bed. "Would ye let me disrobe, my love? We shall both enjoy this more."

"Aye, and I can trace every muscle ye have." Laughter gurgled in her throat as she helped pull the shirt upward and then ran her hands down his thighs to help remove the trousers. It was glorious to have a man with her and nay a woman.

They began to explore every Thalian zone that heightened their arousal. Their ability to exchange emotions while in physical contact added to their pleasure. Within minutes their nerves were tingling and neither could wait any longer.

Two hours later, both were gasping for breath as they lay side by side. Llewellyn rolled over and then propped himself up to look down at her. "In theory we should make an appearance, but tis nice to be here and look at a magnificent Thalian lassie."

Brenda looked up. "Ye dinna ken how I suffered without a Thalian male all these years. How did ye stand it?"

"I was wed for fourteen years. At times my counselor was able to connect emotionally with me. Nay in our manner or the Justine, and it would be brief. It was as though she possessed some mystic quality. It helped soothe the yearning for Thalia."

Llewellyn little realized the pain that statement gave Brenda. "Ere I wed her, and after her death there were always willing lassies; although they nay had Anna's abilities. I did nay suffer the same pangs as ye."

"They were nay Thalian."

"True, but dinna ever refuse an Earth being a bedding. Ye may be surprised."

He ran his index finger down her middle. "If we bed again, I will have to Walk the Circle with ye."

She pouted. "Your memory tis false. We already must Walk the Circle. Did ye nay take pleasure from the bedding?"

He smiled. "My dear, the pleasure was such that I lost track." He reached for her again when the com began beeping.

"Llewellyn, they would nay ring without a reason." She walked to the panel and touched the audio.

"Maca, there are twice as many armed Sisters here than tis necessary."

"Have they started anything?"

"Nay, but I think ye should be here. People are becoming edgy and are asking if ye are avoiding them."

"Aye, give me twenty minutes."

She turned to Llewellyn and made a face. "It's time for showers. The Macas must make an appearance.

* * *

Lorenz frowned as Llewellyn walked off, and then he collected the boys. Laten, Dolo, and Ki he did not worry about.

"Okay, men, let's go see what's in the tents. Andrew, are y'all coming with us?"

"Of course, it's always interesting to see how another culture celebrates."

They watched wrestling, bending the bar, and gymnastics. When they were at the wrestling tent for Daniel's age group, the two in charge felt Daniel was older, but let him proceed. Daniel emerged triumphant with red blotches on his body and a blackened eye.

"I dinna want the salve." Daniel felt the black eye was a badge.

Lorenz laughed and they returned to the food stalls, this time buying from the Don venders. Lorenz favored the yeasty concoctions that reminded him of the bakeries on Earth.

"This pastry is delicious!"

The man beamed. Lorenz started to reach for another one when the hairs on the back of his neck began to prickle and he whirled around to see six black clad Sisters, their faces taut, bearing down on them. He dropped the pastry, picked up Daniel and dumped him behind the stall.

"Stay there."

He pulled his knife from the boot sheath and leaped forward. A Texas cattleman's scream, half rebel yell, half Native American war cry, erupted from his throat, overriding the noise. People stayed their steps and stared.

The Sisters stalled for just one moment and it was enough. Lorenz slashed at the one on his right and whirled to face them in the classic knife fighter's stance. One Sister tackled his knees and he slashed downward impaling her arm. Sisters grabbed at his arms, forcing him to the ground. Someone started kicking him in the ribs. He'd given his father and grandmother his word that he would not use his mind here, but the red rage started in him; the blind fury that sustained him when he was little and physically defenseless. He felt the fury building when the weight holding his right arm suddenly lifted.

Daniel had jumped from the vendor's counter and had one arm around the Sister's neck and the other pulling her arm upward. No one noticed the small, seed-like silvery piece of metal skittering over the tarmac. The Sister stood, roaring, pulling at the body clutching her hair and neck.

Andrew, Kahli, and Pillar were watching with sick looks on their faces. Andrew hadn't fought anyone since he was a teenager, but he and Pillar jumped into the fray to rescue Daniel as more Sisters arrived to join the ones on top of Lorenz.

A crowd of Betrons and visiting Thalians was forming. They, like the Maca of Don, had heard the savage yell.

Llewellyn had been sampling the sausages with Brenda when he'd heard the sound of long years gone.

"Lorenz." He turned and ran, unmindful of those he pushed out of his way or trampled to get to his laddie.

For a moment Brenda frowned. The morning had been most fulfilling. She had planned on the whole day and night with Llewellyn. For another moment she watched his huge body shoving the milling crowd out of his way when she heard someone yell, "Fight!" She sped after him while giving orders into her wrist com to her enforcers and troopers.

Llewellyn used fists and feet to beat away those on top and surrounding Lorenz. He almost hit Brenda before he realized she was fighting beside him.

A fist caught him in the temple and he turned back against the other Sisters taking the place of those that were down.

Within moments the green clad enforcers arrived and the troopers behind them. Other Betrons and visitors from Don joined the fight to protect their Macas. Finally, order was restored and Llewellyn began to assess the damage. The Don stalls were smashed and pushed over. Lorenz had a black eye, split lip, and a cracked rib.

"He used his mind," a Sister was screaming. "Arrest him."

"He did nay." Llewellyn roared. "If he had, ye would be dead, and he would nay be injured."

"They attacked him," Libi, the vendor from the Don pastry stand yelled.

"Lorenz, are ye able to walk?"

"Medical will nay treat alien scum." One of the Sisters was yelling at them. "I have called them and warned them about the interloper."

Llewellyn started toward them, but Lorenz held onto his arm.

"Fither, I don't need their damn doctors. This is like when that bronc got me or the fight in Sedalia. Just pretend you're supporting me like when Daniel and Jeffries arrived at the Rearing Bear."

Llewellyn looked at the swollen, determined face and knew Lorenz was planning revenge. He could feel his body trembling with controlled rage.

"There tis nay proof of anyone planning this."

"Fither, I'm betting I know who inspired it."

"I'll help ye to the crait and help the rest of Don pack up. Then I will come with ye to try out that zark ye have been training for me. Luman and Lavina have another air combo."

Lorenz shot him a quick, pulled up grin and turned to his grandson.

"Andrew, I'll need y'all along to wrap me up. Kahli, y'all find Ki, Lamen and Dolo. Daniel and Pillar, help the others pack."

Chapter 25

Thwarted

In the excitement no one had seen the rat-like bawd creep out of its hole and scoot out to grab the silver, seed size, quivering bot that had been ejected from a med needle when Daniel slammed onto the Sister's back.

A few minutes later, the Keeper of Kine on Rurhran noticed the bot was activated. She quickly used the com to call Rocella at Rurhran's Beltayne celebration.

"Tis activated."

"Excellent, now assign someone to watch its movements. Should it head toward Rurhran, they are to inform us and the field keepers immediately. The rest may truly enjoy Beltayne as the mutant has been injured and will nay bother us this eve."

At midmorn of the next day, a Rurhran technician noticed that the bot had nay moved all morning. The previous watcher had stated, "It was most curious. The Laird spent his time running around the waterfront of Bretta. He must have visited every brew hall and pretty there."

Something was wrong. He contacted Rocella.

"Director, the bot tis still in Bretta. Did the La…" he switched titles, "mutant nay return to Don?"

"Quick, have the Master Keepers do a count of the kine: now!" The technician could not see the anger in Rocella's voice, but he could hear it.

Chapter 26

LouElla

LouElla was reorganizing Flight. Lamar helped her locate instructors, the buildings once used for manufacturing the war vessels, and was polling the Houses and Don's elite to find the needed students. He was outraged when Llewellyn refused to consider Ribdan, Ravin's and Rollie's younger as the Director of Flight.

"He kens how to pilot our vessels."

"Nay favors are granted to Rurhran till our beasties are returned."

LouElla, of course, agreed with Llewellyn, and Lamar was left a baffled man. He could not remonstrate against Llewellyn's decision for LouElla as Guardian had the final say. Lamar stood and bowed before leaving the room.

"Ye are having much better luck locating instructors for Flight than I have been for the schools in Donnick, Mither. Why would their elders consider their children ready for Flight without an education?"

"I dinna."

Llewellyn stood. "I have another problem. There tis nay armor vests or clothing in any of the storage areas. I was hoping to outfit Don's enforcers. Are there any records of what was done with Flight's armor?"

"Aye, the Sisters took any the Justines did nay destroy."

"That tis worrisome. After Beltayne, I agree with Lorenz. The Sisters will attack. We need armor. Tis it possible that Ayran would have some?"

"Aye, but I am the one that should go see her. She seems a bit cool to the rest of Don."

The com came to life.

"Maca, tis a call from Ravin, Maca of Rurhran."

Llewellyn brought the screen up and smiled at the angry Ravin.

"Your laddie with the help of your Directors has stolen Rurhran's kine again. There were two air combos here last eve."

"My dear Ravin, that tis nay possible. The kine are Don's, nay Rurhran's." Llewellyn's smiled broadened. "Your delay in delivering them simply meant that we needed to collect them."

"I will file charges at the next Council of the Realm." Ravin's face disappeared.

"I shall go see Jolene now. Tis already past the working hours and a good time to visit. Nay will suspect the purpose. I will let ye ken what develops." Both stood and embraced before she left.

LouElla requested permission to enter Ayran for a visit as she neared land. The Keeper of the Watch transferred her to Jolene.

"My head tis spinning with details, Jolene. I have brought the brew as I need to relax and there tis nay ready to relax in Don."

"Don tis nay welcomed here till your younger apologizes for bringing up such a hurtful subject."

"Jolene, I was nay aware of this."

Jolene's voice snapped out. "And right now Don needs friends. Rumor has it that Rurhran is so upset about losing seventeen hundred kine in one night that they are plotting to forestall any implementation of the old Thalian rule. There are also rumors that the Sisters feel they can attack and nay will help."

"Jolene, we should have been sisters-by-Walking the Circle. I owe ye much for your honesty. Lorenz will ken how deeply he has hurt ye."

She turned the fliv towards the Laird's and Lady's Station. Jolene, she kenned would nay negotiate if she were in an uproar over some ill chosen words spoken by Lorenz.

* * *

The lessons were in full swing when Lorenz heard the beeping from the console. "Now what?"

He swiveled in his chair and brought up the audio and viewer. LouElla's face appeared.

"Lorenz, we need to talk. I'm landing on the padport out by the pond. Meet me there." The screen went blank.

"Carry on, boys. I'll be back in a minute."

Lorenz went through what he would have called a great room and people back home had started to call a family room. Thalian comfort chairs and small tables were scattered around and colorful blue, black, and white pads were stacked by a table. He let himself out the wide doors and met LouElla walking up the path.

LouElla was dressed in the formal black uniform of Flight, the sleeves wider than usual and a satin like sash of black enclosed the waist. Lorenz smiled, and reached out his arms for the ritual greeting.

"Hullo, Grandmère," he said and kissed her on the cheek. "What's so important that we can't talk inside?"

"What did ye say to the Guardian of Ayran to upset her?" LouElla's anger had evaporated with his kiss. He had taken her sorrow when still a laddie and his eyes always lit at the sight of her.

"I tried to determine if she wanted her grandson or if it was all right if he stayed with me. She practically spat at me for saying her lassie had conceived, let alone carried a child. It seems Thalians are a little less enthused about their own than Papa told me. Is she complaining to Lamar?"

"Nay, I've heard she has armored vests, clothing, and possibly weapons stored. Ye must attempt to put Don back in her good graces."

"How much trust do y'all put in rumors?"

"Enough truth tis spread in Thalia through gossip that tis best nay to ignore it. Raven tis plotting revenge. I was on my way to cajole Jolene into trading armor for beef with us when she refused permission to land.

Lorenz leaned back and lit a cigarette. "Y'all can't make peace with Jolene?"

"Nay, it must be ye."

"Maybe there's another way. I'll never forget that day Papa took me to see the *Golden One* for the first time. I was fifteen when I saw that ship, and I wanted to run. Things got worse. He turned on the viewscreen and audio, I would have run except my legs wouldn't have held me up.

"Then all those strange beings appeared. At least the Thalians looked like us, except y'all sure didn't look like my idea of grandmother. I could feel empathy for Lamar when it showed what the Justines had done to him. Next was a Thalian male right after he won in the arena. I've never forgotten that face. It had to be the most brutal, killer's face I'd ever seen in my life. The Comancheros didn't compare to him. Now I'm seeing that face again. It belongs to one of the kids sitting right in the communications room."

LouElla's eyes narrowed. "Are ye trying to say he looks like Jason? That tis nay possible. Jason's vessel was pulverized and the pieces scattered into space."

"I'm not saying he's Jason's child, or that Jason survived the battle. I'm saying there's a kid in there that looks exactly like him. He has to be Ayran."

"Which means what? That Jason fathered someone before the battle?"

"No, remember I looked so much like my Uncle Kasper that no one bothered disputing the fact that I was Papa's stepson. The only thing that saved Daniel from being loaded with buckshot from Tante Gerde or Mama was the fact he looked even more like Uncle. Ur could be Jolene's son."

"And why would the Guardian of Ayran nay have acknowledged him or named him Maca?"

"That's your call. For that matter, why hasn't she named the daughter with her as Maca?"

"That tis another problem with your theory. Thalians canna birth that quickly. There tis always a period of at least twenty-four years between births."

"Y'all know Thalians better than I do. I do know he looks like Jason and the Sisters don't have him. They couldn't condemn him to Ayran as an Ab if he's already running around pretending to be part Ab. Thalians don't really look at an Ab. It's like an 1880's Texan saying all Mexicans look alike. Maybe she figured he'd be safer that way. House might recognize him as a look-a-like, but Abs and Tris wouldn't remember Jason."

"Why did she nay claim him that first night when all of the Abs were at the Guardians Council?"

"He wasn't there. He was hiding from Martin. Since Jolene's so angry with me, why don't y'all take him back and use him to trade for armor. I don't see the point of clunking around in armor though."

"Tis nay armor like knights wore. Tis a cloth-like material woven from the refined ore deep within Ayran. It wards off the low fire from a stunner and will protect one from the first blast of a stunner set on high. Tis the protection that our Don Enforcers and any Don that assists will need."

Lorenz snubbed out his cigarette. "Want to take a look at this young man before y'all make up your mind?"

"Aye, if he tis as ye say, we will take him back tomorrow, but Llewellyn will go with us."

"Will he be back? He's courting Brenda and he stays overnight." Lorenz opened the door and they walked towards the communications room.

"Do ye object?"

"Why would I? Mama's been dead for almost eighty years."

Lorenz touched the pad with his finger and the door slid open to reveal Daniel chewing on his stylist and frowning at the screen. Pillar and Ur were busy working out more complex math problems and trying to help Kali with his. They all looked up when the two entered and then jumped to their feet, clasped their hands behind their backs and bowed.

Lorenz shook his head. "At ease, men, this isn't an inspection."

LouElla took three steps and Ur found himself lifted from the floor and the greatest warrior of Thalia enfolding him in her arms.

"Dear Gar, ye are a magnificent laddie."

Fear, resignation, then pride swept through Ur. LouElla had recognized his true worth and he laid his head on both shoulders.

LouElla did not loosen her grip when she returned Ur to the floor. "Ye were right, Lorenz, Jolene should nay have rejected her younger."

"Uh, Grandmère, he isn't the Handmaiden's laddie. That would be Pillar; the tallest of the four."

LouElla looked in Pillar's direction as Lorenz pointed at him.

"Perhaps he is the cleverest one here. Daniel and Ur have two things in common. They both want to be in Flight as Warriors. Kahli hasn't decided yet."

"Pillar feels I should have waited with naming as I'm supposed to have the Maca's blessing to do so."

"Well, aye, tis true, but I'm nay going into that this eve. Tomorrow we all visit Jolene, except for Daniel and the other one. The Director of the Laird's Home may watch them.

"This one," she nodded at Ur, "goes home with me and will be dressed in a Warrior's outfit or Don's blue.

"Ye are also to have him," she pointed at Pillar, "with a Don's House sash."

"Why?"

"Because if Jolene does nay wish him, he stays here."

"Y'all really need me along?"

"Aye, nay to apologize, but as Laird."

"Doesn't Council have to rule on that first?"

"Bah! Ye are Llewellyn's laddie." She squared her shoulders. "That makes ye Laird and it will serve as a reminder to Jolene. Be at the Maca's Headquarters by nine a.m."

Chapter 27

The Exchange

Llewellyn and LouElla were seated in the front of the cairt. Ur, dressed in Don's colors, and Pillar, in the Don's Tri's with the dark blue sash. They were in the back and both were grimed-faced. Pillar because he kenned his elder mither would nay acknowledge him, and Ur because he wasn't certain what would happen.

He had tried a variety of arguments, but LouElla had snapped, "Get dressed!"

Ur desperately wanted to be known as a Warrior. He realized that he could posture all he wanted and declare he was a Warrior, but until he was in Flight or won in the Arena all his shouting would convince nay.

Daniel had protested at being left at the Station. Lorenz had ignored him and dropped him off to be with Kit and Kali with the admonition, "Put him to work. There will be extra brew for y'all this evening." He had renamed them under the premise she'd work twice as hard to earn that lease if she knew he was serious.

The sprawling complex of Ayran's Maca's residence came into view. It set on the edge of Ayran's main city and backed up against an old mine, proclaiming to all Thalia that this was the source of their wealth. Ayran's red color gleamed from every window, from the rounded domed roofs, and Lorenz swore the pad-ports looked like tarmac made from rubies. Rose-crystallized light from below was gleaming against the grey gloom of the over-cast skies.

Llewellyn used the com when they crossed the border, and Jolene's voice came on.

"Who tis with ye, Maca of Don?"

"My mither, my laddie, who has words to say to ye, and two laddies ye need to see."

"If this concerns what your laddie said to me, Don tis nay welcome."

"I believe this can be a profitable visit for us all. Why nay hear us out before ye leap to judgement? Tis a curse among Thalians. We battle, then we think. Will ye listen to our words as there are things Ayran possesses that we need to purchase."

Jolene's voice became harsh. "Ye may land, but if I dinna like who emerges, I will order my guards to arrest that one. It will make any bargaining dear to ye." She slapped the circle and marched towards the front, her shoulders straight, and her long hair swinging. She had defied the Justines with her long hair and now defied the Sisters.

She paused at the front to watch through the viewer. Her guards were out in a semi-circle, weapons ready, waiting for her command. If the Laird was up to his tricks, she'd toss all of them in the mines.

LouElla, the Maca of Don, and Lorenz stepped down from the cairt, and then she saw a blocky laddie emerge from behind the Maca. For a moment Jolene was stunned. How dare they dress him in Don's blue? Her voice wouldn't function and her guards raised their weapons. Jolene ran out the door, hair and long red side skirts flowing behind her. As she drew along the first guard, she bowled the man over and screeched at the rest.

"Ye fools, put down your weapons!"

Ur was staring at her stupidly, his arms at his side, not sure whether this was a welcome or rejection, and then he saw her wide opened arms and raised his arms in time for her to grasp him under his arms and pull him into her.

Jolene was murmuring, "My laddie, my laddie," while running her hands through his hair, over his arms and back, not caring whether the greeting was proper. She kept a firm grip on him and looked at the other four.

"Ye will excuse us." She looked at the guards and retainers staring at her with their mouths agape. "Show them to the east garden and provide them with brew."

She turned back to the visitors. "I will attend ye directly."

Without another word, she carried Ur through the massive stone doors and into her chamber. "Ye, into the shower and I will order your clothes." She pulled him close again to reassure herself that he, her laddie, was here and safe.

Jolene released him and bellowed into her room com. "Bring me Jason's clothes from when he was a laddie of sixteen and dinna forget the sash." She paced the room until a naked Ur emerged from the cleansing room, his hair fluffed by the dry blowing air. He grinned at her.

"Ye are impudent." Jolene smiled back and swept him into her arms again. "Where were ye the day the Maca landed? I could nay find ye."

Ur buried his head on her shoulder. "I stayed outside. The Council tis boring and Martin tis detestable. I dinna why he does nay die."

The knock on the door put Jolene into action. She slid the door open and took the clothes. "What size boot do ye wear, Jarvis?"

Ur smiled, the gap in his teeth showing. "I have nay idea, Mither. Abs are lucky to even have shoes."

"Send someone to bring me several pairs of boots for someone about five feet, eleven inches." Jolene snapped at the keeper at the door. "This tis our Maca, Jarvis, and he will be properly clad."

She watched the re-named Ur pull on his clothes. "I am so proud of ye, my wee one. Ye survived as I kenned ye would and the Sisters dinna have ye."

"Aye, Mither, but they will try to destroy all male Macas if they can. Don must win this fight."

He finished pulling on the last of the clothes, stood, and turned around for her, his smile showing the gaps between the wide teeth. The red material outlined every muscle he possessed. Jolene eyed him critically.

"I do believe ye will be even more magnificent than Jason." She smiled at him and tied on the scarlet sash.

"Why were ye at Don? And how were ye recognized?"

"The Laird took pity on me when I was running from the Sisters and offered me work even though Laten warned him I might nay be eld enough."

"Thank Gar for the Laird, continue. Who recognized ye? Lamar?"

"Nay, it was LouElla, but mayhap the Laird. I dinna ken how as he nay saw Jason."

Jolene had her hands on his shoulders and was studying his face. "Did he use his mind on ye?"

"I dinna think so. I have nay had a headache. That's what happens when a Justine does that, isn't it, Mither?"

"Aye." She grew thoughtful. "Why tis that other laddie along? The one the Laird claims tis my lassie's." She snorted.

"Because he tis the Handmaiden's laddie."

"How? She does nay bed anyone."

"She was forced by a land Ab that did nay care that she was the Handmaiden."

"And who told ye that?"

"Tis common knowledge to the Abs and Tris." Jarvis shrugged.

Once again the discreet knock and Jolene allowed the keeper in long enough to deposit several pairs of boots made of the softest leather.

Jason nay lacked for clothes, thought Jarvis as he tried different pairs and selected three that fit.

Jolene's face was troubled. "I dinna want another one of Ayran's House living as an Ab, but if we keep him, some may claim he tis the rightful Maca or Laird. Tis best we send him back to Don."

Jarvis stood. "Nay, Mither, the Laird tis right about Pillar being clever. The Laird renamed him as Pillar and Ka as Kahli, but will claim Wee Da as his own." He was still bitter over not having been selected by the Laird for this honor and bitterness had crept into his voice.

"When LouElla was over last eve, the Laird said Pillar tis clever. If so, tis better that we have him. I may need him someday when ye are gone." He deliberately left out that the Laird had declared Pillar the cleverest.

She looked at him. "Are ye planning on your Mither dying so soon?"

Jarvis laid his head on her shoulder. "Nay, Mither, but I will be a Warrior and command a ship just as my elder did. Then I will need a Guardian I can trust."

Jolene considered. "Why do ye think ye can trust him?"

"Because the Laird does."

"And ye trust this Laird of Don's opinion?"

"Aye, Mither, he tis the kind of man that should be my fither. Why dinna ye wed him?"

Jolene stared at him. "First, he has nay shown any interest in any lassie that I ken."

"He was married on his planet."

Jolene smiled at him. "Right now tis nay the time for Walking the Circle. Tis said in Thalia that the Laird has been bedding the laddies he has at the Laird's Station."

"Nay, for one of them would have spoken of it if he had."

"Yet nay name any lassie he has bedded. Can ye?"

Jarvis shrugged. "Nay, Mither. Ki tis there, but she does nay dwell at the home. Although Kahli said the Laird named her Kit."

Jolene filed the information away. Perhaps the man had bedded the Ab woman, and she changed the subject.

"I still am nay certain the other should be here. He may cast doubt on your status."

Jarvis smiled at her. "My mither can arrange it. Ye will think of a way to bind him to Ayran and to me. Tis my first order as Maca."

"Dinna think that ye will give the orders here. Ye are nay anywhere near the Coming of Age ritual, and ye have years of schooling. Now, we shall attend the Maca of Don and his House." Jolene gathered Jarvis into her arms again.

Chapter 28

Rules of Trade

The visitors stood as Jolene and Jarvis approached. They were in an arbor fed by a hidden drip system. Years of constant mining had left much of Ayran barren and stripped to its stones and Jolene chose to keep the Maca's home near the mines. Arable land was scarce and the climate bitterly cold in winter and summers brief.

"We have nay properly greeted ye, Guardian of Ayran."

"Tis I who shall lay my head on your shoulder first, Maca of Don, with the deepest gratitude. Ye have restored my laddie."

The formal greetings finished, Jolene poured herself a mug of brew and lifted it. "To Jarvis, the Maca of Ayran." Her voice rang out.

She lowered the mug and saw with satisfaction that Llewellyn and LouElla had downed a goodly portion. The Laird, however, had barely sipped at his, his grey eyes watching her every move. Jolene turned to Pillar.

"It seems that ye are my younger." She held up her hand as Pillar's head snapped higher and his brown eyes sought hers.

Jolene's face was hard, her large eyes showed no emotion, and her voice was low. "Do ye claim to be Ayran?"

"I am Ayran!" Pillar's voice was adamant. He clasped his hands behind his back and bowed to her.

As he straightened, Jolene's voice became louder. "And are ye willing to give up any claim to being Laird of Ayran and be content to be kenned as JayEll, Lad of Ayran?"

Pillar swallowed and nodded his head.

"Then ye will lay your head on your Maca's shoulders and swear to him: Now!"

Pillar drug in his breath, stepped up to Jarvis, and laid his head on each shoulder. He then took one step back, put his hands behind his back and bowed to Jarvis. "I acknowledge ye as Maca of Ayran, and I will serve ye and Ayran to the best of my abilities. I so swear by Gar."

Jarvis grinned and pulled him close. "We are House, JayEll." Then he released him and laughed. "I'm sure there are many ways that ye'll be able to please your Maca."

The newly named JayEll swallowed. He was sure Jarvis would somehow find ways to humiliate him, but Jarvis was right. They were House.

"Ye are to be clothed as a Keeper with a red sash for now. We must still settle with your mither.

"Jarvis, ye take him back to my quarters and order his wardrobe." She studied JayEll's narrow shoulders and wider hips and legs. "At least the bottom half says Ayran."

"Ye will excuse me while I walk a bit with them."

They were at the door when Jolene pulled Jarvis close. "Now what else prompted this visit?" She lowered her voice and turned to both. "Do either of ye ken?"

They shook their heads no and JayEll cleared his throat, licked at his lips, and whispered. "They dinna say, Elder Mither, but they may wish armor. They expect the Sisters to attack."

Jolene eyed her grandson. Mayhap the Laird was right. This one was clever.

"Mither, ye must help them. Ye canna let the Sisters win. They will separate us again and I will nay be a Warrior."

"Nay so loud, Jarvis. Nay ere let those who come to negotiate ken that ye are willing to accommodate them." She patted both on the bottom and returned to the arbor.

"Shall I order more brew?" She eyed the tall pitcher and the Maca and LouElla.

"Ye are most kind, Guardian, but we still have a full day's work ahead." Llewellyn's brown eyes and lips smiled.

She returned the smile. "Ye wish something for bringing me my Maca and younger. What would that be?"

Llewellyn leaned back as though offended. "Don does nay charge for uniting a mither and her young." He smiled again before speaking.

"We do wish to make a purchase, but we will use credits. We dinna expect your merchandise to be free."

Jolene made a show of refilling her mug before sitting and smiling at Lorenz. "We have a darker brew if that tis nay to your fancy."

"Thank y'all, ma'am, but I'm fine." He smiled at her, but his eyes were more amused than friendly.

Jolene was mildly irritated and turned to the Maca of Don. "Tis a new thing to have guests during the day's light. This canna be like your visits to Brenda." She smiled and sipped her brew.

Llewellyn smiled at her and set his mug down. "Tis nay like that. We came mostly for the laddies."

"That answer means your real reason for being here tis greater." She smiled a tight smile, her eyes gleaming.

Llewellyn straightened. "We have heard that ye possess the armored vests and suits to protect against the stunners. Your production has nay stopped as ye continued to supply the Sisters. Now we and our allies are in need of such protection for the Sisters will attack. I ken that ye prefer to remain neutral and refuse to help either side in any fighting. Don will honor that. However, I feel that since the Sisters have bought from ye, then we should be able to buy from a neutral House."

Jolene sipped a bit more of her brew. "I dinna believe in Thalians killing Thalians." She tossed her long hair back. "The vests and suits were sold at the price set by the Justines as being fair. Fair or nay, I will offer them for the same amount."

"I had hoped ye would exchange some of the vests for your own protection."

At Jolene's snort, he continued. "Since ye feel so strongly, would ye nay accept the butchered meat at the same value of credits?"

Don tis getting low on credits, thought Jolene, and she glanced at the Laird. He was listening with no emotion showing, his grey eyes were almost frightening in their coldness.

"That would depend on how many vests or suits ye require."

"One hundred vests today, possibly more once I've made arrangements with Betron."

"That would amount to ten butchered kine. Can ye spare so many? Your laddie has taken but fifteen hundred kine, mayhap less, from Rurhran, and Rurhran has nay intention of returning any of the others."

"Thank y'all, ma'am for saying what I've been saying since we got here, but what Rurhran does, or doesn't do, has no bearing on the number of kine we have. Don has taken far more than they have admitted; plus, there are well over five thousand head that are easily accessible on Don and more on the other side of Don's mountains. I haven't had a chance to tally them."

Jolene stared at the Laird. She kenned he said that Don still had kine that the Justines and Kreppies had missed. He had also thanked her for stating the obvious.

Lorenz rose. "And why are you all haggling over buying this armor? I just turned two young men over to your House. If we don't defeat the Sisters when they attack, they'll go after any male around. That includes those two, and eventually they'll go after Rurhran too. The result will leave Thalia at the mercy of the Krepyons when they regain their strength. If y'all want to throw their lives away, just hand them back. At least they would have a chance to fight the Sisters."

Jolene tightened her lips and glared at him. "Ye need nay worry about Ayran fighting. I have held Ayran together all these years. It was here a Justine died, nay elsewhere in Thalia."

"Yes, ma'am, and I ken y'all were smart enough to trick the Justines and somehow withstood the pain from their questioning. That doesn't change the fact that Jarvis will be hunted down if y'all ever try to hide him again. The Sister who was chasing him was ready to emasculate him. JayEll's smart enough to survive as an Ab, but he was starving when I took him home. Are y'all saving your House for when the Krepyons return?"

"My laddie tis correct. Somehow Thalians must think about being Thalians and be ready to protect all that Thalia once meant and could be again. It means we need to pool our resources, and Gar kens that Thalia has few."

"Ye make a fine speech, Llewellyn. The two of ye take all the joy out of negotiating. The ten kine are acceptable. I will trade complete suits for them. Are ye sure ye have one hundred Warriors?"

"It depends on your definition of Warrior." Llewellyn stood. "I learned a lesson in my laddie's land. Training is essential, but when your land tis attacked the very least of them can turn into a ferocious warrior. Thalians will do nay less."

"If we go down, how do those two boys survive?"

It was the Laird again with his infuriating questions. She whirled on him. "Are ye ready to die here?"

He grinned. "No, ma'am, no one's ever ready to die, but I'll take my chances."

Dear, Gar, thought Jolene. Llewellyn has found a skinny bodied Warrior. She pulled out her handcom.

"Jackie, the Maca of Don has just purchased one hundred sets of armored clothing. I'll direct them to the loading zone."

She turned back to Llewellyn. "I'll expect the butchered kine by the end of the week. My workers need their pay and kine meat tis pay."

"When this tis over, I should like to view how ye have your production set up, Guardian of Ayran. It may help in setting up production for the new ships we must build." LouElla spoke as she rose.

"Llewellyn, Maca of Don, and LouElla, there tis one more thing ye must ken. Ye will have to fight with nay but Tris. Lamar has seen to it that what tis left of your House will nay participate."

LouElla's eyes widened and Llewellyn felt his stomach knot. Had his elder really betrayed him?

"Guardian, Tris have always been the bulk of our Army, and they are the bulk of the Sisterhood." LouElla felt her brither must be defended. "Plus there are those youngers who have signed on for the upcoming flight school."

Jolene shook her head. "Tis nay enough; therefore, I suggest that ye, Maca of Don, Brenda, and Jarvis issue a Call to all that are in the Sisterhood to return now. If they dinna, they will become Abs when they fight against us. Ye will also take with ye two of the trainers from my compound. At least the Tris ye have will learn discipline.

"Now if ye will excuse me, I need to tend to the business of Ayran."

She stepped out of the arbor and gave orders to a pink clad worker standing at attention on the path. "Show these three where the loading zone tis."

Jolene held up her hand to stop the ritual good bye. "Tis Troyner strong enough to reclaim his House?"

"Aye, and one of his Directors and two of his Keepers have joined him. They reported that many of the Tris have slipped into the hinterlands. The harvest of pina pods will be down this season"

Jolene smiled. "That has been down since the Sisterhood condemned Troyner. They just refuse to admit they are nay agrarians."

"Then, Guardian of Ayran, I suggest we issue the Macas' Calls in three days' time. It will give me time to speak with Brenda of Betron."

Jolene's full lips parted in a rakish smile. Speak indeed. She kenned the two were already bedding. "And I, Llewellyn, look forward to seeing ye collect your debt from Beauty."

Chapter 29

Found

Levin looked up to see Levi enter the shop and noticed there was a set look to his face and he was walking with a more determined step than she had seen when he was collecting his food rations. She looked at Andrew and he nodded for her to go ahead and wait on her only customer.

"Good morrow, Levi. Tis there something ye are wanting today?"

"Aye, but I see ye are busy. I can wait." His dark eyes darted to Andrew and back at Levin.

She smiled. "Tis but an accounting lesson. What tis it ye wish?"

In response, Levi opened the case he held and pulled out a pair of soft slippers and a small leather case.

"I have crafted these to see if ye would allow them to be sold here. Tis made by Don, nay Rurhran."

Levin took the slippers and turned them in her hand. "How did ye craft these? The Leather Works has nay reopened."

"I ken they are crude, but I was the Head Keeper. I managed to keep some leather, among other items ere the Kreppies arrived. I stripped as much as I could without being noticed. I ken how to run it, if ere it reopens." He kept flicking his tongue at his lips.

"Where was Leonard, the Director?"

"He had already fled."

Levin looked at him, hope growing in her voice. "Without the main crystal or the lesser ones, do ye ken how to make everything functional? The Kreppies destroyed all the crystals and damaged some of the equipment."

Levi took a deep breath, opened the small case, and held up a medium sized, many sided blue crystal. "I took the main crystal and left the others there. Aye, I can do all that, but I wish credits."

Andrew was beside them. "Did I just hear you say that you can make the Leather Works a working factory again?"

Both were confused. His words were puzzling and they were nay sure what caused his outburst.

"I mean, can you start up the factory and produce leather goods by using the hides from the cattle being slaughtered?"

Levi nodded, his dark eyes flicking from Andrew and towards the door.

"This is a fantastic development. Grandpa Mac needs to know." Andrew stopped, clenched his teeth and started again.

"Your Maca will reward you, but first we must meet with him. Levin, you're doing great on those accounts. I'll be back as soon as we've met with the Maca."

He turned to Levi. "I'm Mr. MacDonald, the Maca's youngest."

* * *

Llewellyn and Lorenz were waiting at the silent factory. Andrew's abrupt message came through just as they arrived back at the Maca's Tower.

"Grandfather Mac, this is important. Don't ask questions. Just meet me at the Leather Works."

Levi walked behind Andrew, trying to be unobtrusive. He almost looked like he tried to shrink when Andrew finished greeting his two grandsires.

"This is Levi. He was once the Head Keeper of Maintenance. He has a gift for you."

Once again Levi pulled the crystal from the case and held it in his hands.

"What tis it?" asked the Maca.

Levi realized he would need to answer. His voice squeaked out. "It tis the main crystal to start the entire factory, but we can't do that until I've made sure all the parts are clean and not broken. I haven't been inside since the Director of the Factory told me to leave."

"Was this the only crystal that existed?"

"Oh, nay, this tis the spare one. It was kept in a safe in the Maintenance Department. All the other crystals can be made from this one. We were told to leave everything and exit the building. The other crystals were left in position. It tis said that they were all destroyed."

"Why did the Director nay take this?"

"I dinna, Maca." By now Levi was glancing to the left and right.

"Y'all," and Lorenz rephrased the question. "Ye said this starts the entire shebang-uh factory. Does that mean the tanning area too?"

"Prep area tis what he means," Llewellyn translated.

"Aye, but all must be ready." His voice dropped to almost a whisper. "Ye could use this crystal to create the one for the prep area while I clean it."

Realization hit Llewellyn. This man was desperate for employment, but feared to ask for it. Why?

A smile went across Llewellyn's face. "And why have ye nay greeted your Maca properly?"

Relief flooded Levi's face and he held up his arms.

Chapter 30

Rumor Confirmed

Warrior's Haven was incised on the stone above the wide entrance to Lamar's favorite brew hall. According to Leta this was where Lamar met with Rollo, Counselor of Rurhran, to discuss the return of the kine.

Llewellyn entered the doors and noted that several House members ranging from young to those in their declining years were sitting in the leather booths. Strange, he thought, this could pass for a high-class bar in the U.S. Lamar and Rollo were nowhere in sight.

"Where tis Lamar, the Guardian of Don?"

Silence greeted his question. Leck, appointed by Lamar as Dispenser, looked up and swallowed. This was the Maca and he did nay look pleased. The man filled the doorway and his voice boomed through the staid quiet.

"Have ye nay answer for your Maca?"

The fury in the voice convinced Leck he must answer and he looked at the middle door leading to one of the private rooms. Inwardly, he heaved a sigh of relief when Lamar appeared in the doorway.

"Llewellyn, I thought I heard ye. Will ye nay join Rollo and me in a brew? Then ye may sign the papers about the kine and the sheep."

"Ye have arranged their transfer to Don?" Llewellyn was ready to pull his elder into his arms and ask forgiveness for listening to the gossip of Thalia and Lamar's and Beatrice's failure to tell him about the House members relocating to Rurhran.

A puzzled look came over Lamar's face. "Llewellyn, my laddie, ye dinna really want the beasties. Ye are a Warrior. That kine nonsense was the twaddle of the one named Lorenz who tis a kineman."

"Who do ye think taught him to be a kineman?" The roar made Lamar step backward and Llewellyn followed. "Where tis Rollo?"

"Right here, Llewellyn." Rollo answered. Both men had been seated in round leather chairs by a table strewn with the unplaced pieces of a crystal tower game. An almost empty pitcher of brew sat on a serving tray and a blue mug was at each place.

"I am sure Lamar and I can settle this amicably."

"I am nay interested in settling. I want those beasties, all of them delivered by morning's light." Llewellyn was no longer shouting, but his voice was hard and insistent.

"I am nay empowered to turn over Rurhran's beasties."

"They are nay Rurhran's. They are Don's!" Llewellyn's voice returned to a roar.

"Ye are accusing Rurhran of being thieves."

"Ye are continuing the rape of Don by the Justines. If the beasties are nay returned we will take them."

"Ye are declaring war between the Houses. Rurhran will bring this before the Council of the Realm."

"There tis nay legitimate Council without Troyner."

"Llewellyn, Llewellyn, bide a minute. Ye are a Warrior, nay a herdsman. Leave that to the people who are nay Warriors." Lamar was desperate to salvage his friendship with Rollo and bring Llewellyn to his senses.

"Are ye suggesting that I am nay a Warrior?" Rollo was shocked. "I served honorably in the Justine War."

"Well, aye, but so did all of Thalia. It was after the War that Don and Ayran continued their resistance. That tis the way of a Warrior." Lamar ran his good hand down his chest and turned back to Llewellyn.

"Admit it, Llewellyn. Returning the kine and the sheep was the idea of that mutant alien ye brought with ye."

Llewellyn's fists clenched and he gritted his teeth. "Lorenz tis my laddie, a living child of my Counselor Anna. If he tis a mutant alien, what then am I, or my other Earth descendants?"

He turned to Rollo. "I shall step out of the way and ye will leave. Now! Ye are nay welcome on Don until our property tis returned."

Rollo shrugged, retrieved his hat, and left. He did not even bother to nod at Lamar.

Llewellyn directed his ire at his elder. "As for the beasties, Don needs them. Rurhran tis the House that has prospered and their prosperity tis from Don's beasties. They are needed to rebuild Don."

Lamar shook his head. "Ye have your House and LouElla."

"My mither tis rebuilding Flight. Where tis my House? Except for the ones at the stations and the Centers, nay have come forward. Others have fled to Rurhran and bleed us. That tis ended. Tis the gossip of Thalia true? Did ye tell the House members nay to apply for the open positions?"

Lamar's throat was beginning to constrict with anger. "I may have mentioned that ye were dreaming of a Don that was and those dreams were fueled by that—by Lorenz. Soon ye will come to your senses, and Don will return to the Warrior society we are."

Red flushed Llewellyn's face and he stared at his elder. "I dinna ken ye." He turned and reentered the main room.

"The free brew has ended. If ye wish to remain House, then I suggest ye check the list of positions that are open and apply at the Maca's Tower by tomorrow. Tis your choice." He swung on his heel and marched to the door. Before he could touch the circle to swing it open, his com began pulsing.

He touched the unit. "Aye."

Leta's words were clipped and hurried. "Maca, five Sister fighters and one Rurhran carrier were logged coming across the plains toward the Laird's and Lady's Station. Medicine has received an aid request from the Sisters in Don. Do ye have orders?"

"Meet me at the Maca's padport. Bring your weapon and mine." He ran out the door as he spoke.

Lamar stared at the empty doorway. "He dinna ask me to attend him." The whisper did not carry to the others in the room.

Chapter 31

Raid

It was well after high noon when Lorenz went to the barn to retrieve his zark. After leaving Levi with Andrew, he and Llewellyn directed the distribution of the armor clothing to the Section's Centers, Flight, and the Maca's Tower. About Lamar, Llewellyn remained tightlipped. Lorenz could almost feel sorry for Lamar as Llewellyn had confirmed Jolene's words with Linan. Linan admitted that Lamar had advised the Directors of the Center to beware of Lorenz and the one named Andrew. All three Directors had ignored his advice.

"Mr. MacDonald (as Andrew preferred to be called) has been instructing me in the ways of accounting that I nay kenned. The man tis a genius." Levin had nothing but praise for the Earthman.

Lorenz was running late and didn't change from the armored clothing that his father insisted he wear while in Donnick. He would have preferred his ranch clothes and boots. He planned on moving the range kine into the yard pens today and had left instructions for Laten and Dolo to wait for him. He found them cleaning out a section of the huge barn.

"Forget this job. The cattle, kine need moving. I'll saddle up and meet you all at the lower field. Those range kine have tamed down. We'll put them in the corral next to the first batch. I don't want to mix them just yet."

By mid-afternoon, they were trailing the last of the kine into the main yard section when Lorenz felt the old tingle in the back of his neck that something was wrong. His eyes automatically swept around the countryside and then he scanned the sky. There were little black dots surrounding a larger yellow dot coming towards them.

"Laten, is that what I think they are?"

Laten looked upward. By this time the specks were closing in on the barn and the corralled kine.

"Someone tis coming for the kine."

"Take cover," Lorenz yelled at them and pulled up his rifle as the gold air combo of Rurhran landed with the aft facing the corral and the double doors swung upward. Rocella jumped to the ground. Several Tris clad in pastel yellow began walking down a walled ramp which they extended to the corral gates.

The Sisters were jumping from the fighters, two-at-a-time, holding their stunners. Lorenz cut loose with his cattleman's yell and fired his rifle into the air. The range kine behaved as range cattle. They snorted, bawled, mooed, kicked up their heels, jumped, and ran straight for presumed safety.

Rocella heard the savage screech and gunfire. The herd and dust were billowing towards her and her craft. She jumped back in the combo screaming for her Tris to get aboard. She gave them all of ten seconds. As the first of the kine began to sweep around her combo, she was airborne; the ramp and screaming Tris dangling from the back. Rurhran Tris on the ground were jumping to, clinging to, or climbing up the fence, and shaking any free fist at the departing combo.

Kine are inclined to avoid the unknown and the combo's lifting upward parted the herd. A small group ran between where the combo had landed and the corral, the rest turned and ran towards the Sisters. One or two Sisters fired their stunners and the smell of burnt hair mingled with the dust and odors of the yard. Other Sisters were screaming while they ran. Lorenz fired the rifle again and the kine found fresh reason to run towards the beckoning green beyond the barn. He used his heels to spur his zark to greater efforts, trying to keep to the right and between the kine and the corrals.

He saw two Sisters coming out of the dust from where the lead kine had passed. The first one aimed her stunner at Lorenz and realized more kine were coming straight at her. She fired at the kine's head. The stunner was set to stop a man, but the kine's bony head simply showed a burn and the kine swung its horns at her and kept going. The Sister was flung into the air, her stunner landing several feet to her left. The kine swept through the area and the downed Sister with a bloodied head went scrabbling after the stunner.

Damn, I don't have my boots on, thought Lorenz. He shoved the rifle down into his scabbard and turned the zark. He swung over the side of the saddle, leaned towards the ground, and grabbed the stunner on his pass. Another Sister appeared out of the dust, swung her stunner upward, and fired.

Her shot hit the zark in the chest and the animal rose on its hindquarters, its hoofs flailing the air. The Sister, unaccustomed to zarks, thought the beast was attacking her and fired again. This time she jacked the stunner up to full flame turning it into a killing weapon. She hit the underbelly and moved the flame up to the face. The zark crumpled, screaming in pain as the flames ate inward. She fired again at the saddle area where she'd last seen Lorenz.

He had jumped for the ground the minute he realized his zark was hit. These animals were not horses. They were like enough, but they were more highly bred than quarter horses. A quarter horse could take a bullet and keep going, maybe, but it wouldn't do anything stupid. A high strung thorough bred was an unknown.

Lorenz rolled over and was up on his knees. He stood to use the stunner and saw the Sister aiming at him while Dolo's Ab knife flew through the air and impaled her arm.

The Sister screamed and dropped her stunner, tugging at the knife. Lorenz turned and saw Laten running towards him.

"We made it to the barn. I'll take these two and secure them."

No other Sister appeared through the dust and Lorenz tossed his stunner to Laten. Then he tugged his rifle out of the scabbard and turned the rifle on the two Sisters who were staring at him and Laten. The carcass of the dead zark continued to smolder.

"How many more are there?"

Laten answered instead. "There were five fighters, Laird. That means ten Sisters, and they've scattered."

They took the other stunner and hurried the two Sisters into the barn. Dolo closed the huge door behind them.

"Can these things burn through those doors or any portion of this place?"

"It would take a while, Laird, but the doors are all vulnerable."

"Then lock 'em down." He looked at the Sister with the knife wound. She was clutching at her arm and the blood was running freely.

"Is there any cloth or light twine around here?"

Laten stared at him. "Why?"

"To tie up her wound and then tie them both up."

Dolo had the scan and com on. "Medicine has landed their cairt and are tending to three of the Sisters. There are five Sisters running this way."

"Laten, Dolo, I want you all to hold this place. I'm going out the back door. Relock the door once I'm out, and see if y'all can get a call through to the Maca. Use rope to tie those two."

He ran out the back before Laten could protest. This time he took the Thalian weapon. A rifle was handy, but he had learned to use stunners before boarding the *Golden One*. They could inflict more damage and cover a wider area.

Dust still hung over the ground from the stampede, but the winds off the coast were strong today and the air cleared rapidly. His hat was long gone. His movements slowed in case a Sister came charging around the side. These pens held kine and he felt the Sisters might hold their distance. Some of the range kine might take an exception to a two-legged being in their pen. He'd chosen this side as the fence was solid and not an open weave like the other side.

One peep over the top of the fence brought a stream of fire. He ducked in time and ran back the way he came. He could hear the shouts behind him and doubled his speed.

The high pitched whine of the Krepyon fighter brought more yells and shouts from the Sisters.

What the hell's going on, thought Lorenz. He'd heard those sounds when they'd practiced with the Krepyon ship on the larger asteroids surrounding the Justine Refuge. Laten appeared at the door he had just left.

"Laird, the Maca tis in that craft. He has requested we detain the Sisters on the ground."

Chapter 32

The New Guardian

Lorenz sat in the chair opposite his father's at the Maca's desk; a sky-blue molded piece that curved around the chair. "I just called Daniel and told him I'd pick him up soon."

"Good, I need ye to do something for me."

The door slid into the slot and Lamar walked in with a determined look on his face. Both men looked at him in surprise.

"Have ye come to apologize?"

"Tis ye who owe me an apology, Llewellyn. Ye had nay right to berate me in front of Rollo or the lesser of our House."

"Nay right? Ye have done everything possible to sabotage my plans. By now we should have teachers, trainers for Warriors, someone who kens about manufacturing and designing new products."

"How can there be any to do those things? There have been nay schools for over one hundred years. Our plants were shut down and everything imported from the Kreppies. Our knowledge tis gone."

"We have the crystals' dimensions from the Justines. Knowledge can be re-learned. Surely there are those left who taught."

"Someone taught Levin to do the rudiments of accounting." Lorenz observed.

"She tis a Tri by birth. Gar kens how they learn things."

Llewellyn rose and his voice raged out. "Lamar, accounting tis a complicated procedure. Someone taught her. Are ye blind? The schools are ready to open and someone should be planning the re-opening of Don's factories. Why have ye nay brought any of our House into these enterprises? We have Tri's willing to do what House shunned. Do I need to appoint Lorenz as my Guardian to accomplish these things?"

"What?" Lorenz rose from the chair.

"Ye canna appoint him. He tis nay House, nay Thalian."

"He tis my laddie and he tis my House." Llewellyn roared.

Lamar stepped back. His dark eyes were troubled and he looked from one man to the other.

"Fither, Lamar is better suited to be Guardian than I. Maybe Beatrice can convince him how serious these problems are. There's someone teaching the children something or Lecco wouldn't know how to run the ops room at his Center."

Lamar swung around to face Lorenz. "Do ye truly think ye could find instructors for the wee ones?" He put all the contempt he felt for this skinny interloper into his voice.

"Yes, since Levin and Linen both mentioned someone who was qualified and that his son is at the Laird's Home. Didn't they give y'all his name?"

Lamar ignored the question and turned back to Llewellyn. "Ye canna be serious."

"Jolene spoke the truth; nay idle Thalian gossip. Ye have been sabotaging my efforts to rebuild. Lorenz can appoint Laten Director of the Station and return at times to bring our kine and sheep back."

Lamar shook his head. "Ye have changed. I and my counselor will retire."

He turned his back and walked stiffly to the door. There he turned. Anguish covered his face and resided in his eyes and voice.

"We are Warriors." The door slid shut behind him.

"Papa, see if y'all can't convince Beatrice to stay, and then let her talk Lamar into staying. I don't have time to pull all the elements together that she does, run down a Superintend of Schools, and get your cattle back too."

"Lorenz, I need someone to check the schools, the businesses, and someone that will inspire others to work. When will ye have the educator in here?"

"When I know where he is."

"Ye need to stay in Donnick and help with the Leather Works."

"What about the cattle?"

"Would ye do a raid this eve?"

"No, they'd be expecting one. They need to stew awhile. Let's keep them on edge. Then I can go in when they think we've given up or are too busy."

"Good, when ye check with the Center Directors, ye need to see about raising a guard unit from each. We can use Lena for training them and the trainers from Ayran. She tis bored with enforcer work."

"I need to check in with Andrew too. Why didn't y'all send him to the Laird's Home to live?"

Llewellyn smiled at him. "I thought ye might need it"

* * *

Lorenz landed at the Laird's Home padport. He noted the outdoor swimming pool that flowed into the covered indoor pool. The room facing the outside was filled with huge rounded chairs with rests for drinks.

He stepped inside and was met by the Keeper, Lesta. She wore the blue of House, a shortened blue sash around her waist, and a worried look on her face. "Welcome, Laird. Were ye planning to spend the night and dine here?"

"Yes to both questions, Lesta. I'll be bringing Daniel back with me"

Lesta's face froze. She had met Wee Da, now Daniel on her quick visits to the Station. She struggled for words to explain why this was nay possible when an elderly woman entered. She was dressed in House colors, her hair was completely white, her face wrinkled, and her hand holding the doorway for support was gnarled and covered with bulging veins.

"According to the reports I have, he tis Ab. That tis nay allowed in this home." Her high voice quavered.

"And who are y'all?"

"My mither, LeAnn, Director of the Laird's Home. Mither, this tis the Laird of Don."

"He tis nay."

"Ye are leaving, now. I dislike throwing someone as old as ye out, but this is where I live, and what I say goes." He turned to Lesta.

"I am looking for your counselor. He kens where the educators of Don are. Will ye answer that or are ye leaving also?"

"Laird, nay, I mean, I will be happy to work for ye. Please, my mither tis declining and she canna change her ways."

"Then she is retired." At this panic seem to set into the elderly woman's face. "In fact, convince her of that. Y'all can take her place with the same credits and hire a keeper. Right now I need to know, ken, where your counselor is. I have employment for his father."

Lesta's face became one of hope, disbelief, and hope within seconds. "My counselor, Stann, tis below in the ops room with our lassie." Her words died away. How could she say he was teaching her on the systems with the banned crystals?

Lorenz's face cleared and he smiled at her. "That's the best news I've heard. Is he a teacher for the young? His father taught him, right?"

"Aye," Lesta whispered as Lorenz headed for the lift.

Lorenz looked both ways in the lower hall. A door to his left opened into a huge gym area. That meant the door in the opposite direction was the ops room. The hall, like the rest of the walls, was a light blue with dark blue strips for molding. Scenes from the arena decorated the walls. Lorenz looked at the slot and the door slid open.

The two seated at the screens tried to look innocent. The man and girl were slender. Lorenz gauged her to be about fifteen. *Lesta warned them that I was coming*, thought Lorenz. He stepped into the room.

"Sorry for the intrusion, but I'm in a hurry. My name is Lorenz."

The man and girl rose, clasped their hands behind their back and bowed.

"I am Stann and this tis my lassie, Lania." Both wore the blue of Tris.

"Don needs someone to run the schools and I've been told your father is qualified. Why hasn't he gone to the Maca and offered his services?" At least these two hadn't called him Laird and asked for the hugging ritual.

Stann stared at the two blind eyes that were not blind and decided truth was his only ally. "My fither was told that it was all a sham to fool the Sisters while Don prepared to fight them. The people hired are actually being trained as Warriors. The talk of Don's beasties tis just that, talk."

"Just why do you think the schools are being cleaned, the Centers expanded, and where do you think the meat comes from?"

"The meat comes from Rurhran, and nay of House go to the schools as that tis for Tris."

"Son-of-a..." and Lorenz stopped his words. "The meat is coming from Don. Are ye and your father interested in restoring the schools?"

"Aye, Laird, but Lamar would nay hire us."

"You all will talk with the Maca. What's your father's name?"

"My fither tis called Miken." He waited for the inevitable question of why the strange names in his family.

Lorenz smiled his thanks, looked at the screen, put his hand on the pad, and touched the com button. The display came to life and he entered the Maca's code.

Llewellyn's voice came over the sound system. "Aye, Lorenz, what now?"

"What time do y'all want to meet with the school administrator, Miken, and his son, Stann, who is also an educator?"

The Maca's face appeared on screen. "Right now."

"Not possible, Papa, as Stann needs to take his mother-in-law home and then tell his father that the position is truly open. How about early in the morning?"

"Eight o'clock in the morn." The display went blank.

Lorenz grinned at Stann. "I've just fired your mother-in-law as Director and hired your wife." He was looking at a very blank face and Lorenz changed his words to mither-by-marriage and counselor. He was going to need to adjust his language just as his father had for Earth.

"Your counselor will be hiring someone to help her. Daniel and I will be spending a few days here. Since y'all are teaching your lassie, y'all can teach Daniel too until the classes are operating."

"How eld tis this Daniel?"

"He is twelve. In my land he would be fourth or fifth grade. I have no idea what the levels are here. I've already told your counselor that we'll be back for the evening meal. If we're late just leave a note where it is. I'll take care of the morning meal."

"Laird, ere ye leave, we need to welcome ye." Stann and Lania bowed again. "I canna promise about the classes tomorrow as I dinna ken how long the meeting with the Maca will be or when I will return. Will the Guardian be there?"

Lorenz shook his head. "I'm afraid all he can talk about is being a Warrior."

"Laird, he tis a Warrior." Stan and Lania then gave the ritual welcome.

As Lorenz turned to leave, he stopped. "Y'all are a great teacher, Stann. That's exactly what Lamar is: a Warrior." Lorenz smiled. Maybe if he dealt this hand right, Lamar would be Guardian again.

Two hours later he was back in the Maca's office after dropping Daniel off with Lesta. "Here are the names of the people being recruited at each center. Lena will train the Third Sector volunteers.

"Who tis directing all the training."

"That's where Lamar comes in."

Llewellyn looked at his son. "He just quit."

"Yeah, well, Papa, he wasn't listening to y'all, but we weren't listening to him. When he said, 'we are Warriors,' he meant himself. He is a Warrior and ill-suited for anything else. He should be Director of all the training and visit each Sector. The trainers Jolene sent can do the First and Second. Hopefully, this will bring in the reluctant people of House. If they don't show for that, Lamar is going to kick them out himself. That way y'all can put Beatrice back in charge of things and I can go back to the ranch, uh, Station."

"Nay for awhile, Lorenz, I still need ye here."

Chapter 33

The Maca's Call

Lorenz was greeted by a wet, thong clad Daniel flinging himself up into his arms.

"Lug, y'all are going to knock me over one of these times."

"I am nay lug."

Lorenz grinned. "In my land it means a big, likeable guy: a man." He set Daniel down. "Where's the Director?"

"I dinna, I think she thought I was nay to work since I am your laddie. So I went swimming."

Lorenz put both hands on the boy's shoulders. "Wee Da, y'all are my laddie, but y'all still work when it's necessary. Go get dressed and come inside. Lesta will have dinner ready for us.

After the evening lessons, Daniel stood looking at Lorenz checking over the movement of kine, the calves born, and the feed needed. Daniel's hands were clasped behind his back and he considered the possible outcome of what he was about to do. This man was his fither, he kenned it, yet he did nay act like a Thalian fither. Nay ere had his thumb caressed Daniel's neck or back, nay had he bathed with him, and they had nay massaged each other's muscles pink while bathing.

Instead, Fither tousled his hair as though rubbing hard, scalp bone was enough. Did touching the head mean something special in his fither's world? Wee Da didn't care. What he wanted was a fither in this world. Finally, he approached and sat on Lorenz's lap, threw his arm around his neck, and issued a big sigh. "I have been wanting to do this since I was wee."

Lorenz smiled. "Y'all never sat on a lap before, my laddie?"

"Nay on my fither's," he said simply. Then Daniel looked up, his face quizzical. "Did ye nay hold your other laddies?"

For a moment Lorenz was quiet. "Probably not as much as I should have. I wasn't home." He couldn't help but wonder if Kendall or Randall would have been different if he had. Kendall, maybe; Randall, he decided, never.

"In Thalia, parents stay with their children till they are grown."

"Had I done that, I would have been too old and we would have been poor."

"What tis poor?"

"No money, no credits."

"Oh." Adult answers were cryptic and Daniel was too tired to consider why. He was in his fither's arms and his eyes closed.

* * *

Breakfast was interrupted by a call from Llewellyn. "Ye are needed here at ten this morn. Tis important." The connection went dead.

Damn secrecy, thought Lorenz.

At the Maca's Tower, he found Llewellyn, Troyner, and Marta in the gym room. The two men were practicing holds and Marta was emerging from the showers wearing a robe.

"Come join us, Lorenz."

"It's almost ten, Papa, or haven't y'all noticed?"

Marta and Troyner greeted him, but they ignored Daniel. Llewellyn had picked Daniel up, hugged him, and drew Lorenz into the familiar embrace. "Aye, tis time for guests. Troyner and I need to shower."

Lorenz left Daniel happily playing in the gym area climbing, swinging on the bars and ropes, and lifting the weights.

"Check in on him every so often, please," Lorenz asked Leta. "I shouldn't be long."

Leta's eyebrows rose. "There tis one Maca and a Guardian coming for this meeting. Do ye really think it will nay be long?"

Lorenz grimaced. "I owe y'all a brew."

He entered the Maca's lounge through the sliding door. The huge rounded widow looked out over the bay of Donnick and the door to the office was closed. Llewellyn was busy pouring brew into mugs.

"Do ye wish one, Lorenz?"

"No, thanks, and it's too early for whiskey." Lorenz nodded to Troyner and Marta who were seated on one huge chair. "According to Leta, y'all are expecting more company."

Before Llewellyn could respond, the com announced: The Maca of Betron and Laird of Betron. The Guardian of Ayran with two laddies and a lassie.

Brenda and Benji swept in and the greetings started again. Lorenz far preferred the handshakes of Earth, but his promise had been to follow Thalian customs as his father had followed Earth's.

Jolene and her entourage appeared. Jarvis and JayEll forgot protocol and surrounded Lorenz. A sharp jab from Jolene reminded Jarvis and he grinned. He positioned JayEll behind JoAnne, kenning that his mither would introduce her first. His tight-fitting red clothes outlined his muscles and the black sash proclaimed that he was training to be a Warrior. When the greetings stopped, everyone but Lorenz and JoAnne had a brew.

"Why don't the younger ones use the gym," Lorenz suggested.

"Tis good training for them to remain here." Jolene settled herself on the long sofa. "Are more expected?"

"There tis nay," said Llewellyn as he set his brew down. "This meeting tis called to coordinate our Call to those of our House that serve the Sisterhood. I am of the opinion we should consider Troyner as the true Maca of Troy and let him issue his Call with us. Do any object?"

"He should refer to Marta as his Counselor of Troy." Jolene swung her hard eyes on Marta. "Tis nay against your Mither, but it should make her realize that her support of the Sisterhood denies ye your true role in Thalia. Right now, those in her House would nay let ye serve as her Guardian of Medicine. It will make our position look more logical."

"I approve," said Brenda. "Where tis your Guardian, Llewellyn?"

"Lorenz tis my Guardian." An awkward silence fell over the group.

"They're right, Fither. It should be Lamar in here, just like he should be in charge of training the defenders. He's the Warrior, not me."

"The cast will show nay but the Macas except for Troy and Ayran." Llewellyn face was set. Lorenz shrugged.

Jolene smiled sweetly and leaned forward. "Jarvis will need to sit beside me. If ye prefer, I will introduced him, and then he will make his Maca's Call."

"What if Jaylene should come forward and deny it?"

"Brenda of Betron, ye ken better than that. Dinna mention that name in my presence. I shall make clear that I am still Guardian and in charge of Ayran whilst he tis a laddie."

Troyner set his mug down and stood. "I have regained most of my strength. I can issue my challenge to the false Maca during the cast."

"Ye are nay thinking, Troyner." Jolene wanted the objections away from Jarvis. "The appointed Maca tis nay one hundred years. She will ask Beauty to be her champion."

"Then he can plead ill health, and I will be his champion." There was a certain relish in Llewellyn's words.

Jolene eyes lit up. "Then mayhap we will see the missed bedding."

Lorenz stared at the group. Why the hell were they talking like that in front of a young girl?

"If none here have any objections, I have work to do. There's no need for me in this cast. Too many would consider me an alien interloper."

"I want ye here." Llewellyn turned to the group.

"Tis his way of saying we've talked enough. Tis everyone ready?" He looked at Jarvis while the others nodded and stood. "Have ye practiced what ye will say?"

A wide grin slashed across Jarvis's face and he stood and bowed.

"I, Jarvis, Maca of Ayran, issue my Call to all Ayranians stationed with the Sisters. They are to return to Ayran within the next sun's cycle. All who remain with the Sisters will be cast out as Abs and subject to arrest." There was not the slightest waver in his voice. He was Maca, something he knew Daniel would never be.

* * *

The Maca's Call caught Thalia's attention and their discussions were heated. Beauty fumed during the cast and kept dropping Belinda's hand to make a fist. When Jarvis stood and delivered his speech, she laughed.

Betta gasped. "Tis Jason reincarnated. Where did Jolene find him?"

"Bah, for him to be Maca she will need to deny JoAnne." At the end of the cast, Beauty stood and paced.

"Who do they think they are? Mither, did ye hear them? They act as though they are the Council of the Realm." She waited for words from her mother and when none came, Beauty turned to look at her. Betta was sitting with her head in her hands.

"Mither, what tis wrong with ye?"

Betta raised her head, her eyes filled with despair. "We must leave before nightfall."

"Leave? Leave to go where? What are ye talking about?"

"Did ye nay hear? Brenda has issued the Maca's Call. We must obey."

Beauty stared at her before speaking.

"Nay! We remain here in Ishner. Our philosophy tis sound. Nay of our Sisters will depart if we dinna. We shall attack Don ere the week tis out. It will take a few days to finish altering two of Ishner's flivs into fighters. More important, we are staying because our concept of a Maca tis correct. The so-called Maca's hands are nay but the nerves of a highly sexed Thalian demanding a bedding. We need a governmental system based on enlightenment; nay blind obedience to a sex call"

Betta stood. "Ye are wrong. My lassie has nay demanded a bedding from us. I will nay ignore my Maca's Call."

* * *

The Sister's discussion in the barracks began to verge on mutiny. Most were Tris from the various Houses. Many like Lasa of Don had joined the Army to provide for their families. The barricks had been set up in one of Ishner's closed schools and the bunks were from ships no longer needed or used. Most resented being in this cool, misty region.

"I was thinking of visiting my family anyway," Lasa announced. The wide gap in her teeth revealed that her family was not able to pay Medical for straightening. "We can heed the Maca's call and return here when needed."

Babara was on her feet. "Nay will go anywhere without approval from me. That was but a transparent mockery of fakes playing at being Macas." She glared at them all. "Who believes that Troyner tis Maca of Troy, or Llewellyn tis Maca of Don?

"The exit doors are locked till morning. If any of ye try to sneak away, your fate tis sealed." She stomped out to her private quarters.

Silence fell over the room. Then groups fell to chattering about whether they thought the cast amusing or if there could be any truth in the threat. Had the

Macas truly returned to power? The more heated discussions concerned the parentage of the Maca of Ayran, and whether their Director had the right to lock them up like criminals.

Lasa stood and saw Tela of Troy at her bunk. She walked over, sat down, and put her arm around her shoulder. "Tela, should we nay take a walk around ere retiring?"

Tela nodded. "The cast has made me edgy. I need to exercise."

Chapter 34

The Tunnel

Lorenz entered the gym to find Daniel high in the air swinging from bar to bar. He was tempted to shout, but he feared that would break Daniel's rhythm and cause a fall. Daniel grabbed the end bar, whirled around, caught sight of Lorenz, and yelled.

"Watch me!"

He swung out, let go of the bar, and somersaulted in the air. He landed with both feet on the mat, locked his hands behind his back, and bowed, first to Lorenz and then to the imaginary audience. He looked at Lorenz, a wide, happy smile on his face.

"Was I nay magnificent?"

"Breathtaking. Where did y'all learn to do that?"

Daniel was still beaming. "Right here, I would practice at night." His words stopped and the smile left his face and eyes.

Lorenz was beside him in two quick strides. "Here at night? How did y'all get in?" He gripped Daniel's shoulders.

Daniel was looking upward, his face suddenly frightened and then he brightened. "I'll show ye. Pi does nay need to come here to find food. He tis safe now."

Daniel took Lorenz's hand and led him to the equipment cabinets and lockers set against a wall. "See, there tis where they keep the cold food." Daniel pointed to one of the cabinets. "The packaged foods are stored on the other side. If we were rushed, Pi would just grab them and we would leave. Mostly the Sisters were elsewhere. Only when the Council of the Realm met here did they bother to go to the Ops Room."

He bent down and opened one of the lower side cabinets and began to move out the extra towels. Then he crawled inside and pulled up a piece of molded slate.

"See, fither, this tis where we entered. The last time we came, Ur was scratched around his shoulders."

Lorenz knelt down and used his hand to check the smoothness of the tunnel. Then he dropped down and squeezed his shoulders through the opening. As he came back up, he stifled a curse. "Who else knows about this?"

"Kahli."

Lorenz stood. "Now we find Papa."

He stopped Daniel from crawling into the cabinet to replace the slate. "No, Daniel, leave that section out. He needs to see this."

Lorenz touched the com on the panel and asked. "Fither, will y'all join us in the exercise room? I want to show y'all," he paused for a second, "one of Daniel's tricks."

The door slid open. "I was returning from bidding our guests farewell. What has the laddie been up to?"

"Come and see."

Llewellyn squatted and looked at the hole leading into a tunnel. "Damn! How long tis that been there and where does it start?" He stood and looked at them.

Daniel looked up and swallowed. "Uh, ye go in the water below the docks and piers. I can show ye. Pi, ah, JayEll, said it looked like the tide may have washed it out because when ye swim down and enter the hole there tis a ledge and washed out space where we would sit and get our breath. It was fun."

"I don't believe the tide did it all, Papa. I think it's been there a long time. It might have been made so long ago that Thalians have grown larger. I might be able to crawl through that, but not many of Don's House could. I checked the rock around the opening and below. It's been smoothed out. According to Daniel, Jarvis was scratched when he came through the last time. Was Kahli with y'all then?"

"Aye, fither, he was."

"Does this tunnel run in a straight line?"

"Nay, Elder Fither, it curves up and around after we leave the ledge room. We hurry as the air tis stinky."

"Who else kens about this tunnel besides ye four laddies?"

"Nay else ken, Elder Fither."

"By now Jarvis has told Jolene, and she will have confirmation from JayEll. He won't lie to her, Papa. Y'all need to close it off. Put a weight on there for now. Someone from Medicine or Ishner would be able to get through and blow this place apart."

"We'll use a scanner that will show us where it runs. We can drill down and fill it if I can find the necessary equipment. Mayhap Linan would ken. Will ye find out for me?"

"If y'all promise to put Lamar in charge of the troop training."

"He resents ye and he has nay followed my orders."

"Anybody that could sweet talk Mama like y'all did can make him listen to reason. Just agree that he's a Warrior and this is a job he should have."

"Ye are confidant of that."

Lorenz grinned. "Hell yes, the man wants to fight.

"Now watch this young lad. Go ahead, Daniel, show the Maca a Warrior in training."

Daniel ran for the ropes.

Chapter 35

Daniel Is Missing

Daniel and Kahli had investigated every nook of the waterfront and were looking at the various shops inside the First Center. They found things much different and wondered how these goods had miraculously appeared. The Laird had given everyone at the Station a day off. Kahli stayed with Daniel while Kit went her own way.

"Mayhap fither will buy us one of those sweet rolls." Daniel looked at Lorenz sitting in the open office and saw that he was deep in conversation with someone on the com. The smell of the brool laced rolls with spices was making his stomach growl.

"Wee Da, we breakfasted nay two hours ago." Kahli didn't think the Laird that generous.

Daniel frowned. "It was more fun when we snitched them."

"Tis nay worth the risk now."

"And there are nay pina pods."

The vender with the sweet rolls nodded. "There tis plenty of pina leaves, but tis nay as good as brewed from fresh pods. The Sisters send any they have to Rurhran." He eyed Daniel as he edged closer.

"I'll tell ye what I'll do. I'll put two of these rolls back and when the Laird comes through, I'll ask him if he wishes them for ye two."

Kahli and Daniel looked at each other and shrugged. They couldn't snatch from this man. "Thank ye." They both chimed the words and headed outside.

"Let's go back to the waterfront. It looks like some new sails coming in."

"There tis nay else to do," agreed Daniel. They ran and walked the five blocks and watched the new arrival.

"Tis Bi," shouted Daniel. "Mayhap he has a new toy for me."

Both boys watched with interest as the boat slid into an open spot and one of the crew leapt overboard to tie off. Bi appeared on deck and waved before directing the other two aboard to drop anchor. After that, he swung out the board and walked toward the boys.

"Tis the Laird here?"

"Aye, fither tis here. Did ye bring me a toy?"

"Ye are nay patient. First I must see Linan and the Laird about any trade goods. Come back at the noon meal and dine with me, Wee Da. Ka, if your elder Ki tis here, ye are both welcome too."

Kahli didn't miss his using their Ab names, nor the fact that he wasn't welcome without Kit.

"We are expected elsewhere then." His answer was stiff and Daniel looked at him like he'd lost his senses. To Daniel it would be a lost chance to explore the boat and eat sea fare. He'd noticed that his fither didn't really care for fish and it appeared rarely on their plates.

"Come back in the afternoon. I may nay finish till then. See if ye can't bring Ki back with ye."

Kahli did not bother looking for his sister. He kenned she was at some brew hall or at the First Center enjoying the pool and the brew. Both boys took their time before returning and delivering Bi's message.

Kit was busy looking at the merchandise arranged for buyers.

"Kit, Bi was asking for ye. Did ye talk with him?"

"Aye, I've seen him, Kahli, and he tis angry. I have nay intention of returning with him." She held up a light blue, low cut blouse with sheer sleeves and sighed. "By the end of summer I will buy this if the Laird doesn't charge too much for seed."

Kahli blinked. When did Kit buy seeds and nay clothes?

Lorenz stuck his head out of the office. "I have to meet with Fither. Kit, would y'all see to getting the boys something to eat? I've left plenty of credits with Andrew here. Have y'all met my grandson; my younger?" He quickly amended his words.

"Kit, Kahli, this tis my younger, Andrew MacDonald. Andrew, y'all know, Daniel. The other two are Kit and her brother, Kahli. They work at the Station."

Andrew looked at them and murmured, "Hello, nice to meet you both. Daniel, you'll have to join your father at dinner with me one night this week." He turned back to Lorenz.

"Paw-paw, I need to talk with Beatrice about what provisions she's made for those new recruits from the Sisters. I've entered the modified fliv they brought into the accounts of Flight with Grandfather Mac's approval. Let me know what night you and the boy are coming." He nodded at all of them as he left.

Lorenz looked at Kit. "My apologies for his behavior. He has his mind on accounting and he won't come out of that fog until tonight. Will y'all see to their lunch? I'm not sure when I'll get back."

"If ye call the Warrior's Haven, I'll gladly take them. I've always wanted to eat there." Kit's brown eyes lit with pleasure at the thought.

"Done. I'll be back sometime this afternoon before five o'clock. I'll fly you all back to the Station or Laten will if he's here." The thought of Kit and Kahli dining with some of the nabobs of House amused him. He warned the new Keeper of the place to be damned polite to these three.

Daniel and Khali showed up at the dock about two o'clock. Bi was pacing back and forth. "Where have ye two been and where tis Ki?"

"She will remain at the Warrior's Haven till time to return to the Station." Kahli grinned as he imparted the news and watched Bi's face redden.

Bi turned away from Kahli. "Wee Da, come aboard. I have something to show ye."

He purposely blocked Kahli's way and smiled, but his eyes had no liking in them. "Just the wee one."

Kahlie straightened. "Daniel, dinna. Ye are to stay with me."

Daniel grinned. "I'll be back as soon as I get my toy. Bi would nay hurt me, would ye?" He smiled at the man.

"Nay ever. Ye are the Kenning Woman's laddie." He put a hand on Daniel's shoulder and led him towards the door to the lower deck. To one of the crewman, he barked an order, "Cast off."

Kahli saw the man leap overboard and start to untie. "If ye dinna let Daniel off, I will summon the enforcers." He yelled as loud as his throat would permit.

Bi whirled around at the door to below. "Go on down, laddie, I will be right there." He hurried back to the side. "All right, come aboard then. Ye'll see we are just making preparations to leave."

Kahli hesitated, but he could nay leave Daniel. The Laird had given him a charge. He ran up the plank and headed straight for the doorway to below.

Bi stepped in front of him. "Ye go nay further. I will call Wee Da." He turned and bellowed below.

"Wee Da, come and assure Ka that we mean ye nay harm." He turned back to Kahli and folded his arms over his chest.

Instead of Daniel appearing immediately, they waited. The crew continued to haul up the anchor and unfurling the sails. Kahli kept looking at them and the shore. Two hands appeared; one on each side of the doorway as though someone was holding on for support and leverage to pull upward. A bulky figure was outlined in the dim light behind Bi.

"Tis all right, Bi. Let me speak with him."

Bi stepped aside, but made sure his form blocked the view from the port. Kahli found himself looking into Daniel's face, but it wasn't Daniel. This was a full-grown Thalian with massive shoulders and arms. The face was female with deep brown, sun-red tinted waves of hair surrounding the high cheek bones. A brown scarf covered her hair and the sides of her face. Kahli's eyes widened and he began to bow.

"Stop that," she commanded. "Ye canna do anything to show tis me."

"But Kenning..."

"Hush, dinna name me. Are ye Ki's younger?"

"Aye, lady."

"Then I owe ye both my life. She left ye in charge of the Handmaiden and cared for me on the trip to the village. Now I reclaim my laddie. Will ye keep this secret for me as Ki has kept the other? Ye ken that they will try to kill me again. I need ye to swear by Gar." Her light-brown eyes stared into his and her low voice stroked at his ears and held his heart.

Kahli was almost sobbing. His stomach was turning into knots, but he could nay refuse the Kenning Woman. "I swear by Gar, lady. I will tell nay that ye live and that Daniel tis with ye."

She smiled then, her eyes lighting with a glistening from within. "Thank ye, my young friend. Be assured that my laddie tis safe with us. Go with Gar." She slowly lowered herself down each step.

Kahli watched, fascinated. He realized she held to the bars at the side for support. Her left leg was useless. Bi stepped in front of him.

"Get out of here. We must sail now." He was growling, his eyes glaring at Kahli.

Kahli half-ran, half-stumbled off the deck. His heart was filled. The Kenning Woman lived and his elder had nursed her. Nay wonder Daniel would stay with her. Kahli's mither was gone forever. Her dead body must have burned on the pyre as the Kenning Woman and he remembered crying when her touch was gone. What a tale he would have to tell, and the thought made him stop. He could nay tell. He had sworn the oath of a Thalian Warrior. The Laird would demand to ken where Daniel was and he could nay tell. Mayhap if he found Kit; nay that wouldn't help, he realized. The Laird would still find him and demand to ken where Daniel was. Kahli ran up from the pier area and headed for the grassy glade where the Ab signing was held, changed his mind, and ran towards the Second Section. He had to hide, but where? And where was he to live? How was he to pay for his food? The Abs had gone. He began to think it would have been better to stay on board Bi's ship. He turned to run back to the docks when the view from the hillock he was on showed Bi's ship sailing out of port. His legs collapsed and he put his head on his knees. Just a few hours ago he was dreaming he would someday be House and a Warrior sailing among the stars with Wee Da. Kit would have her home. Now he could nay face the Laird. He could nay tell the truth for then he would break his oath. If he broke the oath he was nay worthy to be a Warrior. Somehow, deep inside, he sensed that the Laird did nay give his word lightly.

If he went into a Center to spend what few credits he had left the Laird would trace him. He would have to go into the woods and land around Donnick. Mayhap he could live as the land Abs, but he kenned that was nay likely. The four times he went inland with Kit, he discovered he could nay hunt like those his own age and he had nay of their special weapons made from wood, leather, sometimes metal, and sometimes stone. Abs ate the rodent bawds when they caught them, but he was nay as good they were in catching them, nay did he like the musty taste of the dark meat.

He began to walk slower. Mayhap if he returned, they would send him to Ayran, or just make him Ab again. His mind raced. JayEll had fared ill at the mines, and JayEll had been one year older. If he was sent to the Abs because of his age, Martin would surely punish him as he had JayEll. He sighed. There was nay answer. He realized he was getting thirsty. At least he could find some running water and drink. Then if he sat, mayhap he could think of a solution. He noticed the shadows lengthening and the sun sliding towards the west. Soon the Laird would be looking for Daniel.

Chapter 36

The Hunt

Lorenz attended a meeting at the Third Sector with Lamar, Lecco, Lena, and one of the returning Sisters named Lasa. She had accepted a position as Sergeant.

Lelan arrived with five more recruits and younger Thalians carrying large sized rocks. Lasa sprang at him. "Fither."

"My lassie, I can quit worrying about hurting ye." He swept her into his arms and turned to one of the recruits. "Lili, come greet your sib."

One of the teenage girls ran up. Like Lelan and Lasa her face was wide, the dark hair bobbed short, and the smile showed a wide gap in her teeth.

Lamar had ordered rocks gathered by the younger citizens of Donnick. He insisted that the Trainers and older trainees keep their weapons with them and that they wear the armored clothing at all times. Lorenz thought them mad. The armor clothing was worn instead of the usual outfits, and while fairly light it felt like a sweat box to Lorenz. He was accustomed to the cotton clothes of the plains and the wind blowing through worked as a cooler when it hit the body's perspiration. He had not argued with Lamar. In fact, he had to admire the man's ability to quickly create some sort of order with the Tris that Lecco and Lelan had gathered.

He spent the rest of the afternoon training Lecco, Lelan, and the other adult Tris to use the long stunner while Lamar, Lena, and Lasa trained the others in throwing and had the piles of rock placed in strategic locations. When the younger ones went for more rocks, Lamar and Lena drilled the adults in marching as a unit. Lasa remained at the head relaying commands.

It was late when Lorenz arrived at the Laird's Home and found a worried Lesta waiting for him.

"The laddie's have nay returned, Laird. I kenned ye were busy and contacted Levin, but she has nay seen them."

"Has one of the workers from the Station named Kit contacted y'all?"

"Nay, Laird."

"Go home then, and thank y'all for waiting. I think I know where Kit is. Maybe Daniel and Kahli are there."

"Laird, your fither would like to speak with ye ere ye return to the Station." She gave a quick bow. "I must leave. My mither tis upset that my fither forgot to clean the pool today, and she tis yelling at him and Stann."

Why, wondered Lorenz, did families always have one that could be disagreeable, and where the hell had Daniel and Kahlie gone this time?

He touched the com by the door. "Papa, y'all wanted to talk?"

"How did things go with ye and Lamar?"

"We didn't quarrel. We were stiffly polite, but the training went well at the Third Sector. Are the two boys there in the gym?"

"Nay, why do ye ask?"

"They're not here. I'll catch Kit at the Warrior's Haven. Maybe they're there."

"Kit, tis that the new Tri from the Station?"

"That's her."

"She tis here waiting for ye. I think Lettuce said the lassie had indulged a bit much and the Warrior's Haven requested her removal."

Lorenz was silent for a moment. "Weren't the boys with her?"

"Bide a moment."

The console went blank for a few minutes and Lorenz lit a cigarette. His hand had traveled automatically to his pocket. He drug deeply and paced. Finally Llewellyn returned.

"Lorenz, she has nay seen them since they ate. She thinks they went to the waterfront."

"Thanks, Papa, I'll start there."

"I'll join ye."

Both were at the water's edge within minutes. Kit was with Llewellyn, her face more concerned than theirs. She showed them a number of places the boys had frequented during the Justine rule, but always the results were the same: Nothing. They stopped every stroller they encountered with the same question, but none had seen two laddies.

The moons began peeping over the eastern horizon, one small, one huge. Both were whitish, half-round globes creeping steadily upward. Gradually, they began to supplement the fading daylight. At the beginning of the Second Sector, they ran into one of the vendors from the First Center heading for the docks with his fishing rod.

"Aye, I saw them this morning. They were to come back for a roll if I did nay sell out. They nay came back, but I saw the taller, skinny one walking towards the hills of the Second Sector. He was alone."

They thanked the man and eyed each other warily. "What's up there?" asked Lorenz.

"Nay much. The hills skirt the First Sector. There tis a view of the Maca's Tower, the Guardians of the Realm Compound, and the ocean. When I was younger, it was a place for the young ones to meet whenever the Kreppies forgot to send a patrol to enforce their curfew."

Lorenz looked upward. The description was apt. These were hills, not mountains, covered with deciduous and fir trees. Here and there the empty houses exposed a blue masonry corner not over-grown with vegetation. "Is there a trail then? Do we call for transport?"

"He tis deliberately walking away from us. A transport this late in the evening would alert him that we are searching. Tis better to find the trail which I remember."

Llewellyn set a brisk pace, the moonlight outlining the buildings, shrubbery, and trees with a surreal glow. At the end of a row of houses, Llewellyn pointed towards a dry fountain and basin. "Just to the left and into the trees a bit, we should find the trail. It will switch back and forth, but we will avoid the boulders while going upward."

It was rapidly approaching the ninth hour and Kit was tiring, her lips held in a tight line. A short distance into the woods and Lorenz dropped to his knees.

"Stand back out of the light." He searched at the trail's edges and found a broken twig and the footprints of someone going upward in a slow methodical manner, almost shuffling at times.

"See, here, he's dragging his feet. Here he turned around, took a couple of steps back towards town, turned, and then started up again." He stood. "He can't make up his mind if he is running away or not, and there is no sign of Daniel."

"Something tis wrong, and there tis nay way of kenning what." Llewellyn was perplexed.

"He went up the path. I'll walk the right side to see if he left it. Y'all can take the left side."

In silence the three started upward, passing under trees that had been left untouched for over a century. Some had crashed from age, others had lost limbs in a storm, and others towered over them cutting the visibility to zero.

It took nearly an hour to reach where the trail wound around a point and they could look up at the flattened top. A lone figure with arms wrapped around his middle stood on the edge of the cliff staring out towards the waters.

"Dear, Gar, he tis getting ready to jump." Kit whispered in horror. "Stop him."

Llewellyn started forward and Lorenz's grabbed his bicep. "Papa, y'all will shake the ground and make all sorts of noise while running." His voice was low. "Move slow or let me go. I'm lighter than y'all and move quieter when running."

Llewellyn nodded his head, and Lorenz disappeared around the point. No sound came as he ran upward. For once he was thankful he had worn the Thalian half-boot. They were supple, light-weight shoes that fit the foot like a moccasin, and he ran like Uncle Herman had taught him to do on the trail.

As he neared the top, he slowed to a walk, carefully lifting each foot and setting it down. He was almost in reach of Kahli when Kahli heaved a sigh and turned.

Kahli's eyes opened wide in fear and then anguish washed over his face.

"My Laird, I sorrow, but I could do nay different." His voice was a deep wail, and he turned back towards the embankment.

Lorenz took five quick steps and put his arms around Kahli and pulled him away from the edge. "Crazy kid, why didn't y'all come to me? Where's Daniel?"

Kahli kept his face hidden and his body rigid. "I canna say. I promised."

"Promised? Promised who? Daniel?"

"Nay, Laird, I swore the Warrior's oath."

Lorenz felt the anger rising, and he placed both hands on Kahli's shoulders and shook. Not hard, not yet, for something was wrong.

"Kahli, y'all are not a Warrior. Y'all are snot-nosed kid." His voice rose.

Llewellyn appeared behind him. "Let me, Lorenz. I am Maca." He stepped alongside of the two and swept Kahli into his arms.

"Shh, shh, laddie."

A long wail erupted from Kahli's throat and his body shook.

Llewellyn hugged him tighter. Dear Gar, why now? Had he nay raised one skinny-bodied laddie? But there was nay mistaking the unspoken message between two Thalians. This was his laddie.

"Shh, laddie, tis all right. Your fither tis here."

"I am nay worthy."

"Is Daniel alive? Is he hurt?" The hard voice of the Laird hammered at Kahli.

"He tis alive. I would nay ere let him be hurt." Kahli muffled voice emerged from Llewellyn's chest.

"Then where tis he?" asked Llewellyn.

"I promised." Kahli looked up at Llewellyn. "I swore the oath by Gar. I canna say."

"Kahli, did ye swear the oath to anyone in authority?"

"Well, aye, nay has authority like…" Kahli's mouth hung open on the last word.

"Do ye mean Martin?"

"Nay." Kahli hung his head and his shoulders slumped.

"Did Daniel go willingly?" Lorenz interrupted. He ignored Kit standing slightly behind him.

"Aye, else I would nay have promised."

"Damn, the Kenning Woman came back. He wouldn't leave me except to go with her."

All eyes turned on Lorenz, and Kit took a cautious step backward.

"What?" Llewellyn turned towards his Earth son.

"Bi brought in a wooden toy that projected an image of a woman that I figured was either acting or the Kenning Woman. I'm saying it was her. Kahli knows it. Look at him. And, Kit, y'all know it too or y'all wouldn't be backing away. Now the question is: Why did she return?"

"Abs dinna have that technology." Llewellyn was puzzled.

"Uh huh, and yet Kit knows how to run the lander and any mechanical tool we have. There's a whole technology and economy out there that the Houses have ignored."

Llewellyn placed Kahli on the ground. "Has he spoken true? Does the Kenning Woman live?"

Kahli swallowed. "I promised," he whispered.

"Oh, for Pete's sake!" Lorenz turned to Kit. "Kit, was Bi in town this afternoon?"

"Aye, Laird, I saw his ship." She had stopped backing away and stood shifting from foot to foot.

"Kahli, did y'all promise Bi anything?"

"Nay, Laird, nay to him. I dinna like him."

"Were y'all on his boat when y'all made that promise?"

Kahli hung his head and nodded.

"I've noticed sea laws are pretty much the same here as on Earth. The captain rules, yet Kahli made a promise to someone with more authority than the captain. Still want to tell me it wasn't the Kenning Woman, Papa?"

"Who could have deceived the Sisters like that?"

"I'm not sure of the details, Papa, but Kit and Kahli's mother died the same day as the Kenning Woman. I'm guessing their mother was burned at the Burning House and Kit went with her 'mother' to where the Land Abs live for a burial that never happened. She left Kahli with the Handmaiden because she was too busy caring for the Kenning Woman." He gave one of his slashing smiles to Kit.

"That pretty well covers why y'all left your little brither in the tender care of Martin, doesn't it?"

Kit gave an abrupt nod of her head. "I would nay have left him else."

"So where is Bi taking Daniel and his mother?"

"To his village, Laird."

"And where would that be?"

Kit shrugged. "I dinna. It tis about two days sail down the south coast of Don when the wind tis high, more if nay. His town tis after the Skye Maist Mountains and twixt two smaller towns."

"Let me speculate. Bi runs the big village and probably controls the smaller ones. Is that correct?"

Kit nodded. "Aye, Laird, that tis right."

"Papa, do y'all intend to take him home, uh to House?"

"Aye, but nay this eve. I will, however, take the lassie and him back to the Laird's Station. I assume ye are following Bi. Ere ye go, ye still have the kine deliveries. Right now Don needs the meat distribution. Ye canna stop him on the seas. Tis too much danger of swamping the boat and ye are nay a sailor."

Lorenz grinned at his father. "I'll leave by tomorrow night or the next morning. Laten can run the ranch without me." He started to turn.

"Laird," Kit's voice was low, "will ye change our agreement?"

"Hell no, y'all are one of the best farmers I've seen. Your hay field and garden are superior to the other ones. Why would I change it?"

She closed her eyes and shook her head. "Others would send me to Ayran for helping the Kenning Woman."

"We are nay others." Llewellyn still had his arm around Kahli. "I intend to claim this laddie if ye dinna object. Ye will need to have a certain level of prosperity."

"Papa, I'd like to bring Daniel's mother back with him."

"Aye, if she will allow it. In the meantime, this information goes nay further."

They turned and started downward. Kahli and Kit were exhausted by the time they reached the bottom; Kahli from an afternoon of worrying, steady walking, and missing the evening meal. Kit had spent her time drinking and her head was throbbing. Lorenz saw them to the Maca's fliv and left for the Laird's Home.

It took less then five minutes to arrive at Kit's home, but Kahli was asleep. "I will carry him in."

Kit was fighting to keep her eyelids from covering her eyes and nodded. She stumbled to the door, pressed the panel, and stepped aside for the Maca to carry Kahli inside.

"Which room tis his?"

"The one to the right." She sank against the doorframe waiting to bid the Maca goodeve and thank him. She wasn't sure if this was reality or a dream. Nay House, nay Maca, would ever look at an Ab or offer assistance. When Llewellyn did not return right away she started towards the hallway. Dear Gar, tis he bedding him? She looked with wide eyes at the Maca returning with Kahli's clothes.

"I removed these. He will sleep better, but I dinna what ye do with them." He smiled and placed them on the chair. "Ye have nay sworn allegiance to your Maca."

Kit looked and saw the hard, brown eyes measuring her and swallowed. At least this Maca preferred lassies and she went willing up into his arms, laying her head on his shoulders.

He slid his hands down her back and lowered her to a standing position, but kept her hard against him.

"Nicely done, lassie, now will ye permit me to claim your brither as my own or do ye object?"

She laid her head on his chest, heard the two hearts, and felt his hardness swelling against her. "I will nay object, Maca. Kahli has always wished to be a Warrior. Our Mither could nay have provided so well." She felt her thighs trembling and she desperately wanted to put her arms around him. A small groan came from her throat and she heard his deep chuckle.

He stepped away and put his hands on her shoulders. "Ye are a bonnie lassie, but if I claim your brither, our bedding may upset him. I have another chore for ye. My laddie, Lorenz, tis a very lonely man. Has he tried to bed ye?"

Surprised, she shook her head no. She couldn't repeat any of the gossip about the Laird.

"I thought nay. He tis a very proper nineteenth century man." His words meant nay to her. As if reading her thoughts, Llewellyn continued. "In his beliefs, bedding someone outside of marriage tis a sin. Many do it, but hide the act. Lorenz tis far too honorable, but he tis a man. He walks at night by the river that flows by his home. Did ye ken that?"

A speechless Kit shook her head no. The Maca's eyes softened and he smiled at her. "I wish for ye to walk there some evening and go for a swim. Whilst ye are there find an excuse to entice him with your Thalian charms."

His hand gripped her lower jaw and she felt his thumb run over her lips and she started to sway towards him. Once again the deep chuckle rose up from his throat.

"Oh, ye are the right lassie. The musk rises off ye and makes a man's head spin. Take away that lonely look in my laddie's eyes and ye will want for nay."

He released her and walked for the door, the wide shoulders moving back and forth and he was gone.

Kit leaned against the chair, her breath coming in and out in small sobs. Dear Gar, she wanted a bedding. She straightened and walked toward her room with the bed and built-in clothes cabinet. Why, why had the Kenning Woman chosen this day to return?

Chapter 37

The Ab Land

Lorenz woke while the moons were hanging low in the sky. It had taken two days to accomplish the distribution of meat. His impatience mounted as he scanned the maps of Don and sent a com wake-up message to Laten and Dolo to have four zarks waiting, one loaded with camping gear for three people and a supply of emergency food. Another message went to Lesta and Stann informing them of his absence and instructing Stann to continue Kahli's lessons by com if the Maca did not bring Kahli here. Lorenz had smiled at the thought of that statement perplexing two members of House.

He rummaged in the well-stocked kitchen and hastily threw dried meat, bags of pina tea, protein bars, and four brools into his sack. Within minutes after leaving the Laird's home he was at the Station talking with Laten.

"I want y'all to let me off near Bi's sea village, but far enough away they won't think anyone is coming their way. Can y'all or Dolo locate it?"

"Aye, Laird, but why?"

"Bi's abducted Daniel, and I'm going to bring him back."

"By yourself? Dolo and I should attend ye."

"Thanks, Laten, but I'll take my com. We'll use the carrier and y'all can mark where any kine are feeding. I'll call if I need help or when transport is needed."

"Ye will run into trouble if ye try to bring Bi back."

Lorenz's lop-sided smile appeared. "Now there's a thought. Let's load these zarks."

As they skimmed over the Skye Maist Mountains, Lorenz saw in the distance a field of corn and a fort like the history pictures showed of eighteenth century

America. "Who built that fort surrounding the buildings and planted crops and pastures around it, Laten?"

"Tis said that they are Tris who fled ere the Justines installed the Kreppies, Laird."

"Log their coordinates. We'll be trading directly with them instead of Bi."

They landed several miles north of the coastal village in an area hidden by a series of low hills and trees growing along the East Fork of the Valiant River. Both forks flowed south, one to the mouth of the bay where Bi's village was located.

The two men quickly saddled the three zarks and loaded the pack animal.

"Laird, I dinna think ye should be out here alone. There are other land Abs that ken the ways of the wild. They will take ye captive or steal your zarks."

Again that wild light was in Lorenz's eyes. "We are going to have some serious jawing about my past when I get back, Laten. This isn't my first trip away from town." He swung up and left a very puzzled Laten staring after him.

Lorenz topped the crest of the hills and looked across the virgin-like prairie of Don. For the first time in almost forty-five years he felt content. He'd been aimless since Antoinette's death. All his boyhood dreams were fulfilled. He'd married the woman he loved. They had raised their family and together built one of the finest ranches in Texas. After her death, his life continued, but inside he was dead. Cattle were no longer king. That crown went to oil. Nothing would replace his dreams of an open land filled with cattle instead of the barbwire, oil derricks, and huge cities intruding everywhere. The smell of prairie grass was almost overpowering and he breathed deeply. The emptiness fell away as he pushed his zarks southward. He was free, free to ride the open range. The air, sweet and slightly humid, filled his lungs and his being.

Several hours later, he was near the village. He'd gone over different scenarios for rescuing Daniel and the Kenning Woman. He finally settled on hiding his horses in the prairie grass, and crawling up to the village for a closer look. If Bi's ship wasn't there, he would cold camp this evening. Either way, he would need to decide whether to ride in or to use subterfuge to lure Daniel away from the town area.

Bi's village was unlike the one they had flown over. That one had fields and pastures. Here they'd seen some small garden plots and a few cattle and sheep scattered about. Laten was probably correct about the land Abs going on raids. The Tris built their houses within the fort area. That meant the inhabitants were worried about an attack. They'd flown high enough to avoid detection, but the fort remained a warning. According to Laten, land Abs and the dispersed Tris possessed zarks and cattle. The fortified village was powerful enough to fight off raids, but open villages like Bi's were vulnerable. So far, Bi's trading had protected his village. And this time, Lorenz knew, there were few trade goods. Bi had been too eager to set sail with his prize.

He fell easily into the pattern of switching between the prairie, the rocks, and the river. At times the grass was over his head and the zarks found it hard, slow going. He paused, switched back to the river to let them drink, and he bent low to sample the water. It was sweet and clear, although warm in the midmorning sun. When he stood, he sensed something in the air and stood listening, but no sound came but the zarks drinking, the rustling of the grasses, and the occasional bird. And yet, his senses were tingling. It was as though he was young again and something was wrong somewhere.

He went forward one slow step at a time. The village couldn't be more than a mile or two and he could smell the wood smoke. He began to look for a place to hide the zarks and to camp when he noticed the brush ahead had a freshly broken limb.

Lorenz led his zarks back behind the low growing willows and shrubbery. He had been careless. The heady smells of the open prairie and free flowing river, the sounds of unknown birds, and the unfenced land diverted him from observing everything. He knew the zarks had their own sense of smell and they snorted and stamped, yet he had to risk whoever broke that limb was paying less attention than he had been. He hobbled the zarks and edged forward by skirting along the willows and away from the bank towards the broken limb. When he was within several rods, he dropped down and crept forward. Every nerve in his body seemed to tingle and he kept listening to the birds and insects, to the wind, and smelling the scents in the air, but this was a different land. It was difficult to tell if there was more than the sense of danger. He crept closer and heard a boy's voice.

"Look, Mither, the fish are very close. Mayhap I can catch them with my hands." And his laugh rolled out.

A slow smile tugged at the corners of Lorenz's mouth and he stood to walk the rest of the distance.

Chapter 38

Lies Reputed

Di sat up and watched a sleeping Wee Da. She smiled and then the worry began. They landed late last night, and she wished she had left him with the blind-eyed Laird and nay listened to Bi's lies.

Bi had returned with a wild tale of a dissipated Laird. Her vision had been wrong. The Laird was blind-eyed, but that was a natural eye color of his world. He was a man who bedded laddies: Wee Da and his friends. When she tried to comfort her laddie for endangering him, Wee Da had protested.

"Mither, that tis a lie. My fither did nay bed me, nay anyone else. Sometimes he acts like a Martin from his world."

Di closed her eyes. The Laird had accepted Da. He had taken him to House and renamed him. Her vision had been true, but what of the latest vision where she saw Wee Da in terrible danger? Had that been wrong? She tried to see again that brief, blurry moment of Da surrounded by armed men.

She opened her eyes and her body grew rigid, the scene in focus. Da was in an Ab village, nay in Martin's Ab Quarters. There were men dressed in leather or brown clothes. Other men were clubbing and striking anyone in their path. The village was in flames, and the room came in focus again. When she was able to breathe, her breath came in sobs. This attack, she kenned, would happen today.

Di rolled over and pushed herself up enough to crawl out from under the cover and dress. She crawled over to Da and shook him awake.

"Come, my laddie, I must gather herbs ere it grows any later. We must hurry. Ye will need to support me. We'll eat dried fish for our sustenance this morning."

Hurrying seemed to do no good. Da dawdled while he dressed and while he ate. At least he did not dawdle while helping her to the latrine area.

Di's crutch was fashioned from a heavy-grained limb. Various bags were tied around her waist for the herbs. The villagers were accustomed to her searching for herbs to help with their healing. It was her way of paying for her keep. She had learned early that all must contribute to this village and the visions seemed to come less and less. Those that came tended to be personal or so blurred there was nay sense to them. Her time as a Kenning Woman was drawing to a close. She kenned a new one had been birthed at the Tri stockade. It was safer to keep that information locked away.

It was slow moving away from the village. Di was following the river but she could go no faster. It was still too early in the season for most of the new crops and villagers were nay in the gardens. Bi did nay send his smaller boats upstream for he had brought nay trade goods. By the time they were out of the villager's eyes, her leg was tiring and the pain constant, but she kept going. Wee Da supported her on one side, but she kenned he too would tire.

"Da, I need to check over there." She had to rest her leg.

"We shall go into the clearing near the river. I will rest and see what grows along the banks. Be careful, for some of the shrubs are drambleberries and the stingers seek their flowers."

Once they were behind the brambleberries she sat on a low rock, wiping away the beads of sweat. Why wouldn't the clouds produce rain and wash away the imprint of her crutch? Anyone could follow her. Di realized they needed to keep going. The river was too deep here for them to cross and from the talk at the village she kenned any caves were on the other, higher side several legs away. Soon she would have to make a pretense of searching for plants and then urging Da on again. Now he was enthralled with the river and was yelling something back at her about fish.

"Hush, we must be quiet."

"Why, Mither."

"Because y'all are out in the wild and there is something wrong." It was a male's voice.

Wee Da whirled away from the river. "Fither! I kenned ye would come! I told Mither!" He landed with a thud up in Lorenz's arms.

Da had been elated when his mother's arms enfolded him. They had arrived last night and he was entranced by the strangeness of a village, but regretted the lack of fancy food. For the moment, he was content to be with his mither as he kenned his fither would come.

"Lug, y'all are going to knock me down one of these times."

Wee Da felt the strong arms close around him and then he was lowered to the ground. "Now introduce me to your mother."

Daniel grabbed his hand and led him back.

Di was staring at him, her mood swinging from great joy to deep despondency. The Laird was here. He would take Wee Da back and she would nay see either again. She struggled to her feet and the Laird was beside her, steadying the crutch and her other arm. His grip was warm and hard. His skinny body belied his strength.

Lorenz found himself looking into a pair of light-brown eyes filled with joy. Her eyes and face changed from elation to complete sorrow, and for a moment he could think of nothing but how this woman could fill his empty life.

"Mither, this tis Fither. Fither, this tis Mither."

The man's grey eyes lit with amusement and he smiled. "Madam, I assure ye that such an introduction was nay necessary for my other children."

He raised her hand to his mouth and gave a light kiss. "Tis a pleasure to meet the mither of my son."

"Ye must take Wee Da and go. Tis danger here! Bi's village will be attacked."

For a moment the grey eyes stared at her and he seemed to be listening to the wind. Then Lorenz pulled out his com and called Laten.

"Pick up now, Laten. It seems the land Abs do not love each other."

"Laird, close the circuit. The Sisters will find ye. They've boxed the Maca into his tower. We are forbidden to fly." The sound vanished and the circuit closed.

Lorenz stood frozen for a moment. He had to get back, but first he had to get these two out of here.

"If we went to the village, would Bi take us to Donnick in exchange for four zarks?"

"Laird, he will do nay for ye. He hates ye."

"Is there anyone else that would chance it?"

"Nay, Laird, I am considered too vital for this village. My presence gives Bi status." Her voice was bitter.

"Then we use the Zarks." He looked down at Daniel. "Gather up some of those sticks in a bundle while I get the zarks."

"Laird, leave now after I hug my laddie goodbye. Ye canna worry about sticks."

"Y'all are going with us." He disappeared through the brush.

Di was left leaning on her crutch staring after him. This tis madness ran through her mind. A cripple canna ride a zark.

Within minutes Lorenz was back riding one and leading the other three zarks. He rode over to the taller tree that to him looked like the cottonwood of his own world and dismounted. He lashed the reins of all the zarks to the tree and walked back to the now sitting Di.

"Have ye ever ridden?"

Di looked up, amazement etched across her face. "Nay, and I canna ride now. My legs will nay straddle the zark like ye just did. Take my laddie and go. Ye have my blessing."

"Lady, either ye let me help ye into that saddle, or I'll lasso y'all and drag y'all behind in a travois. That way, we'd leave enough tracks for a tenderfoot to trail us."

Complete incomprehension was on Di's face and in her eyes.

Lorenz sighed. "Either ye let me help ye up into the saddle or I'll drag ye roped down on a blanket. That will take precious time and anyone who kens the way of the land will be able to follow us."

"That tis why ye must take Wee Da and flee."

"He'd hate me forever if I did that. Right, Daniel?"

"Aye, Fither, Mither must go with us. Please, Mither, let him help ye." Daniel was pulling at her right arm.

"Ma'am, I going tie those sticks behind my saddle and then I'll be back. One way or another, y'all will leave with us."

Di watched him perform the mundane task, her mouth set in a stubborn line.

"Come, Mither." Daniel was pulling at her kirtle this time, and the Laird was walking back.

"Daniel and I will help boost ye up into the saddle and then I'll tie ye in there so ye won't slip off while we're riding. It won't be comfortable and ye are going to be sore." He smiled at her. "I know ye can handle it."

Di took one look at the tears on Daniel's face and let the man try the nay possible. Somehow she was in the saddle, sitting with both legs on one side, and the rope lashed over her legs, around what he called a saddle horn, and a cantle. He patted her legs when he finished and smiled up at her.

"I'm sorry that I have to put ye through this. Ye are valuable to Bi, but ye may not be valuable to that other crew when they attack." Then he turned to Daniel.

"If y'all find yourself slipping, hang on tight to the horn, and don't fall asleep. Do y'all need some help getting up there?"

Daniel flushed. "I can do it." He started towards the zark.

"Mount from the other side, laddie. The zark will throw y'all from that side."

Daniel whirled to see if Lorenz was joking and decided he wasn't. Fither was suddenly beside him.

"I'll steady ye. By tonight y'all will be as stiff and sore as your mother."

Chapter 39

Flight

They rode steadily for two hours with Lorenz leading the zarks with a rope linked from each bridle to his. He would trot the zarks and then fall back into a walk. Grey clouds were building to the northeast and he would pause to look at the sky. Every so often he would turn to verify that they were still back there. About three hours into the ride, he pointed back in the direction of the village.

"There's smoke. The attack has started. How long will it take them to discover ye two aren't there?"

"I dinna, Laird. I told them my laddie and I were hunting herbs. They dinna expect us to return til this eve."

Lorenz gave a tight lipped smile and then guided them towards the river away from the path.

Di was hurting into her bones, but she held her tongue. The zarks drank from the river and then Lorenz rode into the shallow water near the bank. They followed the river until it narrowed and Lorenz turned.

"Hang on tight. We're going to cross here. We'll make it to the Tri's fort by tomorrow."

The water swirled around them and Daniel's horse slipped. Daniel slid into the river.

"Wee Da! Laird, stop!"

Daniel's hands were firmly wrapped around the horn as Lorenz had told him, and he was vigorously thrashing his legs in the water.

"Daniel, act like you're swimming or floating, not running. Hang on until y'all can pull yourself back up into the saddle. We can't stop now. Don't let loose."

Lorenz gritted his teeth. Zarks were touchier than horses at times and right now he didn't want to lose anyone, rider or Zark. The current wasn't swift, but it was swift enough to tumble an inexperience rider. He felt his zark going upward when he heard Daniel's shout.

"I did it, fither." Daniel was mounted and grinning from ear to ear when Lorenz looked back.

Lorenz led them up onto the pebbled sand. "Everybody hold tight. These zarks are going to shake that water out of their manes and blow a bit. We'll ride for another hour or so and then we'll find a place to camp."

The sun would remain up in the sky longer in early summer just as on Earth, but they needed a secure place for themselves and the zarks. It was quite probable that someone was trailing them.

Once the zarks settled down, he ordered. "Daniel, can y'all get those reins? Lean forward and grab one side and pull it up and then the next side."

He watched as Daniel did as instructed.

"See, fither, I will be a great Warrior."

"Y'all are working on it. Ye are taking this like a man."

Daniel's chest expanded with pride. He had won his fither's approval.

Lorenz led them upward and started southwest before turning northwest again towards the mountains. The ford had been at the bend of the West Fork of the Valiant River and he preferred using the trail already there before striking off in another direction. If the clouds thickened enough there would be rain to hide their tracks. He kept checking the others and the clouds as they rode.

"Laird, how do ye ken where we go?" Di was thoroughly lost. She'd not been this far from the village in seven years. She knew it was well past midday, and she had to say something to keep from moaning in pain.

"When we flew over, I saw the fort. That and the route to Bi's encampment are in my head." He smiled at their confusion. "I grew up in a land that looked like this. No roads, no flying machines, and the paths might or might not go where y'all were going. Your mind automatically creates a map."

"Nay, tis Justine," said Di, her words stiff.

"There's nothing Justine about it. Y'all either think like an Indian or y'all don't."

As usual, thought Daniel, fither's words nay made sense, but there was no chance to ask as Lorenz pulled up and dismounted.

"There really isn't any place to tie the zarks here, but I need to go up on that hillock and check things out. If I take ye off, are ye going to be able to go back on?"

Di looked at him, her pain almost overwhelming, and shook her head. "Ye should leave me, Laird."

"Not a chance. Do y'all know anything about the Tris up ahead?"

"Nay, Laird, they keep to themselves. They dinna like Abs."

"What about the Kenning Woman and her laddie? Will they welcome her?"

"I dinna, Laird. Bi trades with them, but only if they see his flag raised at the upper river joining the East Fork. They dinna allow him to come to their village. Tis said they have look outs to drive all away."

"That means Bi is the only one who knows whether they welcome visitors or drive them away."

Di was too exhausted to answer. Lorenz grabbed the hobbles for the four zarks. It was wasted time, but he couldn't chance the zarks running off.

At the top of the hillock, Lorenz could see the smoke to the northwest. He might have made it by riding most of the night, but Di needed to come off that zark. Finding a place to camp was paramount and the prairie offered little cover. About a mile ahead the land swelled to a higher hill with trees. Perhaps there was an underground spring feeding the tree roots. There could be fresh water. He gave up trying to cover his tracks. He'd worn his working boots from the Texas ranch. There was no way to obliterate his walking marks or the zarks' hoof prints. A good tracker would find the sign.

Chapter 40

The Scout

The trees were fed by a clear spring. The signs said others had camped here over the years, but not recently. Struggling vegetation was growing over and around the stones surrounding the fire pit. The grass was stunted, deprived of sunshine by the leafy canopy and the ground stonier, the deep prairie sod held behind a damn of limestone and granite. Someone had drug in a couple of boulders for a windbreak.

Helping Di down was first. Her weight was considerable and her legs had gone to sleep. Lorenz untied the rope and coiled it before jamming it into the saddlebag. They'd need it come morning.

"Daniel, grab her reins to steady that zark.

"Kenning Woman, put your arms around my neck and then slide down."

Doubt rose in her eyes for a moment before doing as he said. Had he not been holding her, she would have collapsed. Fire needles were shooting through her feet and legs and they were unmoving wood. Pain made her grit her teeth. Lorenz pulled the crutch down and handed it to her.

"Just hold unto it. I'm going to help y'all over to that tree and help y'all to sit down before anything else.

"Daniel, take those canteens, uh blads, and fill them. Watch out for the zarks. They'll be drinking too. After that we'll see about where we'll locate the latrine area."

He led Di to the tree and eased her down. "Has the blood stopped circulating? There'd be sharp, needle like pains if it has."

She nodded, unable to speak. How could a Laird ken?

His hands were massaging her legs and her feet, easing the pain and driving it back. Di put out her hands to stay him.

"Laird, I canna bed ye. The pain tis too great this eve." The years of no bedding had been a torture, but who would bed a cripple? "My laddie can do the rubbing."

Lorenz looked up and smiled his crooked smile. "I'm not doing this to put y'all in a complacent mood. I'm doing it to make it easier for y'all to make it to the latrine when it's ready."

They heard the zarks blowing and looked up. Lorenz went running. The zarks had finished drinking and were eating at the grass, moving away from the camp. Daniel was jogging towards them, confident that he'd done as instructed. He stared after the running man. He realized he had somehow done something wrong, and Daniel instinctively knew this was not the time to do wrong things.

Daniel watched Lorenz gather up the reins and lead the Zarks into the trees, tie each one to a separate tree, and then extract the things he called hobbles.

"Daniel, y'all are going to learn how to put these on. Then we'll take the saddles, bridles, and packs off and stow them where we'll be camped. The zarks can feed and we won't need to worry about them spooking and running off."

Daniel wasn't quite sure what his fither was saying, but those strange things meant the zarks would stay. He hurried over and the lesson began.

Once the zarks were hobbled, they carried the saddlebags and packs over to where Di sat and Lorenz put out a blanket for her before setting up camp.

Daniel had never left the Ab quarters during the work season. He had been guarded by the Handmaiden. He had heard Kahli's tales of the land Abs, but deep down hadn't believed half of them. He looked at Lorenz in disbelief when Lorenz began rolling a large boulder nearer the two already in place.

"Daniel, see how many large stones y'all can find."

"That large?"

"No, I want stones as big as y'all can carry. I've already located the other large stone I want."

"Why nay use the zarks?"

"They're tired and we'll be in the saddle most of tomorrow." Lorenz looked at Di lying on the blanket he'd put out for her. Her face was strained and her eyes closed.

He took the blad and gave her some water.

She swallowed a few times, said, "I must rest," and fell back.

The blanket eased the hardness of the ground, but now he had to devise a cave like place for them to sleep. The clouds had continued to build making the afternoon warm and humid. The wind had increased, and he hoped the storm would blow over as it swung in from the ocean. Dusk was falling when he tied the tarp over the improvised shelter.

Daniel was kneeling by his mother and saying, "I will help ye."

Lorenz looked and saw Di using Daniel as a prop for rising with her crutch. "Where tis the latrine?"

"Just follow the path through the grass where Daniel and I walked. Uh, ma'am," he used the polite address of his land, "it depends on what y'all are doing. Y'all might need some leaves."

"Ye forget that I've lived as a land Ab these seven years."

She tried to walk with dignity, but the crutch, the limp, and the soreness of her muscles made her pathetic.

When they returned Lorenz had a small fire going and the moons were losing their fight with the clouds. "I have pina leaf bags. It's supposed to be nourishing. Y'all can have most of the tea. We'll share the cup. Our meal will be these delicious bars and some dried meat." Daniel made a face.

"Sorry, but it's the same emergency supplies and a couple of brools for breakfast. I slipped up. I thought we'd be back at the Station or in Donnick on the day I found Daniel and y'all."

Di stared at him and sank down on the blanket. "If ye thought that, why did ye bring so much?"

"I didn't know how long it would take to get ye both out of Bi's village."

"It does nay matter. Here, Wee Da, ye may have mine. I will sleep now." All Di wanted to do was hide: hide the pain, hide her broken body.

"No, he can't. Y'all need it. Tomorrow will be just as rough." Lorenz's voice was gruff. "Daniel, your mither is being a mither. Y'all said ye are a Warrior."

Daniel stood, bowed, flopped back down, ate the bar with relish, and reached for some of the dried meat.

Di was too tired to argue. She choked the bar and tea down before crawling into the shelter. Smaller rocks were piled around the four boulders and laced with twigs. A tarp, anchored by rocks and stakes, covered the shelter. She could hear Wee Da and Lorenz rinsing out the pot, and the Laird mentioning the zarks and she remembered nothing, not even the rumbling thunder.

"Daniel, make sure y'all and your mother stay alongside those barriers we built."

"Why fither?"

"Because if someone sneaks up and starts shooting, the rocks may offer protection long enough for me to get there."

"Where will ye be?"

"Up in the biggest tree around here." He pointed towards the spring. "It's the one closest to the spring. I'll tie myself up there so I don't fall during the night if I doze off."

"Ye will nay sleep?"

"Not as much as y'all. Someone can trail us just by following the grass our zarks have beaten down."

"But we were in the river and along the banks there was nay grass."

"Four zarks leave plenty of tracks. If the rain had hit this afternoon, it might have washed out some of them, but a good tracker could still find us."

Daniel looked doubtful. Lorenz reached out and tousled his hair. "Go to bed my laddie. We all need our rest. We'll leave as soon as we can in the morning."

The clouds had obscured the moon and stars. The air was heavy with moisture. The tree Lorenz had selected looked like a cottonwood. The brush looked a great deal like willows, and the other trees like the ash trees that grew throughout the Midwest and West.

The storm erupted from the clouds during the night. The wind drove the rain downward and sideways, slammed it into the ground, and poured it over the landscape. Lorenz had tied himself in the stoutest tree, but the leaves did little to break the rain. He managed to pull the water shedding blanket up over his head, but worried about his ammunition getting wet. He'd chosen this as a good place to keep watch. Sleeping in the shelter would put him in the opening; a risky place to be if someone were tracking them.

Sleep became impossible as the rain and wind kept tearing at the blanket. He climbed down to finish sleeping in the shelter, but even there the rain blew in. As dawn spread grey light he crawled out and headed for the latrine. His wet clothes and Daniel's tossing had awakened him.

When he finished, he adjusted the thong and buttoned the Levis when the old nagging feeling of danger alerted his senses. He drew his gun. Had the rain gotten to it? It was impossible to judge. He began to listen. The prairie grasses rustled, but no other sound was detected. Whatever he had sensed was drawing nearer. Of that he had no doubt, but the wind still waved the grasses obscuring any unnatural movement in the grass. Lorenz took one soft footfall at a time to return to the camp area. Every few steps he would stop and listen. The sound of the zarks snorting came from the correct location. Then one of the zarks whinnied, and he heard the sound of an arrow thudding into the shelter and Daniel yelling.

"Mither!"

Lorenz ran as silently as possibly on the beaten down, wet grass. He had warned Di and Daniel to stay low and up against the rocks if they were attacked, but sleep can rob a person of good sense when the unexpected happens. Now he could smell the smoky presence of another being living in the open. He was about to emerge from the pathway when the slippery grass proved his undoing and he fell headlong into the opening and his handgun fired into the air.

Perhaps it was the sound of the shot for the arrow zinging towards him also missed its mark and sank harmlessly into the ground. Lorenz sensed someone leaping at him and he rolled, pulling at the knife in his right boot, and stood.

The scout was upright, a knife in his hand. The two men circled each other, each feigning a thrust and withdrawing, then closing. The scout whirled in and slashed. Lorenz whirled away and slashed back, his boot heels catching firmly in the ground, and he slashed again. This time blood appeared on the man's arm. The Ab ignored the gash and moved in, slashing at his midsection. This time he caught Lorenz near the hip, but the rivet on the heavy denim deflected the blade. The man was caught by surprise and his eyes moved up to Lorenz's face. For an instance he froze, and Lorenz slashed at the man's middle and ripped upward, his left hand reaching out to grasp the other's knife arm and push it to the side.

The man sat down and held his abdomen, his intestines and blood oozing between his fingers. His eyes were glazing and he looked up at Lorenz.

"How can ye see?" Blood bubbled out his mouth and he crumpled to the side.

"Wee Da, come back!" Lorenz could hear the Kenning Woman screaming. He stepped backward and looked over towards the shelter.

Daniel was running towards him with both hands holding a rock. His mouth determined, and his eyes wide. Di was trying to pull herself out of the shelter. Soft yellow light crept over the world and illuminated the blood flowing into the earth.

"Daniel, put the rock down. He's not going to hurt anyone now." He started to move towards Di to help her when he realized that danger was still all around them.

"Daniel, get your mother back into the shelter."

It was too late. Ten armed men came over the other side of the hillock. The lead man carried a stunner. Two men had bows strung with arrows, but the majority carried long knives that looked like machetes. These men weren't dressed in buckskin, but were wearing a combination of light blue or butternut colored clothes that Lorenz knew as homespun. They wore a boot like shoe, but they were not the soft, pliable boots of Thalia's Houses. These looked like the cobbled boots of his youth.

He stood with his hands away from his sides. If he used his mind, he would break his promise to his father. Using his mind against ten men, however, was not a good idea. He couldn't control them all.

One man stepped forward. Like most Thalians, he appeared to be about thirty-five, but he was not muscled in the same manner of House members. Once again, the reminder was of Lorenz's own country: a stocky, determined man of the earth. These men were farmers.

"We saw the smoke from a village fire and feared it might cross the river, or those who were raiding were headed towards our village. What tis the state of Bi's village?" He stopped speaking. He stared at Lorenz's range clothes and then at his eyes.

"Who are ye? From where do ye hail?"

"I am Lorenz Adolf MacDonald from the state of Texas in the USA of the planet we call Earth."

The man shook his head over the strange words and outlandish string of names as one trying to clear his mind.

"Ye are blind, yet ye fought a man and won. How?"

Lorenz's eyes brimmed with amusement. "I am grey-eyed as many of the people from my world are, but that doesn't make us blind. It's just an eye color like blue, green, or brown."

The group seemed to take a deep breath. "And how many are here from your world?"

"Right now there's just me and my younger."

Another man stepped closer. "Langford, the Kenning Woman tis here as fore-told. We are to return with her. Do we take these two with us?"

216

Daniel started to move and a man raised his fist.

"Daniel, attend." Lorenz snapped the words out. "Don't move."

Di moved forward on her crutch and none stopped her. She put her arm around her Wee Da. "This tis my laddie. I go nay without him. Ye came for me, but these two are part of me."

Lorenz couldn't help but wonder at her statement. The men were now looking at her and realized they'd forgotten him. The one called Langford turned to the man on his left.

"Do ye think the Select Man and Council will wish to see them too? If we dinna take them, we need to put them afoot or kill them."

Another slimmer man named Spence decided. "The Council will decide their disposition. We are on Zarks and all will ride. Milon, Liken, bring up the zarks."

Langford turned on the man. "I was appointed to lead this expedition."

"Aye, that ye were, but that was for any fighting there might be. There tis nay fighting, and I sit on the Council. This tis a Council matter."

Spence shouted at the men going for the zarks. "Bring me some rope too."

"That's not necessary." Lorenz feared his anger might override his thinking if tied. "It's very difficult for the Kenning Woman to ride. She'll need assistance. She's too stiff from yesterday to have her arms bound and then be tied to the saddle too. I pledge my word by your Gar."

"Bah! Tis but an excuse."

"Right now she needs someone to assist her to the latrine area. I suggest ye permit her laddie."

Spence was puzzled. "What gives ye that authority and why are ye with them?"

"Bi took my son from my ranch. I came after him and found him with his mither."

Spence's eyes narrowed. "What are ye saying?"

Lorenz smiled broadly, the smile transforming his hard face into that of one that drew attention and respect.

"In your words, he tis my laddie given to me by Gar. Bi took him from Donnick. I came after him and found him with his mither, the Kenning Woman."

"Why was he with ye in Donnick?

"My fither wishes me to take over the Guardian duties of Don."

Langford was on his other side and snapped. "Who tis your fither?"

"In this world he is Llewellyn, Maca of Don."

Langford tightened his grip on his stunner and swallowed. "Then why do ye call an Ab your laddie?"

"Langford, we waste time here. The Selectman can ask him those questions. There may be more of them coming after her." Spence jerked his thumb back at the dead man. "The Council will do the asking and deciding."

Lorenz felt certain that "selectman" meant this group was electing their leaders. Perhaps they were reasonable men of Don who were farmers.

"The Kenning Woman is still in agony from yesterday's ride. She needs sustenance before we leave and someone to support her in the saddle."

Chapter 41

LouElla's Town

Di was white-faced and biting her lips when they approached the fort. The moons had appeared in the East as white caricatures of their usual yellow night brilliance.

Lorenz noted that there were both men and women stationed above as watchers. When they'd flown over, the scanners had shown images of houses away from the fort, but no smoke rose from them. The inhabitants must have been called in. None of the men surrounding them had been talkative. He'd spent his time tending to Di. Daniel had been allowed to ride untied also. These men probably operated on the theory that as a child, he would be too fearful to flee. Daniel would have been insulted at such a conclusion.

They pulled up in front of the gate. Langford waved his stunner in the air and someone at the top responded in the same manner. The heavy gate doors swung inward in slow motion and the group rode through.

"What is this place called?" Lorenz asked the man riding beside him.

"LouElla's Town."

Once again that transfiguring smile spread across Lorenz's face.

"Grandmère will be pleased."

As usual, no one understood his words. Inside, a large man, resembling an old Langford, stood waiting for them. They all stopped in front of him. A quick glance showed Lorenz that it took two men on each side to operate the gates.

"Who are the others with ye?"

"Selectman, the younger tis the Kenning Woman's laddie. The other claims to be the blind-eyed Laird of Don."

"I made no such claim. I am Lorenz A. MacDonald. The Maca of Don is my fither, but no Council of the Realm has ruled on whether they accept this." Silence greeted his statement, and Lorenz could see the doubt on the other man's face.

From the walkway around the fort came the sound of a horn blast.

"Tis the hour for sustenance. Lock these three away and the council will see them in the morning. Langford, tend to it. Have sustenance sent to them. Both ye and Spence will give your report this evening."

Langford led the way to a small log structure with one narrow rectangle for a window and one door for access. The four men surrounding them watched as Lorenz helped Di down and held her while Daniel retrieved her crutch.

"We all need to use whatever you all use for…" Lorenz hesitated. "Whatever ye use for natural body functions. The Kenning Woman is hurting badly and canna go far."

Di's face was drawn with pain and her eyes almost closed. She barely managed the crutch and clung heavily on Lorenz's shoulder.

"Ye are prisoners. We will bring ye something." Langford wanted rid of them.

Lorenz noticed three of the men looked uncomfortable, and one cleared his throat.

"She tis the Kenning Woman. We will bring pallets, the pots, and sustenance."

"Our comforts are Ab like. Ye'll find everything far different from what ye are accustomed to having." Langford was sneering.

Lorenz smiled. "Not true, my world was the same as this one when I was a laddie." Di's eyes flew open and all looked at him.

Langford motioned them inside. The place was barely large enough for three pallets. It would be a long night Lorenz decided, but at least he wasn't tied. Overcome by weariness, Di sank to the floor.

"Careful, this place is probably bug infested."

"What else can we do, Laird? I canna stand and must stretch out. It will make nay difference when they bring the pallets."

Half-light spilled through the rectangle creating grey light. Daniel and Lorenz squatted, one on either side of Di and they began massaging her legs. After a few minutes Lorenz spoke.

"Let me take over, son. Y'all are tired too."

Di turned to him. "Laird, I canna be a woman to ye."

"I wasn't expecting that. Besides, Daniel's here. That wouldn't be right."

Di closed her eyes. The man made nay sense.

They woke her when the food arrived. The men deposited the pot of what Lorenz knew as samp: green corn cooked in milk and a bit of butter. Instead of bowls, they were given three spoons, two blankets, and a large, metal thunder mug without a cover. Lorenz doubted if the container was large enough for all three come morning.

"Would it be possible for those two to be taken outside to your privy or whatever ye call the bathroom quarters here? From what little I saw, ye have them located outside of the homes."

"They are nay available." The man's voice was gruff, and he looked embarrassed.

"Kenning Woman, nay all here are against ye." He backed out, one of the others tugging at his sleeve.

"Here, Daniel, help me spread this blanket. We'll set the pot just on the outside of it and share."

They flapped out the rough, woolen material. It wasn't as well woven as some of the Navajo blankets Lorenz had seen, but was on a par with the blankets out of Mexico and parts of his own country.

"What tis it?" asked Daniel, wrinkling his nose.

"'Tis podding, my laddie, at least that's what I've heard it called. I sorrow, Laird, tis nay fit for House, but I'll nay eat if ye need it all."

Lorenz shook his head. "Lady, I call it samp, and it's not the first time I've eaten it. Everyone shares. Now let's eat." He tried to keep the irritation out of his voice.

Di fell silent and crawled onto the blanket. The man was a total puzzlement. When he rescued them, she felt he was everything she had seen in her vision. Now she wasn't sure. She could see nay way for them to flee this village. If the Laird remained here it meant that Thalia would be destroyed. She barely ate any of the podding. Her appetite was gone and her bones and muscles ached from two days of riding. The night air this close to the mountains was cooling rapidly and the aching in her left side and leg increased with the cold. She crawled over to the thunder mug and used her crutch to support herself. Modesty was nay part of an Ab's daily living. Lorenz's voice startled her.

"Do y'all need some help?"

"Wee Da can help me." Her voice was stiff to her own ears.

"He's not big enough." Lorenz ignored Daniel's protest and walked over to her.

"Laird," Di tried to protest.

"My name's Lorenz. Try using it once in a while. I'm sick of the Laird thing." His hands took the thunder mug. "I'll hold it and y'all use that crutch and me as brace."

Di found she needed to comply. Soon the odor of urine filled the small space. Lorenz gave a wicked smile in the darkening room and placed the empty podding pot over the top.

"If need be, we'll use that too if they haven't retrieved it by morning." He returned to the blanket.

"Kenning Woman, or Di, ye take the middle and Daniel and I will be on either side. We'll use the second blanket for cover. If it gets too cold, I'll sit up."

Di found herself annoyed with his order for her laddie. "Wee Da should be in the middle. He tis the laddie."

"His name is now Daniel, and he's in better physical shape than y'all. Your bones are going to hurt tonight with the cold. In my land we call it rheumatism or arthritis."

Di gave up arguing and let him help her. Daniel snuggled next to her and the blanket floated over them.

Lorenz lay down beside them and closed his eyes. He had to rest. Tomorrow he needed to get them out of here and the woman smell of her rose up to fill his senses. Damn, he thought, as he felt the erection start and the body heat rose from his midsection. He knew he'd been too long without a woman. Suddenly her hand slipped down inside his Levi's and grasped, slowly working up and down. His hand clamped over her hand.

"I canna be a lassie to ye, but I can ease your pain."

"Not here," he whispered. "Daniel is next to y'all."

"Why does that matter?" Di was perplexed. What sort of customs did this wild-eyed man have?

"He's a child." There was desperation in Lorenz's whisper. Then he shuddered as he felt his organ explode with release. His body lost its rigidity and he slumped back against her and wrapped his arm around her.

"Woman, y'all will drive me mad." His voice was gravely. He breathed in the smell of her and it was good. "Just wait until we're safe."

Di felt her body trembling, yearning for what she'd been denied for seven years. And what did he mean by just wait? Was he going to force her? Right now she ached and ached from her bones and her want of a man. Sleep would be in fits and starts and her eyes closed.

Chapter 42

The Hearing

Breakfast was some kind of cornmeal porridge that needed a good dose of salt. Lorenz decided that was one condiment they didn't waste on people locked away. The place was reeking from the dank quarters and the overflowing thunder mug.

Four men came for them at what Lorenz judged to be about seven or so in the morning. People were watching from doorways and then following them as they walked toward a larger, center log building. This one had window spaces with shutters that could be closed or opened. Wooden steps led up to the door. Lorenz noted the wooden latch. These people were surviving, but comforts must be slim, and none of the people here were heavy muscled like the Thalians of House or their Tris. These people were leaner, tanner, with the long, smooth muscles of farmers.

They were ushered into a large, square room set with benches on the left and right creating a center aisle leading towards a table. The five men and one woman seated on one side of the table were staring at them as they entered. A square frame with brown fabric was spread out behind them and a large, tanned cowhide hung over the top. It was, Lorenz decided, their attempt to signify this was not an ordinary room. The middle man had on a dark blue, well-worn House shirt. The garment stretched across his chest and forearms that still bulged like a House member. His long, black, grey streaked hair was slicked back and tied with a string. The others were all clothed in shirts and trousers of brown homespun or Tri blue. All of them kept their faces impassive, but they were staring at Lorenz's grey eyes and strange clothes.

Three feet from the table, the group stopped. The middle man took his gnarled fist and whacked the table.

"Ye, who claim to be the Kenning Woman, step forward." Labin, the Selectman kept his face hard.

Di moved forward a pace and stood as straight as possible.

"Do ye still have your visions?"

"Nay as often for I decline."

"But Bi's village still values ye. Why did they let ye go?"

"I and my laddie had left the village. I warned them that it would be attacked and nay there took it seriously."

The seven looked at each other.

"Why was that?"

"Bi had told them lies about the condition of Don and Donnick. He told even more lies about the Laird. I did nay ken he lied till my laddie was with me, but the people there believed Bi. They felt my kenning was false."

"Ye believed a wee one over a grown man?"

"The village was attacked. The Laird took us out of there."

The man looked at Lorenz. "Why did ye nay call for a carrier to pick ye up?"

"It seems the Sisterhood attacked Donnick while I was gone. My fither, your Maca, is in the Maca's Tower and they can't get to him. I must get back there. I would prefer to take these two with me, but if you all could house them safely, Don will pay well."

They stared at him, not believing the audacity of his words.

"Ye just said the Maca was trapped. What can ye do?"

Lorenz grinned, the right side pulling higher than the left. "I won't know till I get there, will I? But I can assure everyone that I will get him out of there."

"Preposterous!" Labin turned to the others and they held a whispered conversation. Finally he looked up.

"It seems the Kenning Woman's vision of a restored Don tis false. Ye are nay the Kenning Woman. All of ye may leave, but we keep the zarks. Ye will die if ye return."

For a few seconds Di stood with her eyes half closed, her body shaking. Finally, she looked up, raised her right hand, and pointed her right index finger at the Selectman.

"Hear me, people of LouElla. I am still the Kenning Woman of Thalia, but I will diminish. The new Kenning Woman tis behind that screen and she needs my blessing. She has told ye the same thing. She will become the Kenning Woman without my blessing, but she will nay ken her mission." Her body relaxed and she leaned on her crutch.

The people seated at the table took turns swallowing and all focused their eyes on Di. Finally, the woman spoke, her lined face and lips taunt.

"Were ye given the blessing by an elder Kenning Woman?"

"Aye, one such ancient came to me. All of Thalia thought her dead, but she was in hiding. The lassie must ken her mission."

A child stepped from behind the screen. Her dark hair was clubbed back and her dark eyes were clear, her lips pink and soft. Her clothing was a loose blouse top and trousers of leather. She lifted her arms to the Kenning Woman.

"Ye must come to me, Wee One, as I canna pick ye up."

The girl almost skipped to Di, her face shining, her brown eyes opened wide. Di bent down, and the child laid her head on each shoulder. Di did the same, but on the second time she whispered something into the child's ear.

"Kenning Woman, how will I find that?"

"I canna say." Di straightened, a soft smile on her face. "Ye will have to follow your visions."

The child's look became almost adoring. "Thank ye, Kenning Woman." She bowed and turned to walk past Lorenz when the Selectman banged his fist and shouted at her.

"Dinna go that way."

The child did not turn, but continued towards the spectators. Lorenz heard the rustling behind him as if someone were walking toward the child. He did not see the child stop.

Her small body trembled and she closed her eyes as she swayed back and forth. The sounds behind Lorenz stopped, and all looked at the child. Within a minute, her eyes snapped open and she whirled, her right index finger pointed straight at the Selectman.

"Ye canna stop the Laird. He must return to the Maca, or we will burn when the Kreppies come again."

Her eyes closed and she shouted. "Mither!"

Someone shoved past the guards and picked up the child, soothing her. The Council sat stunned.

One cleared his throat and looked at the Kenning Woman. "Did ye do that to frighten the wee one or us?"

"Ye are wrong. I canna give her a vision. It was her own." Di's voice was clear and strong. "The visions can be frightening, but she tis right. In mine, I saw the Laird with the Maca, and he carried a Justine sprayer, nay that other world weapon that ye took from him."

Once more the Council spoke in low whispers. Finally, the Selectman looked up. "We find it best that the Kenning Woman and her laddie walk back to Bi's village. The stranger may leave. If ye do nay make it back to Donnick, it will nay be our doing."

"I don't leave here without those two being safe." Lorenz took a step forward and the guards moved closer. "The Kenning Woman cannot walk that far. If you all permit us to use the zarks to get over the mountains or down to the coast and find us a boat, the zarks are yours. No demands for payment when the Maca is in control again. Otherwise, if I make it out, I'll be back and payment will be harsh."

"We nay use credits. Ye dream, man."

"I wasn't talking about credits." His voice was hard.

The Selectman looked into the grey eyes and swallowed. This was a Warrior like the Thalians of almost one hundred and forty years ago. He had seen them then and marveled, thankful that his technical work kept him at the power ops center and not on the ships heading for Justine.

"Why do ye care," asked the man next to the Selectman. "They are Abs."

A look of puzzlement filled Lorenz's eyes. "Haven't the years of living and working like Abs taught you that there isn't any such separation in the beings of a land? You all are Thalians. What's the matter with your perceptions? Do you all really want to be known as those that killed the Kenning Woman?"

Unease filled their eyes. "There tis nay to take ye to Donnick if Bi refuses."

"I saw other villages when I flew over. Some of them had small boats. Surely someone here can convince them to sail us around the mountains to the Zark Station. There's four prime zarks in the bargain, plus when my fither and elder mither come here he'll be offering you all the same square deal he's offered the other land growers."

Disbelief was in their eyes and on their faces. LouElla was dead and what Maca offered anything to a Tri?

"LouElla tis dead. Do ye think us fools?

"My elder mither lives and she tis in Donnick."

Labin rose. "Why would we believe LouElla lives?"

"The Justines couldn't kill her and neither could the primitive conditions in my land. She doesn't think like other people, beings, when it comes to any kind of fight."

Labin looked at Di. "Did Bi tell ye any of this?"

"Aye, he said LouElla had returned and was trying to restore Flight. Bi was nay too clear about the last part."

"Why have we nay heard this?"

"Because Bi has nay told ye." Di silently cursed Bi into Darkness.

"She has held me and she tis magnificent." Daniel's head was up and his face determined.

"Ye are a laddie, and an Ab; hold your tongue," commanded Labin.

"I am a Warrior." Daniel roared back.

"Daniel, hush now." Lorenz wished he was close enough to throttle him.

"Ye named an Ab?" Labin was looking at Lorenz as though he were mad. "And ye expect us to believe a Maca would allow this?"

Lorenz smiled. The transformation startling to the six seated in front of him. The man changed from a Warrior to someone trustworthy.

"My fither spent many years in my land. He saw the wisdom of our philosophy that all men are created equal. My people possessed the right to pursue our own destiny. We built the most prosperous country in my world. Names are just that: names. But Daniel as my son, my laddie, has the right to bear my brither's name."

Labin glared at him, but went back to the subject of LouElla. "If LouElla lives, why tis she nay in the Maca's Tower?"

"I can't tell you why or where Grandmère, Elder Mither, is. I'm not there, and if I call on the com, which you all have, the Sisters will know my location and they'll be here. I suggest no one use it unless far away from here."

"Why do ye call LouElla by another name?"

"In my land, Grandmother or Grandma is our word for Elder Mither. My late counselor thought her much too magnificent for plain Grandma and christened her Grandmère."

Once again the Select Council conferred.

"We do nay believe your words. LouElla died years ago and no Maca allows others to produce credits. A Maca grants credits."

"My fither witnessed the benefits of letting the credits from the grain or beasties sold by those working the land be retained by those beings. In my land, people, beings, in your terms, get to keep the credits that their hard work earns. The Maca was no different from anyone else there. He saw how much more productive beings are when it's their own agra-lands they are working or their own businesses. Since he's the administration part of Don, he would receive a certain percent and require a certain amount of record keeping. Beings that continue to work for Don would receive a wage credit like everyone does now; however, what you all earn will depend on the work and the weather. You all would have your own place with the right to pass it down to your children. They won't be able to sell it to others. If they don't want to raise crops the land goes back to the Maca at a fair price and the Maca chooses the next lease holder."

He could hear the murmurs behind him.

"Why would a Maca be willing to give up his land?"

"It's not giving it up. It's called rewarding the citizens of the land and acknowledging their inalienable rights. He's already granted that type of charter or rights to different Thalians willing to take him up on the offer. There are Tris in town he allowed to continue selling their produce or handcrafted products. He was about to open the schools and start up the plants again when the Sisters struck.

"Right now the Sisterhood has him pinned down, but they don't have him. They can't get to him, but I can."

"Ye can do what the rest of Thalia canna?" Labin was dubious.

Lorenz's lopsided grin appeared. "I can."

The seven conferred again. This time Lorenz heard the woman state, "We canna do harm to the Kenning Woman. All here and the land Abs would turn against us."

Her words must have convinced them as Labin raised his head and the others straightened. "We have decided the three of ye will be taken to the coast. We will try to convince someone to take ye, but make nay promise."

"Fair enough, because if I don't make it back and anything happens to my fither, Grandmère will take her revenge out on Thalia this time. She's already snapped the neck of Bobinet for betraying the Thalians fighting the Justines. If her laddie dies, I wouldn't want to be in her way."

Labin sat back and once again the seven spoke with lowered voices. Finally, he looked up.

"Laird, ye said ye would be satisfied to get to the Zark's Station, aye?"

"That would suit me fine. I can make it to Donnick from there."

"We have a cairt left from when we arrived here. We dinna use it as it would have drawn the attention of the Kreppie monitors. The land Abs ken we have it and some of the old stunners. They leave us alone except for some minor raids. We can fly low and take ye around the York Delta to the Zark Station. We will keep the zarks. Kenning this, do ye still want the Abs?"

It was Lorenz's turn to be surprised. He'd been a fool. Of course, they had to get here somehow. "Agreed, and, yes, the Kenning Woman and the laddie come with me."

Chapter 43

The Houses and the Sisterhood

Jolene seated herself on Ayran's Guardian Chair. For this meeting, she had stationed Jarvis, JayEll, and JoAnne in the viewing room. They were to listen and learn. The Laird had been correct: JayEll was clever. She kenned that Jarvis lacked the same analytic intelligence, but his brawn, intuition, and ego made up for the lack. He possessed the driving force of a Warrior that even she did nay possess. She dared nay let the Sisters win this war. They would destroy her laddie. Her renegade lassie could protect him, but she did nay trust Jaylene since she refused her own laddie. The woman was mad. Jolene fingered the blue icosahedron crystal in her pocket, and pressed the audio.

"Ye may admit Ishmael now."

Impatience had hardened Ishmael's face when he entered Jolene's salon. Why would the Guardian keep him waiting? She had to ken why he was here.

Jolene rose from the ruby carved chair piled with red cushions and opened her arms. Ishmael dutifully laid his head on each shoulder. She pulled him closer, and ran her hands over his back and buttocks before letting him go. Her red overskirt floated downward and her brown hair gleamed. Her smile was almost sweet.

"Ye are young to take such a risk."

Ishmael's smile was forced. "I've faced worse. Are your troops ready? If so, I'll sail immediately to Donnick. Brenda had seventy trained troopers ready when I landed at Bretta."

"I can spare but fifty troopers. If they attack here, we are ready. The Sisters are using about a quarter of their strength in Donnick. The remainder tis ready to be sent against any Maca or Guardian going to Don's aid. They are less likely to suspect an attack from someone sailing one of Ishner's ships. Can ye make Donnick in twenty-four hours?"

"It will be forty-eight hours as I intend to fool the Sisters by nay sailing directly for Donnick."

"I suggest ye put in at the Zark Station. The Sisterhood will think ye deliver the fish the Sisters refuse."

Jolene's voice became grimmer. "I believe both the Laird and the Maca have eluded them. They claim they have information that the Laird was killed in an Ab fishing village, but they have shown nay screens of him or any transport he used to go there. They are guessing. If they had proof, they would show it like they have shown Lamar and Beatrice. They have nay mentioned Llewellyn. My scanner picked up a message from Don that claimed the Maca was in his Tower. The Laird is somewhere in the wilds of Don." Jolene's eyes were as hard as the dark ore her workers extracted.

Ishmael nodded and moved forward to lay his head on her shoulders, but stopped as she held up her hand.

"I have one more thing for ye to deliver to Llewellyn." She pulled the leather bag from her pocket and extracted the blue crystal. "This crystal tis for Llewellyn. Tell him that this tis nay as powerful as the red crystal the Justines ripped from Don's Tower, but tis effective in a one hundred mile radius. Nay of the Houses have the red. He will ken where it goes."

"If the man tis barricaded in his Tower, the Sisters have a guard around it. How can I deliver it to him?"

"Ye dinna use the normal entrances. Ye will use the seaway to enter a tunnel." Jolene smiled in satisfaction at the stunned look on his face. "I suggest all the troopers disembark at least six legs from Donnick. Ye can then proceed to Donnick with your fishing nets and drop someone clad in the oxy garment with supplies sufficient for twenty-four hours. If the Sisters search ye, there would be nay troops. This bag also contains a map of the southern portion of Donnick's piers and the underwater location tis pinpointed."

"If ye ken this, surely the Sisters do."

Jolene's eyes were bright. "All of Thalia has secrets, but some are held by the Abs. My position means I ken what many in the Houses ignore or nay ken."

"I was an Ab and nay heard of a secret entrance to the Maca's Tower, or…" his words ceased for he had heard of secret entrances to certain places in all of the Houses' older cities. Most were rubble or water filled, but still the tunnels and underground domains were there.

Jolene stood and smiled. "Tis my kenning that whoever enters this way must be slight like a laddie or a lassie still below one hundred. I could nay enter." She studied him. His shoulders had broadened and he had gained weight since he had rejoined Ishner. "Ye may be too large also. Pick someone ye trust."

She dropped the crystal back into the bag and opened her arms. "Now lay your head on my shoulders before ye go." Her hands were itching for the touch of his young male body and she took her time.

* * *

The Maca of Rurhran, her counselor, Rollie, and their three lassies, Rennie, Rocella, and Roberta, were seated at their Maca's Tower conference room table. Joining them were Rennie's counselor, Rhodan, and their laddie, Ribdan, and their lassie, Rolla. Their clothes were the golden hue of Rurhran and all wore worried looks on their faces.

Ravin spoke to them all. "We are agreed then. The Sisterhood has gone too far."

Rocella shrugged. "It looked so promising at first. What tis wrong with Beauty that she defies her Maca? Mayhap if we were to appeal to her..."

Ribdan broke in, his voice bitter. "Why would ye do that, my elder? I canna even plead my case to be taken into Flight with LouElla, Guardian of Flight, or her Counselor of Flight as long as the Sisters hold him in his Tower and Rurhran holds his beasties. I am condemned to remain here, a useless appendage to any of your enterprises as ye control all the agra-business details. Mither and Fither tend to what little diplomacy Thalia conducts. Someday Rolla hopes to join them."

Rollie looked at his younger and swallowed. "When this tis over, I am sure LouElla will find a place for ye."

Rennie looked at her parents. "Ye are fooling nay but yourselves. LouElla scorns anyone who does nay honor her laddie. Mither, ye agreed with us just minutes ago. LouElla will turn her vengeance on Thalia if her Llewellyn tis destroyed."

Ravin's shoulders sagged and she closed her eyes. Her lassie spoke truth, and she had foolishly thought Beauty had listened to her and Rocella.

"Mayhap if I threaten to issue my own Maca's call she will listen to reason."

Rollie looked at his counselor and reached for her hand. "My dear, I rarely say against ye, but all ye will do is raise her enmity and they will attack us once Don tis subdued. If we help Don, and Don succeeds, Llewellyn will still want his beasties back."

"If they attack, I will have to issue such a call."

"That, Mither, would be too late. Ye would be wiser to issue the call now. When ye do, make sure it reaches into all of Thalia." Rennie stood.

Ravin nodded. "It will be for all of Thalia. Rollie, will ye accompany me? I need ye beside me."

The two ascended by lift to the third floor. The conference room was on the second level. The third floor housed the stations for communications and defense.

On the third level, Ravin seated herself in the speaker's chair. Rollie sat beside her, his hand resting on her thigh.

Ravin opened the display screen and began. "I Ravin, Maca of Rurhran, issue my Maca's Call. All of Rurhran's inhabitants are to return to me and Rurhran by any means possible. This applies to anyone stationed in any other Maca's land or those who have entered the Sisterhood's Army. Fighting against the Maca of Don and the inhabitants of Don tis forbidden. Refusal will mean ye are considered an enemy and banishment to Ayran." She sat back waiting for the storm.

Beauty's response was immediate. "Are ye switching sides? We had an agreement."

"Which ye have nay honored, just as ye have nay honored your Maca's Call."

"I intend to challenge her when this tis over."

"That tis nay legal under Thalia's laws. Ye should have issued the challenge long before she issued her Maca's Call. Now ye have broken the laws of Thalia and are an open target. I will nay have any Rurhrans in your command."

Beauty was staring at her in disbelief. "Did ye expect us to allow Llewellyn to destroy Thalia?"

"Ye forget, Beauty. LouElla will be avenged."

"She will submit to our rule or be banned."

"She will blow Thalia out of the galaxy the same as she did the Justine planet."

"Tis ye who forget, Ravin. LouElla does nay command the *Golden One*. Tis the Justine mutant that captains it. He does nay care who rules Thalia."

"What of the other mutants on that ship? They are related to LouElla from what she said. The woman mutant stayed with her. They may nay care who rules Thalia, but they will object to a dead Llewellyn. Be reasonable and recall the Sisters from Donnick. Then I will rescind my Call."

"Any Sister leaving for Rurhran will be shot down." With that, Beauty darkened her screen.

* * *

Ishmalisa, Guardian of Ishner, rose from her seat. She had taken over the duties of the scanner while the Keeper of Ops went to an early lunch. She needed her counselor, Illnor. He had insisted it would be safe for him to work on the accounts without the Sisters or one of their spies waiting for him to do something wrong. She kenned Illnor was of the opinion that all of Ishner's Keepers were members of the Sisterhood and all would report everything they did.

She hurried down the hall towards the office area, past the gym, and neared the school area when she heard their lassie, Ilyan, screaming. Ishmalisa ran to the schoolroom and pressed her two fingers onto the carved fish and charged through the door as it slid open.

Iwanda had Ilyan by her left arm and was raining blows with a strap on her backside and legs with a wild, satisfied look on her face. She looked up as Ishmalisa dove for her.

"Your lassie tis a sassy lot with nay respect." She stopped talking and tossed the child away to bring the strap upward to slash at Ishmalisa diving at her knees. Iwanda went down as rapidly as she had when Llewellyn tossed her out of Don.

"Ye fool, I will issue a challenge to this child Maca and ye will be out!" Iwanda was screaming at Ishmalisa.

Iwanda had not considered the fury of an enraged mother fighting for her child. The meek, obedient Ishmalisa did not answer, but slammed her fists into Iwanda's face and chest area over and over again. And then, Iwanda stilled.

"Here, use the strap to tie her." It was Illnor's gentle voice. "We must flee. They will condemn ye."

"Mither, Fither, she hurt me." Ilyan was still screaming.

"Shush, lassie, till they finish." Issing had entered from the gym and was trying to put her arms around Ilyan.

Issing had pleaded with the Sisters that she needed to recoup her strength after being with the Abs for eight years. She had nay been given the Confirmation Rite to commerate the fact that she was a mature Thalian with the rights and obligations of an adult. They could nay enlist her till the Confirmation Rite was administrated before the Council of the Realm.

Ishmalisa and Illnor descended on their child, touching her, soothing her, and cooing over her. Ilyan started sobbing.

"She's horrible. Don't let her near me again. I'll hate ye if do. Send her to Ayran!"

Issing made a face and thought, *spoiled brat,* but aloud she said, "We must go. The Sisters will condemn all of us as Abs if they catch us. Thank Gar Ishmael tis on his ship."

Ishmalisa straightened. "I'll have Ilyan issue a Maca's Call."

"They will ignore ye on the grounds that she tis a wee one."

"She tis right, my counselor. The Sisters will take over this House and our lassie will nay ever be Maca. Mayhap Brenda will give us refuge." He picked up Ilyan.

Ishmalisa nodded and they ran for their House cairt. It was powerful enough to withstand the first onslaught of the Sister's converted fighter lifts.

Their cairt was on the padport at the back entrance to their home. None of the Sisters were lounging in the back during the noon hour. They were in the dining area, intent on eating and socializing. Once inside the cairt, Ishmalisa set a straight course for Betron. They were near Betron when two black fighters came into view.

Ishmalisa continued to speed towards Bretta. The fighters dove at them, their mounted stunners sent white streams of intense heat and power into their cairt. Ilyan began screaming.

"Get down all of ye!" Ishmalisa's voice was hoarse. The cairt bucked, but the systems remained up and they continued to fly at maximum speed. The fighters circled and came at them again, this time firing at her head-on. She yanked the controls sharply upward. She ignored the cries from Ilyan and Issing. Illnor was on the floor trying to stay by Ilyan. The control panel started blinking red warnings to land immediately. She banked towards the shore and the fighters turned with her.

Two green Betron fighters appeared and dove at the black ones, their firing power ripping black panels and sending the Sisters' fighters spiraling.

"Brenda welcomes ye, House of Ishner. Your cairt appears to be damaged. We will accompany ye to a landing and then transport ye to Bretta."

Tears filled Ishmalisa eyes. Illnor was holding Ilyan. She could hear the soothing noises he made. Was there ever such a considerate counselor? She kenned how wise she had been to marry him.

* * *

"Director, Iwanda has been injured. There tis a lump on her head, she does nay respond, and her skin tis yellow. She needs Medicine immediately."

"Stay with her, I'll attend." Babara cursed the Sister called Ivana under her breath as she redirected her com to Medicine. Why hadn't Ivana called Medicine?

Magda's face appeared and Babara explained the situation on Ishner and about the downed fliers. "We need a rescue Medicine there when we pick up our injured fliers. "The coordinates are…"

"Ye and your leader have ignored your Maca's call and ye have nay right to destroy Don. Ye are attacking Thalians. Nay of Medicine will be sent to assist till ye leave Don."

Beauty's face and voice replaced Babara's. "Magda, we are on Sisterhood business. Your allegiance tis to us. We need ye now and when we attack Betron for this flagrant violation of downing our fighters."

"Ye are Army. The Council of the Realm has nay directed ye to fight. Ye have disobeyed your Maca. I fight for the rights of Thalia."

Millay, Director of Medicine, broke in. "Maca, I beg ye, let me attend my Sisters."

"If ye try to go, I will order ye confined. Failing that, I'll shoot ye down. My Maca defenses are intact. If Beauty wishes to dispose the Maca of Don let her challenge him. She has brought this shame on Thalia to hide her own shame of welshing. If any leave I will issue my Maca's Call." Magda ended the cast.

"I'll order two flivs to rescue the downed fliers." Babara's lips were white-rimmed with fury. "Tis this how our Sisters welcome our ridding Thalia of mutant males and rebellious Sisters?"

"Magda must be in her decline." Beauty was perplexed. "Mayhap Millay can talk some sense to her or Melanie."

"Bah, I hear Melanie tis friendly with Ishmael and the blind-eyed one."

"Enough gossip, Babara, we are at war. The blind-eyed one may be making for the Maca's Tower. Double the patrols around it."

"He canna be there. That Ab attack on Bi's village must have caught him."

"That message was sent after the attack. He was nay in the village."

"Bi claims he has the Kenning Woman's laddie."

"Bi tis a lying Ab. There was nay Kenning Woman. That mutant canna survive in a primitive area. Our fighters searched the coast for a day. They found nay man or laddie wandering along it." Beauty turned her back on Babara. She was tired of people contradicting her. She needed Belinda's soothing hands. Why hadn't Llewellyn surrendered? Mayhap as a mutant he would nay starve, but what of the others caught in the Don Tower? They were Thalians. They needed sustenance. Two days had passed since the occupation and the Houses were in open rebellion. Reports from Ishner claimed the lower ranking Sisters were complaining. Nay saw her vision of an all female Thalia governing without the Maca system. Worse, how had Brenda managed to salvage two of her fighters? Taking Betron would nay be as easy as she had planned.

Chapter 44

The Zark Station

The blue cairt piloted by Lisa, the elderly member of the Select, landed about a quarter-of-a-mile from the main buildings of the Zark Station. "Quick, get out." She had seen something on the horizon and wanted the safety of the mountains and her own town.

Lorenz handed Daniel Di's crutch and helped her down from the cairt. "We thank you, good woman and all of your people. May God's blessings fall on all who live there."

For a moment surprise flickered across her face and she slid the door shut before bringing the cairt upward and turning back towards York Delta..

"Laird, why did ye bless them when they kept all your traveling items?

"Call me Lorenz. It's my name." Annoyance was in his voice. "And in answer to your question, it's the way I was raised. They are decent, honest people and they are going to feel guilty about certain things when Papa, Grandmère, and I go visit them."

Walking was a slow process. The grass here was mown, but Di's crutch sank into the moist ground and Lorenz found himself steadying her. Her arms were powerful, but pulling the crutch upward put her off balance.

"Daniel, run on ahead and tell Luman or Lavina we need a transport of some kind."

Daniel shot him a quick grin and turned to run.

"Nay, the Tris will run him off, Laird.

"Wee Da, stay here!" Di stumbled as she turned her attention to Daniel.

Daniel stopped. Which parent did he obey?

The problem was solved as a dark blue lander came barreling towards them. In the front were Luman and his Keeper of the Grounds. Lorenz raised his left arm in greeting and the lander stopped in front of them.

"Laird, we heard ye were killed by Abs."

"It's surprising what one can hear on the news these days." Lorenz was smiling broadly. Sometimes this planet was very much like Earth.

"It's good to see y'all, Luman. I don't think the Kenning Woman could have made it on this ground. Y'all must have had rain."

Both had exited the lander and were staring at them. Finally Luman found his voice after stifling the words about her death and advising the Laird that House dinna give Abs a ride. The man dinna think like House. "Welcome, Laird, but landers seat but four."

"We'll ride in the back and Daniel can sit on my lap. Di can't walk in this terrain."

Leslie, the Keeper found her voice. "I have some zarks to check. I can walk back." Her back was very straight as she walked towards the largest stable.

"When things calm down, fire that woman or demote her." Lorenz helped Di into the back. "Daniel, ride up front. I'll sit back here and steady your mother."

Luman felt the Laird's words harsh, but he and Lavina kenned that the Maca needed to win or their life together would be over. He turned the lander around.

"We could nay discern whose cairt that was. It looked like one of Don's."

"It is. It belongs to the Tris that refused to kowtow to the Justines. They've kept it hidden during the years of occupation. It probably hasn't been used since the Justines landed."

"Dear Gar, was there a man named Labin?"

"Yes, he's the Select Man of the group. It seems he was selected to lead their council and help decide legal and land issues for their settlement."

"He tis my elder, my fither's sib. He swore he would nay submit to the Justines and the Kreppies. He fled ere they landed."

He started to drive toward the empty Ab quarters.

"Where are y'all going?"

"The Kenning Woman will need a place to stay."

"She'll stay at the main home. She and Daniel will need protection while I'm gone."

Luman swung the lander to his left and remained quiet. As they approached the home, Lavina and Leman walked out.

"Laird, ye are safe. Welcome." Her words stopped and she stared at Di.

"The Kenning Woman, she lives. Laird, do ye ken what a prize ye have?" She moved closer to give him the Thalian greeting.

Daniel had jumped out as soon as they stopped and went running to his mither's side. He held the crutch as she grasped the side and slowly slid down, her cheeks flaming.

It took Lorenz a moment to disentangle himself and respond. "I don't have her. I rescued her and Daniel. Whether she stays after we drive out the Sisters is up to her. Right now we need showers, clothes, and food. Then I'm riding for Donnick. I'll need two zarks, food for four days, more dried food to deliver to Papa, and a weapon if you all have any extra. The Tris at the village didn't trust me and took mine. Frankly, I think they intend to use them if attacked."

Leman now offered his greeting followed by Luman. It was, Lorenz decided, a bother, but something they considered essential.

"I have a room in the back for ye, Laird, but I fear the Kenning Woman will need to sleep in the great room if ye dinna wish her at the Ab quarters." Lavina led the way into the home and through the hall.

"She and Daniel can have the back room. I'm not staying. I'm leaving as soon as I shower and eat. It's going to take days to get to Donnick unless you all can figure out how I can do it without the Sisters shooting down anything that flies."

"I fear ye are correct, Laird. The Sisters have sent warning that all are safe, but if any attempt to fly or approach Donnick, they will destroy them." Lavina opened the door and led them to the back.

It was the usual rounded room with a circular bed placed towards the far end. Everything was done in varying shades of blue. Blue-grey drapes covered most of one wall, but revealed a rounded patio out the double door inset with peri-glass.

"I dinna if we will have House clothing to fit ye, Laird. I can find Tri clothing for the Kenning Woman and her child. According to Thalian tradition, the Kenning Woman has automatic Tri status in any House home where she resides. The Sisters and the Justines refused to acknowledge her."

"Right now, I don't care, but if I make it to Donnick, Tri clothing would be a good disguise. These clothes shout alien."

Lavina nodded. "Aye, they do."

"I want Daniel to shower elsewhere. He's too old to see his mother nude."

Several pairs of uncomprehending eyes blinked at him.

"It's my custom, not yours." His voice was testier than he meant to be. Daniel was too old. Antoinette would never have allowed their sons to see her, but in truth he wanted to be alone with Di.

Lavina's face cleared first and amusement sparkled in her brown eyes. "Of course, Laird, I'll bring the clothes in discreetly. Do ye think that the Maca would object if I gave Daniel Leman's old outfit? We have nay Tri children's clothes."

"Why would he object?" Lorenz tossed his hat onto the bed. "He's been wearing that color of clothes at home."

Lavina shrugged, put her hand on Daniel's shoulder and led him out of the room. "Ye can use the gym shower. The pool tis right next to it if they take longer." She was certain they would take much longer.

Di looked at him. "Laird, I canna be a woman to ye until the pain decreases." She knew that he as Laird could take her, but did nay wish to believe it of him.

"I understand that." His voice was gruff again. "We still need to shower and according to Papa, Thalians manage to find a great deal of pleasure in that."

"Ye have nay showered with a lassie?"

Laughter erupted and his arms were around her, bringing her close. "My dear, in my upbringing, it wasn't even considered." His hands were busy disrobing her. When her clothes were on the floor, Lorenz shed his.

"How did your fither survive there?"

"He managed. It was Grandmère that suffered the most; until she found Red. That's the person more or less in command of our *Golden One*."

Di shook her head. It was too confusing. She looked at him and drew her breath in sharply. The faint scar that ran down his face and neck became a large, rose-colored line descending from the neckline almost to the stomach area. "Who put that horrible gash in ye? Why hasn't Medicine healed ye?"

Lorenz shrugged. "That was done when I was thirteen. When I was fifteen, Papa found me and took me home. The scar looked worse then. There wasn't anything in my world to take away the proud flesh. It's actually faded some since I drank the Justine nectar."

Di was puzzled. How old was this man? He had her by the arm and was leading her into the round shower. The door closed behind them and the warm soapy spray shot out from the sides, descending on their bodies. By turning their backs, the spray automatically adjusted for the head height. Then the water gradually cleared and pure water rained over them. His hands were on her and he pulled her close again.

"Di I promise y'all that Medicine will mend what is wrong. If they don't, my grandson, Gary, will do so when the *Golden One* returns." His mouth found hers and he tasted the freshness of her while the water sprayed over them.

Chapter 45

The Ride to Donnick

True to her word, Lavina had laid their clothes on the bed while they showered. When dressed they walked to the main part of the home and the smells of food. A Tri silently pointed to the table.

"Where are Luman and Lavina?"

"Luman tis in the Ops room and Lavina tis working with the Zarks. She said that ye needed sustenance; plus I am to prepare more for traveling."

"Thank y'all. Di sit here and I'll fetch Daniel."

Di sank into the cushioned round chair, grateful for the comfort. She hadn't used such seating in over seven years. She refused to think about being in the House of Don. It wasn't safe, and yet the Laird claimed that the Maca accepted Wee Da. She kenned as long as she was here she was safe, but Lamar dwelled in Donnick.

Daniel came running into the room, his face flushed from the sun and his hair still wet. Lorenz followed behind.

"Mither, they have a wondrous gym here, and Leman will teach me some of the Warrior moves he has learned. Tis a wondrous place! Almost as good as the one at the Maca's Tower." He slipped into his chair.

"Fither made me put on my clothes. He says tis wrong to sit at another's table without them. He tis very Justine about such things." He smiled, beaming at her and then Lorenz.

Di smiled at her laddie as she remembered the Laird's hands on her. "Ye are wrong, Wee Da. In private your fither tis very like a Thalian."

Lorenz choked on his swallow of milk. "That is not the proper conversation for a child at a table."

Di's eyes widened and she was about to protest when Luman appeared in the arched doorway.

"Laird, I just heard from Ishmael. He tis pulling into a cove five miles from here to drop off some of his catch. He will have to dump it else. I told him that the fish was welcomed, and that I would like to see him again. I promised to meet him there with help and a lander."

Lorenz stood. "Y'all did right. I can get to Donnick a lot faster even if he can't enter the port there. I'll grab what I need and meet y'all outside." He speared a slice of roast beef and slapped it between a roll. Then he saw the stricken look on Di's and Daniel's faces.

"We should go with ye, Laird."

"No, y'all can't go where I'm going." His tone was too short, too abrupt, and he gave a half-grin. "You all are far safer here. I'll make sure Luman and Lavina ken how important both of you are."

He turned, bent and wrapped his arms around Di and whispered. "I swear y'all will be healed when I get back, if not by Medicine then by my grandson."

Before Di could answer or ask what a grandson was, he moved over to Daniel who was standing with his arms out.

"I could lead ye, I ken where ye go. I am a Warrior." Daniel's face was grave and his head high.

"Yes, ye are a Warrior, but nay one word about where I go. Promise me."

Daniel nodded his head. "Aye, fither, I ken."

Lorenz picked him up and hugged. "Someday, yes, y'all will be with me, but today y'all have to stay with your mother and help her." He left the room at a run.

It took but seconds to pick up the supplies the kitchen Keeper had put together and he ran out towards the building housing the vehicles. Luman had the lander out and was coming to pick him up. On the seat was a Tri's hat.

"If ye put on the Tri hat, ye will fool all."

Lorenz grinned. "Why? Do y'all expect a Sister to fly overhead or be on board?"

"I trust nay anymore."

They rode in silence the last of the distance. As they drove into the cove, a small boat bearing Ishmael and another man approached. Once they docked at the metal pier, Ishmael swung ashore and ran towards them.

"Lorenz, they claimed the land Abs had killed ye." His Thalian greeting was enthusiastic.

"Have ye heard? The Maca of Rurhran has issued her Maca's Call. They have finally come to their senses."

Lorenz smiled and greeted him. At least this man called him by his name. "I need a ride as close to Donnick as possible, Ishmael."

A huge smile lit Ishmael's face. "I was about to suggest the same. I canna sail into the port, but it will be close. If the Sisters spot us, they will have a hard time trying to decide who they should follow with their scanners."

He turned to Luman. "I hope the part about needing the fish was nay serious. There tis enough for two meals for all here. We've spent little time trolling. I canna explain. I do advise ye and your family to be ready for any event."

"We had already planned on that. The Laird claims he can rejoin the Maca."

Ishmael's eyebrows elevated, but the other person, clothed in Ishner's Tri aqua, had brought up the box.

"Give my best to all. We will see each other at the next Council of the Realm." Ishmael and Luman performed the Thalian ritual.

"Luman, please keep those two safe for me. Lavina realized the importance of the Kenning Woman to Don and to Papa." They too exchanged the Thalian embrace.

Chapter 46

Plans

"I thank ye for nay asking questions till now." Ishmael pulled out two brews and set them on his desk. They were in the Captain's cabin. To Lorenz, this ship was strangely silent. No sounds from engines, no sounds of a crew, and yet the ship sliced through the waters like a rocket through space. The interior was in various shades of teal and aqua: teal and aqua walls, floors, curved desk, and cushioned, round chairs. The illusion of colorful fish swimming in the walls was the Thalian idea of art. At least, thought Lorenz, the fish aren't teal colored.

Ishmael looked at Lorenz. "Will ye join me? Tis an excellent Rurhran brewing."

"I'll take one." Lorenz knew there was no whiskey here and Thalians valued their companionship over a brew.

"As a precaution, I did nay wish to speak while Ikean, the seaman, was with me. He kens what tis happening and the others have guessed. However, some things are better said where nay else hear." He settled himself into the captain's chair.

"There are one hundred and twenty troopers from Betron and Ayran aboard. LouElla was visiting Bretta when the attack occurred and she tis here."

"Grandmère, here? Why didn't she greet me?"

"She tis resting right now. We will pull into a cove at nightfall for the troopers to disembark. The distance to Donnick from there tis about seven legs. They will march on Donnick and are armed and wear the armored clothing. I intend enter a submersible and get as close to Donnick as possible. I will be wearing light-water proof clothing and have a supply of oxygen. I've been given this to deliver to the Maca."

Lorenz had straightened when Ishmael mentioned the troopers. Now he leaned forward as Ishmael slipped out the blue crystal.

"Jolene gave me this and assured me it was for Don Tower's defenses. The Justines took all the red crystals, but somehow Jolene has configured a new one in Don's color. Medicine was the only House the Justines permitted to retain any defenses and they have the yellow. Jolene dinna say, but I'm certain she has equipped Ayran's Tower. Tis nay any other reason she would risk giving me this."

Lorenz picked up the crystal and a wild light appeared in his eyes. "Just how did y'all plan to hand this to my father? Walk up and knock on the door?"

"Nay, Jolene also gave me this map. There tis a tunnel that leads into the Tower."

"And directly into the gym." Lorenz added. His face grew grim. "Jolene's been busy prying secrets out of Jarvis and JayEll. At least she used the knowledge for a good cause."

"Do ye ken if it tis still open?"

"There wasn't time to seal it. We had just found out about it the day before Daniel disappeared. We were scheduled to fill it when I left and the Sisters attacked Papa. The tunnel is still intact. By the way, I'm the one going up the tunnel." A smile lit his face.

"I'll need a weapon wrapped in something to keep the water out, and the food I brought with me. Papa may or may not be running low. Y'all have put on weight since that night at the Guardian's Council. That tunnel is a tight squeeze for Jarvis according to what Daniel told me. Jarvis was scratched the last time they raided the larder in the Tower."

Ishmael took a deep breath. "I think we both shall be going up the tunnel. If we make it anywhere near the opening, the Sisters are apt to spot us. A disabled submersible tis an agonizing death."

"If y'all can't fit in that tunnel, the Sisters will be waiting if y'all go back up."

"What guarantee do ye have that ye will fit?"

"I doubt if I'm wider than Jarvis."

Ishmael shrugged. "It tis a risk for both of us. Why nay stay on board?"

"I've already said why. That's my father in the Tower. If I have to blow the entire planet apart and use my mind on people, he's getting out of there."

Ishmael nodded. "Ye nay look Thalian, but ye are a Warrior."

"There's no need for y'all to risk your neck, Ishmael."

"If the Sisters win this one, I am already dead."

"I'm beginning to regret I avoided saying more at the landing."

"Why tis that?"

"I've found two reasons for staying here; the land and a woman. I wasn't going to give y'all a chance to change things."

"What are ye talking about?"

"Do y'all have any idea why I was in that part of Don?"

"Nay really, we thought ye were checking on stray kine."

"Bi, an Ab seafaring man, had kidnapped Daniel, Wee Da as y'all know him. I went after him. I found Daniel and his mother."

Ishmael's eyes widened. "She lives then. Ye mentioned the Kenning Woman at the cove, but I thought it had to do with the prophesy. How did the Handmaiden manage that? She was nigh death."

"That's true, and she still cannot walk without a crutch. It looks like the pain is constant. She needs medical and that's not possible until Papa is back in control."

Ishmael was puzzled. "That will nay help. She tis Ab born."

"The hell with that, I'll have my grandson and the Justines work on her when the *Golden One* returns." Lorenz leaned back, his eyes narrowed. "Are y'all saying ye aren't interested in her? I thought y'all were living together when the Sisters tried to kill her."

Ishmael shook his head. "We were nay always together, just when we needed each other. She was helping me on the theory that if I returned to good standing, I would be House again. Di tis an ambitious woman."

Lorenz looked at him for a moment remembering Antoinette. His wife had no intention of ever being poor. Perhaps she had chosen him over his brother for that reason. It didn't matter. He had had her all those years. If he was truthful, he would have to admit to being ambitious and he smiled.

"Ishmael, y'all are talking to man from a land of ambitious people. I couldn't hold that against anyone. All I care about is that y'all are not interested in her."

"Have ye nay been listening to the gossip of Thalia? Melanie and I have been seeing each other. We are too young to Walk the Circle, but that changes in less than a decade. Tis very important to us that the Maca of Don wins this fight."

"Captain, we are approaching the fishing area ye selected." The voice came over Ishmael's com.

"Aye, I'm there." Ishmael stood.

"This tis where the troops will disembark. It will take about twenty-four hours for them to reach Donnick. We will sail out far enough to cast nets, haul in fish and sail closer to Donnick during nightfall. I dinna wish to attract the Sisters' attention. If they send a fighter, we will start to sail towards Troy. That tis when we lower the submersible. We will need to supply ye with one of our suits for underwater. One of mine should fit. Tis nay Don's color, but I dinna think ye care."

"No, I don't."

Ishmael nodded and they headed for the deck where over one hundred people were milling back and forth while others were being loaded aboard five smaller floating units. They were waiting for their turn. As they emerged, LouElla grabbed Lorenz and pulled him close.

"Ye must come with me."

"I can't, Grandmère, I've something I have to take to Papa."

"We are going there." Her voice snapped out.

"But I'm going into his Tower."

"Through the Sisters? How?"

He raised his head from her shoulder and grinned. "I know how. I'll get by them, but how is my secret."

She stared at him and pulled him close. "Ye are wise, my younger. I must leave now in the first boat. Gar go with ye."

"And with ye, Grandmère." He touched her face.

One of the Ayranians walked over to Ishmael, her dark Warrior clothes made it difficult to see her physical outlines until she was almost next to them.

"We all offer our thanks to ye, Ishmael. Balen of Betron tis among the first group landing. He tis third in-command and will run the scanner while we march. Do ye have any instructions or suggestions?"

"Do y'all have maps of Donnick?"

"Aye, plus, LouElla will help guide us. We are nay sure how many of the Centers remain open."

"They were all three open when I left. I don't know what the Sisters have done since they've been there. The largest population is in the second Sector. The people there support the Maca."

She nodded. "If we come through the first or the third Sector, the Sisters would wonder at the jump in population. LouElla," she nodded at her," selected the second Sector to hide our arrival."

"Your biggest danger is from their fighters. Can they swoop in between the streets?"

"Aye, if the Captain piloting tis very good." She turned away as someone called to her.

"I must go. Gar go with ye."

"Via con Dios." Lorenz grinned. "It means the same thing."

"I can have one of the Keepers show ye to your cabin. Ye should get some rest ere we head inland."

"And what about yourself?"

"I shall continue to give orders here and man the scanners. Would ye like a brew sent to your cabin?"

"No, thanks, I still don't care for it that much." He grinned. "I'm not much for resting. I'll follow your schedule."

Chapter 47

Underground

Lorenz looked at the submersible and gritted his teeth. He had assumed it would be like the submarines of Earth. It was an underwater craft, but its capacity was no more than six or eight Thalians. He could feel the sweat building under his arm pits and on his chest. The crystal, dried food, a lume, a hand com and small hand stunner were strapped to his chest and back underneath the tight fitting suit. To him, the underwater clothing felt binding. They were meant to shed water and minimize drag.

"The material tis the finest that Ayran produces for being underneath the waters." Ishmael assured him. "I told ye my clothes would fit ye."

They were about to enter the submersible when the com crackled to life.

"Ye are too close to Donnick. Return to Ishner by passing on the east side of Rurhran. We shall be flying overhead. The slightest deviation and we attack."

Ishmael motioned Lorenz to silence and pressed his speak button. "Pilot set your co-ordinates for Ishner via the far route. We will nay deliver to Troy this trip."

He grimaced and turned to Lorenz. "Are ye ready?"

"Will this thing launch from below without sinking your ship."

"Aye, it should. The crew will ken to be ready to man the lifers if it goes ill."

"Let's go." Lorenz didn't relish the idea of being inside that elongated tube of confinement, but he followed Ishmael, wishing he had his tobacco. One last cigarette before the... and he closed his mind to the thought. He was almost grateful when they entered the submersible. No more waiting.

"If my ship does go down," said Ishmael as the submersible seat straps snapped over their shoulders and legs, "there will be too many boats in the sea for one fighter to track. They will nay look below the surface."

"What if the ship remains intact?"

"They will nay think of it. This has nay been used since before the Justine War. All major ships have them, but there has been nay reason to use them. I've arranged the signal with the next in command." Ishmael pressed the com button on the board.

"Bring up the nets."

Lorenz watched as the back of the boat opened and Ishmael guided the submersible into the waters. It was like launching a Scout from inside a *Golden One*, but this time there was weight all around them and the waters almost as dark as space.

"Can y'all keep this thing from hitting an obstacle and still make Donnick?"

"We should be safe. It automatically adjusts for any object too near and I entered the coordinates this afternoon."

"How long will it take?" Lorenz realized his throat was tighter than normal. Ishmael looked at him, his eyebrows lifted.

"I've spent my whole life avoiding being confined. It seems all it takes is being around a Thalian and four walls close in."

Ishmael grinned. "Aye, this does take a bit of acclimating."

"Will they let y'all know if your ship is all right?"

"Nay, I've forbid all com links. The Sisters scans would register them.

"The waters are normal. I believe it righted itself and they pumped out any excess water. Tis a fishing boat, ye ken?" He returned to watching the display.

They lapsed into silence until Lorenz felt the upward movement of the craft. Light grey seem to penetrate the waters as though daylight was beginning above them.

"Tis but a couple of more miles now, Lorenz. I did nay speak sooner, but I ken how anxious ye are. We need to put on the breathing units now."

The straps slid away and Lorenz stood. He hooked the unit over his head and slid his arms through the straps holding the air containers. Ishmael did likewise and went back to watching the screen.

"There tis the shoreline with an old pier less than a mile away."

"That's probably it. I've seen it from the top, but I didn't go into the water. Y'all should stay here and take this vessel back to your ship."

"There tis nay enough…"

Fire struck through the top. Another streak landed to the side of them.

Ishmael pointed to the right and pushed the circle to open the side door. Both men dropped and met the water with the arms and hands outstretched and kicked off against the seats. They barreled out into the bay. Lorenz followed Ishner downward and they swam along the bottom toward what he hoped was the right direction.

Water began rolling and tossed them upward and then down. Ishmael was the better swimmer and turned to grab onto Lorenz's side. It was enough to right him and they spread slightly apart to swim towards the shore.

It took thirty minutes to reach the metal posts. Lorenz went underneath the pier and through an opening below a protruding boulder. It took all of thirty-nine seconds to enter the chamber Daniel had talked about. He hoisted himself onto the self-like space and Ishmael followed. Both took off the breathing apparatus and Lorenz stripped his top garment. Light in here was a dim grayish-green blending with the walls and the pool of water. The air was musty.

Ishmael pulled out the lume and hand com. "Did ye want anything else?"

"The stunner."

"It will nay stop them."

"I'll feel better." Lorenz pulled on the shirt and went forward to shine the lume around. A dark opening was just ahead. A tunnel of rock and stone awaited them. He turned the lume back on Ishmael, careful not to shine it on the pool that marked where they had entered.

"I'm wondering just which one of those kids had the guts to go up there first. Do y'all have any idea?"

"Tis hard to say, but JayEll was the leader for a long time. Jarvis was trying to supplant him, but I dinna if he was able."

"Do y'all want to take a look before we start?"

"Nay, I will follow behind ye. The thought of all that earth around me sits nay better than water with ye. Besides, where else do I go? The Sisters will be patrolling outside and they will find my craft."

Lorenz nodded. "Will the coms work down here long enough for me to tell Papa to open the panel without giving away our position?"

Ishmael looked at him and then at the pool. "If ye are on but for a few seconds, it may work. If they find this, they will come after us. Plus, when the tide comes in, this will be water covered. Ye can see where the tide has ebbed and flowed. Nay doubt it washes into the tunnel for a certain distance."

"I'll go into the tunnel first and call from in there. Then we'll start upward."

Lorenz bent and scrabbled forward. The tunnel was fairly wide here and the air breathable. He shined the lume along the tunnel as far as he could see. It seemed to narrow and he shuddered. The breathing unit would take up too much space and there would be no way to dispose of it. He pressed the com button.

"Papa, open that damn panel. I'm coming in Daniel's way." He closed the unit. He was just inches inside the tunnel and already sweat had appeared on his forehead. He stuck the com into the wristband and went forward, holding the lume and weapon. Soon he was down on his knees and crawling forward, pushing the lume and stunner ahead of him. He could hear Ishmael crawling behind him.

Time lost meaning for both men. Neither could gauge how long they were in there or how long this scrabbling crawl would take. All that mattered was getting out.

Lorenz knew he couldn't crawl back. How had those four boys done it? He could feel the rock scrapping at his knees and stomach when he pulled himself forward. At least his shoulders hadn't scraped the sides—yet. They continued to inch forward and upward, both men drenched with sweat and silently cursing at the walls below, above, and beside them. It was dark, hard rock, but the passageway remained wide enough to slither and hump through like some creature out of the darkest hell. He kept shoving the weapon in front of him, sometimes using it to push the lume so he could contort his body, slump his shoulders, or try to bring them together, and still the rock clawed at him. At times he could be up on hands and knees, at other times he used the imbedded rocks to pull himself forward. His breath was coming in pants and the rock seemed to be closing around him. Sweat covered every part of him as though he had run miles during the heat of the day, and the air became heavier and thicker. He could feel the thumping of both hearts. The sound of Ishmael wheezing behind him seemed to drop away, and he paused long enough to feel Ishmael touch his ankle before moving again. Lorenz wasn't sure how much longer he could continue when the tunnel seemed to end. He raised his head and realized somehow the air was better. He went up on his knees, surprised at the room, and ran the beam from the lume along the wall. The metallic bottom panel of the cabinet met his eyes. Damn, hadn't Papa received his message? His hand went upward and banged into the smooth panel.

Chapter 48

The Battle for Donnick

"Did ye hear that? The blind-eyed mutant tis right there." Bonni pointed at the space on the map that had lit up. "He just told the Maca to open a panel."

Beauty had jumped and swiveled her chair at the sound of the male voice over the com scanner. She had entered the Ops room when the fighter's report arrived about a submersible in the bay area. It was eliminated, no survivors had surfaced. She was directing the search for any survivor. Had Ishner been aiding Don? That the mutant had been in the craft was now evident. How had he made it to shore and avoided the patrol? She pressed her command audio to talk with the fighter that had destroyed the submersible.

"Tele, do ye have the coordinates of that last transmission?"

"Aye, Commander."

"Fire."

"At what? There tis nay there."

"Your eyes are bad. Fire."

"Aye, aye."

There was silence.

"Well, what did ye hit?"

"The ground, Commander." The voice was strained.

Beauty stared at the screens. "Do we have that area covered by scanners?"

"Nay there, but closer to the Maca's Tower there are scanners."

"Use them." Beauty accessed another channel.

"Llewellyn, what are ye up to? If ye try anything your elder Lamar will suf-fer."

There was no response and Beauty fumed. LouElla, on a mission for more instructors and students at Flight, had flown to Bretta just prior to their attack. Beauty was certain that if LouElla had been captured, Llewellyn would have capitulated.

"Send a patrol out to search that area and bring Lamar here. I intend to settle this today if I have to kill every male in Don's House."

Bonni looked at her with a stricken face.

"Go," shouted Beauty. "Bring Lamar here. I want him in front of the screen and Llewellyn hearing his screams. I'll alert Captain Bilan to expect ye."

Bonni ran out of the room in a show of obedience, but partially to hide her face. Lamar was Beatrice's counselor. Both had been kind to her as a child on Betron. Great Betta had always praised Lamar for his bravery and skill as a Warrior. Bonni had discovered she did not like being part of this and the possibility of killing more Thalians. Where could she hide? Nay here on Don, nay could she return to her Maca now.

It took her but minutes to find a fliv and fly to the Don Guardian's Home. Bonni was relieved to find Bilan waiting for her. Bilan was sensible; a Betron Tri who had been claimed by the House of Army and given commanded of a squad. Her duties here consisted of guarding Lamar and Beatrice and keeping the First Sector of Don quiet. Perhaps Captain Bilan could advise her.

Captain Bilan met her at the padport and snarled. "Why dinna ye bring a cairt. We will need more than two to guard them."

"The Maca of Don has control of the vehicles."

"There tis nay Maca of Don. What tis the matter with ye?"

Bilan turned and snapped orders at two troopers. "Bring Lamar and Beatrice. We'll fly Lamar to our Center and march Beatrice there."

She turned back to Bonni and noted the doubt on her face and in her eyes. "Now, what tis bothering ye?"

Bonni looked up. Bilan was impressive in size even for a Betron. The face was broad and square and her brown eyes did nay miss much. Bilan had always expressed a concern for the troopers under her and she extended the courtesy to others like Bonni, a technician.

"I fear that Beauty means to harm Lamar in some manner. He has always been a gentle counselor for Beatrice."

"Ye worry needlessly. Our Commander kens that would turn the rest of the Houses to Don."

Bilan patted Bonni's shoulder. "I now order ye back to our Center. Mala and Teona will go with ye. I and the rest of my troop will be there within twenty minutes."

"Why so many? Lamar tis aging and has but one arm."

Bilan looked at her. "Tech, I gave ye an order." She walked to the back of the home. The tech dinna ken how dangerous Beatrice and Lamar could be: dangerous and treacherous.

* * *

Llewellyn heard the blow as he reached for the panel and lifted it. Lorenz's hands grasped the sides and Llewellyn reached in to grab his laddie's forearms and pull him out of the tunnel and up into his arms.

"It took ye long enough to get here." His voice was rough and he held Lorenz closer than normal.

Lorenz was still gasping, and his body shook at the thought of ever being entombed again. Sweat still ran from his hairline, but his breathing gradually returned to normal. He was surprised to find he was hanging on to his father's biceps.

"Papa, Ishmael, he's still in there." He panted the words out.

Llewellyn released him and knelt in front of the open cabinet. Ishmael was partially sprawled over the cabinet floor. His wet hair was plastered against his skull and like Lorenz, he was taking great gulps air. Llewellyn pulled him out and then enfolded him in an embrace, not as long, but heartfelt.

"Ye took a great risk helping my laddie, Lad of Ishner. Don thanks ye."

"That's not all y'all have to thank him for, Papa."

Llewellyn turned to see Lorenz stripping off the underwater clothing and lifting a bag hanging around his neck.

"Ishmael brought this all the way from Jolene. As Laird, he insisted I carry it."

Llewellyn took the bag and dumped the contents onto his hand. He ran his thumb over the twenty-sided blue crystal Jolene had crafted and sent.

"Jolene said ye would ken where it goes." Ishmael was speaking. "It tis nay as powerful as the red icosahedron, but nay of the Houses have that crystal. The Justines destroyed them all."

Lorenz was stripping out of the tight binding pants. "Sure, and it never snows in the winter." He tossed the clothes aside. "I'm betting Jolene has one if she can make that one."

Llewellyn looked up and smiled. "Lorenz's clothes and shoes are in the closet. It looks like they will also fit ye, Ishmael. I'll be in the Ops room. Mither, Beatrice, and I had repaired Don's shields when the Sisters landed." His smile grew broader.

"They are about to lose their fighters." He turned and ran out of the room, his broad shoulders barely clearing the door.

Ishmael was busy stripping off his garments. "Where are the showers?"

"Behind us." Both men bolted for the door.

"Tis big enough for both if ye dinna object."

"Hell, I've bathed with many a hand in an open space."

Lorenz slammed the door and the warm, soapy spray descended, gradually changing to the clear stinging rinse. Warm air blew over them as the water stopped.

Lorenz hit the panel beside the shower door and the closet door slid back. The clothes hung in graduated sizes. Lorenz's were among the smallest. He handed a spare to Ishamel and grabbed a pair of his soft boots. They were narrower than most arrayed on the wall. "Find a pair that y'all think will fit."

He hurriedly pulled on the clothes and headed for the cold food cabinet. "There's probably a brew if they haven't drank or eaten everything here. Would y'all like one? Then we'll need to tell Papa about the reinforcements." He opened the door to an almost empty space. How long had they been on short rations?

The com sprang to life and Beauty's face appeared. *She looks like a gloating politician*, Lorenz thought.

"Ye mutant from another world, the man ye call Elder has words to say to ye."

Her face was replaced by Lamar with two guards on either side. It looked like they were there to keep him from falling.

Lorenz heard the intake of Ishmael's breath. "They have used the rods on him. It tis forbidden by law."

Lamar raised his eyes. Lorenz grimaced. It was plain to see the man was in pain and his lips were bleeding.

"Llewellyn, my laddie, they wish me to tell ye how and where ye are to surrender." He straightened his shoulders. In a movement almost too quick to discern, the old Warrior knotted his good hand and swiveled his body to slam his fist into the midsection of the guard on his right.

"Thalia!" he screamed and tried to raise his fist again as three Army Sisters piled on top of him.

In the background they heard another voice. "Commander, we need reinforcements. We have been attacked by a troop twice our size. Send a fighter to these coordinates."

For a moment the screen went blank and then Beauty was back.

"Llewellyn, your elder will die if ye dinna speak. Do ye see that fighter rising now? Whatever ye had planned will nay work."

Lorenz and Ishmael glanced at the blue, tinted round windows and saw the dark fighter rise out of Flight Center. A blue streak reached out and slammed into it, bits of metal flying in all directions, and burnt, flaming bodies tumbling earthward.

"He has installed the crystal." Ishmael's voice was hushed. "Dear Gar, what would the red one do?"

Llewellyn's voice came into the room over the private com link. "Why do the Sisters assigned to the Secong Sector need reinforcements?"

Lorenz stepped up to the panel and pressed the circle for intrabuilding communication. "Brenda and Jolene sent extra troopers. They figured y'all needed some help. Grandmère is leading them."

Llewellyn's voice boomed out over the city com. "People of Don, attack the Sisters holding the Centers."

Beauty was back on the screen yelling at him. "Llewellyn, if ye take out the fighters ye will have destroyed Thalia's defenses. Tis all Thalia has."

"Ye, Beauty, have already destroyed Thalia. Do ye surrender? If nay, the remaining fighters and any Sister that tis in or near them will die. Fight me in the streets and we will end this. If I win, I will bed ye in the streets for your debt."

"We are Thalia's Army!" Beauty's voice rose to a screech. "After the fight, Llewellyn, ye will have less manhood than your Elder."

The screen went blank and both young men stepped to the window. Blue strobes of light went out and down into the Flight Center. Flames and debris went flying over the wall. Suddenly the blue light arched towards the First Center, then the Second. Flames swept down and around the perimeter of Don's Maca Tower, scattering the circle of Sisters guarding it. Some were holding their arms, others were limping, and two were being carried. A voice suddenly came over the city com.

"Maca, dinna take out the fighter at the Third Sector. We have secured it." It was Lasa's voice.

"Good work, Sargent. Keep it on the ground. What of the Sisters guarding it?"

"They are our prisoners."

"See if ye can unite with the force near the Second Center. That tis where the reinforcements are."

"Aye, aye, Maca. Revenge for Lamar!" The last words were a battle cry.

The screen filled with Ravin's face and voice. Rollie sat beside her, white faced and his mouth drawn in a tight line.

"Beauty, ye have tortured one of our Warriors from the Justine War. Your actions are despicable. I call upon all Thalians to destroy ye."

Jolene's round face replaced Ravin's. Her brown eyes were large and gleaming. "Ye, Beauty, are marked. Surrender now or be taken and sent to my tender care."

Llewellyn had turned all of Don's screens on from his upper defense Ops Room knowing the Houses would watch all casts. "People of Don, we will have the traitors by nightfall. The screens will remain open for ongoing reports."

Brenda's plain face appeared next. "Llewellyn, our troopers report that they have secured the Second Center and are marching on the First. There tis one casualty. Do ye have any agreement with Medicine?"

Magda responded. "We will support Don. If the Maca approves, I will send a recon for your trooper."

"Approved, and thank ye, Maca of Medicine." Llewellyn's face lighted by a tight lipped smile, appeared.

Lorenz expected the casts to end when Betta suddenly stood beside Brenda. "Beauty, my lassie, what have ye done? Ye must command the rest of our Sisters to request permission to leave Donnick. As the Guardian of the Realm, I abhor your actions against one of Thalians finest Warriors." Tears streaked her face.

Beauty stared at her mother and sister for a moment and slammed her finger against the Ishner circle.

"Iwanda, send the rest of our troopers here."

"Aye, aye, Commander."

Llewellyn's voice came over Don's com again. "Director Leta, do ye have any to attend the manning of our Tower's front area?"

"Aye, Maca, Lettuce and Lena are available."

"Good, assign one of them and ye repost to the Ops room. I intend to fight."

"Lorenz, would ye two care to join me? Ye'll find the armor in my office. I will join ye there in a moment." The com went silent.

Lorenz looked at Ishmael. "Like I said, this isn't your fight."

Ishmael smiled. "Ye forget, Lorenz, I am Thalian."

Lorenz shrugged. "The office is this way, or are all of the Maca's Towers built the same?"

"Aye, I dinna believe there has been a change in design for at least five hundred years. Ops can be located in differing areas."

"Architects must have a hard time of it."

They were out in the hallway heading towards the office. Leta went running by them, barely pausing long enough to nod before running down the half flight of stairs to the Ops Room.

"What are architects?"

"It's an important profession in my world." Lorenz opened Llewellyn's office and they stepped in. The huge, contoured desk was flanked by three blue chairs. The large windows looked out towards the open space heading down to the bay. "In fact, they would have rebuilt this at least two times."

"By themselves?"

Lorenz laughed as he placed his hand on the panel and it rolled away revealing mostly empty shelves. He reached in and pulled out two of the armored uniforms, *they look like tight-fitting long johns without buttons*, he thought, and handed one to Ishmael.

"No, the architect designs the new buildings and the construction people figure out how to build them." He and Ishmael pulled on the uniforms. The material adjusted to their clothing.

"This will be warm. I've nay had occasion to wear one ere now."

Llewellyn came charging into the room and grabbed his uniform. Lorenz reached in the closet and pulled out the Justine sprayer.

"The Kenning Woman says I will be carrying this. I don't know how she even knew we had one."

"Are we ready? Ishmael, ye should stay here and help guard the premises. Don owes ye a debt as tis."

"I dinna do this for Don, but for Thalia."

Llewellyn nodded and led the way out of the office and down the short hall leading to the back doors.

Chapter 49

The Debt

"Our fighters are destroyed, Commander. Do ye wish to set up defenses here?"

"Nay, Babara, I intend to defeat these interlopers. Assemble the troopers. I will lead them. At least Don will ken their mutant Maca has nay courage enough to meet us as equals."

"Commander, tis best if ye command from here." Babara's voice was strained. "There tis too much risk that someone outside will miss a needed element."

Beauty pulled her transparent globe over her head and fastened it to the armored shirt. "Donnick will fall to us and with it Llewellyn." She grabbed her stunner. "Line those troopers up now."

Bonni sat very still at the scanner. She hunched her shoulders to look smaller hoping both would quarrel and ignore her. She was sickened by what Mafy had done to Lamar. It was wrong, very wrong.

Suddenly a desperate Iwanda was on screen. "Commander, the troopers are refusing to uphold ye. They are taking the fighters back to their own Macas. They are preventing our Sisters loyal to us from boarding the fighters."

For a moment Beauty stared at the display. "Why?"

"They honor Lamar." Iwanda looked as incredulous as Beauty at the thought.

Beauty turned and ran out of the building as she yelled, "Troopers, rally to me. We fight the males of Don!"

Babara whirled on Bonni. "Are ye just going to sit there?"

Bonni's lips were dry. "I canna fight for a torturer." The blow from the stunner smashed into the back of her head and she fell forward.

Babara followed Beauty yelling, "Thalia, all Sisters forward for Thalia!"

* * *

As they came abreast of the hall doors, Llewellyn looked up at the outside scanners. For once the black uniformed Sisters were not standing there and a wide smile creased his face as he laid his hand against the panel. The doors swung outward and the three men raced outside to crouch by the half-wall.

"Maca," it was Leta's voice, "Beauty and Babara are running towards this building. They have stunners. There are about five troopers behind them. I will join ye."

"Tis best for ye stay there, darling lassie. If they try to burn through here, ye are to stop them."

Lorenz glanced at his father. Was the man bedding her too?

"Papa, y'all can't really intend to rape her."

"I meant it as much as her threat to take every bit of me that tis male."

He was looking straight ahead, but motioned to Ishmael. "Would ye make a run for those buildings to the right? We will cover ye as we nay wish to be blindsided."

Llewellyn and Lorenz stepped forward with their weapons held waist high while Ishmael ran towards the vacant shop buildings. Once he was safely behind one, Llewellyn started forward, Lorenz on his right side.

"Forcing her in the middle of the street would negate everything y'all ever taught me."

"I taught ye for Earth. Here certain customs are looked at differently. On Thalia forcing anyone for control tis wrong, but this tis caused by her refusal to abide by the rules of the Arena. She welshed on her promise and asked for the Med Scan, hoping that the Justines would eliminate me. She kens what she has due."

They could see Beauty and her guards running towards them with their stunners in firing position. The afternoon sun splashed golden light over the tarmac and smooth walls, beating back any shadow trying to establish a foothold for nightfall. It was unreal, decided Lorenz. Light breezes from the waterfront toyed with their hair.

Lorenz let loose with the Justine sprayer when the troopers were twenty feet away. It gouged an open space in front of the Sisters.

"That's far enough," he yelled. "Any closer and everyone is dead."

Ishmael stepped forward and looked with disbelief at Lorenz and at the Sisters. He had assumed they would take cover or all would toss aside their weapons to physically fight. Thalians did nay kill Thalians. Instead the range of the Justine sprayer meant that the Sisters were in danger. What was Lorenz doing? Proving he was a deranged mutant?

The Sisters coming towards them stopped. From the area of the First Sector's Center the sound of stunners and shouted commands could be heard. Suddenly a troop of green, light green, brilliant red and pink came around one end and started towards them.

"Beauty, ye are surrounded. Do ye submit?" Llewellyn's voice roared out.

She removed her globe, motioned for the others to stay back, and started bounding towards Llewellyn, her fists in the air shouting, "Thalia!"

A tight smile lit Llewellyn's lips, but the black eyes were obsidian. He handed his stunner to Lorenz. "Dinna fire that unless the others start forward."

He rocked forward on his toes. When Beauty was about nine feet from him, he leapt forward, his right fist upraised, shouting, "Thalia!"

Lorenz, like the others watched the two leap at each other. Beauty had drawn a small knife and held it in her raised right hand. That's a stupid move, he thought. Papa's reach must be six inches more than hers.

The two met in mid-air, Llewellyn's right hand opening and grasping her right wrist. For a moment they seemed to be suspended and then crashed earthward. Llewellyn's heavier weight brought him down on top. He slammed her knife hand into the tarmac. The crowd could not see Beauty's face turning white. Her right arm was useless.

She struggled to extract herself, to gain some sort of advantage, but he was too heavy and his hands ripped her trousers downward. Then he rose on his knees to drop his own trousers, Beauty managed to roll to her left and then back, using the momentum to swing her left fist into his face.

In response Llewellyn dropped his knees on her midsection and rammed his elbow into her face. Then he rammed himself home.

Babara scooped up her weapon and started forward when the red suited commander of the relief column sent a low stun ray into her side. Babara's weapon went clattering to the ground while she grabbed at her wounded side. The other Sisters glanced at the House troopers, and decided to remain stationary.

The crowd watched in silence as the huge, muscled back moved up and down and Beauty's legs flailed and beat helplessly against the hard surface. Abruptly,

Llewellyn stood, the white stream from his manhood spurting up and then down, splashing over Beauty's midsection. His voice carried to the watchers.

"Ye did nay think I would let ye carry my seed just to destroy it." He stepped back and away, and then reached down to pull up his trousers.

Beauty rolled over and realized she could not use her right hand or arm to push herself upward. She rolled to the left, went up on her knees, and stood. She whirled to face him, but only her left hand would go into a fist. Beauty was desperate for revenge, but the sound of cheering filled her ears and she whirled to see a crowd of House troopers yelling.

"Llewellyn! Llewellyn, Maca of Don!"

Rage filled her and she shook. Worse, Llewellyn had a satisfied look on his face while calling Medicine. There were two pink suited troopers around her and she heard Llewellyn talking.

"When ye finish caring for Lamar and the troopers, we need someone to check on Beauty. She has a broken wrist."

The red suited Ayranian commander stepped forward. "Maca, we need Medicine at all three Centers. One or two of my fighters were injured, and some of yours; nay badly, but they will need care."

Llewellyn relayed the message to Medicine, and turned to the Ayranian trooper. "My deepest thanks to ye, your fighters, and to your Guardian. May I ask your name?"

"It tis, Joycene, Maca. It was our pleasure. My parents told me how ye were cheated of your victory so long ago. It tis a shame they are nay here." She bowed. "Where do ye wish to confine these Sisters and the others we have captured?"

"They will be confined in the lower cells of my tower.

"I was told Mither was leading the troopers. Do ye ken where she tis?"

"LouElla tis at the First Center tending the wounded till Medicine arrives."

He brought up the handcom again. "Leta, are ye and Lettuce prepared for prisoners?"

"Aye, Maca, the cells are empty for now as the others were sent to Ayran."

Beauty blanched at the news. She had failed. It would take years for the Sisters to regain their strength. Iwanda, based on Ishner, had to hold and build.

Chapter 50

Cultures

"Are ye leaving, Lorenz?" Llewellyn stood in the doorway of the office watching Lorenz remove the armored uniform and slinging it onto the lower shelf.

"I'm heading to the Zark Station." His voice was strained and he kept his back to his father. In his mouth was bile, and his stomach knotted from the spectacle he had just witnessed. He didn't know this man he called father.

Their mission was complete. Llewellyn was Maca of Don and in control. The debt that he owed him for saving his life was fulfilled, but this man was Papa. He had helped teach him right from wrong, how to trust again, and how to love. Why had his father behaved in the manner of a wild bull? To return to Earth wasn't possible for another ten or twenty years. He had no intention of riding around the universe trading God knew what and he would not share responsibilities with Red. Where was there a place for him?

Llewellyn moved towards him as Ishmael appeared in the doorway. "Maca of Don, would ye speak with my Guardian? She and Illnor desperately need your assistance."

"Aye, as soon as I contact Medicine. Lorenz, would ye bide a moment?" He sat in his chair and faced the display.

"Medicine, tis there a report on my Elder?"

Magda answered. "Aye, Maca of Don. He will recover and Beatrice tis with him."

"Thank ye," he replied. The screen filled with Ishmalisa's face.

"Llewellyn, Maca of Don, I and my Counselor appeal to ye on behalf of our Maca, Ilyan. I caught one of the Sisters beating her and trounced that woman. Illnor stopped another from interfering and tended our lassie. We took her and

Issing and fled. They almost caught us when Betron came to the rescue. Now the Sisters hold Ishner, but I have received a message that the people there are in revolt against the Sisters. My people have nay weapons."

"Where are the Sisters located?"

"They were in the school adjacent to the Maca's Tower, but now occupy the Tower."

"Does your Tower have the defense crystal?"

"Nay, Maca, but they are secure in there."

"We shall see if we can induce them to emerge." He smiled at her. "They will run low on food if we close it off for ye."

"Would ye allow me to attend? Illnor will remain with our lassie."

"Aye, and I will bring my laddie and Ishmael. My mither also if she wishes."

"Thank ye, Maca."

Brenda took her place. "Llewellyn, I honor ye for your fight and congratulate ye for settling your debt. Thank ye."

"Ye are welcome, my love."

"Why's she thanking him?" Lorenz asked Ishner.

"For nay leaving his seed in Beauty."

Brenda continued. "I have instructed my troopers to go with ye, and I will join ye when ye pick up Ishmalisha."

Jolene's smiling face was next. "Well done, Llewellyn! That was what the traitorous welsher deserved. I have ordered my troopers to go with ye. I'm adding fifty more. We will meet ye at Betron."

As she faded, Rollo appeared. "Maca of Don, please, how tis my friend, Lamar?"

Llewellyn's face hardened. "He tis recovering. Beatrice tis with him."

"Thank ye. With your permission, I and my younger, Ribdan, and fifty Rurhran troopers would like to accompany ye to Ishner."

"That surprises me."

Half of the screen showed Betta standing beside Brenda. Her face was rigid, her lips white, but her voice was controlled. "Maca of Don, I ken why ye collected your debt, but I despise ye for it, however, I propose that the Council of the Realm meet again in Donnick when the Sister's Army tis subdued. Ye are acknowledged as Maca of Don and Troyner as Maca of Troy. Thalians must nay fight each other. These last few days have been a disaster. Do ye agree?"

Llewellyn's voice remained hard. "Ye left out the part where Don's beasties are returned."

"If that can be accomplished without another fight, aye, it tis agreed."

Raven stepped next to Rollo. "Maca of Don, I fear that ye have nay the facilities, nay the people to care for so many kine and sheep. The people who have been faithful workers in tending them are fearful of returning to Don."

Llewellyn eyed her for a moment. "Maca of Rurhran, kine dinna need that much tending, and our facilities are excellent. Ye are correct: sheep do need tending." *Lorenz despises sheep* ran through his mind.

"Mayhap on the sheep we do have a basis for negotiations as long as ye agree that my youngest, Andrew MacDonald, be part of them. His solution tis apt to be economic, but it will be reasonable."

Raven tried to hide her look of puzzlement. Negotiations she kenned, but what was his meaning of economic? She tried to smile while speaking.

"Tis agreed then. Do ye object to us joining ye against the Sisters?"

"Why would I? Your force tis most welcome. The numbers alone should convince them to surrender. If nay object, I will visit my elder, Lamar, and Don will be in Betron within the hour."

Magda appeared briefly. "Ye will need to let me ken if Medicine tis needed. For now we are busy enough."

There was a chorus of agreement, and Llewellyn switched to the Don channel. Lorenz considered the move futile as each House monitored the other, but politeness required the Tris not ken the conversation of the Houses. Llewellyn leaned back in his chair and proceeded to speak.

"People of Don, your Maca thanks ye for your calmness and your assistance. The Sisters here are defeated and will be judged. We are joining forces with the other Houses to confine the rest of the rebellious Sisters. If your homes and families are missing loved ones, keep in contact here. Nay all the Sister stationed at Ishner wish to be there and your Council of the Realm will weigh the evidence. The Council of the Realm will meet in Donnick ere the week has passed. The troopers that assisted with this fight have forty-five minutes to eat and rest. They will then accompany us to Ishner. I'll keep ye updated on the results. If ye have nay heard, your Guardian, Lamar, tis recovering." He blanked out the display and swung around to face Lorenz and Ishmael.

"Does that improve your mood, Lorenz? Lamar tis Guardian again."

"He should have stayed that way." Lorenz started to turn.

"Ye will need that armored uniform, unless ye have decided nay to accompany us."

Ishmael stared at Lorenz in bewilderment. "Does nay your land honor obligations?"

Lorenz looked at Ishmael and realized that he seemed to be the only one sickened by Llewellyn's raping a woman. What was wrong with these people? Worse, if it had it been him helping Ishmael, he would have felt that there was an obligation to make sure that his family and their possessions were safe.

He turned and retrieved the armor. "As long as I don't need to put it on until we're over Ishner. Let's go grab something to eat and see if Leta needs something brought in."

Llewellyn spoke to their backs. "Lorenz, would ye go with me to Lamar's? I also need information about the Kenning Woman. Has she agreed to return here?" He watched his laddie's back stiffen and Lorenz turned, his shoulders squared, and his chin jutting forward.

"That's right, as Maca, y'all control everything here. It's your say-so whether she returns and gets medical help, isn't it?"

Llewellyn stood. "That tis the way of Thalia, however, if ye say she needs Medicine, I will support ye. Tis she ill?"

"No, her bones didn't heal right. She needs them re-broken and straightened. Right now, she's probably suffering from arthritis too. Thalians or the Justines can cure arthritis; Earth can't."

Llewellyn considered. "I dinna if Medicine will agree." He saw the flash of annoyance on Lorenz's face. "Although, by custom a Kenning Woman accepted by House, tis a Tri. If Medicine refuses, we will ask Gary for medical."

Ishmael stared at Llewellyn like he was possessed. "Maca, she tis Ab."

Llewellyn smiled at them. "There are certain customs that Thalia must admit are too harsh. Now, Lorenz, if ye dinna wish to call upon Lamar, please see to our guest. I must attend."

Lorenz turned to Ishmael. "Would y'all give me a minute?"

Ishmael looked at both, nodded, and withdrew.

"Why the hell is everyone congratulating y'all for rape?"

They faced each other, Lorenz stiff and tense, Llewellyn with that bemused look that he wore when watching people.

"The first fight I won was in the House Arena after the Council of the Realm meeting and the dinner shared among the Houses. Nay but members of House are permitted at the dinner, and the fight was for the bedding, nay the fight. Beauty should have bedded with me ere they turned me over to the Justines, but she demanded I be turned over to the Justines first. Why do ye think she has been so determined to see me kicked out or destroyed?"

"I figured it was because y'all threatened her power."

"Aye, granted, but she kenned people compared her build with mine, and she would lose again. She had to bear the whispers of people calling her traitor and coward."

"It's still rape."

"What I did today tis legal under Thalian law and the debt tis now paid. I would nay dare to do that again, and frankly, I dinna wish to. Tis nay my idea of a proper bedding.

"Since ye are weighing whether to stay in Thalia or nay, once we finish in Ishner, I wish the Kenning Woman brought here to thank her and name her. Then we'll install her in the Shrine of the Kenning Woman. That will validate the status of Tri."

"The what? People worship her?"

"Nay, however, they would go to her for comfort. Usually a Kenning Woman can tell them nay, but she can listen. There are times when she can fulfill their requests for a vision."

"But that doesn't make Daniel eligible for Warrior status, or her for marriage to someone in House, right?"

Comprehension lit Llewellyn's eyes. "So that tis it. Ye looked into a pair of lovely Thalian eyes and wish to wed her. Like a good fither ye are concerned for your laddie's future. That tis why ye are ready to fight me. Ye thought I would oppose any mating. There are solutions to these situations, and we shall find them. Ye will also need help in being a Thalian fither to Daniel, or any other lads or lassies ye may have."

Lorenz was staring at Llewellyn wondering how his father knew him so well.

"How the hell did y'all know about the eyes?"

"And what was your first description of Antoinette? It was, 'She has the prettiest blue eyes. They're so blue they are almost violet.' Now I'll wager this lassie has eyes different from the dark brown of most Thalians."

Lorenz let out his breath. "One more question. Would y'all have done that if Mama were here?"

"Anna tis nay here, nay would she have come here." His voice was hard. "She kenned more about our ways from my telling of Thalia than ye. If she still lived, I would nay be here. She tis still in my heart, but she tis gone and I am here. As I told ye, your customs there, mine here. If I had nay taken what was mine, I would be diminished and Don tarnished. I am Thalian."

Lorenz realized that question had been unfair. What was true for his father was true for him. If Antoinette still lived, he would not be here. Still he persisted.

"That doesn't make it right."

"In your Earthman's moral code, aye. It was the same for me on Earth."

"I figured your moral code was ours. Y'all helped teach me, remember? And I was damn certain I never lived up to it, or you."

Llewellyn shook his head. "Lorenz, I told ye Thalia tis different. Do ye now mean to leave us?"

"Right now I can't. I'd like to object to everything y'all said, but I just re-membered Daniel crawling into my lap. No self-respecting Earth son at the age of twelve would have done such a thing. Randall would have been too proud, Kendall too fearful of being judged a baby, and if Antoinette lived, I would not be here and worried about Daniel and his mother."

Llewellyn was smiling at him. "That means we shall make more arrange-ments than just her living quarters and healing. After a suitable time, I can appoint her Director of something. That will automatically make her House."

"Y'all aren't objecting?"

"When have I ever told ye nay?"

"The time I tried to gut shoot y'all comes to mind, and I still don't like what y'all did. Y'all were always so damn perfect."

"I am nay perfect. Your own beliefs teach ye that. I am a man and nay else. I canna ease your mind on our ways, but ye are my laddie." Llewellyn's voice was rising in irritation.

Lorenz yelled back at Llewellyn's roars. "And you're my father and neither of us can change that."

Llewellyn's eyes lit up. "So your solution tis what?"

"I guess we go see Lamar. He's a brave man. On the way there, I'll tell y'all about the Tri village, LouElla, and the child who will be the new Kenning Woman."

Llewellyn stared at him. "Dear Gar, ye have been a busy man again."

Chapter 51

Aftermath

"The Guardian of Ayran."

Jolene was admitted into Llewellyn's office. Since she had sent the crystal he so desperately needed, Llewellyn assumed she was here to collect her favors for the crystal and the troopers.

"Welcome, Guardian of Ayran. Tis early, but would ye like a brew?"

Jolene smiled. "Of course, Maca of Don, tis never too early for a brew." They greeted each other and she settled herself into the chair.

"I was checking with my Director Jennie who tis overseeing the work of restoring the machinery and electronics in the Flight factory," was her subtle reminder of another obligation.

"Thank ye," she said as Llewellyn handed her a mug and sat across from her. Both were dressed in their traditional colors, but Jolene had added a black sash around the middle. "Jennie needed to be caught up on the workings at Ayran. By the way, where did ye find your electronic technician? I may have need of his services. That, of course, tis nay why I came."

Llewellyn smiled. Jennie had nay doubt told Jolene everything about Labin.

"My visit concerns the future." Jolene smiled a gentle smile and settled back. "I wish to be Guardian of the Realm. Without Don's support that would nay be possible."

Llewellyn found his mouth open and quickly forced words out. "Ye mean when Betta begins her decline?"

"Your political skills need honing, Llewellyn. The next Guardian will be LouElla. I dinna think ye would vote against your own mither. Nay would I expect it. My time tis when LouElla relinquishes her role."

Jolene continued. "Betta will nay be the Guardian to try Beauty. She will step down. Ravin will wish to be Guardian then. I dinna trust her. She will twist some of the laws to reflect the Sisterhood philosophy. She prefers women in charge. Rollo has nay say in what transpires in Rurhran. He follows her blindly." Jolene's voice and face had hardened.

Llewellyn sat back and took a sip of his brew. He was over his initial shock and had wit enough not to say but ye intend to rule over all. His brown eyes filled with amusement and admiration.

"What makes ye think Ravin will try to be Guardian?"

"Llewellyn, that has been planned by the Sisterhood for years. When Betta declines, it tis to be Ravin, then Ishmalisa, then Beauty. Nay would consider me."

And that, thought Llewellyn, tis how they made ye their enemy.

"Jolene, I have one question. How were ye able to produce the crystal and the special clothing when the Justines destroyed technology and the knowledge data bases?"

"They left part of the equipment. They and the Kreppies wished the crystals for jewelry. They forgot that many Thalians retained the knowledge in their minds. Before they came, I mentioned to several how desirable it would be if the duplicate crystals were taken and hidden. I told my people that all knowledge crystals were destroyed and that we needed to teach our wee ones what we kenned. My workforce tis fluid; Tris and Abs come and go."

"Jolene, ye are a true Thalian, but how can ye be certain Mither will take the Guardianship. She tis an excellent Guardian of Flight."

"She tis aging and she kens it. Nay have ever turned down the Guardianship, and I believe ye are better qualified as Guardian of Flight than she or Lamar. Lamar canna administer anything as Beatrice does it all. LouElla tis an excellent Commander and fighter, but she will become bored with the details of training, administration, and manufacturing. Ye handle them well."

"Thank ye, but I do have assistance from my House."

"Aye, the help tis from your laddie, your youngest, and from Beatrice. The rest are mostly Tris who have thrown their support to ye."

"Members of House have come forward."

"Llewellyn, all of Thalia heard the threat to cut off their brew and their food." She smiled at him. "Ye ken who works the hardest, and I believe ye are quite sensible. Too many House members swell with importance and do nay. When did ye learn how hard a Tri will work to become House?"

"My laddie's land tis a country of Tris that beat all the expectations of the old Houses. I nay forgot their lessons."

"Good, now do ye agree to support me as Guardian when the time arrives?"

"Aye, that I will." He was sure Jolene would find some way to retaliate if he did nay agree.

"Ye are right. I will vote for Mither as Guardian, however, I owe ye for the crystal." He leaned forward.

"I ken that I am nay the only House that has requested the red crystal. I have nay heard an answer from ye."

Jolene's face was complacent. "Why, Llewellyn, I'll start work on those as soon as I have the support of all that I need. Ye can secure the votes of Don, Betron, Troy, and Flight."

"I canna promise how Troyner and Brenda will vote."

"My dear Llewellyn, of course, those two will follow your lead. I nay need their word now; just yours."

"Ye have that, Jolene. I think ye will make an excellent Guardian of the Realm."

* * *

"Ye canna permit it." Lamar came roaring in after Jolene left

Llewellyn had started to rise to welcome his Elder Lamar, but the sudden outburst stayed him.

"Permit what?"

"The false Kenning Woman in your House. The gossip tis that Lorenz plans to wed her. He tis trying to prove he is nay and canna ever be Thalian."

Llewellyn neck muscles swelled and he roared back. "He tis my laddie, given to me by Gar and my Anna.

"How can ye say she tis a false kenning woman when I and my grey-eyed laddie are here?"

Lamar's face remained set. "He canna bring an Ab into our House. Ye must rid us of her and her laddie. Lorenz tis nay House. He tis nay but an alien…"

"Stop now, ere ye say more and forever end your tenure as Guardian." Llewellyn's eyes were black obsidian and his voice a full roar. "Ye are serving as Guardian at Lorenz's insistence. Get out now, ere I forget that ye are my elder."

Bafflement filled Lamar's face and he whirled and left. There had been nay greeting, nay goodbye.

Llewellyn let out his breath and sat in his chair. Then his fingers poked at the circles on his desk and a face appeared on the pop-up screen. She was smiling that glorious smile just for him and her white hair was unbound and curling around her face and flowing downward. He'd taken it on one of their excursions to the *Golden One.*

His eyes were intent and slowly his face softened. "Darling, lassie, ye left me too early. Just your eyes and smile can calm me. I ache for ye, my beloved. I sorely need your counseling. Just when I think everything tis settled and the rebuilding commencing, there tis always another problem or fracas in my own House.

Our laddie tis happy again. He has found a lassie to wed. I shall wed too, but that is to have a Thalian wee one. I could nay risk your health again." He smiled at the face and pressed a button. The screen blackened and disappeared into the desk.

* * *

Di sat in her bedroom staring out the glass door at the still water in the outside pool as though it would tell her something, anything. Boredom filled her every waking hour here except when her Wee Da was near or she exercised in the gym room. There were no herbs to gather, no need to hunt for food or firewood. Even the cleansing room was near and required little effort on her part. Da would return when he and Leman finished studying under the direction of someone named Stann.

The pool gave her no answer. Should she risk going to Donnick with the Laird? Could he really stop the Houses from killing her? Lamar was still there and would try to silence her. He wanted nay words about the events of seven years ago. Did Rurhran still fear her hold on Rocella? Jolene was like a queen of an ant colony waiting to take her revenge. If she returned to Bi's village, her status as Kenning Woman would vanish within ninety years or sooner, and she would gradually starve to death.

"A penny for your thoughts."

She looked up at the man standing in the doorway. First surprise, then a wild look of joy washed over her and she tried to rise rapidly.

"My Laird, ye are back."

"Will y'all start calling me Lorenz?" He was beside her, drawing her into his arms. "I've missed y'all. Where's Daniel?"

"He tis studying." And she forgot that this was nay possible. She was kissing him as fiercely as he was kissing her. When they stopped for breath, she looked at him in wonderment.

"Papa wants y'all to meet with him. He wants to give his official thanks and present y'all to the Council of the Realm as the Kenning Woman. You're to stay at the Laird's Home until the Kenning Woman's Shrine is reconditioned. No one has been there for years."

Di made a face. "The old Kenning Woman died but fifty years ago. She had lost her visions and nay did for her as the Sisters forbid it."

"If she lost her abilities, how could she tell y'all your mission?"

"She kenned that vision years ere she found me in a place safe enough to tell me. Laird, uh, Lorenz, I canna live at the Shrine. Wee Da would need to be there too. He must stay with ye, and I will return to Bi's village."

Lorenz shook his head. "Y'all don't understand, ah, ken. It's just long enough for Medicine to heal y'all and then Papa can appoint y'all as a Director of something. After that we'll be wed."

"We what?"

They were the same height and were looking straight at each other.

"Diana, y'all are," he gave a quick grin, "magnificent. I'm in love with y'all. Your laddie is my laddie. Will ye Walk the Circle with me?"

Di closed her eyes. This man took her breath, her heart, her reason, and she could nay tell him nay. All she could do was kiss him again and taste of him before thinking of a way to tell him nay. When they broke apart she saw his smile. His grey eyes danced with warm light and the smile changed the hard planes of his face.

"I've told Papa, the Maca, that I intend to wed y'all."

Lorenz found it easy to continue to hold her close to him. "We need to head back to Donnick. After y'all meet Papa, I need to visit the Laird's Station. I'd like y'all and Daniel to go with me if you all aren't too tired. We'll be back in Donnick before dark. Ishmael and Melanie will be at the Laird's Home tomorrow. She'll do an examination and recommend what needs to be done."

"Lorenz, Medicine will nay be there."

"Ishmael helped set it up. He doesn't need to be there, but it's a good way to be with Melanie. That doesn't upset y'all does it?"

"Why would ye think such a thing?"

"Well, y'all were living with Ishmael when the Sisters attacked you."

"He was from House. He might have returned and then he could have helped my laddie." There was fierceness in her voice. "I am Ab. There tis nay other way I could help Wee Da." To herself she thought, Troyner loves Marta, and she will nay accept Wee Da.

Lorenz let his breath out. "I was hoping y'all would say that. I'll visit the Shrine tomorrow and see what needs to be done. Oh, I forgot, dinner tonight at the Laird's Home. Papa may put in an appearance, and my grandson, Andrew, will be there."

He was about to explain grandson when Daniel burst through the door.

"Fither." He bounded across the floor and embraced both. "I heard ye had returned." His smile was as radiant as Lorenz's.

"When do ye Walk the Circle? When do we do the Claiming Rite? Does the Warrior School start right away? Are we going back now? Will Leman and his family go with us?"

"Whoa, slow down, and for another thing, y'all don't burst in our bedroom like that. Y'all are too big."

Both Daniel and Di looked at him in puzzlement and he stopped himself from grinding his teeth. "We are going back, but Leman and his family are staying here. As for Walking the Circle, your mother needs to be healed first. Then the Council of the Realm has to approve me before any Claiming Rite for anyone. The regular schools will open first. The Warrior School may not start until next year. We all will need to make another trip back to the town of LouElla to listen to their needs, and now we need to thank Luman and Lavina for their hospitality."

Di considered the man mad. The Maca would nay approve and Medicine would nay be there. And why, why did he think she could live in the Shrine? It was too open, too accessible. If she didn't go to Donnick, her laddie would nay be a Warrior, and she would have failed as his mither for the other half of the vision would come true. Her mouth straightened. She would accompany the Laird and Da. If death claimed her, her laddie would be the Laird's and a Warrior. There was nay other decision. Her prophesy had proved true. The

Maca and his blind eyed Laird had revenged Thalia's wrongs by the Justines, the Kreppies, and the Sisters. Don and Thalia would be restored.

* * *

Andrew knocked on Kit's door wondering why Grandpa Mac had considered this assignment necessary at this time. Surely someone else could teach the woman the basics of entering planting and production numbers into the system. The explanation that the Claiming Rites would make Pawpaw and Kahli House eluded him. Why did these people consider House and Tris so much more than Abs? His recommendation, repeated over and over that all Abs in Don should become Tris was met with a raised eyebrow. Grandma LouElla's explanation of, "They dinna want it," was inadequate.

Kit opened the door with a wide smile. "Ye are welcomed here."

The Maca's instructions had been clear. "The situation has changed. Make my younger smile." Kit kenned she could make a man smile, even a mutant from another world.

Glossary

Their symbols for the written word resemble ours, but the letter A would have no middle bar. The letter F would have only the top flag, and the letter E would not have the middle bar. Their smaller case letters are the same as the upper case, but smaller in the written word. Our method was used in compiling this glossary.

Attend: Stop and listen. Also to be an attendant to the fighter in the arena

Bawd: Rat like rodent, but with golden brown fur.

Blad: Canteen

Brither: Brother

Brool: An apple like fruit. Different varieties grow in Don, Rurhran, Betron, and inland southern portions of Ishner.

Bucht: Sheep, surprisingly ewe means female sheep.

Canna: Cannot

Carrier: Large craft for carrying livestock or freight.

Carver: A butcher.

Cleg: Rodent-like creature with fluffy, light brown hair that turns golden on the tips. It is the size of a medium rat with brown "pop" eyes and large front teeth for gnawing.

Concraete: A composite of concrete, silica, and specialized plastic.

Crait: Craft that carries ten people.

Dinna: Do not

Dramelberry: A fruit tasting like a raspberry, but purplish blue in color.

Elbenor: Large bear like mammal (like the American grizzly) possibly some exist in the uninhabited portions of Betron.

Eld: Old

Fither: Father

Fliv: Vehicle that carries four people. By mounting large stunners they can be transformed into fighters.

Handmaiden: Assists the Martin and cares for sick and the dead. A man may not have the title or her functions.

Home: The residents of Thalia's dwellings no matter what class.

House: Family Gens that control a planet: Never refers to a residence.

Icosahedron crystal: A twenty sided-crystal encoded with instructions for releasing energy. Used as a defense at the Maca's Tower. Red is the most powerful.

Ken: Know

Kenning: Knowing, fore knowledge.

Kenning Woman: The formal title of the woman who sees visions. The visions benefit or warn Thalians of impending events. It cannot be held by a man.

Kine: Cattle

Lad: Formal House title for those not Laird or Maca

Laddie: Son, boy, young male.

Lady: First born daughter of a Maca. See Laird.

Laird: First born male of a Maca. The next Maca will come from the Laird or Lady of a House.

Lass: Formal House title for those not Lady or Maca.

Lassie: Daughter, girl, young female.

Leg: A unit of distance: about 11/2 miles.

Lifers: Spare boats on a ship should an accident occur.

Lift: Flying craft for four people.

Maca: Male or female hereditary ruler of a House. When the old Maca dies, the first born of the Lady or Laird or the House after the old Maca's death becomes the new Maca. The ruling house will control a continent of Thalia or a specialized branch like Medicine or Manufacturing.

Martin: Leader of the Abs and religious figurehead. His authority on religious matters is similar to a Pope. This title cannot be held by a woman.

Minirob: Used in medical treatments for surgery, repositioning, delivering medicines. They are absorbed by the body.

Mither: Mother

Padport: Where flying vehicles land

Pina Pods: Grown on Troy and in some hot houses. They contain a creamy, nut that provides oil and protein, and can also be eaten. They are considered a delicacy, especially the ones from Troy as it is their natural home. The leaves and pods are used for a tea like beverage.

Sargent: Equivalent to our Sergeant

Station: Ranch or large agricultural endeavor.

Stingers: Looks like a larger honey bee.

Troller: A listening device and a communicator.

Troller: The fishing vessel of Ishner. Their nets catch everything.

Twas: Was

Twere: Were

Twill: Will.

Twould: Would.

Ye: You

Yere: Your

Younger: (1) Grandchild (2) Any relative that was born later.

Youngest: (1) Great-grandchild (2) Progeny of the great-grandchild

Zarks: The equine of Thalia

About the Author

Mari Collier was born on a farm in Iowa, and has lived in Arizona, Washington, and Southern California. She and her husband, Lanny, met in high school and were married for forty-five years. She is Co-Coordinator of the Desert Writers Guild of Twentynine Palms and serves on the Board of Directors for the Twentynine Palms Historical Society. She has worked as a collector, bookkeeper, receptionist, and Advanced Super Agent for Nintendo of America. Several of her short stories have appeared in print and electronically, plus three anthologies. Twisted Tales From The Desert, Twisted Tales From The Northwest, and Twisted Tales From The Universe.

Author Contact Information

http://www.maricollier.com/
https://twitter.com/child7mari

Lightning Source UK Ltd.
Milton Keynes UK
UKHW011844281220
376048UK00006B/330/J